SAPPHI

Also by Freda Warrington from Earthlight

The Amber Citadel
Book One of The Jewelfire Trilogy

THE
SAPPHIRE THRONE

FREDA WARRINGTON

EARTHLIGHT

LONDON · SYDNEY · NEW YORK · TOKYO · SINGAPORE · TORONTO

www.earthlight.co.uk

First published in Great Britain by Earthlight, 2000
An imprint of Simon & Schuster UK Ltd
A Viacom Company

Simon & Schuster UK Ltd
Africa House
64–78 Kingsway
London
WC2B 6AH

Simon & Schuster Australia
Sydney

A CIP catalogue record for this book
is available from the British Library

1 3 5 7 9 10 8 6 4 2

ISBN 0-7434-0826-8

Typeset in 9½ on 11½ Meridien by
SX Composing DTP, Rayleigh, Essex
Printed and bound in the UK by Caledonian International Book
Manufacturing, Glasgow

Contents

The Nine Realms

RIVERWYNDE

Sepheret

Deirland

Noreya

To
m

SKALD

WHITEVEIL MTS.

Mithrawn

PA

LUSANIAH

Parc

Grey
Ocean

SERPENTINE
MTS.

Azura
Maroc

LAPISZU

Acknowledgements

For their endless encouragement, moral support and love throughout the writing of the Jewelfire Trilogy, I especially wish to thank Mike Llewellyn, Justina Robson, and my Mum and Dad. Thanks are also due to my steadfast agent, John Richard Parker, my incomparable editor, John Jarrold, and to my dear friends Storm Constantine, Anne Gay, Chris Baker, Rachel Baker, Chris Roe, Lolita Soares and Jay 'Alice' Cooper . . . not to mention the Brum Writers' Group, who have helped me through many an awkward chapter. Blessings also upon the Dark Angels of the Nottingham Vampyre Group, for all the fun and good times. Last but not least I salute Vikki Lee France and the Prophets – past, present and future – who know my innermost secrets yet who, amazingly, are still friends with me . . . Thank you for being there, all.

Freda Warrington's web site can be found at:
http://members.aol.com/FredaMike/index.html

Prelude: Eshte

The young man arrowed like a salmon through the water.

This was his element. Jthery relished the crystalline chill on his naked body, the caress of waterweed and the surge of fish startled by his penetration into their green realm. Breaking the surface, he trod water and turned to look back across the lake. A perfect inversion of the sky hung in the water, mauve and rose blending to gold. One small moon gemmed the sunset; Lily Moon, attended by two stars.

In the centre of the lake was an island, on which rose the mansion of his family. The walls were painted softly blue and violet and there was lacy fretwork along each eave and balcony. The house extended long jetties into the lake, with boats bobbing at their moorings on the liquid gold of the water. The long windows, too, gave back the sunset.

Inside was Jthery's family; his great-grandmother the Duchess of Mithrain, his grandmother her immediate heir, his father and mother . . . and all the other grandparents and aunts and cousins, who were too busy with political concerns to notice that Jthery was happier alone in the lake than in their company. When they noticed him at all, they called him fey, and lazy, and shook their heads over him. Affectionate concern, but they still didn't truly see him.

One day Jthery would be Duke of Mithrain, land of amethyst lakes and silver mists. Not until he was a very old man, though. At nineteen, he wasn't sure that he ever wanted such responsibility. Not after what had happened to King Garnelys. He didn't know what he craved.

He turned on to his back and floated, looking up at the sky, his pale red-gold hair fanning out like a halo of waterweed. So peaceful. He was dreaming, desiring something he couldn't even name . . .

The lake lurched. The water in front of him exploded.

He was floundering, gasping as the wave surged over him. The lake was shallow here so he could just manage to find the bottom with his toes. As he flailed upright, coughing and pushing his sodden hair out of his face, he saw her.

A lovely female form, rising out of the water in front of him. Taller than him and shimmering like glass, her body was formed of rippling water, her hair a flowing waterfall. Jthery stared at her in complete terror. An undine, an elemental; the legends told that they seduced young men, only to drown them . . .

'Jthery of Mithrain,' she said. Her voice was the clear music of a spring bubbling over stones.

His own voice, when he managed to speak, was hoarse. 'How do you know my name?'

'You called us.' Her eyes were orbs of bright water.

'No.'

'You don't know it, but you did. You have called to us all your life.'

He shivered. It was true. Gods, she read his mind, she knew him. 'Yes.'

'What do you want?' the undine demanded.

'I – I don't know. To see you, to know you are real. My lady, I didn't mean to disturb you.' He shook his head helplessly. 'I always felt the lake was part of me. Forgive me.'

'The lake *is* yours,' she said. 'But that means that you, in turn, are ours.'

He shivered. He was afraid he would drown in her shining power, yet the fear was seductive. She went on, 'You have not disturbed us; we came to you because we need you, Jthery. One who loves the water as his own life-blood. For who else will speak for us and act for us in the world of air? The earth is in turmoil. Have you not felt it?'

He hardly knew how to reply. He clasped one arm across himself, profoundly cold. 'There – there has been a war. The King of the Nine Realms is dead. We thought peace had returned, but . . .'

'Only on the surface,' she said. 'Beneath the surface, we feel the truth of it. Your war was only the outer sign, the froth on the flood. It was all to turn your eyes and attention away from what lay beneath. Help us, Jthery. Help us and we shall help you!'

'What should I do?' he stammered.

She pointed at him, water falling like rain from her shining arm. 'Someone shall need your aid. You will know. Will you act for us?'

She towered over him, bright and terrifying. He couldn't refuse her. 'Yes. Lady of the Waters, I'll do anything for you.'

'For you know who I am?'

Yes, he knew. No mere undine, this, but a Goddess. 'Eshte,' he whispered.

At that she smiled. Her hand reached for him and caressed his chest, spilling a sudden stream of warmth over him. 'What do you want?' she asked again.

'Nothing, my lady.'

'It's a simple question.' Her voice became gentle. 'What do you want for yourself?'

'I don't know.' He shifted awkwardly, but she wouldn't be denied. 'To be loved, I suppose.'

'And you will be.' Her form was becoming less distinct, her voice fading into the rush of water. 'But beware, Jthery. There are different kinds of love waiting for you. One is true, the other is false and lethal. The wisdom to know the difference lies only within you. And we rely on you, all of the Earth relies upon you to make the right choice! Water is life, Jthery. You are going forth to preserve the very life-blood of the Earth. So tread carefully, and wisely, for your choices may save or doom us all.'

The goddess's water-form surged upwards. She became a silver fountain that rose and fell as an icy deluge. The force of it thrust Jthery under the water. He was drowning, wide-eyed, seeing impossible phantom fish and sea-serpents writhing towards him through a mass of bubbles. Then a great surge of water pushed him. As he was swept away he saw silver ripples in the shape of a dozen hands, pulling at him, dragging him down to sweet death amid the writhing weeds.

When he came back to consciousness he was lying on the shore of the lake. The sand was warm beneath him. He felt dazed. Such terrifying visions . . .

There was something pressing into his palm. Opening his hand he found a jewel there; an amethyst carved in the shape of a carp, with a drop of clear aquamarine suspended below it by a silver link. The carp hung in turn from a round white moon of opal. He sat up, staring in awe at the jewel.

Then he knew.

Eshte had been real. She had given him a gift. Her symbol. Everything Jthery did from now on would be in her service.

He stood up, his long body pale against the violet sunset, the violet lake. It was time to return to the house and break the news, but he wasn't afraid. The Goddess had given him more than a jewel; she had given him the simple knowledge that he did not need the approval of his family, nor a summons from the Amber Citadel, nor any reason greater than his own instinct. He could simply leave.

Chapter One. Shadows at Luin Trest

Eldareth emerged wearily from the Seer's hut and stood blinking in the brilliant dawn. He was in shock. His body still thrummed with the last tremors of struggle, despair and, at the end, soul-heavy resignation. He squinted at the bleached sky and drew a breath, let it go in a long sigh of exhaustion.

He'd had to escape the dark interior of the hovel, with its miasma of animals, smoke and sorcery. He needed fresh air. It was hard to believe, after what he'd seen, that the real world was still here. The steep green slopes of the Serpentine Mountains rolled in every direction, away into the silvery haze of the horizon. Birds were chirping in the trees and goats grazing on the turf roof of the hut, oblivious to what had happened inside.

The world was still here. But Tanthe was no longer in it.

Eldareth the Wanderer sank down on the grass, elbows resting on his knees and his head drooping between them. I let her down, he thought. I failed to keep her out of the portal. I feel as if – damn it, she was not my responsibility and yet I feel as if I betrayed her!

Dull stirring of older, deeper guilt . . .

There was a movement near him. Eldareth looked up.

Standing in front of him was a silvery figure, eighteen inches high, posing with its hands on its hips and a quizzical look in its black eyes. It was the Seer's secretary, Loga, a male of the race called Zampherai or Sub-terraneans or occasionally, by uncharitable humans, maggots.

'Well?' said Loga.

'Is it safe for you to be out in daylight?' Eldareth said

irascibly. 'I thought the Zampherai only felt safe under-ground, or at least in the dark.'

The tiny man shrugged. 'I'm not going to dissolve. I can't see particularly well, that's all, any more than you can by night. Your face is a sort of white blur, with flares coming off it; nasty.'

'Thank you.'

'I meant, nasty as in angry-looking.'

'I am angry,' said Eldareth. 'Not with you, not even with the Seer, though the gods know I should be. With myself.'

'So, you're going to sit here and sulk about it?'

'I'm not sulking. I'm trying to decide what to do next.'

The secretary hopped up on to Eldareth's bony knee and sat there, staring at him with fathomless, mole-blind eyes. 'It wasn't your fault, my lord Eldareth. Tanthe decided to go. You and the Seer tried to hold on to her; she fought you off. It was her decision.'

'Yes, but what does she know? She's twenty-one, lived all her life in the same village, brought up with a ridiculously naive, romantic view of the Aelyr. I am twice her age, I've travelled everywhere, seen everything. I know the dangers. I should have stopped her!'

The secretary shifted, drumming his heels against Eldareth's thigh. 'Nothing could have stopped her. Come back inside, have a drink to steady yourself. We have whisky from the Serpent Isles.'

'If it is not all inside your master by now,' Eldareth said darkly. 'It's good of you to show such concern, Loga. More than the Seer has done. He obviously can't wait to see the back of me.'

'He's mortified,' said Loga.

'So he should be. So am I. What am I going to tell the people she left behind – her friends, her lover, her sister? "I let this happen to Tanthe and oh, by the way, you are probably never going to see her again?"'

Eldareth closed his eyes. He couldn't get the tang of other-world energy out of his nostrils; an earthy scent like

6

rain mingled with electricity and some other intangible perfume. The scene unfolded again through his mind; he couldn't stop it, could only wish hopelessly to change the ending.

They'd been in Parione – trying to restore normality after the civil war – when Tanthe had come to him and asked his help. She was being haunted by visions of an Aelyr male, she said, and must find out what the visions meant. So Eldareth had brought her here, two long days' ride from Parione, to the Seer's remote hut in the Serpentines.

The Seer – whom Eldareth nicknamed Fox as much for his character as his hair – had accepted the usual payment of wine and ralds and given the usual warnings. In the centre of the hut stood a well, capped with a disc of polished crystal. Tanthe would see images in this disc, the Seer told her, but she must not expect him to interpret them for her. Must not even tell him what she saw, he insisted, for he was only a vessel of transmission.

The four of them had seated themselves around the well; the Seer, Tanthe, Eldareth, and even Loga, who normally concealed himself beneath the Seer's chair to make a record of proceedings. Then came darkness and the thick stench of animals rising around them . . . Fox and Tanthe chanting, sinking into mutual trance . . . lines of light swirling in the crystal disc . . . a picture forming of another world, the realm of the Aelyr, deep green and blue . . . And although this was meant to be Tanthe's vision, Eldareth saw it too. In growing amazement he had watched Tanthe reaching out, speaking urgently to the young Aelyr man who formed and floated in the light . . .

And then it all went wrong.

A pair of hands came bursting up through the crystal as if through water, and seized Tanthe. The crystal dissolved, green light flared from the shaft of the well, and the auburn-haired Aelyr hung there in the glow, gripping Tanthe's hand and begging her to go with him.

7

The well had turned into a portal between worlds. Tanthe was being dragged into it.

Eldareth had caught hold of her, struggling to keep her in the hut. Voices echoed in his ears; his own, the Seer's dismayed horror, the soft desperate pleading of the Aelyr male, Tanthe's confusion. The whirling column of energy, the electric scent. Panic.

She'd turned to Eldareth, wide-eyed, asking desperately for his advice. He'd tried and failed. He'd been so stupid; told her a secret he should have kept to himself. That had done it. His unguarded words had sent her diving into the portal, insisting that she *must* know the truth, whatever the risks.

So it *was* his fault. If only he'd kept his mouth shut – too late now. She had ripped herself out of Eldareth's hands, stepped into the waiting arms of the Aelyr. The peacock light had swallowed them both. It flared, narrowed to a taper, and was sucked into the well. Then the crystal reformed, a thin hard barrier, and all was dark once more. Tanthe was gone.

Eldareth shuddered. The memory was so violent, so vivid. It had only happened a few hours ago.

All night, he and the Seer had laboured to reconjure the portal, to no avail. The Seer was only that; a visionary, not a sorcerer. In truth he hadn't the faintest idea how a portal was to be created, and neither had Eldareth. Some powerful interaction between Tanthe and the Aelyr had created it, and those conditions could not be recaptured in a thousand years. Fox, of course, already knew that, and as a result had been in an increasingly foul mood all night. But Eldareth had refused to give up until dawn broke, finally forcing him to accept that the well of vision was dark and cold, and bound to remain so.

He rubbed his forehead with the heel of his hand. He loved Tanthe as a friend, almost a daughter. He felt responsible for her, and simply couldn't believe he had let her down so drastically.

He looked up and saw Fox in the doorway of the hut, leaning on the wattle frame, flask of whisky in hand. He was a slender, nut-brown man in his mid-thirties – so it appeared – with a white streak in his long russet hair and a sour expression on his face.

'You don't care about this, do you?' said Eldareth. Loga jumped down as he stood up. 'It wouldn't be so bad if you cared. If you had put some energy into finding her instead of making it so obvious you want me gone.'

The Seer gave a sneering *hmph*. 'Could you explain to me how I should care about someone I do not know? I didn't solicit her business and I certainly did not ask to have my Well of Vision abused by the creation of a portal. *I* didn't create it – *she* did. And it was her decision, I seem to recall, to pass through it. So she got what she paid for, and more, did she not?' He raised the flask to his lips.

In two strides Eldareth reached him, gripped the hand that held the whisky, snarled into the Seer's pinched face. 'You may drink to forget all your other visions, Fox, but by Nuth and Anuth, you are not going to forget this one! Gods, I held you in such awe the first time I came here. A visionary who could draw images from the ether or from the deep subconscious; I thought you so wise, so mystical. Living here in isolation, with your record-keeper writing your secrets in arcane runes. Now I know better. You are a fraud, Seer. You spend your life running away from what you know. Have you any idea what has happened of late in the outside world?'

'I try to know as little as possible, but news still seeps in,' Fox sneered. 'Civil war, or something.'

'King Garnelys conceived a mad scheme of building a ridiculous monument to himself, and turned Aventuria upside down to do it! We had to make war on him to stop him. Surely you would have seen that coming, had you not drowned your memory in liquor and turned your back. You could have saved lives. Thousands of lives!'

The Seer looked up at the taller man, his narrow face

burning with anger. 'Have you finished?' he said thinly. 'Now I am more than a coward and a fraud – I am a murderer? I must take more than the blame for your friend's disappearance – I must take it for all of Aventuria's ills? Don't you dare to presume you know me, Eldareth. I cannot see into the future. The first thing I tell all those who come here is that *I cannot see into the future!*'

He was so fierce that Eldareth let him go. The Seer rubbed his wrist, glaring at him. 'When they come to me, I open up the world to them – but they see only the narrow little fragments that their minds allow them to see. Yet to deliver each of those tiny visions, I have the whole of present time rushing through me. All that exists to be known, channelled like a great gale roaring through your mind – have you ever experienced that?'

'No,' said Eldareth.

'Then don't presume to judge me! It is madness, chaos, pain, howling anguish. I know Seers who have killed themselves rather than endure it. I am still alive, and I have not gone entirely mad, purely as a result of the measures I take to protect myself. I live alone. I shore up walls in my mind to keep the visions separate from my consciousness. And yes, I drink, to blur those that seep through – and still, and still they seep through. My last defence is not to care – that, or be destroyed. Don't begrudge me that until you have lived an hour in my mind!'

There was a pause. Eldareth said, 'Have *you* finished?'

'Come inside and I'll give you a vision of your own! I'll even waive the fee.'

His eyes glittered ferally. Eldareth shivered. 'Thank you, no. It's been a long night.'

'Scared? You should be.'

'I dare say my vision would be as narrow and useless as those of your other clients.'

The Seer sighed through his teeth. 'Well then. At least come back inside and have a drink.'

Their tempers burned out, they looked at each other awkwardly. Eldareth relented. 'All right.'

They sat on a pair of rickety stools in the hut's entrance, with chickens pecking around their feet and goats trying to chew their sleeves. Eldareth drank sparingly of the whisky, but its golden fire took the edge off the night's misery. Loga declined but sat cross-legged between them, leafing through sheets of thick, rough-edged paper that was covered in tiny runes.

'Forgive me, Fox,' said Eldareth. 'I didn't mean to heap the blame for Aventuria's ills upon your shoulders. But do you feel no curiosity at all about what you see?'

'Curiosity would do for the fox as it did for the cat,' said the Seer, poking at the earth with a stick. He showed no sign of the alcohol affecting him. 'They came here, you know.'

'Who?'

'Her parents. Your friend Tanthe's parents. A year ago, or was it two?'

'Are you sure?'

'As sure as my intuition ever is. I'm breaking my own rules, telling you this. Two Aelyr, a man and a woman, veiled head to foot in silk the colour of dusk – as if that would hide them from me.'

Eldareth was fascinated. Perhaps Elrill had been right about Tanthe after all, though none of it made sense. Her parents were human and lived in Sepheret, and yet— 'Did they ask about their . . . daughter?'

'No. They asked only to see human affairs in the world. And that, I gather, is what they saw, although how much sense they made of it was their problem. The things they saw may have been connected with Tanthe, though they probably didn't realise it. But the one thing I perceived about them was that they were fleeing from something. Very afraid, and fleeing.'

'Anything else?'

Fox shook his head. He frowned, and looked suddenly exhausted. 'Nothing.'

Eldareth was frustrated, but his will to argue was spent. 'Well, this information is of no help to Tanthe now. Fox, I apologise for the trouble and I thank you for your help, but I had better be on my way.'

'As you will,' said the Seer off-handedly, rising and vanishing into the darkness of the hut. 'I have animals to feed.'

Shaking his head, Eldareth stood up wearily and went outside. As he reached the two horses, which were tethered to a tree on the hillside, Loga followed him.

'You're wrong about my master, you know,' said the Zampherai, hopping on to a boulder so his head was on a level with Eldareth's. 'I have these arguments with him endlessly. He will never admit it, never; but he behaves as he does because he cares too much, and can't bear it. Why does he employ me to record all that is said during the visions? Habit, he claims, but I know better. It's for posterity, just in case he turns up something of use.'

'Ah.' Eldareth turned to Loga, suddenly understanding. 'So, while he has deliberately forgotten most of it, you know it all – because you have written it down?'

'I didn't say that. They're just words. I can't interpret them.'

'But?'

'You don't understand. If he told what he saw, what if people acted in a particular way – and it was the wrong way, and disaster followed? His responsibility is to stay quiet as much as to speak – only to observe, not to precipitate events!'

'But?' Eldareth repeated.

'What we see is a pattern,' Loga whispered. 'Warnings. The *roths* of the Earth and the Jewelfires of Verdanholm are uneasy, and the Aelyr are restless.'

'Restless, why?'

'Because a change is coming.' Loga's black eyes shone, watering in the too-bright light. 'My master can't bring himself to say the words deliberately. Perhaps he can't

12

admit it, perhaps he doesn't even consciously *know*, but he has said it in trance. And I believe your little war and your mad king were just a tiny part of it, just the beginning. And the Seer denies it because he is only human, and no human wants to believe that it's happening.'

'That what is happening?'

'The Bhahdradomen,' Loga whispered. 'The Bhahdradomen are rising.'

An hour later, Eldareth was on horseback, riding north. His horse, Gany, was a glossy dark chestnut of Paranian blood, solidly built with an arched neck and a long golden mane and tail. Eldareth was leading Tanthe's horse, Redbird, the lean and beautiful red bay mare that she'd ridden all the way from Sepheret. He hoped Tanthe would forgive him for taking her, but two horses would make his journey easier.

Patient and hardy, the horses cantered steadily through the green valleys of the Serpentines while the summer sun ached above. Eldareth was glad of Gany's gentle stride. His back ached, the price of wear and tear on his long spine from years of travelling. He was a lean, tall figure in his well-worn riding gear; breeches, jacket and boots of dusty black, with touches of green and brown. His face showed the ravages of a life spent mainly outdoors, angular and weather-lined, the nose and cheekbones like blades, and a couple of days' beard sprouting on his scarred cheeks. His straight raven hair was tied back with a leather thong. He could hardly be called handsome, although Helananthe liked him well enough . . . or had, until he'd let her down.

Eldareth had thought hard but swiftly about what to do next. He could have ridden straight back to Parione – two days to the south – to tell Rufryd, Saphaeyender and Ysomir of Tanthe's disappearance. And then what? There was nothing any of them could do. Rufryd might well insist on a long, arduous ride to Silverholm – home of the Shaelahyr – to demand Elrill's help, only to be coldly refused. Yes, Eldareth could see him doing exactly that. He shook his head. Rufryd was a good lad at heart, but hot-headed was an understatement.

Meanwhile, Eldareth had another task. He had promised Helananthe – soon to be crowned Queen of Aventuria – that he would go to Eisilion and fetch her mother Princess Ghiseyma and her brother Venirryen out of exile. They were hiding at Luin Trest, the house of Ghiseyma's friend and distant cousin, Lady Nietriya. To return to Parione first would set him back four or five days. Since there was no point, he'd decided to press on to Eisilion.

He could still barely believe that Ghiseyma had had to flee. That King Garnelys, Helananthe's grandfather, had turned on anyone who opposed his plans, even his own family. That he'd run his only son Galemanth to ground and had him murdered. At least Prince Galemanth had had the foresight to send his wife and son into hiding before it was too late.

Why had Garnelys changed? He'd been a kind man, a benevolent ruler for many years. And then that sudden, terrible transformation. His obsession with building the insane Tower, his willingness to conscript his subjects into slavery and waste thousands of lives in the process.

It had been hard for the Aventurians to rebel. Eldareth had ridden all over the Nine Realms trying to warn people of the King's delusions. Usually failing. The King's subjects loved and trusted him, with good reason. The monarchs of Aventuria had served their people well for centuries, keeping the Nine Realms peaceful and prosperous. The notion that the King would betray them was unthinkable.

Still, they'd been driven to it in the end. Helananthe and Eldareth had rallied the rebels, defeated Garnelys's army at Hethlas Rim, and ridden victorious into Parione and the Amber Citadel – only to find Garnelys dead, murdered by Tanthe's sister Ysomir. And so the mystery of his cruel behaviour went unsolved. There were theories, but no facts.

Eldareth wished he had company. *I should have brought a retinue*, he thought, *suitable to accompany a princess and prince back to their palace*. He had hoped that Tanthe might be making the journey with him, at least. Someone to talk to, to keep his mind from grinding at these troubles.

With Garnelys and Galemanth dead, Helananthe would soon take the throne. Eldareth could barely imagine it. He had been her friend, travelling companion and lover for years. They'd slept on the ground together, got drunk together, ridden into battle together . . . And she would make a fine ruler, he knew it. The problem was, he couldn't imagine himself on the Sapphire Throne beside her.

She had asked him to marry her. He had said no.

Helananthe had been furious and upset, which was part of the reason he'd left Parione. But the truth remained; no matter how deeply they loved each other he could never, in a million years, imagine himself King Eldareth of Aventuria.

Ludicrous.

He'd never wanted power. He'd seen such desires destroy people. And when he berated the Seer for evading responsibility, in truth he was berating himself. He'd made too many mistakes in the past to trust himself in such a position. The prospect of kingship made him flee. And so, must he abandon Helananthe and lose her for ever?

Ten days of travelling brought Eldareth over the trail of the Serpentines and into Eisilion. The boundaries between the realms were not clear-cut, but Eldareth observed the subtle change of landscape and atmosphere; the lush verdancy of Paranios giving way to starker hills. The slopes were covered in rough bronze-stemmed grass, with feathery seedheads that made a shifting red haze over the slopes.

As he stayed in a village one evening, a town the next, all the talk was of the Battle of Hethlas Rim, the death of

Garnelys. The people of Eisilion had obviously received news of events in a haphazard way, so no one knew the whole story and speculation filled in for the facts. Eldareth did his best to correct the rumours in passing. It made him smile, to hear them singing the praises of Lord Serpeth, their Duke, such a brave and courageous leader whose actions in battle had saved Aventuria. Eldareth hardly had the heart to point out that Lord Serpeth had gone into battle on King Garnelys's behalf, only to swap sides half-way through when he saw that Helananthe was the more likely to win. Still less that Serpeth had not actually had to engage in any fighting.

He'd always liked the Eisilians, though. You couldn't help it. Devious, changing with the wind, yet unfailingly charming.

Leaving the town, Eldareth reckoned he had another three days' travel to reach Luin Trest. His road – if this vague track could be termed a road – wound high over rough moorland, bringing him down through a river valley then up again into rusty, heather-patched hills. He passed a number of farms and villages, but decided to press on. Towards evening, he regretted it; a summer storm was boiling in the sky. Rain began to fall in huge, lukewarm drops.

Eldareth looked up at the sky and cursed. Clouds massed black and ominous, washing the landscape with an eerie luminosity. Lightning flickered behind great swollen anvils of cloud. Then came thunder, making the horses shy and dance as it lumbered noisily across the sky.

The rain grew heavier. On the horizon he saw long veils joining the clouds to the earth. No shelter anywhere, dangerous to huddle under a tree. Eldareth dismounted, to make himself less of a lightning target, and began to lead the miserable horses at a run towards the hillside. An outcrop of rock offered at least a partial refuge.

As they made for the outcrop, the rain became torrential and blackness rolled in. Lightning tore the sky; Redbird reared, pulling Eldareth almost off his feet. He struggled on, hardly able to see the ground in front of him. Their climb brought them on to a saddle that ran between this hill and the next. As he glanced into the valley beyond, a sustained lightning burst illuminated the bulk of a building.

It stood high above the valley, fused into the hillside; a ruin of dark spires surrounding the faceted cone of the roof. Rain and lightning slithered over it, turning the ancient roof-tiles to iridescent scales. A temple. No ordinary temple, though; Eldareth knew by the look of it that this was a place dedicated aeons ago, not to Eisilion's snake-goddess, but to the Aelyr.

It stood long-neglected, crumbling, with creepers veiling the walls and tree-roots entwining the foundation stones – still an enduring reminder of age-old conflict, misunderstanding and anguish.

He hesitated. The temple looked sentient, shining black and silver, its solid bulk reaching skeletal fingers into the sky . . . but Eldareth wasn't superstitious. He had Aelyr friends. Unlike the Eisilians, he did not think of them as demons. He grasped the horses' reins and led them towards the ruin.

The hillside was steep below the towering walls, treacherous with loose soil and shale. Sliding, stumbling on tree-roots, blinded and wet through, he brought the horses safely to the front of the edifice. Here he found a portico with tapering columns like long, thin cones supporting what was left of the roof. Behind the portico the front wall was intact but the doors were long gone, fallen from rusted hinges. The massive doorway framed a black void.

Redbird and Gany balked, nearly pulling Eldareth's arms out of his sockets. Biting back the curse that broke from him, he spoke gently, coaxing them over the threshold and into the temple.

Inside, the space felt vast. It was not quite dark; he made

out faint patches of sky above. The roof was laced with holes, but intact enough to shelter them from the worst of the storm. There were smooth flagstones underfoot. Lightning revealed walls of blue-black stones festooned with tangles of undergrowth, rows of stone seats along the sides facing in towards a dark, round block of marble that must have been an altar. Along the rear of the temple were stone partitions behind which, he guessed, the priests' private sanctum had lain.

Relieved to be out of the rain, Eldareth led the horses to the driest corner of the temple and tethered them to a stone rail. He unsaddled them, dried them as best he could with cloths from his saddlebag, then left them to graze on tufts of grass that sprouted freely through gaps in the wall. No poisonous plants within their reach, that he could see. There was nowhere comfortable for him to sleep, so he lay down on a stone bench with his pack under his head, and tried to make the best of it.

No sound but the rushing rain – but the moment he dozed, the air was suddenly filled with dozens of voices whispering.

Eldareth's eyes flew open. His senses were confused. Unable to see or hear clearly, he felt suspended in darkness with the whole temple spinning gently around him. His heart leapt. That scent again, the earth-and-lightning aroma of strange forces, and those illusory voices whispering, soft and maddeningly unclear and yet deafening . . .

He half-sat up, trying to orientate himself. Then he knew for sure that he was awake – and not alone. Leaning up he peered over the back of the bench in front of him, hoping desperately that it shielded him from sight.

In the centre of the temple, light shimmered in a dim bluish column above the altar. The column rippled, ever-changing, ethereal. Against the light, figures moved. A mass of veiled forms, blue black like the temple itself, as slender and insubstantial as ghosts rising up under death-shrouds; each outlined by an aura that reached every sense he had. Cold, weird fingers of light entered his mind. These were not humans. Shimmering power flowed from them and he knew.

They were Aelyr.

Not damping down their natures, so as not to alarm humans, but unselfconscious, gleaming with the terrifying *otherness* that humans could not bear.

Paralysed, Eldareth watched the procession pass.

They were coming into the temple from outside, bringing the scent of rain with them. Some of them passed within a couple of feet of him and he couldn't move even to duck behind the bench; could only remain there as if a spell were on him, praying they would not see him. Some of them seemed to look straight at him with veiled yet glowing eyes, and his heart nearly failed. Yet if they saw him, they ignored him and moved on, dark and intent and purposeful.

And as they drew near the centre of the temple and were silhouetted against the light, they grew smaller and smaller. Far tinier than they could possibly have appeared at the altar, which was only a few yards from him. It was as if they were staying in one place while he moved away from them. As if the glow contained another world entirely. They were passing through a portal to their own realm, and the mystery of it suffused Eldareth with awe and terror.

He thought he heard a cry. A human cry.

He started up, and the temple lurched around him. The figures were gone. The light vanished, sucked back into the altar with a soundless *whoosh*; all was dark and deserted again. And Eldareth fell instantly into a deep, dreamless sleep as if he had been drugged with milk of poppies.

He woke to blinding daylight and a headache, with the horses blowing hot grassy breath into his face. Memory came slowly, painfully.

'So, I saw the Aelyr engaged in some secret business last night,' he said, stroking Redbird's soft nose. His voice was rough with sleep. 'Did you see them? Shame you can't talk. I can only thank Nepheter that they didn't take any interest in us.'

The temple was deserted; just an overgrown shell. But an atmosphere lingered, and he knew that whatever power and *roth*-spirits had been summoned here by worship, centuries ago, still lingered.

Eldareth began to move his aching limbs, to make ready for the day's journey. Breakfast of dried meats and fruits from his pack. A perfunctory shave and wash. Checking the horses over, saddling them, Gany standing patient, Redbird sighing and fidgeting and making her usual attempts to nip him.

He thought of Elrill as he rode. Elrill's folk, the Shaelahyr of the Whiteveil Mountains, had chosen to live on Earth rather than in the Aelyr realm, Verdanholm, and they were relatively benign to humans. But he couldn't forget that Elrill had enemies; other factions of Aelyr who were less than sympathetic to humans. Perhaps with good reason, he reflected. And what if Elrill was right, and Tanthe had some connection with those unfriendly Aelyr?

Eldareth rode on, pushing himself hard to reach his destination.

Two more days passed without incident. On the third, he came in sight of the long narrow valley, a stream rushing white against the copper of the hillsides. And poised above it stood the great stone house, his destination, Luin Trest. He'd lived here once, as a child, just for a short time during his mother's endless flight from his father . . .

Here lived a noble family, cousins of Lord Serpeth, cousins also of the monarchs of Aventuria and the dukes of Mithrain – all the noble houses were interrelated in some way. Lady Nietriya, a good friend, had sheltered Ghiseyma and her son here during Garnelys's madness. A beautiful place, but bleak and remote, especially in the winter; how glad Ghiseyma would be to go home. Still, she was a strong character, not given to complaining. Unlike the boy, who was her only weakness. She let him get away with too much. Maybe a couple of hard winters here would have changed his character.

Eldareth shifted his aching body in the saddle. 'Nearly there,' he told the horses. 'Nice warm stables for you, a good night's sleep in a bed for me. Gods, we've earned it, eh?'

People came out to meet him as he rode into the courtyard; stable-hands, kitchen staff, and with them several excitable hounds. Redbird reared in alarm as the dogs came bounding forward, barking. Eldareth quickly dismounted from Gany to calm her, shouting at a couple of stable boys to restrain them. The lads scrambled to obey. Then came older women and men, senior members of the household, dressed in the intricate diamond patchwork that was unique to Eisilion; the material made into stiff, quilted garments of gorgeous hues. And following them, Lady Nietriya herself, tall and graceful, her dress all tiny lozenges of blue, green and bronze.

Her chestnut hair had turned white since he'd last seen her, but otherwise there was little sign of age in her strong face. Only a few lines around her deep set blue eyes. Her expression, though, was anxious. In fact everyone around her seemed edgy, rather than pleased by his arrival.

'My dear Lord Eldareth!' she cried, coming forward to embrace him. 'How wonderful to see you. I can't tell you how glad I am that you're here. Ah, we are both grown much older since last we met.'

He laughed, embracing her and kissing her cheek. 'My Lady Nietriya. Has the news reached you?'

She pulled back, the tension in her eyes approaching dread. 'I know that Lord Serpeth took his armed men to aid the King. They have not returned. We hear rumours that there was a war, that the King is dead, but we haven't known what to believe.'

'It's true,' Eldareth said. 'I was there. A long story which

21

I will gladly tell you over a good meal. The King is dead, and Helananthe is to take the throne. And she asked me to come and fetch her mother and brother home. It's safe for them now, and she wants them at her coronation.'

Lady Nietriya's face turned whiter. There was silence; her staff gave each other grave, difficult looks.

'Alas, Eldareth.' Tears crept on to her lashes. 'Ghiseyma and Veny are gone.'

'Gone? Where?'

She began to tremble; he'd never seen her afraid before. 'It happened five nights ago. They were abducted. It was over before we knew what was happening. I have racked my brains to think what we could have done to prevent it, but—'

'Abducted?' Eldareth exclaimed. 'But why? Who would do this?'

'They were veiled, the ones who came to take them.' Lady Nietriya lowered her eyes, her voice quickening with fear. 'They came in force, they seemed to fill the whole house and to cast a trance upon us. There was nothing we could do to resist them. Why they wanted Ghiseyma and Veny, they didn't say, and we have heard no word from them since. This has been the most grievous calamity.'

Eldareth gasped, remembering his night in the deserted temple. 'They were Aelyr, weren't they?'

She glared at him, stiff with anger. 'Don't speak that word. Demons!' She sketched the sign of the snake-goddess in the air, a protective S. 'How did you know?'

'I think I saw them entering their portal, three days' ride from here. Are you sure they told no one why—?'

She shook her head. 'I have no idea where the demons came from, nor how they knew Ghiseyma was here, nor why they should have done such a thing.'

'Damn it! They must have had Ghiseyma and Veny with them, and they passed by me close enough to touch, and I didn't know.' Eldareth groaned. 'I heard a boy cry out, and I did nothing. Ah gods, and what am I to tell Helananthe?'

Chapter Two. The Forest Hall

Tanthe was falling into a well of green light.

The world dissolved, spinning; she felt that she had always been here, drowning in blue-green ether. Travelling a long loop of time that hung suspended from the instant in which she had stepped into the portal . . .

Her thoughts and memories swirled like dreams.

She was back in Riverwynde, running across a golden field with her sister Ysomir at her side. Searching desperately for something. Her mother Aynie appeared; small and slim, her burnished hair lifted by the breeze, her eyes crinkling in the bright sunlight. Laughing, she held out her arms to her daughters.

'Tanthe!' she cried. Her voice was faint and Tanthe strained to hear her. 'Thank the Goddess you're home! You've been away so long.'

'Mum,' said Tanthe. 'I'm sorry, but we're not really here. I must find the mirror.'

'What mirror?' said Aynie, her smile fading.

'The little crystal mirror Grandma Helwyn gave me. It's really important that I find it.'

'You can't have lost it!' said Aynie, and she was Helwyn at the same time, silver-haired and forbidding, the orb glowing green upon her staff. 'Oh, you careless girl! How can you learn what truly matters?'

Aynie and Ysomir vanished. Tanthe was alone in the field, which seemed so real she could feel the stubble cracking under her boots and smell the hot earth. Yet the mountains were rushing up like white flames into the sky. She thought, I can't be here, I travelled two thousand miles to Parione to find Ysomir, I can't be back home with it all to do again!

She began to run across the field. She must find Ysomir. Her sister was here somewhere, she knew, concealed in a sun-warmed hollow with Lynden, her lover, but although Tanthe searched and searched, she couldn't find her. Ysomir was gone. Snatched away by the soldiers of King Garnelys, conscripted to the mines and then to labour on the dreadful Tower . . .

The journey unrolled again. Tanthe was riding through an endless forest with Lynden and his brother Rufryd, and sometimes she and Rufryd were arguing and sometimes making love and sometimes being pursued by hideous pale creatures with seven-fingered hands . . . but the forest went on forever.

Now Saphaeyender was leaning over her. Her idol, the great writer, the genius she'd worshipped from afar all her life. Living flesh and blood. His face was bathed in light, his black hair flaring around his shoulders, the streaks of white at his temples shining like exotic plumage.

'Tanthe,' he said softly, 'how could you leave me? I had so much still to show you. Don't go. I need you, my goddess, my muse.'

Saphaeyender changed. He stood before her in battle gear, sword in hand, wide-eyed and covered from head to foot in blood. 'Lynden, Lynden,' he said in a hoarse whisper that filled her with horror. 'I couldn't save him.'

Suddenly they were in the midst of battle. Horses were thundering around her. People falling on all sides. Dark reptilian birds gliding overhead. Redbird stumbled, pitching Tanthe off so that she fell, again, down through green-tinged darkness from one world into another . . .

After what seemed a year or two, Tanthe became aware that the world was no longer spinning. There was firm ground beneath her and a soft light glowing into her eyes. Framed against vague shapes of green and bluish shadow, someone was leaning over her. Not Saphaeyender, not Rufryd . . .

The visions slipped out of her grasp. She surfaced to find she had no recent memories, no idea where or even who she was.

The face looking down at her was at once strange and poignantly familiar. A young man with golden skin and innocent, deep brown eyes. His dark auburn hair brushed her face as he leaned over her.

'Tanthe?' he said.

She couldn't answer. Her mouth was dry and solid, as if she'd been unconscious for hours. The stranger held her hands; his were warm, strong, long-fingered. 'That is your name, isn't it? It was hard to hear you,' he said. He had a slight, strange accent, as lovely as music. 'Your real name was never known to us, so I'll call you that. I'm Auriel.'

And she knew, although she couldn't remember anything else, that he was Aelyr. *Aelyr.* The mysterious other-race who looked human and yet were not.

'Auriel,' she croaked. That meant something . . . She struggled to sit up and he helped her, putting one arm round her shoulders and holding her close to him. Even her own clothes seemed unfamiliar; where had she got them from, the breeches and tabard of fine emerald-green cloth, the shirt of soft ochre linen, the red-brown riding boots of such fine leather? Auriel wore a tunic of gossamer-soft grey silk, which revealed the sculptural beauty of his lean and silken body. He seemed too beautiful to be real. And there was something of the forest animal about him, an acute wariness, as if he might flee at the slightest hint of danger.

'What happened?' she said. 'Where is this place?'

Concern darkened his eyes. 'Don't you know? You must remember.'

She shook her head vigorously. 'I don't! Where the hell am I? *Who* am I?'

'Tanthe,' he said again. 'You are in the realm of the

Aelyr. You came through from Earth. I've tried to reach you for years. We made a portal together, don't you recall?'

'When?'

'A minute ago, hardly more. Don't be afraid. I've heard it said that crossing over can have this effect, the first time.'

She saw that they were in a woodland glade. There was lush grass beneath them and dense trees around them in a rough circle, the branches so interwoven and thick with leaves that she could see only a few lozenges of sky. A sun was shining, though she couldn't see it. Everything looked strange. The greens were too intense, while the blue of the shadows and the inky flowers in the grass was as rich as lapis lazuli. The scents of greenery, damp earth and dew were almost musky, intoxicating. Every leaf was outlined with light. Her senses were overwhelmed.

'Can you stand up?' he asked.

'I think so.' Her limbs tingled. As he helped her to her feet, her blood began to flow, her strength to return. 'This is . . .' The word hung on the edge of her memory. 'Verdanholm.'

'Yes, Verdanholm!' he said, smiling for the first time. 'I can't believe you are here at last. Sister, beloved sister.'

And he kissed her, full on the mouth.

That breached the dam. Her memories came surging back in lines of fire. Auriel stroked her dark hair and they both wept, clinging hard to each other.

Of course she knew him. Hadn't he haunted her whole life? A face in a strange little crystal mirror, that she'd lost in childhood. A ghostly figure in the woods, there and gone; a reflection in pools and lakes and quartz walls, begging her urgently to go to him, but she didn't know how . . .

'Auriel,' she said, hardly able to believe she was touching him. He'd been a tantalising phantom and now he was real and warm in her arms. Silken skin and muscle under her fingers, and the new, delicious, subtle spice of

26

his body . . . She was speechless with joy and terror.

'Do you remember now?' he said.

'Yes – yes, I know how I got here.'

'And you know who I am?' he asked urgently.

'No.' She pressed her head into his shoulder. 'I mean, I've seen you many times, I know your face and name and that you claim to be my brother. I feel that I trust you. But, Auriel, that's not the same as knowing who you really are.'

'You don't remember—?'

'What?'

'Anything more than your human life.'

'No! Stop trying to confuse me. I've only had a human life.'

He gave a faint sigh. 'I understand.' Hugging her, he said into her hair, 'I'm sorry, Tanthe. Forgive me. Please forgive me.'

The pressure of his body was waking flames in hers; startled at herself, she pulled away. 'For what?'

'Bringing you here.'

'Why? You didn't force me. Is it dangerous?'

He touched her cheek, and she saw anxiety in his eyes. 'It can be.'

In sudden alarm, Tanthe looked round at the glade. There was no sign of a portal; no window on to her own world, with Eldareth's anxious face framed in it. Only a stump of bluish stone half-hidden in the grass. 'Gods, what have I done?' She pointed at the stone. 'Is that where the portal was?'

Her question seemed to make him uneasy. 'Yes.'

'How come you were here, just when I happened to be . . . where I was? Bit of a coincidence, isn't it?'

He was frowning at her. She wondered if Paranian wasn't his first language, and he didn't understand. Then he answered, 'I have lived for days at a time in this glade because the portal *rothanamir* is here. Waiting, in the hope that you would call to me.'

27

'Oh,' said Tanthe, taken aback. 'Then how did you open it?'

'With this.' He took an object from a pocket in his robe. It was an orb of clear quartz the size of his palm. 'The *anametris* sphere. It's so hard to open the portal. I've only done it twice before, and only for a second or two. I can't go through it. So you had to come to me. It was only together we could open it long enough for you to come through.'

'I see . . . I think. There's so much to talk about, I don't know where to start. Why can't you go through it?'

He slipped the sphere away. 'We should go now,' he said quietly.

'Auriel, I can't help noticing . . . You seemed frantic when you begged me to come to you, as if you were in terrible danger, or about to be captured. Now you're just, well, a bit edgy, but not panicking. What's going on?'

He clasped her hand. 'The urgency was to bring you through the portal before it closed. But the danger's still there,' he said softly. 'Come with me.'

He was leading her on to a path that wound out of the glade and through the woods. Where the path began, a stone squatted beside it like a giant toad. She had the uneasy impression that it was watching them. As they went, Auriel looked around anxiously in a way that made her more nervous than ever. 'Where are we going?'

'Somewhere you can rest, and I can explain.'

It seemed a habit with him, Tanthe noticed very quickly, to say, 'I'll explain,' or 'I've so much to tell you,' but these promises were followed, so far, by mysterious silence.

They walked through the forest for a time, enveloped in its deep blues and glowing greens. The trees seemed to lean over them – actually moving, Tanthe suspected, if only she could look round fast enough to catch them. Occasionally a strange bird call would boom through the canopy; otherwise the silence was intense. Presently she noticed a background noise, a rushing like that of a waterfall, except that it was too even in pitch. It contained an unearthly music that reminded her of the Shaelahyr.

'What's that sound?' she asked eventually.

'The stars,' replied Auriel.

'Stars? In the sky, you mean?'

'Of course.' He looked at her in disbelief. 'You hear them singing on Earth, don't you?'

'Er . . . no, we don't.' Speechless, Tanthe decided it was safer not to ask anything else for a while.

The forest didn't feel friendly. They crossed a clearing, open at one end onto a landscape that seemed oddly bleak, with silvery grass vanishing into the mist of the horizon. Several tall, jagged blue stones stood in the clearing like priests. They had a cold aura that unsettled her. Looking up, she saw the sky for the first time. It was a rich cobalt blue and the noisy stars were scattered as thick as snow-flakes across it, visible in daylight. Light fell in diamond nets across the weird rock sentinels, unlike any light she'd ever seen on Earth.

She ventured a question. 'What are those?'

'Just stones,' said Auriel.

They walked through the forest for what she judged to be twenty minutes; but time was deceptive here. She felt it wasn't passing in a straight line but in curves and clumps, sometimes in knots that went back on themselves, then forward again. And this, like Auriel himself, felt so familiar yet so unspeakably strange that her head ached with trying to understand it.

'Here we are,' he said.

She couldn't see anything at first. They walked on a few steps and then it took shape from the trees themselves. A great house, rising up into the canopy of the forest.

It was tall and wide, like a mansion, but its walls were formed by living trees, their tall trunks as supporting pillars, their living branches woven into a curved roof, panels of loose-woven twigs between the trees to complete the walls. Its appearance was simple and awe-

29

inspiring. No rustic construction, this, but a lofty, timeless edifice that might have housed gods. Tanthe was breathing fast. She was truly in the faerie realm, from which no one came back unchanged.

Auriel led her through an open doorway to the interior. She looked up into a great, dark space, hearing the branches of the roof creaking and rustling above, feeling the air moving through the lattice walls, sweet and green scented. There was a great central hall with a long table in the centre, with three chandeliers of rough branches that resembled stag antlers suspended above it. Along the far wall were wattle screens that seemed to have other rooms behind them. A rope ladder hung from a balcony that overlooked the hall; beyond it was darkness. More rooms? she wondered. There was a greenish material like canvas on the floor, and scattered on it, rugs of a rich dark blue speckled with silver beads.

Auriel went to the table, where a single lamp glowed, a white orb. She couldn't quite see what he did but she had the impression he scooped fire out of it with his fingers, and went along touching that fire to glass or crystal lamps all along the walls.

He came back to her and touched her cheek; she thought she felt the cool flame of the lamplight lingering on his fingertips. 'Are you thirsty?'

'Yes, and starving,' she said.

He smiled. 'Sit down.'

The table and the wooden bench on which she seated herself were rustic in shape, yet the creamy grain of the wood was satin-smooth under her fingers. New scents kept coming to her; the crushed herbs on the rugs, the spicy incense of the wood. This was so vivid and yet . . .

Tanthe kept feeling that time was slowing down, stopping, curling back on itself, then suddenly rushing ahead in a flurry of steps. Parts of the hall seemed to blur and glimmer, settling back into focus when she tried to catch them out.

Auriel went to a shadowy construction – some kind of cupboard or dresser she couldn't see properly – and came back with a plate of round white cakes, a slim carafe and a goblet of deep blue glass. As he poured, the clear stream caught the light like diamonds, bringing her thirst to ravenous life. The same glow played around his gilded form and fiery hair, and she couldn't stop staring, dumbstruck by the reality of him. He sat down beside her, smiling. He watched her all the time, she noticed, as if he couldn't believe she was real, either.

As she lifted the goblet, she found it was not glass at all but some kind of carved mineral, cool on her fingers. She drank deeply. The liquid was delicious, flavoured with honey and elderflowers, with a herbal bitterness beneath.

'Aren't you having a drink?' she said.

'I'll share yours.' He wrapped his hand round hers as she held the vessel and lifted it to his own lips, taking a sip then planting a kiss on her thumb. The sensuality of the gesture took her breath away. He called her 'sister' yet he wasn't treating her like one. Normally she would have been angry by now but it seemed sacrilegious to lose patience in the Aelyr realm. Half of her didn't want to believe they were related, purely because of the disturbing lust she was beginning to feel for him.

She took a mouthful of cake. Rice, almonds and rosewater, dissolving on her tongue . . . that was all she could compare it to. 'Is this where you live?' she asked. 'Have you always been here? All the times you tried to reach me?'

'Some of the times. Not all of them.'

'Are we safe here?'

He hesitated, as if surprised by the question. 'Yes, of course.'

'Only you said outside that there were dangers, and this house is hardly the Amber Citadel. Anything could come in.'

'It's all right,' he said, stroking the back of her hand.

'Really? Oh, good. Why don't I believe you?'

He looked down, studying her fingertips. 'If only you could remember, this wouldn't be so hard. If you hadn't lost the mirror!'

Now she was becoming impatient, despite herself. 'How do we know we are talking about the same mirror?'

Reaching into the pocket from which he'd taken the sphere, he produced a round mirror, eight inches across; a disc of clear silvered crystal set in white quartz. He placed it on the table in front of her and she stared at it.

'Did it look like that?' he asked.

'Yes,' she breathed. 'Exactly like that.'

'This is what I used to call you. A *silvenroth* mirror. You know what *roth* is, don't you?'

'Yes, energy. Hundreds of different forms. *Silvenroth, liroth, ethroth* . . .'

When he looked at her, his face was warm and alive; but now and then he would glance away with fear darting in his eyes, as if watching or listening for something. 'What happened to the mirror?' he asked, low and quiet.

Tanthe bit her lip. 'If you must know, I hid it, because seeing your face in it scared me to death.'

'I'm sorry. I didn't mean to frighten you. You frightened me, sometimes; came so close to me that I lost my nerve, and ran from you.'

Tanthe laughed. 'Like a nervous young stag. That's what you remind me of.'

He smiled, but his eyes were all shadow. 'I tried so hard to pass from my world into yours, but I couldn't. The most I could do was press close to the barrier between us so that you saw me, if only for a few seconds; but it took so much of my strength, and I was never really there.'

'You must be powerful, though.'

His beautiful eyes widened. 'What do you mean?'

'To be able to make me see you, even though I'd lost the mirror. Is that a normal Aelyr power, or are you a mage of some kind?'

He looked horrified. 'No, I'm no mage. I've no power at all. Not enough, anyway. If I had that sort of power, I wouldn't . . . it doesn't matter.' She touched his hand, but he didn't elaborate. 'I hoped that when you passed from your realm to ours, it might bring back your lost memories.'

'Of what?' she said.

'Being my sister.'

'Well, it hasn't. How could we possibly be related? We don't even look alike. Your hair's red, mine's black, your eyes are brown, mine are blue—'

'Green,' he said. 'Bluey-green.'

'Whatever. For Breyid's sake, you're Aelyr and I'm a peasant with too many wild ideas for my own good. I can't be your sister. You must have made a mistake.'

'No.' He held her hands and gazed insistently into her eyes. 'You must recall something. You must know, in some deep part of you, or you wouldn't have come to me.'

Tanthe rubbed her forehead. Little spirals of dizziness and half-remembered dreams were dancing through her skull. 'If only my grandma Helwyn had explained something about that mirror when she gave it to me. Perhaps she didn't know what it was herself. After you scared me, I put it under my bed and when I looked for it, it had gone. I haven't seen it since. Sorry, but I was only a child! Next time I saw you was at harvest last year, just before the soldiers came. This beautiful man drinking from a pool in the woods . . . I knew you were Aelyr. I just knew. And after that I saw you often, and you gave me this—'

She took out the little Aelyr knife, a pale blade with a crystal sphere on the pommel, which had warned her of danger and even saved her life. Auriel placed his hand on hers, gently pushing the *mnelir* away. 'No,' he said. 'I didn't mean your conscious memories. I meant your unconscious ones.'

'There's only one,' she said uneasily. 'A recurring nightmare of being pulled backwards into the darkness

33

and feeling that I am going to suffocate. What's that about?'

'That's it, Tanthe.' The intensity of his eyes startled her. 'You can remember passing out of the Aelyr realm and into the Earth.'

'How old was I?'

'You were newborn.'

'Then how could I possibly remember anything?' she nearly yelled.

'Because the Aelyr exist before we're conceived,' he answered simply. 'You know that, don't you?'

'I've heard it, yes,' she said, her jaw set.

'So we come into the world knowing what we are, remembering the Jewelfire . . . the place we were before.'

'Well, I don't.' She was suddenly close to tears. 'So, if I was newborn, how old were you?'

'I was four. We count the years by Earth's time, as best we can,' he answered, to her surprise. 'I remember mother and father a little. Mother's name was Fiomir and father was Talthaliorn.'

'Was?' She choked on her shock. Just to hear him speak these unknown, resonant names. 'What happened to them?'

Auriel paused. 'They were in danger, fleeing for their lives. They knew a daughter was coming to them, but they couldn't flee with an infant, so they put you in the care of a human family, where you wouldn't be found. They gave the family a *silvenroth* mirror, so one day you might know the truth. They tried to take me with them but it was too hard, so in the end they left me behind as well.' He sounded sad. 'They did it to save our lives, and their own.'

Tanthe began to cry, dry sobs of shock. 'But I'm human,' she said, pinching the flesh of her forearm. 'I am.'

'But how do you know what it feels like to be human, or Aelyr?' He put his arm alongside hers. 'Does my flesh feel different to yours?'

She stroked his arm. Warm, like hers, and sprinkled

with soft hairs, like Rufryd's. 'I don't know,' she whispered, wanting to do a lot more than touch him and wishing she didn't. 'I lived with the Shaelahyr last winter, and they had bodies like us – very long, pale, silver-white bodies, it's true – but still, they had all the same needs we do and yet, they were different. You're different. I'm not like you.'

'Tanthe, I don't know how to explain. I'm not sure I understood what Fiomir told me. But somehow you were put in human flesh so you wouldn't be noticed. And your memory must have been clouded for the same reason. So yes, your body is human, and all your experiences. But your spirit-*roth* is Aelyr.'

She pressed her hands to her forehead, rubbed her temples. 'I don't believe it.'

'Your bad dream. You know it's true.'

'This is horrible. This is not fair. Aynie and Eodwyth are my parents.'

'Yes, they brought you up and loved you. That's more than I have had. But your true parents are Fiomir and Talthaliorn. Is it horrible, to think you are one of us?'

'No, of course not! I mean it's the lying, the betrayal that's horrible.' She took a long drink. 'I need to think about this. Gods, I really need to speak to my parents but I can't! They're thousands of miles away – no, another realm away.'

She got up, walked slowly around the table. It seemed to be getting dark outside. The lamps gleamed like moons. When she came back to Auriel she hopped on to the table itself and sat with her feet on the bench.

'What was this terrible danger that Fiomir and Talthaliorn had to flee from?'

He tipped his head back and looked at her. His face was like the statues of beautiful gods she'd seen in Parione, his eyes shining darkly. Her head swam with the urge to forget everything else and kiss him . . . 'I don't know.'

'You must have some idea. Was it the Bhahdradomen?'

Auriel looked shocked that she spoke the name so easily. 'I didn't realise you would ask so many questions.'

She laughed. 'What did you expect? Your sister is the nosiest person in the Nine Realms. You can't drag me into this mystery and not give me answers. I want to know why you're trapped here, what sort of danger we're in, everything!'

He gave a faint groan. 'It's complicated. I . . . I lived with Fiomir's friends for a time but I ran away, trying to find you and our parents. Then I found I couldn't leave this part of Verdanholm. That's all.'

'It can't be.'

He looked so innocent and distressed, a forest creature severed from its wild power, that she longed to reassure him. She leaned down and stroked his hair, held him against her. He caught her hands and kissed them. 'Auriel, you brought me here and I'm going to help you. But you've got to be a bit more forthcoming. I don't know this place. I think it's best if I take you back to Earth. I've got friends there, powerful friends who'll help us. I know the Queen.'

His eyes were awash with wild hope and terror. 'I'd love to. But I can't. I can't. I don't know how to send you back, either.'

Her stomach twisted coldly. She stared at the carafe, the cakes. Only superstition, she knew, but she couldn't put it out of her mind. *Don't eat or drink in the faery realm or you'll be under their power for ever.*

'What are you afraid of?' No answer. 'Don't play games with me, Auriel, please. There must be something we can do.'

'There's nothing.'

She leapt to the ground. 'Then what the fuck did you bring me here for?'

He didn't react. If this had been Rufryd, he would have yelled back at her. She couldn't cope with Auriel's long-suffering evasiveness.

'I'm sorry, Tanthe,' he said, catching her hand. 'I'm so sorry.'

'Never mind sorry. So you're stuck here by some spell and you brought me here to keep you company? This is ridiculous. I feel like I've walked into one of Saphaeyender's "Collected Folk Tales of Aventuria". Perhaps the Woman Made of Bones will walk in next.'

'Tanthe, please,' he said gently, tugging at her hand until she sat down beside him. 'Everything will make sense soon.'

'It had better!'

'It will. Have some more wine. Tell me what has happened to you. You said something about soldiers?'

'I suppose you don't know what's happened in Aventuria.'

'I know a little,' he said, 'but I want to know about you. Tell me.'

She felt the honeyed liquor going to her head. The walls shimmered, and she couldn't hold on to her anger. So she began to tell him of her own adventures. Her life in Riverwynde as the daughter of peasant farmers, her dreams of living in the great city Parione among writers and artists . . . the terrible way her dream had come true. How Ysomir had been conscripted to work on Garnelys's Tower, how Tanthe had travelled two thousand miles and fought in the Battle of Hethlas Rim to get her sister back . . . only to fail.

Auriel listened, but she couldn't help noticing that his gaze kept darting warily to the door. He seemed to grow more and more tense. Eventually she trailed off and said, 'Look, I may be cut off from my Aelyr wisdom, Auriel, but I'm not stupid. I get the feeling you're waiting for something.'

He said nothing.

'You are complete rubbish at lying!' she snapped. 'What is going on, really?'

'I'm waiting for the others to come home,' he said.

Her heart began to pound. 'What others? I thought you lived alone here!'

'I never said that.'

'You—' She stopped. He was right, he hadn't said it; she had jumped to conclusions, as usual. 'Who are they?'

'They're part of our family, Tanthe. Our family.'

As he spoke, Tanthe's whole body jolted in a violent start. She felt, an instant before she looked up and saw, that there was a figure in the doorway of the forest mansion.

He was quite tall and as beautiful as Auriel, but seemingly older, with pale golden skin, black hair that curved over his shoulders to his waist, eyes soft and grey as the spectral lakes of Mithrain. He wore a black and violet robe and over it a cloak, purple as night, clasped on the shoulder with a white jewel set in silver. He looked magnificent, like an elemental that had taken shape out of the twilight.

For a moment she had an immense shock of recognition. She thought, *that's my father*, then just as quickly thought, *no*. The moment had gone. This was a stranger.

'She's here,' said Auriel.

The stranger smiled, came striding towards her and gripped both her hands, almost before she had time to stumble to her feet.

'Oh, Tanthe,' the stranger exclaimed. 'I have your name right? Good. This is wonderful. We've longed for this moment for – oh, years. You're among friends now, among Aelyr who love you. I am Falthorn, your uncle. Your father's brother.'

Chapter Three. The Poet and the Birch Tree

In the non-physical dimension known as *ezht*, where even space and time folded upon themselves, two Bhahdradomen waited.

Adepts, they projected their astral selves as images true to their physical forms. Zhoaah was pale and delicate and precise in his movements, Gulzhur vulturine, his face a sour skull webbed with translucent skin and gnarled veins.

They waited on a featureless black plain; above them a bowl of inky night hung starless, with only the faintest glow around the horizon to distinguish sky from ground. Beneath their feet, a luminescent path bisected the plain, coming from nowhere, dwindling to nowhere.

Along this path, under the black sky, came their master Vaurgroth; a tower of dark cloud.

Vaurgroth.

In the Bhahdradomen tongue, his name could be translated as Master of Light, Lord of Creation, Ancestor of Spirits, Overlord of Universal *Roth*. His name was his title, and his titles were many. Vaurgroth of the Fire, they called him. The fire that would burn the world clean.

Zhoaah's soft features stretched in a nervous smile, but Gulzhur was grim, revealing neither fear nor triumph.

The thunderous cloud split open, like the two sides of a cloak being flung back, and a dazzling white light spilled out. The two Bhahdradomen recoiled, shielding their eyes. Colours rippled up through the light, like reflected fire. Through the blaze they glimpsed the hint of a bone-white face, long serene eyes, a spider's web of red tattooed on the great skull, which was bald but for a single rope of white hair.

'So, my friends,' came the voice, deep and rich and resonant with the music of thunder and the whirring of a million insects. Zhoaah and Gulzhur made obeisance in turn as he greeted them by their name-titles. 'Facilitator, Enabler. Have you gifts for me?'

'Master of Light,' said Gulzhur, trembling a little. 'We bring ripe fruits, indeed.'

'Ahh.' Vaurgroth came close to them, so close they felt his heat, smelled the metallic crackle of his energy. 'Enabler . . .'

He fed on Gulzhur first, sucking from him all the human pain, confusion and grief that he had accumulated during his time in Aventuria. To Gulzhur, it was like the tearing away of a warm cloak. He endured it. He'd known he would have to make this sacrifice to his master, who gathered more *gauroth* energy to himself every day, sucking it ever more thirstily as his power grew. It was a sacrifice he made gladly.

Afterwards, Vaurgroth held Gulzhur's face between his hands for a moment before letting him go. The Master of Light's face filled his vision, pulsing with radiance. Smiling. Every mote of energy he had taken, he gave back in approval.

Then Vaurgroth drew Zhoaah to him. Facilitator's head fell back and he uttered a cry of loss as the Master fed. The column of light throbbed, shimmering with colours and emitting faint moans of delight.

When it was over, Vaurgroth pushed him away. 'You twine the pain too tightly to yourself, Zhoaah,' he said. 'That's why it hurt you to surrender it to me. It is not a possession. Be as Gulzhur; wear it lightly and give it up easily.'

Zhoaah's form wavered. He visibly gathered his strength to hold himself in the *ezht*. 'Forgive me, Master. I shall take your advice.'

'Still, I understand. Ancestor is merciful.' Vaurgroth's tone was kind. His was a benevolent and expansive character, so different to his dried-up predecessor Aazhoth. 'Enabler's *gauroth* was of a generalised kind, garnered from dozens of small fights and battles and deaths between strangers. Solid meat, nutritious but lacking subtlety. Yours, though was of a different order. The agony of the King's own victims, and the crowning glory; the anguish of the King himself as he died, confused and betrayed, in a lake of his own blood. Now that was a truly unique and exquisite delicacy.'

'Ah yes, great lord. You understand completely.' Zhoaah nodded, pleased to have his achievement recognised.

'And a prize near-impossible to give up. So I want you to know how greatly I appreciate the gift you have given me.'

'Master, giving the energy to you is an honour greater by far than the mere pleasure of acquiring it.' Zhoaah smiled.

'That is Ancestor's will,' said Vaurgroth.

'There is an infinite supply of *gauroth* awaiting us!' added Gulzhur. He saw that Vaurgroth was pleased with them. For once, Gulzhur allowed himself to relish their victory. 'We have gained an excellent foothold in Aventuria. We seduced the King into trusting us and unleashing our *ghelim* upon his own people. We have made contact with Bhahdradomen in hiding all across the continent. We provoked the humans to make war on each other, and then at the last moment withdrew our aid, leaving the King's side floundering in defeat. We tore the rug from under his feet, as humans might say, in the most spectacular fashion!'

'The Tower is begun,' Zhoaah added, preening. 'The King was such easy meat, it was almost too cruel—'

'Is the Tower finished?' Vaurgroth cut in.

Zhoaah started. 'No, Master of Light. Surely it was not the intention to actually . . .'

'Is the war still continuing?'

'No,' admitted Gulzhur. 'It was bloody, but brief.'

41

'No conscriptions? No more slavery? No battles?'

'No, great lord.'

'So the humans are at peace? They are no longer fighting, killing and hating one another? They have a new monarch? While you have vanished, and withdrawn the *ghelim*, just as if you were never there?'

Enabler and Facilitator looked uneasily at each other.

'Well?' Vaurgroth's voice held the brassy heat of rage. 'Have I made an accurate assessment of the situation?'

'Yes, master,' Gulzhur said reluctantly. 'But—'

'Alas, I was hoping for good news. Instead you summon me here to tell me that Aventuria is at peace and all is well with the humans!'

The light swelled red and ochre with Vaurgroth's fury. How unutterably terrifying and bitter it was, to have disappointed him. Gulzhur sank into grim silence; Zhoaah looked at once indignant and horrified.

'So your work is far from finished. It has barely begun. You lack both the time and the reason to stand here congratulating yourselves, and I have not the stomach to listen to it.'

Deflated, humiliated, the two made deep gestures of regret and obeisance. Zhoaah said quickly, 'Our only wish is to serve Ancestor, Master of Light, and to restore our *domenim* to our rightful . . .'

'I know,' Vaurgroth said coldly. 'And you will. But never think you are indispensable, nor by any means the greatest of my adepts and spies and *ghelim*. Already I have more in motion than you can imagine and you have a great deal of work to do even to keep up with your fellows, let alone to impress me. Leave the *ezht* now; I can see that you are tiring. Return to your bodies, and wait for my aide to find you and instruct you. We knew it would be no easy matter to claw our way back from two hundred and fifty years of exile, while humans and Aelyr hold all the advantages.' He relented a little, bestowing them with a look that was firm and challenging rather than critical.

'But our time is coming. Our time is coming – only if each and every one of us pours his full self into the fight!'

Vaurgroth flowed away from them, a seething pillar of cloud crackling with the energy he'd taken from them. He vanished, and the light was gone from the plain.

'This is unfair,' Zhoaah whispered. 'After all that we've done!'

'No,' Gulzhur said harshly. 'He's right. We have been lazy and complacent and lo! Apart from a scattering of dead humans, what have we achieved? Nothing. Come, Facilitator. No self-pity. We begin again, and this time we do not rest until Vaurgroth has just cause to be proud of us.'

Rufryd awoke to a familiar sense of emptiness. For the first few moments, cocooned in sleep, he didn't know quite what was missing; the bed was comfortable, the walls of creamy marble safe around him, the morning light tranquil through the lattice shutter . . .

Then he remembered. Gods, all of it. He turned on to his back, groaned, rested his hands on the pillow above his head.

He thought he'd fallen asleep in Ashtar's huge soft bed last night . . . but no, she'd shaken him awake and banished him to his own small room on the lower floor of her house. As she always did. Lady Ashtar was a celebrated actress, who had far more important business to concern her than a mere lover.

Tanthe didn't behave like this, he thought. She used to be there in the mornings . . . Sod Tanthe. I won't waste my time thinking about her.

What the hell was he doing here in Parione? He asked himself that question a dozen times a day. Living with an actress of Saphaeyender's legendary theatre company, in her luxurious villa in the shadow of the Amber Citadel? He didn't belong here. It wasn't real.

Ashtar was using him, Rufryd knew. He had met her

when Eldareth had brought him, Tanthe and Lynden to a safe house where Saphaeyender and his actors were in hiding, having offended King Garnelys with a satirical play. Rufryd had disliked her at first. But after Tanthe had rejected him in favour of Saphaeyender, Ashtar had taken him under her wing, seduced him, invited him to live with her. He'd had nowhere else to go. And she was attractive, with thick dark hair, sensual heavy features, an eloquently curved body with which she expressed more (on stage and in private) than by speaking any of Saphaeyender's lines. All the men in Parione were in love with her, it was said; in which case at least three-quarters of them, Rufryd observed bitterly, trailed through her bedroom to prove it. If he'd thought he was special to her, he was quickly disillusioned.

Still, she was good-natured. By nature as sensual as she looked, when the mood took her she gave Rufryd very little rest, for which he couldn't complain. Yet whenever they made love, exciting as it was . . . each time after the golden moment of orgasm, when he opened his eyes and saw Ashtar's face, not Tanthe's, there was always that dreadful pang of emptiness.

They didn't love each other. He didn't belong in her world. But he had nowhere else to go, so he said nothing, and drifted through the days trying to *think* of nothing, if he could possibly help it.

It had all fallen apart after the Battle of Hethlas Rim. Before that, at least he'd still had hope that Tanthe might see sense and come back to him. He'd been surrounded by friends and comrades, wrapped in the excitement of Helananthe's rebel army, working together to defeat Garnelys. Saving Aventuria, yes.

Then afterwards.

Helananthe and Eldareth were gone to the Amber Citadel, too busy to bother with their lowly friends. Saphaeyender had returned to his villa, taking Tanthe with him and inviting Rufryd to stay also, as if Rufryd were an object of pity – no, it would have made him ill to stay around them. And Lynden – his dear younger brother, who had been the reason for making the long journey to Parione in the first place – Lynden was gone.

Killed in battle by a stray arrow. Stupid mischance. Killed, without fulfilling his quest to find Ysomir and bring her home, without even seeing her.

Rufryd didn't weep; it was his reluctance to show his feelings that had first alienated him from his father, years ago when his and Lynden's mother had died. But as he woke each morning, his first thought was of Lynden.

Rufryd flung back the covers, rose and began to dress. Same travelling clothes he'd worn from Sepheret to Paranios; black breeches, linen shirt, quilted black jacket sewn with blue silks and beads. These had been good clothes once, but now the embroidery was threadbare, the black fading to charcoal. He refused to put on the fashionable robes that Ashtar had given him; the last thing he wanted was to look like a citizen of Parione.

As he entered the living area, the scene looked like a painting. A chamber of glowing golden marble giving on to a lushly verdant courtyard; Ashtar framed against this background at the breakfast table, immaculate in a white dress that was stiff with boning and rich with gold embroidery. Two of her staff waited in the recess of an open doorway. Rufryd gave them a brief, hostile glance; from the beginning they'd made it silently obvious that he was beneath them.

Ashtar looked at Rufryd in surprise. Her red lips were poised around a moist apricot. Slowly she lowered the morsel back to her plate.

'What on earth are you wearing?' she said. 'I did ask you to put on a robe today. Saphaeyender is holding a meeting to decide the future of the theatre company. You can't go dressed like that.'

Rufryd's mood grew darker. He went to the table and leaned on it, facing her over the elegant crockery. 'I'm sure

Saphaeyender has more important things to think about than what I'm wearing. It was good enough for him in Enhavaneya.'

'Well, we are not in the forest playing warriors now.' Her expressive face became stiff with fury. 'After what he went through in battle, it would be worse than bad manners for you to walk in looking as if you have just wandered off the battlefield. It would be downright offensive.'

'What *he* went through?' He shook his head. 'Anyway, there's no need to get so worked up about it, Ash. I'm not going.'

The actress looked coolly at him, showing no reaction. He guessed she was torn between relief, and anger that he would not follow her everywhere like a hound. 'It's almost as rude for you to refuse. Why not?'

'Oh, come on. I don't want to sit there like a spare part while you lot talk about your precious theatre. I'd feel like your blasted stable-hand, or something.'

Her lips curved. 'Not my groom, Rufryd. My stallion.' He started to turn away in exasperation but she caught his hand. 'Now don't be so touchy. I'm only teasing. Tell me the truth; you're not still jealous of Saphaeyender and Tanthe, are you?'

'No, of course not!' he said, too fervently.

'It won't last, you know,' Ashtar said archly. 'Saphaeyender has one affair after another. He tries it on with practically everyone who crosses his path.'

'So I've heard,' Rufryd said bitterly. 'But that's Tanthe's problem. Let her find out the hard way.'

'I'm sure she will. He's been, shall we say, distracted at least once since he's been with her.'

Her words were only making him more helplessly angry. 'I don't know anything about that, and I don't want to.'

'You should. It was with your brother.'

Rufryd froze. He stared at her, shocked and furious. 'I don't believe you.'

'I saw them together myself once, Saphaeyender and Lynden in the woods; very cosy they looked.'

'You're lying!' Rufryd shouted. 'Lynden loved Ysomir. He loved her so much he wouldn't look at another woman, let alone a man. As if Saphaeyender hasn't taken enough from me already, you're telling me he even took advantage of my brother? He was just a boy! It wasn't him!'

Ashtar rose from her chair, alarmed at his reaction. 'Rufryd, calm yourself. I thought you knew. It's not important now, surely?'

'Then why mention it?' He pointed at her. 'You're lying. Do you get some perverse pleasure out of it, or is it just that *you're* jealous of Tanthe?'

Ashtar's servants, a man and woman, stepped forward out of the shadows. 'Do you need any assistance, my lady?' the man said softly.

'No, it's all right,' she said, composing herself. 'Leave us.'

'Don't bother,' Rufryd said. 'Finish your breakfast. I'm going. Have fun with your charming theatrical cronies, Ashtar; you deserve each other.'

He strode past her, crossed the shaded marble loggia and went across the courtyard to the stables. A narrow cloister gave on to a smaller yard enclosed by marble walls, with large loose boxes along two sides. At the sound of his footsteps, a fine-boned dark head swung over the stable door to greet him, nostrils flaring, large black-tipped ears swivelling. Honest company, at last. His horse, Halcyon.

Or rather, his brother's horse. Rufryd still thought of the blue stallion as Lynden's. His own horse, Sunhawk, had been killed underneath him in battle. So Rufryd looked after Halcyon instead, for Lynden. The stallion was of Sepheret stock, a tall, fine creature as swift as fire. Dark and light hairs roaned in his coat to make him seem slate-blue, the colour emphasised by the kohl-black of his slender hard legs and his mane and tail. He was good-natured, highly-strung, willing. Lynden had adored him.

The summer sky over the city was perfect; deep blue hazed with gold, the air soft and sweet like blossoms. The flagstones shone like pearl; the mansions gleamed pale gold and ivory round Rufryd as he rode between them. Trees swayed, dangling exotic flowers from their branches. There were birds everywhere; blue-doves clustering along the tops of walls, pointers like little white arrows in the sky, noisy bright red pipers squabbling in the treetops. Away to his left, the Amber Citadel shone down in golden splendour. Parione was the most beautiful place he'd ever seen, he couldn't deny that.

But the scars of the King's last days had not been erased. Silt in the gutters, which still snaked down from the building works on the hill, would eventually be sluiced away by the autumn rains. But the stump of the unfinished Heliodor Tower remained, louring over the city, out of proportion and graceless.

Rufryd looked away. For the sake of that useless monstrosity, their lives had been wrecked.

He found himself on the outskirts of the city, at the burial ground again. He was standing on a quiet hillside, with the birch trees softly sighing around him, Halcyon placidly tearing at the grass beside him. The sapling that marked Lynden's grave was in full leaf.

'I don't belong here, Lyn,' he said. 'It's what Tanthe wanted, not me. Now she'd got her pretentious literary friends and her hero as her lover, and I've got nothing. But tell me, where am I supposed to go? The only reason for going back to Riverwynde was to take you and Ysomir home, and now I can never do that. I've nothing else to go back for. They'll never understand what we saw and went through together. I had no friends at home. How can I go back and tell Father you're dead, when you were the only thing in life he loved? He'll only hate me more than ever for not saving you. Anthar's balls, Lyn, what in cursed Hellaxis am I supposed to do?'

He stood there for a time, staring at the silent tree.

Cursing dead Garnelys for taking Ysomir away. Wishing with all his heart that none of it had happened, then Lynden would still be alive.

Some way off, a woman cleared her throat. He looked round and she called, 'Rufryd? You weren't at home. I thought I might find you here.'

It was Dawn. Dressed in the blue livery of an Amber Citadel officer, she came picking her way over the dewy grass towards him. She'd been an actress in Saphaeyender's company, but as different from Ashtar as could be. Dawn was a warrior now. Her hair was red as copper, her fresh face sprinkled with freckles. Rufryd was glad to see her. Now if she had seduced him instead of Ashtar . . . but no, she still wasn't Tanthe. Dawn was more like a sister to him than anything.

Besides, she and her lover Mirias were the most devoted couple he'd ever seen. They were everything he and Tanthe should have been. Kind, noble, open-hearted, idealistic, they'd fought bravely in the rebellion, then given up the luxury of theatre life to dedicate themselves to Helananthe's service. Rufryd half admired them for it, and half resented them. To give up fame and wealth in favour of serving the Queen, simply because they put Aventuria's welfare above all else . . . who could be so self-sacrificing, so sickeningly *good*?

'I hope I'm not disturbing you,' she said.

'No, it's all right. I come here to get some peace.'

Dawn smiled. 'Dear old Ashtar not giving you any peace, then?'

He sneered. 'She must think I'm an idiot. She keeps me for sex and in return I get fed and housed.'

'Are you boasting or complaining?'

He turned on her. 'Yeah, great joke. I feel like a bloody dog in a kennel!'

Dawn looked shocked. 'Goddess, Rufe, why do you stay there if you feel like that? I tried to tell you what she's like but you wouldn't listen.'

'No, you're right. It was my own vanity that took me in. Now I'm too proud to admit it. That and trying to get back at Tanthe. Don't say anything to Tanthe, will you? I want her to keep thinking I'm having a wonderful life without her.'

Dawn slipped her hand through his arm, her tone sombre. 'Actually, about Tanthe. That's why I'm here. I've just been to see Saphaeyender and she's not there any more.'

Rufryd turned to her, the corner of his mouth twisting. 'What d'you mean, she's not there?'

'Apparently she just upped and left. But she left letters. One for Saph, one for Ysomir and one for you. Only Saph, the lazy sod, didn't bother delivering yours and Ysomir's. So I said I'd bring it to you. I've got them both, actually. I know he's still depressed after the battle but he really could have—'

'Where's mine?'

Dawn took a folded parchment from the folds of her cloak. Halcyon snuffed at it before she could snatch it out of his reach. 'Halcyon! Oh, he's slobbered on it, Rufe. Sorry.'

'Don't wipe it, you'll get grass stains on your lovely royal uniform. Here.' Rufryd took the letter, blotted it on his sleeve and broke the seal.

Dearest Rufe,

By the time you read this I will have gone away. I don't know how long I'll be; a few days at the very least, but in case I'm longer, this is to explain why. I hope we still care for each other enough for you not to think it strange that I wanted to let you know. Anyway . . .

Remember the little knife with the white stone, that I believed an Aelyr had given to me, even though you insisted I'd just found it? I've seen him again, the mysterious Aelyr. Several times in fact, each time begging more desperately for my help. So I'm going to search for him. I'm hoping Eldareth will help, but if not, I'll go alone and I'll search until I find an answer. As for Saph, he won't understand why this couldn't wait. I don't really understand it myself. All I know is that if I don't do it now, it will be too late. Wish me luck!

See you soon. Lots of love,
    Tanthe.

Rufryd gave a strangled gasp of despair. 'She's just gone off on her own? Why the hell didn't she tell me? I would have gone with her.'

'Hmph. Why *would* she have asked you, when you went to such lengths to make her think you didn't care?' Dawn threw back.

'Damn it, this is ridiculous! Hang on, when did she leave?'

'I don't know, actually,' said Dawn. 'Didn't she date the letter?'

Rufryd opened it again, deciphered the scrawled numerals at the top and swore. 'She's been gone ten days! Saphaeyender's sat on this letter for ten days and couldn't get off his arse to send it on to me.'

'I know, Rufe,' Dawn said grimly, touching his arm. 'I'm annoyed with him too. But isn't it Ysomir we should worry about? She's the one who has no idea why her sister hasn't visited her for so long.'

Half an hour later, Rufryd was storming into Saphaeyender's villa on Temple Hill, aflame with rage and oblivious to Dawn following and trying to calm him down.

Saphaeyender's living area was a cool, blue-shaded room of white stone and lapis, edged with lattice screens and glowing green ferns. The gentle sound of fountains floated in from his garden. Here he was holding court, encircled by a score of sycophants; some of them reclining

51

on couches among the ferns, others on marble benches or even sitting on the floor at his feet, to Rufryd's disgust. The man himself was stretched out on a long divan, dressed in a white robe sewn with silver leaves, that fell around his long slim form in perfect folds. He was looking down into his wine glass, laughing at something one of his hangers-on was saying. The scene was one of perfect tranquillity and refinement, everything Tanthe had dreamed of . . .

Rufryd went surging into the room, tearing the peace to rags. He stood over Saphaeyender and grabbed the silver-worked edges of his robe. 'You bastard!' he snarled. 'You Goddess-forsaken, motherless *bastard*!'

The poet stared up at him for an instant, stunned and indignant. Then Rufryd dragged him to his feet and punched him, sending him flying backwards over the couch. Saphaeyender crashed into a tall plant, sending leaves and earth raining over his polished floor. 'That's for Tanthe!' Rufryd yelled. 'I haven't even started for Lynden!'

He dived after Saphaeyender, and his hands were around the poet's throat, thumbs pressing into his wind-pipe, and the great one was flushing purple, eyes bulging with hopelessness and terror. Yet even to have him at his mercy like this seemed meaningless. Rufryd's mouth opened and tears stung his eyes, and then a dozen hands were pulling at him, dragging him off, helping Saphaeyender to his feet. The rest of the followers were on their feet, exclaiming. Ashtar was among them but staying out of the way, her arms folded.

'Rufryd,' sighed Dawn, a long way off.

Saphaeyender rose, swaying. His long dark hair was in disarray, and blood dripped from his mouth to stain the pristine weave of his robe. He gathered himself into a semblance of dignity and said evenly, 'I take it I've done something to upset you.'

There was the faintest ripple of amusement. Rufryd knew what it meant: '*How witty our master is and how foolish you are!'* He glared round and caught Ashtar's eye; she looked livid. He took the letter out of his pocket and waved it in Saphaeyender's face.

'This.'

'Ah,' said Saphaeyender.

'You bastard. You knew Tanthe had gone and you did nothing. Couldn't even be bothered to give me this fucking letter!'

The poet opened his hands. 'Rufryd, I'm sorry. I forgot. I was going to send it to you but I didn't think you would even be interested—'

'Oh, really?' He produced the second letter, still sealed. 'And what did your great mind conclude about Ysomir? You didn't think she'd be interested, either?'

Saphaeyender's hectic colour drained away. 'I've had a lot on my mind. I forgot, truly. I'm sorry.'

'I'll tell her that, shall I? "You've lain awake worrying for ten nights but never mind, Saphaeyender says he's sorry"?' He looked round at the others again, despising the way they mocked him, wanting to sear their arch amusement to ashes. 'Any of you going to explain to *her* why that's funny?'

There was silence. Saphaeyender stood gasping for breath, dishevelled, hurt and lost for words; just the way Rufryd had wanted to see him. And yet it hadn't changed anything. 'You couldn't even leave Lynden alone, could you?' he said harshly.

'Ah. So that's what this is about. Who told you?'

Rufryd half-turned, meaning to point at Ashtar, but changed his mind. This was all pointless. His rage was spent. 'Doesn't matter,' he spat. 'Hope all your acolytes know how you use people and throw them away. But you're the one who's got to live with what you are.'

He began to walk towards the door but Ashtar stopped him. She put her hand on his chest and her eyes were glittering with rage.

'How dare you embarrass me like this?' she hissed. 'This

is not an idle party. We are trying to salvage what's left of the company; don't you know how important that is, after everything I've said to you? If you ever behave like this again—'

'What?' said Rufryd. 'You can't threaten me. I'm leaving you.'

'Oh, no, you're not. I'm throwing you out.'

'Fine.' He glanced around the faces of the company, who were rivetted by their exchange. Perhaps they could use it in their next production. 'I know what I am to you. It's a novelty, having a bit of peasant rough around, isn't it – as long as I don't dare come out of my stable while your friends are there? Forgotten what it's like to sleep on a forest floor and drink out of streams, have you?'

Ashtar's eyes spewed fire. 'You've got nowhere to go.'

'It's all right,' said Rufryd, looking into Saphaeyender's horrified eyes. 'I'll sleep on my brother's grave.'

'Rufryd, wait,' Saphaeyender said, following him as he strode to the doorway. 'Let me take the letter to Ysomir.'

'I don't trust you.'

'Then we'll go together. Please. It's the least I can do.'

'All right,' Rufryd said icily. He took the letter from his jacket and placed it in the writer's long, fine hand. 'You take it. But I'll go to see her later, to make sure you turned up. And if anything happens to Tanthe – I'll hold you to blame.'

'Rufryd.' Saphaeyender took another step after him, and his voice was hollow, desperate. 'I loved your brother. But nothing sexual happened between us.'

'Nothing?'

'I swear. But only because he wouldn't allow it. I wanted to, but he wouldn't. Because I am everything you said, and worse.'

Rufryd let go of a breath between his teeth, a snake's hiss. 'So that's why Tanthe left you. Came to her senses, at last.'

*

'It's not true that you have nowhere to go,' Dawn said as they walked along the street that wound away from the villa. Rufryd was leading Halcyon. 'Why don't you come to the Amber Citadel? Helananthe would give you a position just like that, I know it. She would love to have you there.'

'She had a bloody funny way of showing it. She seemed to forget Tanthe and me existed, once the battle was won.'

'Rufe, have you any idea how much she has to think about? Garnelys left the most unbelievable mess for her to sort out. But you could be at the heart with us, helping to rebuild things.'

Rufryd felt only cold, indifferent. 'With lots of charming Parionian courtiers? I don't think so, Dawn. I don't belong there.'

'Well, where do you belong?' she said, exasperated. 'I'm trying to help you.'

'Don't bother! Go on back to your wonderful queen and leave me alone.'

She stopped, her knuckles planted on her hips. 'You know, I'm trying very hard not to get angry with you. I'm not Ashtar, I'm your friend. Shall I get Mirias to talk some sense into you, or would he be wasting his breath as well?'

'I don't need any sense talking into me,' Rufryd said savagely. 'I'm not a specimen for Ashtar to keep as a pet, or Saphaeyender to patronise, or you to "help" like I'm some poor wretch you found in the gutter.'

Dawn gaped at him, but her indignation only made him colder. 'Well, forgive me for caring about you, but—'

'Just fuck off, Dawn. Fuck off back to your palace.'

He walked away, but the cloud of blackness went with him. Even Halcyon aggravated him, striding with such unquestioning trust at his side. Rufryd breathed hard, looking up at the rosy sky and hating it; not knowing why he couldn't seem to get enough air, nor why his heart droned like a heavy drum in his chest.

He found himself going back the way he'd come, leading

his horse up the hill towards the Temple of Nepheter on the summit. Had the village beliefs ever helped him at home? Had he ever looked for the god Anthar within himself, or asked the priestess Helwyn for advice? Never. At festivals, he'd paid lip service to the gods at best. But now his feet led him to the temple . . .

It was a beautiful building, pale golden as the sun, topped by a dome that seemed as weightless and iridescent as a shell. Nepheter and Dyonis were worshipped here, but they were only Breyid and Anthar by different names, the Great Mother and Her Consort, source of all wisdom.

He stood on the threshold, looking inside. The temple was bright, full of sunlight and dappled rainbows. Flowers were strewn on the altar, boughs of white blossom and tiny blue daisies. He could hear priests chanting behind a lattice screen, *'Dyon, Dyonis, Dyon, Dyonis, lord of laughter, lord of joy . . .'* And he saw the two statues, white as milk; Nepheter and Dyonis, looking exactly like two graceful, smiling citizens of Parione.

His stomach twisted. There was no place here for his misery.

A priestess came towards him, dressed in primrose and silver. She was small, sweet-faced. 'Come in and be welcome,' she said, her smile radiating warmth. 'There is a place to tether your horse. He's beautiful, isn't he? There's water for him, and a cup of wine for you. You are troubled, I can see. If you wish to make an offering or just to be silent, none will trouble you here; but if you wish a priest or priestess to talk to you, or if there is anything at all we may do to help you . . .'

'Nothing,' said Rufryd, backing away. 'I made a mistake.'

By dusk he had wandered deep into the lower levels of the city. Here the artisans toiled, and smoke drifted up from smithies and glassworks, and the air was rich by turns with the scents of sawdust . . . fish . . . overripe fruit . . . horse dung, flattened and smeared by cart wheels. He looked in through the wide-open doors of a foundry and saw figures silhouetted against the orange blaze of the furnace. Hammers falling, sparks flying. The heat stung his eyes. Surely it was in a place like this he belonged . . .

'Born in the city?' said the broad, red-faced man who came to the door to see him.

'No.'

'What apprenticeship have you done? What guild d'you belong to?'

'None,' Rufryd said. 'None.'

'Y'don't stand a chance. Try the street-cleaner's guild, they're always desperate.' The man flapped a large hand and vanished back into the blaze.

Rufryd wandered on, Halcyon walking patiently at his side and lipping bruised fruit that had fallen from carts on to the pavement. Street-cleaning, he thought sourly. Has to be done and I'm not proud.

'No, Halce,' he said. 'We'll go into the countryside. Find a farm, maybe. There'll be clear water and good grass, and peace.'

A new odour threaded through the prosaic stinks of the city. Incense, rich and mysterious, catching in his throat. He heard the surge of a river running somewhere out of sight. Here were few buildings, only flat dark spaces and rugged banks lining the unseen river and old, gnarled trees pushing up through the flagstones. And before him rose another temple; twin-domed and black as night, with basalt pillars upholding the wide maw of the portico.

Dim red lights glimmered inside. He stood in the doorway and the incense snaked around him, burning his throat and eyes, wreathing him in musky resins. He heard voices chanting, so mournful that it drew gooseflesh on his back and arms. He tasted darkness, dampness, salt.

The priestess who came out to him was the ugliest creature he had ever seen; four feet tall and almost as wide, her humped back rising behind her grey bedraggled head. Her robe was dusty black, striped with red and white like trickles of blood and milk. She leaned on a staff that was carved in the form of three intertwined serpents, crowned with an obsidian globe. Her eyes were clouded opals but she peered at him as if catching him in her last clear slot of vision.

'This is the Temple of Nuth and Anuth, the beginning and the end,' she said. 'Come inside, and welcome.'

Chapter Four. The Amber Citadel

Helananthe had been steeling herself to this moment for days. She must interview Ysomir; the woman who had killed King Garnelys.

The Queen was in a chamber high in a tower of the Amber Citadel, waiting for the prisoner to be brought to her. Mirias and Dawn – to whom she'd entrusted her personal security – and a couple of palace guards stood silently on either side. She would have preferred to conduct the interview alone, but as monarch she couldn't take the risk. According to reports, Ysomir was calm to the point of apathy, but there was no guarantee that she would not flare into frenzied violence a second time.

Helananthe hated this room. The walls of golden stone and the marble floor, even the light that fell through the windows – all were tainted with death. This was the room to which Garnelys had brought young servants and conscripts, insisting that they amuse him with his beloved board-game metrarch . . . innocent young subjects whom he then betrayed, dragging them into a hidden cell where he tortured and killed them in the practice of a dreadful sorcery.

She closed her eyes. Only now, as the thrill of victory faded, was the truth sinking in. The terrible things Garnelys had done to his own subjects . . . how could she square that with the grandfather she remembered and loved? Above all else she needed to know *why*, but her last chance to speak to him had been torn away.

Garnelys had died in this luxurious little room. She had defeated his army and forced entry to the Citadel, her sole intention to arrest him and demand an explanation. But she'd arrived minutes too late. Rushed in only to find him dead, the room awash with blood, and a young woman standing over him with the knife still in her hand, blood all over her fine dress.

Death was splashed red all over the walls and floor, soaked into the couch where he'd fallen. The whole chamber shimmered with dark energies. Through the diamond panes of the window she could see Theatre Hill where the stump of the unfinished Tower brooded palely over the city, the Tower Garnelys had dedicated to the gods. Now the sight of it made Helananthe ill, but she forced herself to look. How could such a monstrosity be demolished?

The King's funeral had been a grim affair, attended by officials who had helped carry out his cruel orders, and by others who had opposed him and suffered for it. And still the citizens of Parione had wept in the streets; both for the good king he had once been, and for the tragic way his reign had ended. Helananthe had wept with them, but now her eyes were dry and her mood dark.

Someone tapped on the door. The doors of golden oak swung open, and two female warders came in with Ysomir between them. The prisoner was calm and dignified, dressed in a simple brown robe, her tawny hair loose on her shoulders.

Helananthe stiffened. The first time she'd seen this young woman leapt starkly into her mind. Blood dripping from her face and hair, her eyes wild. Voicing insane claims that she had been Garnelys's wife. Claims that turned out, incredibly, to be true.

Now Ysomir was every inch the innocent, unspoiled country girl that her sister Tanthe described. Incapable of harm.

'Sit down,' Helananthe said tonelessly. She was in a gilded chair, but the seat she offered Ysomir was the blood-stained couch. Perhaps she was being cruel, but she couldn't overcome her rage and incomprehension at Ysomir's behaviour.

The prisoner hesitated, then sat on the very edge of the clotted seat. Her warders stood on either side of her.

'Good day, Ysomir,' said Helananthe. 'How are you?'

'Very well, thank you, your highness,' Ysomir answered guardedly.

'It's "your majesty", in fact, but I'll let it pass. Your actions have prematurely made me Queen of Aventuria.'

Ysomir stared at her with guileless green-gold eyes. Helananthe suppressed the urge to strangle her. Why was there no fear in her face? 'Your majesty. I beg your pardon.' How well-spoken she was for a farmer's daughter, how unaffectedly graceful; Helananthe felt too tall and loud by comparison.

'You recognise this chamber, I take it?'

'Of course, ma'am. This is where Garnelys used to bring me to play metrarch.'

'This is where you killed him.'

Ysomir lowered her eyes. She nodded. 'Yes, ma'am.'

'You have never denied your guilt.'

'No, ma'am.'

'You were caught quite literally crimson-handed. You stabbed my grandfather to death with a jewelled fruit knife, inflicting seventeen stab wounds upon his body. You have confessed, verbally and in writing, that when you launched this attack upon him, the King was not threatening you but begging you for help.'

'All that I did, I have freely admitted.'

Helananthe's mouth thinned. She was struggling to be impartial; how could Ysomir be so calm? If only the girl would seem defiant, distraught, anything! 'The Nine Realms have long been peaceful, our people law abiding, and our laws gentle and lenient. However, your crime is of such an exceptional nature that it is one of the very few for which execution is automatic.' She spoke harshly, willing Ysomir to react. 'Since you were caught in the act and admitted your guilt, there is no requirement for you to stand trial. Doesn't this concern you?'

The merest shadow creased Ysomir's brow. 'I accept my punishment. I deserve it.'

'Execution?'

'Yes.'

'Imprisonment for life?'

'Anything.'

The atmosphere in the chamber was gelid with tension. The guards and warders seemed to hold their breath. 'So tell me a little about yourself, Ysomir.'

'All I have to say, I have written down.'

'And I've read it, but I want to hear it from your own lips. I want to understand why you killed him.'

The prisoner gave a slight shake of her head. 'There's not much to tell. I lived in a village called Riverwynde and I was going to marry Lynden. I never asked to come here; Tanthe was the one who wanted to leave home, not me. Last year the King took conscripts from Sepheret, but the quota system meant they could take only one from Riverwynde. They took me because I could carve stone. They sent me to work in the mines. Some of my friends were killed in an explosion there. Then they sent me to the Tower, where people died every day from illness and accidents.

'A figure in a grey robe used to come among the conscripts and if someone caught his eye he would take them away, and they were never seen again. Everyone was terrified of him. They called him "Old grey-bones". One day he took me, and I found the rumours were true. He was the King.

'For some reason he chose not to kill me as he killed the others. He seemed to need my company, and when the Queen died he married me. I never thought for a moment that that made me queen or gave me any claim—'

'It didn't,' Helan said dismissively. 'I checked. It was more in the nature of an unofficial wedding, a hand-fasting.'

'Still, he needed me – yet he never hid what he was

62

doing.' Ysomir's quiet voice wavered. 'He tortured people in front of me. I watched him kill a physician who had been kind to me. Sometimes he threatened to do the same to me, but he always relented, and begged my forgiveness. He seemed to think that if only he could justify himself to me, that would make it all right – but how could it be?'

She stopped. Helananthe said, 'I appreciate that you were afraid of the King and that he forced you to witness terrifying spectacles. However, you've admitted that he never actually harmed you in any way; that he married you and kept you in luxury, and yet never laid a finger upon you, either in love or violence. That you knew he was deeply disturbed. That in the moments before his death he was begging you for help – and yet, in the moment when he might have been redeemed, you stabbed him!'

Helan curbed herself. She mustn't let her anger break loose.

'I did wrong.' Ysomir turned her hands so they lay loosely, palms up on her thighs, as if she was looking for blood in the creases. 'I regret it, but I cannot undo what I did.'

'How true.' Helananthe could be intimidating when she chose. She leaned forward, pinning Ysomir with her eyes. 'The point is this. Since you saw fit to murder my grandfather before I could speak to him, and since my poor grandmother is dead also, you are almost my only link to him. I must know what was going on in his mind.'

Ysomir shifted a little. 'All that I know, I wrote down.'

'Not all, surely.'

'I don't know what was going on in the King's mind! How could I? I only know what he told me.'

'Then what did he tell you?'

The prisoner raised her right hand to clasp her left arm, as if shielding herself. 'Garnelys told me things that should never be repeated. Humiliating things that might reduce him in your eyes.'

'Let me be the judge of that.'

'In front of everyone . . . ?'

'Speak!' Helananthe snapped.

Ysomir spoke, softly but clearly. 'For all his childhood, Garnelys's father King Aralyth told him he would never be a good enough king. Perhaps he meant to make Garnelys strive harder, or perhaps he truly thought nothing of his son. I don't know. But the result was that Garnelys thought himself worthless, and all his life was spent striving to prove his father wrong. The truth is that he hated himself.'

Helan recalled the kind, gracious man Garnelys had once been. 'That's impossible.'

'No. He despised himself. He thought he was a weak king, and that no one would remember him. He felt . . .'

'What?'

'Impotent. Perhaps he literally was; I was never that intimate with him.'

Helan's face turned hot. Ysomir went on. 'That's why he began the Tower. He thought that if he built a great monument to Nuth, Mother of Life and Death, it would give him the power he lacked. And more; he thought that the only way to be remembered, and to control the way his subjects remembered him, was never to die. If he built the Tower forever, he would live forever. And that was why he didn't care if his heirs were dead. He said they were no longer needed.'

'He told *you* this?' Agony to believe he had been so deluded, even though the evidence was blatant.

'Yes, ma'am.'

'And Laphaeome? What part did he play in this?'

Ysomir's voice was quiet and precise as a razor, and it echoed with a strange power that turned Helananthe ice cold. 'Garnelys couldn't bear to hurt those he tortured. Afterwards he would be filled with remorse; he'd weep, and beg me to save him from himself. He said that shedding their blood was the only thing that eased his

64

pain, a compulsion he couldn't control. But when he was torturing them, Laphaeome was always there, smiling. He drank the pain that Garnelys caused.'

'Was Laphaeome controlling Garnelys?'

'I couldn't say.'

'Did Garnelys ever indicate to you that Laphaeome was . . . Bhahdradomen?'

There was a stirring in the chamber, an inrush of shocked breath. But Ysomir showed no reaction. 'I knew Laphaeome wasn't human. It was so obvious, I don't know why no one else saw it. If Garnelys knew, he never admitted it. Or he was blind to it. It seemed to me that Garnelys initiated everything, while Laphaeome just stood in the background, smiling.'

'When was the last time you saw Laphaeome?'

Ysomir thought. 'I can't recall. I was with the King on the day of the final battle. He kept summoning Laphaeome, over and over again, but Laphaeome didn't come. Garnelys grew more and more desperate. I think he knew.'

'What?'

'That Laphaeome had deserted him, and this meant the war was lost. The King couldn't believe his own subjects had turned against him. It broke his heart, I believe, to know that his father had been right and that he'd failed. He couldn't accept it.'

There was a quality of impassive certainty to Ysomir that Helananthe couldn't penetrate. More than that, there was a power about her, a weird inner light. Frustration made Helan want to shock the girl, really frighten her.

'Ah, if only we could ask Garnelys the truth directly! Perhaps now you understand that your action has not only harmed the King's family, but put the whole of Aventuria at risk. You were obviously aware that my army was on its way, that Garnelys had been defeated and disempowered. So why did you choose that moment to kill him?'

Ysomir's lips parted. At last she said, 'I did it for Lynden. It was Garnelys's fault he died.'

'Yet when you stabbed the King, you could not possibly have known of your lover's death!'

'But I did,' said Ysomir. '*I felt* Lynden die. He'd come all this way to rescue me and then he died before we even saw each other. I couldn't bear it. That's why I killed Garnelys.'

Her words did nothing to soften Helananthe. It would have been painful enough to hear that she slew him in self-defence; worse to think it had been done in a rush of selfish passion.

'As your sister has no doubt informed you, I've decided to spare your life. But I can't release you. Whatever the King's crimes, it was not your place to act as his judge and executioner.'

Ysomir looked at her hands, saying nothing.

'You will remain imprisoned in the Amber Citadel for life.'

'Yes. Thank you, ma'am.'

Thank you? What sort of response was that? Helan frowned. 'Take her back to her cell,' she snapped.

Flanked by her warders, Ysomir rose and left the room, her back straight and her face serene. Helananthe slumped back in her chair, drained.

'Mirias, would you pour me a glass of wine, please?'

He obliged. It felt odd to have him waiting on her, when she had used to admire him on the stage; handsome, dark-haired, heroic. She'd long been in the habit of addressing him and Dawn as friends, not staff.

Helan rose and stood at the window, sipping her drink. The interview had peeled back another layer of skin, only to reveal yet more roiling unpleasantness beneath. She was still no closer to discovering how Laphaeome had insinuated himself into the King's confidence, nor why Garnelys had needed him. It concerned her more than she dared admit, to think that the Bhahdradomen had been involved.

Two hundred and fifty-one years ago, in the year 1500, great King Maharoth had defeated the dreaded Ghaurthror of the Flies and exiled the Bhahdradomen forever. He'd turn in his grave to know that a descendant of his had made such a stupid, lethal mistake. Now it was 1751, the centuries counted from the official founding of the Amber Citadel by Queen Silana. A young citadel, by some standards. In a shivery moment of superstition, Helan wondered if it was not fatal arrogance to give up the older Marocian calendar, which would have made the year 36,124. So many of those seventeen hundred years – meant to be a new age of glory – had been overshadowed by the Bhahdradomen. And now she feared they still were.

What a mess her grandfather had left. He'd dismissed most of the trusted staff she'd known in her youth, in favour of self-serving people like Lord Poel and General Grannen. He had even dismissed the Council of the Sun Chamber, one hundred and forty elected men and women who represented the people and tempered the monarch's decisions.

Many of these good people were missing. Secretly murdered at Garnelys's command, she suspected.

Every day she uncovered another ghastly layer of crimes he had committed. And although she was doing her utmost to salvage things, she had no one whose counsel she could trust. Rathroem, her friend from the Serpent Isles, had been found dead just before the Battle of Hethlas Rim. Murdered by Bhahdradomen hands, it seemed. An ominous sign that even Mediators were no longer sacrosanct.

She needed Eldareth. She longed for him to return with her mother and brother. Then there would be life and familiar faces in the palace again.

Meanwhile there was too much to do. There were guilds and temples to pacify, the Sun Chamber to be reconvened. Conscripts wandered miserably in the streets, with no means of going home; Garnelys's defeated army rubbed uneasily against her own warriors, unsure whether to be friends or enemies. Even the palace staff were a problem. She must judge who supported her and who resented her for overthrowing her grandfather. Until her coronation took place, her authority was tenuous.

And worse, several thousand more of Garnelys's men were on their way home, pursued by the furious folk of Thanmandrathor, who had also risen against the king. What was going to happen when they arrived?

Another knock at the door. The aide Lord Derione came in.

'Your majesty, Lord Poel is here to see you. You sent for him?'

'Ah, yes.' She took a deep breath. Another difficult confrontation. 'Show him in.'

Lord Poel had been Garnelys's high chancellor, the one who implemented his most unpopular decrees. He glided in like an obelisk in pleated white robes, his black hair and beard precisely curled. His face was marble, his eyes cold obsidian. Helananthe was tall but he still looked down on her. She was glad, for the first time, that she'd forsaken her favourite travelling clothes for these robes of gold and purple silk. They might be uncomfortable, but at least she looked more or less regal.

'Your majesty,' he said, sweeping a deep bow to her.

'Lord Poel,' she responded. 'You understand why I asked you to meet me in this chamber in particular.'

'Ma'am?'

Oh, he knew, but he was giving nothing away. 'I understand that Garnelys spent much of his time here.' She pointed to the chapel-like recess at the rear of the chamber, where a stone bier stood. 'I understand that he sat and played metrarch while my father Prince Galemanth's body lay upon that bier. That he would take conscripts through that hidden door to torture and kill them.'

Lord Poel's face glistened with unshed sweat. 'Forgive me, ma'am, but I am not sure what response you expect from me.'

Helananthe gritted her teeth. She was trying very hard not to hate this man. 'Lord Poel, I appreciate that in your continuing loyalty to King Garnelys, you can't acknowledge anything that might cast him in a bad light. But I am his flesh and blood, his heir. We are all on the same side. I'm simply trying to discover the truth.'

'I can assure you, ma'am, that I had no knowledge of any such activities by the King. It came as much of a shock to me as it did to you – if, indeed, these allegations are true.'

'I didn't want to believe it either,' she said heavily. 'But I have written evidence. I have spoken to witnesses. You only have to go down there to feel it in the atmosphere. I want to know what made him do it. I must know, for Aventuria's sake!'

Poel went a touch paler. He said accusingly, 'Alas, that the one man who could have given you the answers was savagely murdered.'

Helan took a deep breath. 'My lord, I know that you loved the King. So did I. The last thing I wanted was for him to die. My one desperate wish – his denial of which drove me to such desperate measures – was to speak with him. Now that chance is gone. You understand, don't you, that I need to uncover the truth not for my own benefit, but for that of Aventuria?'

'Of course.'

'You were his chancellor. Didn't he take you into his confidence?'

He bridled. 'Only in matters of state, ma'am. Not in personal matters. Those I believe he reserved for . . .'

'For the mysterious Lord Laphaeome, who has vanished from the face of the Earth?'

'I was going to say, for the Lady Ysomir.' He soaked the word 'Lady' in contempt. 'Laphaeome was the architect of the Tower.'

'Did you know Laphaeome well, Lord Poel?'

'Hardly at all.'

'How did he strike you?'

The obsidian eyes narrowed. 'He was a quiet man.'

'Quiet?' Helananthe felt like laughing hysterically. 'Quiet? You have heard that we believe he was only posing as a Mediator? That he was in fact . . . Bhahdradomen?'

Poel stiffened. Inside the rigid edifice of his body she glimpsed a tiny soul, pompously armoured against his fears. 'Impossible.'

'Why? Because you know for a fact he was human? Or because you dare not believe it?' No answer. She went on, 'Since I can't speak to my grandfather, I would dearly like to interview Laphaeome.'

'He cannot be found, ma'am.'

'But if he should reappear . . . It's unlikely, I know. But I will get to the bottom of this!' She took a step closer to Poel. 'Tell me honestly, my lord . . . How do you really feel about what I did?'

He blinked; it was almost a flinch. 'Ma'am, I . . . I am sure that you acted for the good of Aventuria.'

'I didn't intend to depose him. Only to act as regent in his stead, while he rested. I serve Aventuria.'

'As do I.' He dipped his head. 'And if I may continue to serve you as I did your grandfather, ma'am, I am yours to command, body and soul . . .'

Lord Poel was trying to survive, she realised. Had he relished Garnelys's dark turn of mind and the exhilarating powers it gave him – or had he simply been doing his duty? Helan sensed that Poel hated her, yet he was willing to grovel in order to hold on to those powers . . . perhaps thinking that as she was so young to take the throne, only twenty-eight, he could manipulate her and she wouldn't even know?

Or perhaps he'd be a good, efficient servant. But it was Poel who had ordered the demolition of the Old Royal Theatre. Poel who'd implemented the conscription of thousands of Aventurians to the slavery of the mines, the quarries and the Tower itself. Poel who'd stood barring her way to the Amber Citadel, insisting that Garnelys refused to see his own granddaughter.

'You always hated the theatre, didn't you?' she said softly. 'Hated people who were spontaneous and creative and full of life. You so enjoyed telling Saphaeyender that it was all to be pulled down around his ears.'

His eyes were slots of black fire in the stone face. 'I was merely carrying out the King's orders. If you have no place for me within the Amber Citadel, I shall be gone within the hour.'

'Don't leave yet,' she said ominously. 'You will be informed of my decision by this evening.'

Once Lord Poel had gone, she sent her guards and even Dawn and Mirias out of the room. Then she turned to Derione. He was a sensible, good-humoured man approaching middle age, his thick blond hair streaked with silver at the sides. His ancestors were from Noreya, northern land of forests and secretive but kind people. She was trying to gauge whether or not she could trust him.

'Derione,' she said, 'You worked with Lord Poel. What sort of man is he – beneath the surface, I mean?'

He smiled. 'I found him pompous, vain and aggressive. However, he is extremely loyal; one might say mindlessly so. His main concern is keeping his status now the King is gone; he's frightened, and that will make him malleable. Keep him close at hand and I believe he will prove a dependable aide.'

'Dismiss him, and he could make a dangerous enemy?' Helan added.

'Quite.'

'I see,' she said. 'I heard that Poel's parents were actors. His arrival was a great inconvenience to their careers and so they abandoned him as an infant, to be brought up by an uncle whom he grew to loathe.'

'I heard the same story,' said Derione.

71

'It makes one wonder, doesn't it, whether he had personal reasons for taking such joy in the demolition of the theatre? I wonder how many other irrational personal grudges he holds?'

They looked at each other in quiet, mutual understanding. 'I don't think he's a bad man at heart,' said Derione.

'I doubt Saphaeyender would agree with you. We are all twisted in some way, but . . . do I want someone working for me who would carry out such a heinous command without question? On the other hand, Poel will be expecting me to dismiss him. I don't want him brooding, storing up grudges against me. I could have him arrested, but that would look as if I fear him, which I don't.'

'And it would set an awkward precedent. There were many who worked unquestioningly for King Garnelys. I was among them.' There was a sharp irony in his tone, which she appreciated.

'Lord Derione, I understand that when Garnelys was about to send his army against the rebels, you cautioned him against it. You pointed out that to make war on his own subjects would rupture the Xauroma.'

He looked surprised. 'Yes, I did, ma'am. He didn't listen.'

'But you tried. That shows me your heart is in the right place, even under duress. Derione, I am going to make you my chancellor.'

He seemed stunned, and touchingly happy. 'Ma'am – I don't know what to say. I'm honoured. But Lord Poel?'

'Oh, don't worry about him. I'll find some minor administrative post for him. You will be *his* superior from now on. How d'you think he'll like that?'

Six miles east of Parione, the exhausted army of Thanmandrathor halted and made their last camp. They were in sight of their goal. The straggling remains of Garnelys's army had vanished into the outskirts of the city, or been overtaken and left behind. The

Than'drathians' victory seemed complete.

In the evening light, Mawrdreth and his sister Branq'elin climbed a hill and saw, for the first time, the glorious golden hills of Parione with its magnificent crown: the Amber Citadel.

Mawrdreth put his arm round Branq'elin's waist. She had fought and travelled fiercely, but now, as she rested against him, he felt her profound tiredness. They stood for a long time in silent awe; two tall figures in green and bronze, their hair lying in glossy brown plaits over the leather and gold of their breastplates.

'Here we are,' he said. 'No one has come to stop us.'

They were the son and daughter of Duke Tasq of Thanmandrathor, and they had led their makeshift army in an unthinkable rebellion against the King.

'Do you think the Citadel could be ours?' she said softly.

'That depends on whether they receive us as friends or enemies.'

'All I know is that the Paranians will never do this to us again,' Branq'elin said, soft and fierce. 'Never. I should rather we broke the Nine Realms apart than let them conscript and misuse our people as slaves!'

Mawrdreth was silent for a while, his arm round her shoulders. The Amber Citadel stood bright and impervious as the slow gold of the sunset deepened to apricot. 'According to rumour, Garnelys is dead. We weren't the only ones to rebel.'

'Well?' she said. 'I shall say to the new monarch all that I would have said to the old. Our father deserves no less.'

Helananthe wandered alone through the convoluted layers of the Amber Citadel.

This palace had been home to Helananthe all her life, but now it felt different. Fleeing in fear of her life, returning to usurp her own grandfather, finding him and her beloved grandmother and father all dead . . . These events couldn't help but pull everything out of shape.

Towering walls and battlements encircled the yearning spires of the palace, a shining crown on Parione's greatest hill. The soft sky poured its balm over the amber walls. Inside, the palace was the same as ever. Its lofty corridors were panelled in amber, tiled with swirling marbles, jewelled with priceless works of art framed in gold leaf. As a child she'd run and slid along these corridors and played on the Sapphire Throne itself, making the walls echo with laughter. But now the palace simply . . . echoed.

How empty it felt. Helananthe was painfully aware of the vast responsibilities that were hers. Until Eldareth came back, she had no one to confide in. Since he'd refused to become her husband, perhaps she could not confide him ever again . . .

Eldareth was an enigma, even to her. He'd become something of a legend for his epic travels across Aventuria, his friendship with the Shaelahyr, and his work with Saphaeyender. When Helananthe had first met him, Eldareth had been Saphaeyender's leading actor at the Old Royal Theatre, and (legend had it, though he denied it) the inspiration for some of Saphaeyender's heroes. Then at the height of his fame he'd left; untouched by adulation, and too restless by nature to stay in one place for long.

By then he and Helan were in love. When he resumed his travels, she went with him and embarked on the wildest times of her life.

Against her family's wishes, of course. Eldareth had no noble blood; his past was unknown, and so on. Long ago her father had warned her that he would not make a suitable consort for a future queen. Now she saw that he had been right, for Eldareth was still too restless to marry. The prospect of kingship had made him race in the opposite direction.

Helan cursed. The very attributes for which she loved Eldareth also made him impossible.

She left the state apartments and descended to the lower levels, pausing to chat with any staff she met. She wanted

74

to befriend them, to reduce the risk of unpleasant surprises. Presently she found herself in a long, curved corridor, plain compared to the state rooms but still gracefully decorated. Lamps burned in golden globes along the low ceiling and the walls were lined with closed doors. These were guest quarters, where in happier times the family and friends of the palace staff had been permitted to stay.

She suppressed a shiver. Garnelys had used these rooms for the conscripts he brought from the Tower. Kept them in luxury a few days, until he was ready to use them.

Helan began to open one door after another, finding the rooms empty. As she made her way along, she became aware of a strange sound, a chanting. She stopped, listened; yes, it was a woman's voice, uttering what sounded like an invocation to the Goddess. She went onwards, and as she came round the gentle curve of the corridor she saw a lamp burning and a female warder standing sentinel outside the very last door, which was set facing her in the end wall.

As Helan approached, the warder – a handsome woman of middle years – looked suspiciously at her. 'Can I help you, my lady?'

'What are you doing here?'

'Guarding a prisoner, my lady.'

'Who is it?'

'I'm only allowed to discuss that information with those in authority.'

'I don't believe I've seen you before,' Helananthe said. 'It's obviously rather remote down here, but you do know, don't you, that Garnelys is dead?'

'Yes, my lady, but no one has changed our instructions so we are guarding the prisoner until someone in authority tells us otherwise.'

'Well, I am the new queen,' Helananthe said with a wry smile. 'Is that authority enough for you?'

Realisation dawned on the warder's face. Flustered, she dipped her head.

'Your majesty – I'm sorry, I didn't know.'

'It's all right, it's been happening all day. The prisoner?'

'It is the High Priestess Ariolne of the Temple of Nuth, ma'am.'

Now it was Helananthe's turn to be shocked. The priests and priestesses of Nuth were sacrosanct. 'What? *What*?'

'She was placed here at the late King's command almost two years ago,' said the warder, flushing. 'I don't know why.'

'Two years! Let me see her.'

The warder unlocked the door. As Helananthe stepped through, she saw a woman standing in the centre of the room with her arms raised, her back to the door, her raven hair shining against the dusty-black sheath of her robe. Incense curled around the room; candlelight gleamed on the gilded furniture and silken rugs. Before Helananthe said anything, the woman ceased her invocation and turned.

She was almost as tall as Helananthe, with a very strong, sculptured face for which 'beauty' was too weak a word. Her dark eyes and black brows were striking against the ivory of her complexion; she looked a bit like Eldareth, aquiline. Helan had seen her before at state occasions, spoken to her a few times, but aside from this they barely knew each other. The priestess regarded Helananthe with stony composure.

'Good Reverend Mother Ariolne?' said Helan, inclining her head.

Ariolne returned the gesture. 'Princess Helananthe. Good day to you, and blessings.'

'I understand that my grandfather King Garnelys imprisoned you.'

'He did.' The priestess's mouth twitched sourly at one corner. 'And I have no complaint at my treatment. Only at being deprived of my liberty and contact with my temple.'

Her situation and her dignity embarrassed Helananthe beyond words. The clergy of Nuth were a class apart, as revered and respected as Mediators. Garnelys seemed to have lost his grasp of that concept in the most disastrous way. 'Good Mother, I don't know whether the warders have told you but my grandfather and my father Prince Galemanth are dead, therefore the responsibility of the throne has fallen to me. Please tell me why you are being held here.'

The priestess stiffened. There was pain in her eyes. 'I know that your father is dead, your majesty. Prince Galemanth sought sanctuary in my Temple but was run to ground by the King's henchmen and murdered there in front of me. I am here because I had the audacity to make a complaint to the King about it.'

Helan's eyebrows rose in disbelief. 'He imprisoned you – for complaining?'

'Garnelys desecrated the sanctity of Nuth's Temple in the most obscene manner,' the priestess said softly. 'Then he hid me away as if to hide his own shame.'

'I'm terribly sorry,' Helan said, opening her hands. 'Priestesses from the Temple told me you had vanished, but they feared you were dead. You are free to leave as of this moment, of course. I'm doing everything within my power to repair the damage my grandfather did.'

'Then I wish you luck and Nuth's blessing, ma'am. But if mutual trust between the monarchy and the priesthood is torn apart, I doubt that it can ever be repaired.'

Ariolne's ominous tone made Helananthe uncomfortable. The priestess seemed so much older and wiser than she was. 'Good Mother, I understand your anger. I'm angry, too, especially at my father's untimely death. There is much work to be done, and whatever it takes to restore good relations between us, I will do. In return I would appreciate your counsel, as is traditional between the Temple of Nuth and the Amber Citadel.'

The priestess's mouth softened a little, but her eyes burned. 'Are you sure? People often find the truth unpalatable, and monarchs are no exception.'

'I'm sure.' Helananthe held out her hand. 'Come, you're free to go home. I'll take you up to the royal guest apartments, and you can eat and rest there while I arrange for a carriage to take you back to the Temple. We can talk as we go.'

Ariolne very nearly smiled. 'Thank you, my daughter,' she said.

As they made their way through the Citadel, Helan found herself telling the priestess all that had happened. 'I *must* know the extent of Bhahdradomen involvement in this,' she said. 'There's something Ysomir isn't telling me, but I couldn't squeeze it out of her. I'm tired of questioning the wretched girl. To be honest, I can't stand the sight of her.'

'Why?'

'Because she's no one, and yet in killing my grandfather, she was taking it upon herself to act like a god. Because she gives me the shivers. She's not all there! No, it's not that. She's *too* knowing.'

'But you must face her,' said Ariolne. 'You must do many things that you don't like. Talk to her again.'

'No. I can't waste my time.'

'Then ignore my counsel, but you will regret it. Ysomir is the key to this.'

Frowning, Helananthe looked sideways at her. Ariolne's eyes contained sparks of red, as if they reflected a temple fire. 'How do you know?'

'Otherwise your feelings about her would not be so fervent. If you used your instinct, you would know it too. Ma'am, your coronation hasn't taken place yet, has it?'

'No.'

'I thought not. You mustn't delay it any longer.'

'But I'm waiting for my mother and brother and my . . . my dearest friend to come home. I can't be crowned without them present.'

Ariolne shook her head, her face harsh with disapproval. Helananthe was beginning to find her more intimidating than her own father had been. 'You should. You must.'

'Why?' She had a feeling that she knew what the priestess was going to say.

'The Xauroma. The covenant between the monarch and the land must be remade without delay. Until you have sworn your fealty to the Xauroma during the coronation, the ceremony of initiation cannot take place, and until then you will have no true understanding of the nature of the covenant, and therefore no true authority to act in its name. Your instincts will be awry and your decisions ineffectual.'

Helananthe took a deep, impatient breath. This was the last thing she'd wanted to hear. She so wanted Eldareth and Ghiseyma there at her coronation, wanted it to be a great and joyous occasion, not something rushed like a secret wedding.

'It's just a ceremony. I already know the Xauroma. I've felt it, I've touched the *xauroth* sphere.'

'And that's more than you should have done, without proper initiation. You are deluding yourself, my daughter. A newborn child can wonder at the glitter of jewels, but has no idea what he's looking at. Whatever you think you know, I promise you that until your true entry into the mysteries, you are working with the understanding of an infant.'

Helananthe was offended. 'For an infant, then, I think I'm doing reasonably well so far.'

'I did warn you that my counsel may not be what you want to hear,' Ariolne said crisply. 'Also, you cannot sit upon the Sapphire Throne until you are crowned.'

'I know.' She took a deep breath. 'Very well, good mother, I did ask for your advice. It's not what I planned, but I'd better be crowned as quickly as possible. Arrangements could take weeks, though.'

'No,' said Ariolne. 'Once we set things in motion, you can be crowned within seven days.'

Reeling inwardly, Helananthe decided to ask nothing else for the time being. She couldn't admit it, but initiation into the Xauroma was the one thing she dreaded.

They were entering the upper levels of the palace now. As they walked down the long, bright gallery that led towards the Sun Chamber and other state rooms, Derione appeared and came striding towards her, looking anxious.

'Your majesty, I've just received some news. I couldn't find you.'

'Well, here I am. What is it?'

'The deputation from Thanmandrathor has entered Parione. They are on their way to the Amber Citadel now. They are demanding to see you, and our messengers report that they are furious. What should I say to put them off?'

'Nothing,' said Helananthe. 'Welcome them, feed them, and bring their leaders to the Sun Chamber. I'll be waiting for them.'

Chapter Five. Falthorn

'I am Falthorn, your uncle,' said the dark-haired Aelyr. 'Your father's brother.'

He clasped her hands and the moment seemed to stretch out forever. Tanthe watched in a trance of amazement as the others followed him into the forest hall. Aelyr men and women, fifty or more. She remembered her mother describing a procession of Aelyr she'd seen years ago. *'The light around them was a pale glow and it sparkled like a field of stars . . . All these veiled figures moving slowly against this soft shining light . . .'* and the breathless excitement stirred by those words now rushed through Tanthe like flame. The image was just as she'd imagined yet different; these Aelyr were not veiled in evanescent grey, but dressed in black and blue, violet and silver. They came in like the night sky, velvet-dark but full of stars. The crystalline music of the night grew louder as if it travelled with them, wrapped around them in spirals of light. Suddenly the music seemed to plunge right inside her. This was real and she was in the midst of it! Her whole body thrummed with a rush of wonder and fear.

'Can she remember anything?' Falthorn said, turning to Auriel.

Auriel shook his head. He looked anxious, but so lovely, his auburn hair floating around his shoulders. 'Only her human life. Nothing apart from that.'

'Not even her name?'

'My name's Tanthe!' she said, indignant at them talking across her.

'Of course. A perfectly good human name,' said Falthorn. Two of the Aelyr were coming towards her, a man and a woman in silvery robes. They were as regal as a king and queen, their hair brushed back from long, radiant, alien faces. Falthorn turned, holding out his hand to them.

'My mother Lady Cielemne and my father Lord Valthiell. Your grandparents. Look, here is Auriel's sister at last!'

She felt she should bow, wasn't sure it was correct, ended up giving an awkward slump of her shoulders. Close to, their faces were as smooth as pearl; there was little to hint at their age except their proud carriage, their aura of power and authority. The man's hair was dramatically streaked with black, steel grey and white; the woman's dark brownish-black, like Tanthe's. She had a jewel in the centre of her steep forehead, the same deep blue as her irises, like a third eye.

They didn't smile. They didn't even touch her. They simply regarded her with intense searching interest, until she felt she would melt under the heat of their gaze.

'Can she remember her Aelyr name?' said Lord Valthiell at last. Even his voice sounded alien. High and powerful like a horn, full of strange rich notes. *My grandfather*? Tanthe thought. A very far cry from her human grandfather Osforn, the gardener, self-contained and gnarled as a little oak tree. Even further from her other granddad, the generous but drunken Lan.

'Alas, no,' said Falthorn. 'We are not sure she was ever given one.'

'Of course she was given one,' said Valthiell. 'Talthaliorn and Fiomir must have named their own child.'

The names resonated. *Talthaliorn, Fiomir*. She couldn't think of a thing to say, but they didn't seem to require any response from her. They stared at her as if from a great height, and then they turned away, and others were coming past. People as strange and beautiful as Auriel, some of them smiling, some staring.

'Your cousins, Ostarial and Alviath, Faerlim and Nialorn . . .'

Tanthe was confounded; it would take time to remember all their names, to put them to the right faces. Some of them kissed her hand, some her cheek; her skin shivered where they touched her, as if some of their light had attached to her skin.

She was amazed at being the centre of their attention. All these shining beings, who were no taller than humans yet seemed so by their grace and presence, these soft moving creatures of violet, silver and black, who were one moment like shadows and the next iridescent as dragonflies . . . it was one thing to be told they were her family, quite another to believe it.

Tanthe stood there in sheer disbelief. She felt like laughing. She bit her lip, her shoulders shook. This was absurd. Completely. She tried to catch Auriel's eye but he was looking straight through her as if he'd seen a ghost. *Do the Aelyr believe in ghosts?* she wondered.

Time made another of its odd rushes forward, and now the Aelyr were taking seats all along the central table. Several men and women were passing down the table, setting places and arranging dishes of strange fruit. Not servants . . . two of them had just been introduced as her cousins.

That reassured her a little. It appeared that everyone took turns to do the work, like at home in Riverwynde.

'Come, dine with us, Tanthe,' said Falthorn. 'We have much to talk about.'

'Yes,' Tanthe said numbly. 'Do we?' She was aware of her less than clean travel-gear standing out among their robes. 'I'm not really dressed for dinner.'

'It doesn't matter. Auriel will find you a robe later. There's only one courtesy we require of you, which is to give your sword and bow to Ostarial. He will take them to your chamber for safe-keeping.'

'Oh . . . of course.'

She did as he asked. Ostarial raised his eyebrows as he took the long, silver-white Shaelahyr blade from her in its scabbard, but made no comment. Then Falthorn said, 'Come.'

He led her to the table, and bade her sit down. Valthiell and Cielemne were side by side at the head of the table. Falthorn placed Tanthe at the end of the bench nearest to them, with Auriel next to her. Falthorn sat opposite. Next to him was her supposed cousin, Ostarial, a watchful young man with grey eyes and dark hair. She saw no indication that he was Falthorn's son, nor any hint that Falthorn was even married; how these 'cousins' related to each other or to her was anyone's guess.

The chandeliers were lit, each branch-tip sparkling white. Lamps shone on the woven walls and along the table. The vault of the hall vanished in blue darkness, but the table was an island of light that shimmered on goblets of silvery-iridescent glass and glowed on the shining faces of the Aelyr.

Falthorn took a white carafe and poured pale wine into their goblets. 'To Tanthe, the long-lost,' he said, smiling into her eyes.

All the Aelyr raised their glasses to her. She flushed with pleasure and embarrassment. Food was offered to her – soft vegetable shells filled with grains, pieces of white cheese, strange-tasting gold and purple fruits – but she ate absently, barely registering the succulent flavours, all her attention fixed on the Aelyr.

It seemed to be Falthorn who did most of the talking. She'd never sensed such confidence and power in anyone before. Not even in Elrill, the lord of the Shaelahyr. There was something hypnotic, almost exhilarating about his certainty. Valthiell and Cielemne barely said anything, and she had the impression that Falthorn was testing her, while they sat in silent judgement.

'Our people are called the Valahyr,' he said. 'Have you heard of us?'

She racked her brains. 'No, I'm sorry. I know the Shaelahyr . . .'

There were soft but distinct hisses of disapproval. Ostarial said, 'Ah, that would explain the sword.'

Falthorn laughed. 'You know, then, that not all Aelyr are the same. The Shaelahyr are a small group and there are others; but the Valahyr are one of the main *eretrue* of Verdanholm. You see only a handful of us here.'

'*Eretrue*?' said Tanthe.

'The plural of *eretru*, whose meaning lies somewhere between "race" and "clan", I believe. The Valahyr are your father's folk, but your mother's *eretru* was the Fhelethyr.'

'The Fhelethyr . . . are they very different to you?'

'Not greatly,' said Falthorn. 'They inhabit different areas of Verdanholm and they are more inclined to maintain ties with Aventuria which have a ritual symbolism for them. We are different, as the races of Earth are different, but we are all still Aelyr.'

Again Tanthe recalled her mother's description; a woodland procession of Aelyr whose veils appeared grey, but shone in rainbow hues when you looked more closely. She wondered, were they Fhelethyr my mother saw?

'So none of my – none of Fiomir's family are here?'

'I'm afraid not.'

'And Talthaliorn and Fiomir themselves . . . you don't know where they are?'

'Alas, I wish we did. We hoped that you might help us discover what has become of them.'

'But I told Auriel, I have no memory of anything other than being human. Forgive me, but that's why I find it so hard to accept I could be one of you. Sometimes I think I'm on the verge of remembering, but it goes again.'

Falthorn reached across the table and touched her hand. 'Don't distress yourself. We would be asking you to remember a time before you were even born, or rather to call up the race memories of the Aelyr, which is hard for us sometimes. Would you like to remember, Tanthe?'

'Can you make me?' she gasped.

'It's possible, but I would be reluctant to attempt it. It

could be dangerous, with no surety of success.'

The idea alarmed her. 'I don't think I'm ready,' she said quickly. 'I'm used to being Tanthe, I know who I am. I'm not sure I want my identity to change so drastically.'

'Well, that's wise of you,' he said, pressing her hand as he released it. 'It's probable that when you are ready, the knowledge will return of its own accord. Meanwhile there is no pressure upon you to remember. All we want is for you to be comfortable among us. Feel at home here, for indeed, this is your home.'

'I'm confused,' Tanthe said. The wine was helping her to grow bolder. 'Auriel told me he couldn't leave. So are you all imprisoned here? Is it something to do with the Bhahdradomen?'

There was a ripple of shock as she uttered the word. Valthiell and Cielemne looked sternly at each other, but Falthorn appeared unmoved. 'Did Auriel tell you that?'

'Well no, not as such. I kept asking him questions but he couldn't or wouldn't give me a straight answer.'

Falthorn started laughing, while Auriel looked at the table. 'The truth is, Tanthe, that for a long time Auriel was searching for you in secret. He thought we would be angry at what he was doing – as indeed we were, purely because we were concerned that he might endanger himself. However, even though he feared we'd disapprove of him bringing you here, he persisted in trying to find you. But as you see, we are more than happy to welcome you. In fact, it means more to us than you can know.'

She gave an amazed laugh, moved and ridiculously happy. 'Oh, Auriel,' she said, gripping his hand under the table. 'I have had some extraordinary times lately, but I think this is the best.'

Falthorn looked sombre again. 'We're flattered, but I should add that things are not perfect here. Auriel did not completely mislead you about the . . . the Bhahdradomen. Although Verdanholm corresponds to your world in many respects, it is not solid like Earth. It is a more fluid realm.

This part of it is, shall we say, tenuously connected to the rest and it is difficult, if not impossible as a rule, for any of us to reach Earth from here. However, this is not directly the doing of the Eaters. The Valahyr have done this, isolated ourselves in order to protect ourselves from them.'

Tanthe was alarmed. 'But I thought they were only a danger in Aventuria. Not here.'

Two bright stars shone in Falthorn's eyes. 'They are dangerous everywhere, Tanthe. It has been Aventuria's mistake to underestimate the danger, to ridicule them rather than respect them, to let them live in Vexor rather than destroying them utterly . . . Ah, you shiver. I don't mean to frighten you, but it's the truth. They were never crushed. They have only been dormant, like spores. Now they are stirring again.'

'I know,' Tanthe said. She'd been rubbing her upper arms in a reflexive gesture against his words. Now she lowered her hands and sat up straight, wanting to prove to these people that she was not afraid, not ignorant. 'I don't know whether you're aware of it, but they've been active on Earth, too.'

'We've heard little of Earth for a long time. What has happened?'

She began to tell them all she knew. How she, Rufryd and Lynden had come across a pocket of Bhahdradomen in the Forest of Ardharkria, dead trees and sterile soil spreading like a stain from their abode. How they'd discovered that there were pockets of Bhahdradomen all across the continent, allowed to remain by secret clauses in the peace treaty after the War of the Silver Plains.

'This is not common knowledge,' said Falthorn.

'No,' said Tanthe. 'If it had been, the people living around them wouldn't have stood for it. Some have been paid to keep quiet about it; that includes the Duke and Duchess of Sepheret, my own realm. There may not be many of them but I think they're like pockets of marsh-gas, just needing a touch of flame to explode. But it's far worse. It's believed that the Bhahdradomen were actually helping the King. Their *ghelim*, their shape-changers, came invisibly with Garnelys's troops to enforce the conscriptions. One of them killed my uncle. My human uncle, I mean. And they appeared on the King's side in battle.'

'In what form?'

'As – as dra'a'ks. Great flying creatures that hunt like hawks but have scales like lizards—'

'Yes, yes, dra'a'ks, dragon-hawks. I have seen them.'

'But these *ghelim*. They looked like dra'a'ks but you could tell they were something else. Something . . . horrible.'

'They say that those with eyes to see can always tell,' Falthorn said softly.

Tanthe thought of Lynden, who had become so sensitive to the Bhahdradomen it almost drove him mad. 'And they can make others see, too.'

Valthiell spoke, startling her. 'You say they helped the king? Was he aware of their nature when he accepted their help?'

'Father,' said Falthorn, 'I hardly think we can expect Tanthe to know that.'

They didn't know she'd fought with Helananthe and entered the Amber Citadel; she hadn't reached that part of her story. 'It's believed they must have tricked him, because he can't possibly have summoned them on purpose. Unfortunately Garnelys can't answer because he was killed before anyone could question him.'

'Killed?' said Valthiell.

Tanthe decided not to mention Ysomir, in case they began to think she was making it all up. 'His people rose against him in the end. It was the only way we could stop him. We have a new Queen, his granddaughter Helananthe. But now all sign of the *ghelim* has vanished, and no one seems to know the truth of what went on.'

'It sounds a mess,' said Falthorn.

'No,' Tanthe said defensively. 'We are at peace again. Maybe the Bhahdradomen tried it on, then got cold feet and fled. Elrill said they are fuming because they know they have no real power.'

'Well, I set little store by anything Lord Elrill says.' Falthorn folded his arms on the edge of the table and looked keenly at her, as if debating with an equal. That swelled her confidence. 'They have been dangerous in the past and they will be dangerous again, believe me. For thousands of years they attacked Verdanholm, devouring our realm. Now it's begun again.'

'Devouring . . . ?'

'The Eaters is a deceptively innocuous but deadly accurate term for them. That's what they do. They consume life to the bare bones, even consume space itself, but at the end of it they are still thin, still hungry.'

The hatred and passion in his eyes lashed physically at her. 'Well, if it's true and they are coming back, I'll give everything, I'll even give my life to stop them!'

'I know you will, Tanthe,' Falthorn said more gently. 'I know you will. We didn't realise that you would be so well-travelled, nor so well-acquainted with our enemy.' He looked at his mother and father. 'Is she not brave, your granddaughter?'

Valthiell and Cielemne turned to her, and for the first time there was warmth in their eyes. Obviously their respect had to be earned. They looked so radiant, her heart filled with awe.

'You are brave indeed,' said Cielemne. 'A true daughter of the Valahyr.'

'So, tell us more of this war and the king's death,' said Valthiell.

Tanthe obliged, in her element. As the evening wore on, she experienced a wonderful sense of euphoria. It came in part from too much Aelyr wine, but mainly from being accepted among these people, from their warmth and the way they treated her as an equal; but more than that, it came from inside her. She was not the naive girl who had left Riverwynde last year. She had travelled, fought and learned a lot since then; she had been trained in swordsmanship by the Shaelahyr of the Whiteveils; she had dwelled in the forest of Lusahniah with Helananthe, fought alongside her at Hethlas Rim. Saphaeyender himself had been her lover. She was a woman in her own right. She hadn't come to the Valahyr empty.

When the meal was over and the talking dwindled, the Valahyr left the table and mingled in small groups, some sitting cross-legged on the mats, others wandering outside. Alone for a few moments, Tanthe turned and found Auriel at her shoulder, offering an armful of blue silk.

'I found a robe for you,' he said.

'Oh, thank you. Where should I go to change?'

'I'll show you.'

He led her to the back of the hall, through a door in the woven wall. On the other side, she saw that the edifice was even larger than it had seemed from the outside. Tanthe looked around, marvelling. Where she had thought there would be a few sleeping chambers, there were passages and rooms snaking off in every direction. An arch of stones framed a fissure that led down into the earth; rope ladders led to higher levels, where woven chambers hung like nests in the branches of great trees. Night glowed blue through the interlaced branches of the walls.

'This is wonderful. Is it me, or is it bigger on the inside than the outside?'

Auriel smiled and pointed at the entrance between the stones. 'There you can bathe, if you wish. There are towels to dry yourself. I'll wait here.'

'Are you suggesting I smell?' said Tanthe, grinning. 'Oh, it's all right, it would be incredible if I didn't.'

'You don't,' he gasped, as if afraid he'd offended her.

She shook her head. 'You're not used to being teased, are you, Auriel? We'll soon do something about that.'

Cautiously she entered the dark passageway, and found that it wound down to an underground cave. A couple of lamps gleamed blue on indigo rock. On one side, a waterfall gushed down the wall, falling into a pool that drained away underground. On the far side, behind a wattle screen, there were holes in the rock with the stream rushing away far below. A privy, thank the gods! Tanthe thought, suddenly realising just how desperate she was to use it. The Valahyr were not made of air, then. They ate, and did everything else that humans did . . . although, of course, she should have known that from living with the Shaelahyr.

Having doused herself in the waterfall and feeling much refreshed, she found she'd forgotten to bring the robe with her. She dragged her travelling clothes back on to her still-damp body and returned to Auriel.

'I forgot the robe,' she said, laughing.

'So you did.' He half-smiled back, seeming nervous. 'I'll show you your sleeping chamber, you can change there.'

'I like your uncle,' Tanthe said as he led her past the stones. 'Our uncle.'

'You like Falthorn?' Auriel said non-committally.

'Yes. And Cielmim . . . Cielnin . . . I think I'm drunk. The grandparents.'

'Here,' said Auriel, pushing open a door. The chamber inside was small, with a mattress on the floor, dark blue and green covers thrown over it. The walls were woven of living branches; green leaves filled the gaps and gave privacy. On one wall a square gap in the weaving made a window on to the forest. The room was filled with rich blue twilight.

'It's lovely,' said Tanthe. The door swung lightly shut behind them. Auriel was standing close to her, real and physical, his face carved by shadow to a breathtaking male beauty she'd only seen in statues and paintings.

They stared at each other.

'You look nothing like any of them,' Auriel said hoarsely. 'You're beautiful, really beautiful.'

'No, I'm not. Not like you are. Are you drunk too?'

'No,' he said.

'Don't the Valahyr get drunk? It must be just me, then.'

His eyes were wide, anxious, full of light. He raised one hand to touch her hair. Tanthe felt breathless. The reckless euphoria she felt was more than intoxication.

'I'm going to have to take my clothes off,' she said. 'To change, I mean.'

'I'll leave,' he said half-heartedly.

'You don't have to.'

Auriel's eyes seemed to swallow her. She saw his breathing quicken, the rise and fall of his chest where his loose tunic revealed his silky flesh. She felt she was losing all self-control and reason; trying not to fall on him was killing her.

'I would like to stay and talk to you,' he said.

The robe spilled on to the floor. They seized each other, hands tangling as they strained for each other's lips. Tanthe pulled him down towards the bed and they both lost their balance, falling onto the covers then squirming to press their bodies together.

She hadn't relaced her shirt or put her boots back on and it was easy for her to shed her clothing. And he – he was naked under the thin grey silk. Gods, his mouth tasted so sweet. Everything about him was sweet, innocent, good; she loved him so easily and so completely that she wanted to eat him alive.

He said he was older than her yet he seemed younger, and she still couldn't believe in her heart that he was truly her brother – but so what if he was? That only heightened the excitement. The very newness of his presence increased her desire – she'd only touched him for the first time today – and yet he seemed so familiar. She felt she'd known him all her life, and it seemed the most natural thing in the world to touch and kiss and . . .

'We can't,' Tanthe said, suddenly panicking. 'I brought nothing with me to – to—'

He didn't understand. 'What?' His eyes shone with firefly light.

'To make sure I don't conceive.'

'But you won't. Your body is human, mine is Aelyr. We cannot be fertile together.'

'Oh,' Tanthe breathed. 'You know a lot, don't you?'

'I know that I love you.' Auriel lowered his head to her breasts. His hair fanned deliciously over her skin; his tongue made hot circles around her nipples, his fingers delved warm as amber between her legs. She dropped her head back in bliss.

In Silverholm Rufryd had once been seduced by a Shaelahyr girl, Metiya, and later (after her anger was spent) Tanthe had asked him what it was like. Hopeless as always, he'd answered only, 'I don't know. All the bits were in the same place,' and she'd wanted to hit him; but it was true. Auriel's body as he stretched alongside her was human in every detail – flawless and glistening, yes, but still human-seeming – and the male organs were the same, like plump luscious fruit, and his prick grew long and hard under the pressure of her hand. His mouth arched hot against hers, tasting her. His delight in her breasts, the way his hands slid over her as he were desperate to touch her everywhere at once, and now pressed ever more urgently into her . . . he worshipped her femaleness like a human lover.

He was almost clumsy. As if he'd never done this before. That idea made her almost faint with excitement and she opened herself to him, guiding him, hoping he would not come too soon. With a gasp he pushed into her. He was inside her, this beautiful stranger, her brother. They were on their sides, her supple thigh lifted over his hip. They lay still for a few moments, gazing astonished into each other's eyes, joined by muscular, pulsing fire. She stroked the glaze of sweat on Auriel's skin. His body scent swam into her, spicy like fragrant wood laced with musk and delicious spices. Euphoric, like skeins of drugged smoke, heightening every sensation.

He began to move slowly. Thrusting into her as a human man would but, oh gods, it was different and suddenly she knew why Rufryd couldn't explain or perhaps had not even realised . . . She clung to Auriel in wild ecstasy, her hands on the taut globes of his buttocks, forcing him deeper. Everything was changing. Their heat became a glowing aura that spiralled around them, sucking them into a realm of flame, melting their limbs to liquid gold. They were no longer in the forest hall but travelling outwards through a night sky where stars lay thick as snow in a twisting pathway. Auroras arched over them. She was flying towards a new, wondrous place she'd never dreamed existed, where all veils would be drawn back and all her questions answered.

She felt her orgasm coming, a red spark in the distance reeling in closer and closer on a golden chain. Her breath soared. She was on the edge, the very edge of a flood of wonder, and when it broke unimaginable revelations and untold histories would pour over her and she would touch the fire, the Jewelfire of the Aelyr that powered the universe . . . And Auriel was with her on this wondrous journey, comets flaring in his eyes, her name on his lips.

Now a star was rushing towards her, becoming a white disc, and then a small round face, tumbling over and over, with dark holes for eyes—

'Tanthe, *Fliyet*,' Auriel groaned, moving hard and convulsively now. He cried out, pulsing his seed into her. His release ignited hers. On waves of fire she arched against him, hurtling uncontrollably towards the revelation; then everything was swallowed up, both the physical and the astral worlds, in the blazing spasms of her climax.

It seemed a long time before she could open her eyes. They fell back and lay loosely entwined, panting. She felt her skin zinging, heart pounding, all her emotions unravelling. Auriel's eyes were sightless with awe.

Slowly he blinked and focussed on her. 'I can't speak,' he said, pressing his fingers tenderly to her cheek-bone.

It took her even longer to come back from the plane of sensation . . . but as she did, she found only Auriel and the sky gleaming indigo through the leafy walls. No revelation. The miraculous inner-world had drawn its veils against her.

'No,' Tanthe sighed. 'Oh, gods, it seemed so close!'

He leaned over her, his hair tangled, his lovely face flushed. 'Tanthe?' he said softly. 'Did I do something wrong?'

'No, dearest,' she said, hugging him. 'You did everything perfectly. Couldn't you tell?'

He smiled, boyishly pleased, but his eyes remained anxious. 'Then what?'

'I don't know . . . You were with me, weren't you? We were flying along a – a path of stars, and . . . I thought something amazing was going to be revealed. But when I came all the images vanished. There was this face like a little mask . . . It doesn't even make sense now. I must have been hallucinating.'

Auriel twisted a skein of her hair round his finger, not meeting her eyes. 'No. What you saw was real on a higher level. It happens often when the Aelyr make love. Opens the channels of energy to knowledge. I think you were on the edge of recovering your memory.'

Tanthe sat up, groaning. 'I wish you hadn't told me that. I was so close it hurt!' She clasped her head. 'Gods, if I could have spent one more second there . . .'

'Never mind,' he said, pulling her down again. 'Perhaps you're not meant to remember. Perhaps it's better you don't.'

'I don't know.' She tucked her head into his shoulder. 'What was that name you called me? Not someone else's, I hope?'

'No, it's yours,' he smiled. 'An Aelyr name I made up for you, when I didn't know yours. Fliyet.'

'I like it. You can call me that, if you want.'

'Fliyet, sister,' he said, covering her hair with kisses.

'Don't remind me of the sister part,' said Tanthe. 'So has it happened to you many times, Auriel, travelling to strange places when you make love?'

'This was the first time.'

'Travelling?'

'And making love. They say you have to be an adept to concentrate on the astral side, and I'm no adept.'

I was right, she thought, thrilled. 'But you're so beautiful. How have those Valahyr women left you alone?'

'I was waiting for you, Fliyet.' He sounded sad.

'I hope you weren't disappointed.'

'No!' he said, holding her tight against him. 'You'll never know how much more this is than I dreamed . . .'

'Auriel . . . It wasn't my first time. I wish it had been.'

'It's all right. You're here now.'

'You're so strange,' she whispered into his neck. 'I don't mean it badly, but isn't it a bit weird, to wait for your sister? Is it a Valahyr custom, or something? I feel as if I know you, but I don't understand you at all.'

He raised his head to look at her and she saw that his face was wet with tears. 'I wish I could explain, but I can't.'

'It's all right.' She stroked his cheek, overwhelmed with love for him. 'Gods, don't cry, you'll start me off. Auriel, I don't understand what's happening here, but that's probably because my amazing Aelyr spirit has ended up in the body of a thick human. Be patient with me, because I love you and trust you with my life.'

'You still don't believe it, do you?'

'That I'm Aelyr? Sometimes I nearly do, then part of my brain says, "Nah. It's too crazy." But then why else would you have gone to so much trouble? Haunting me, even giving me gifts . . .'

'Tanthe, do you still have the *mnelir*?' he broke in.

'The little knife? Well, of course.' She stretched over the side of the bed and felt in her clothes until she found it. On Earth it disguised itself as a blunt, grey pocket knife; here it shone, a white blade in a glittering scabbard, with a crystal sphere on the pommel. 'This saved my life. The Bhahdradomen were terrified of it.'

He was suddenly grave. 'Would you give it back to me?'

'Oh,' she said in dismay. 'I thought it was a gift.'

'It wasn't mine to give. It's very old and rare, irreplaceable. I borrowed it from Falthorn, and he's asked for it back.'

She didn't know whether to laugh or growl. 'Borrowed? D'you mean you stole it?'

'I'm sorry. I just wanted to help you. But I must give it back, or Falthorn will be furious.'

'Not afraid of him, are you?'

'That's not the point. The *mnelir* is his.'

She breathed out between her teeth. 'Of course you can have it back, love, if you must. There . . .' She placed it on his discarded tunic on the floor. 'I'll miss it, though.'

'Thank you. And I'm sorry, Fliyet,' he said fervently. 'Please don't blame me for this. Forgive me, please.'

'Hey, it's not that bad—' she began, but Auriel kissed her, as if to change the subject. His tongue touched hers, sending new threads of lust through her. She slid her hand to his groin and he was still hard, a warm golden rod in her hand.

'You can't leave,' he whispered. 'You must stay with me.'

'Love, I'm happy to stay like this forever . . .'

As she spoke, Tanthe began to hear music. It was coming from outside, a strange insistent rhythm even weirder than the music of the Shaelahyr. It grew louder until she sat up and said, 'What *is* that?'

Kneeling up, she looked out of her window at the forest. The air flowed cool and delicious on to her hot face. Between the deep green canopy and the deep blue of the evening, the trunks were tall black sentinels edged with silver; and before them, in a clearing, the Valahyr were dancing.

'Auriel, look!' she gasped.

He knelt up behind her, his arms round her stomach and chin on her shoulder. And to her amusement and pleasure he slid into her from behind, gently making love to her as she leaned on the leafy sill of the window.

The hum that he'd described as the music of the stars was suddenly piercing; other sounds wove through it, a dry waterfall of rhythm like seeds in a gourd, high piping notes and deeper ones like wind-chimes. The music spiralled up, down, round, going nowhere but as thrilling as the very heartbeat of the universe. And the figures she saw dancing were silhouettes against a silver-grey glow.

They moved slowly, unfolding and stretching upwards with slender limbs; and it seemed they danced under veils, like graceful ghosts rising up under shrouds. The veils were translucent, tenting the silhouetted forms like misty light and cobwebs, glittering with dew, diamonds, tiny rainbows.

The music filled Tanthe's ears and her head, until her whole body vibrated with it. She watched in open-mouthed wonder, even forgetting Auriel. 'So lovely,' she breathed. The most beautiful and other-worldly sight she'd ever witnessed was this eldritch ballet.

And it was the last thing she remembered clearly.

Time and memory played cruel tricks on her.

There were colours, voices, snatches of conversation, fleeting moments of clarity. Sometimes she was walking in the forest, or staring at the sky until the music of the stars deafened her. Searching for something. Frightened, but always forgetting why.

She felt food in her mouth, and there was something about not eating food in the faerie realm or you would be trapped there for ever . . . but it tasted so good, and time whirled away from her again. Often Auriel was holding her. She felt the piercing-sweet stab of orgasm many times, but she never knew whether her lover was crying out with pleasure or sorrow.

Her pleasure became an ache, and then pain. She lay in

bed in her leafy chamber, having an endless dream about autumn coming to Verdanholm and all the leaves being torn from the trees. Pain folded her double. She was a book written by Saphaeyender. Just a book. If she could only close, the chapter would end.

The pain slipped away from her anyway and was forgotten. She wandered through the rooms of the forest hall, searching. Stood under the waterfall. Felt the diamond fire of Aelyr wine in her throat and dreamed again. Patchwork of moments tossed into the air and scattered at random like leaves.

Tanthe woke suddenly, drenched in cold sweat.

She was in her bed in the forest hall still, but everything felt different. Night lay black outside, but slivers of light seeped through her walls as if from a lamp in the passageway. All was silent. She had a sudden, violent fear that she was completely alone in this realm. That the Valahyr had gone.

Trembling, she tried to get up. At once she began to shiver; she was weak, and ached all over as if someone had kicked her in the back. Putting out her arms to support herself on the wall she realised she was in a black gown she'd never seen before.

She felt utterly terrified. The leaves on the walls had grown thicker and been trimmed back, as if she'd been here for weeks . . . how was that possible? She saw her old clothes on the floor and gathered them to her, the remnants of her identity. They smelled musty, as if they, too, had not been worn for weeks. If only she could put them on, she would be Tanthe again.

There was no sign of her weapons, she realised with a pang. Hadn't Ostarial been meant to bring them here? She made a quick search. Nothing.

She saw a carafe on the floor and lifted it to her mouth, but the scent of wine made her mouth pucker in disgust. She needed water.

'Either they've fled because I developed some kind of ghastly 'flu,' she murmured, 'or I've got the worst hangover in the history of Aventuria.'

She made for the bathing cave, moving more easily as her circulation returned. As she undressed she discovered, in bemusement, that she was bleeding and that someone had put a pad of soft white material between her legs to absorb it. Who? Had she done it herself, and if so, why couldn't she remember?

She began to sob in a mixture of confusion and fear. She splashed water on her face and drank deeply from the waterfall, but only stood under it for a few seconds. The cold was unbearable. Convulsed with shivers, she dried herself quickly and pulled on her undergarments – with a clean pad she made from a strip of towel – then her old shirt, breeches and tunic. The clothes chafed, and she felt sore all over. But the bleeding was good, it reassured her she was alive and real and not dreaming.

'I must really have been ill,' she said aloud, pulling on her boots. 'That must be it. I must find Auriel.'

Climbing back to ground level, she stood in the many-armed passageway beneath the trees. There was a lamp burning there, but all was silent. Were they asleep, away, what? All she could remember was a single day and evening here, and she had no idea who slept in which chamber or what hours they kept. Now her thirst was quenched she was hungry, but she didn't want their food; she remembered it as like eating nothingness, or mushrooms that contained only water and dreamy poisons.

A flurry of images stopped her short. Walking in the forest with Auriel. Laughing, constantly laughing as if she was demented with happiness. Falthorn and the others always smiling, kissing her, touching her, as hot as the Shaelahyr had been cold; making her drunk and languid on their affection. Only snatches. Scraps of events that seemed to span months.

She drew a quick hard breath against her terror. Mustn't give in to it. I've fought in a battle and killed Bhahdradomen. There is an explanation for this. I'm not afraid, not afraid . . .

She tried a couple of doors near her own, pushing them gently open to find the leafy chambers empty. She looked up at the higher levels, thought of climbing a rope ladder up to the branches but lost her nerve. The same horrible emptiness waited up there too.

Instead she went cautiously towards the door that led into the great hall. When she'd first entered Verdanholm, a single second had passed like aeons. Now she felt that countless days had passed in one night. Panic simmered in her. All she wanted at this moment was to flee back to Earth but she kept hearing Auriel telling her that no one could leave, ever . . .

She pushed open the door and passed into the cavernous hall. All the lamps were out and it creaked with emptiness, desolate in the grey dawn that spilled in through the far doorway. The great chandeliers were lightless, like tangles of dead antlers.

Deserted. She walked woodenly toward the entrance, thinking, why have they left me? What am I going to do? She looked out into the forest but it seemed deathly still and silent. No music, no dancers, no birdsong. Her fear grew. What if she hadn't been here for days, but years? Her disorientation held her one breath away from screaming madness. Was she still asleep, having a nightmare?

She hovered in the doorway, not knowing whether she would feel better or worse outside. Turning, she gazed at the far end of the hall. Upon the balcony that overlooked the hall, she saw a glow.

Her breath quick and shaky, she ran the length of the hall and, with trembling arms, climbed the ladder up to the balcony. Here she found two great chambers that seemed larger than they possibly could be from the outside. The weightless, woven doors were unlocked; in the first, sapphire velvet covered the walls and tented the ceiling, and there was a broad, carved bed canopied in the same lush material. The chamber of Lord Valthiell and Lady Cielemne?

The second was similar, but the velvet hangings were darker, a gorgeous midnight blue. Tanthe immediately felt power in the room, something at once silver and dark, that wrapped itself around her like static. This must be Falthorn's chamber. Suddenly she had the weirdest feeling that she'd lost something vitally important, and must find it. Had he left any clue as to what had happened – either to her or to the Valahyr?

She went along the walls, lifting the velvet hangings and finding clothes stored behind the first two. The third one she lifted, however, revealed a recess whose contents made her gape. It was illuminated by pale light; this must be the glow she'd seen, filtering between the branch-walls on to the balcony. In the upper part of the alcove hung weapons, knives, bows and arrows. And the first thing she saw was her Shaelahyr sword.

It was unmistakable. There were a couple of Valahyr swords hanging up and they were quite different; curved and set with garnets and sapphires. Hers was long, straight and ice-white.

Tanthe was angry. Falthorn demanded his *mnelir* back, she thought, and now he has the cheek to steal my sword. How dare he! I suppose he'd say he put it here for safe-keeping. Well, I'm having it back. Fuming, she strapped the belt round her waist and settled the scabbard. At once she felt stronger.

On the floor of the recess there was a strange chest about four feet wide, three feet deep and three high. It had panels of carving, enamelled and jewelled in deep vibrant shades of blue, and the whole chest was shod in strips of bright silver. This was the source of the glow. Light spilled from under the lid like captive sunlight.

Tanthe stared at it in awe and fear. She guessed that

there were Aelyr weapons inside; not ordinary ones like swords and bows, but mystical ones like her *mnelir* that contained *liroth* energies. Was her knife in there? Did she dare to steal it back?

Cautiously she touched her left hand to the lid of the chest. A savage pain leapt through her arm and a violent jolt threw her backwards. She sprawled on the rugs in shock for a few seconds. Her whole arm had gone numb. She shook it and it filled with the agonising fire of pins and needles.

'Bastard!' she spat, seething now. If she couldn't get the *mnelir* back, perhaps there was something else she could take to protect herself? Careful not to touch the chest again, she slung an Aelyr bow over her shoulder and seized a quiver of arrows. She wasn't the best archer in the world, not a patch on Rufryd, but she wasn't bad.

Tanthe gritted her teeth, thinking how Rufryd would disapprove of her stealing. But at this moment she didn't care. She felt like a cornered animal.

She went out on to the balcony again, nervous but determined. She crossed it and was about to lower herself on to the ladder when a figure came into the entrance. She froze, her heart bounding in alarm.

The figure was Ostarial, the watchful dark-haired Valahyr. Dressed in black, he was framed against the forest with the dawn light flaring his shadow towards her. Tanthe stared; he saw her, too, but she couldn't make out his expression. The sight of him brought her no relief, only sharp, instinctive terror.

'Good morning to you, cousin,' he said, walking into the hall. 'What are you doing up there?'

It was all she could do to speak. 'Looking for someone. Something horrible's happened to me.'

'Has it?' He came closer and she almost yelled at him to stay where he was. But he stopped anyway, before he was too close under the balcony to see her. 'What?'

Now she saw his face and there was narrow suspicion in

his eyes as if he knew something, but wanted nothing to do with it. 'You tell me!' she cried. 'What have they done to me?'

'Tanthe, they've done nothing to you.'

'Then why can't I remember anything since the first day I was here? Where are they all?'

'They're here,' Ostarial said evenly, as if to soothe the madwoman. 'We have been . . . hunting, that's all.'

'I don't believe you. Hunting? You don't eat meat!'

She was breathing hard, caught between rage and terror. Through the tall entrance came the rest of the Valahyr, in ones and twos at first, then in a crowd. Falthorn was in their midst, Lord Valthiell and Lady Cielemne following. And there was Auriel at the very back. A pang of emotion speared through her. He looked like a beautiful woodland spirit and still an enigma, a stranger.

All the Valahyr saw her and crowded forward on either side of the central table, staring up at her. Their eyes were feral. Terror nearly blinded her and she clung to the balcony rail for support.

'Is something wrong, Tanthe?' Falthorn said, walking to the front where Ostarial stood.

'You tell me what you've done to me!' she cried, aware that she sounded hysterical.

For a long moment, Falthorn exchanged unreadable looks with his parents. Finally he said, 'Ah, you're back with us, are you?'

'But where have I been? How long have I been here? Why can't I remember? Have you been drugging me, or something?'

Falthorn's black eyebrows rose. 'That's rather harsh. We are your family. Only a few days have passed. Tanthe, you fell ill the second day you were here and the potions with which we healed you do tend to induce long sleep and colourful dreams . . .'

His words sounded hollow. 'You're lying,' she snarled.

104

'You're upset,' said Falthorn. 'You also appear to have been in my chamber, judging by the weapons you've hung about your person. There's no need for this. Come down.'

'Oh, no. I don't trust you.'

Falthorn sighed. His tone was light but she sensed deep irritation and indifference. Very far from the kindness he'd first shown her. 'Ostarial, bring her down, would you?'

As her cousin started towards the ladder, she slipped the bow off her shoulder and set an arrow to the string. A gasp rippled through the Valahyr. Ostarial stopped, glowering at her.

'Don't try it!' she snapped. 'Don't think I can't use this bow or sword! The Shaelahyr taught me! Whatever you think of them, they never lied, and never drugged me!'

Falthorn folded his arms. 'Still, you can't stay up there forever. Put the bow aside and come down. No one's going to hurt you.'

Tanthe was trapped. The last thing she wanted was to injure any of them; that would put her in the wrong and give them license to do anything with her. She would have to give herself up . . . but the table gleamed between the mass of Valahyr like a shining path to freedom.

She slung the bow on her shoulder. Snatching a breath she hopped up on to the fragile balcony rail and launched herself into space.

Hands desperately outstretched, she grasped at the branches of the nearest chandelier and caught it. Her arms jarred but her momentum carried her and she swung in a long arc, letting go and landing in a crouch on the table surface, behind the Valahyr. They turned in astonishment, but Tanthe was up and running. She leapt off the edge of the table and was through the entrance before they even knew what was happening.

Now she was out in the forest, feet pounding.

The gorgeous colours of Verdanholm – sunrise dripping bronze through the blue-green leaves – blurred past her. Already she was growing short of breath, her limbs dragging. How could she have become so unfit in just a few days? She was a fast runner, but now sheer panic and adrenaline were all that forced her on. She had a wild idea that if she could only reach the clearing where she first entered Verdanholm, she might escape back to Earth before they caught her.

The forest looked the same in every direction. But Tanthe's sense of direction was good and it seemed only the day before that Auriel had brought her this way . . . She crossed the clearing with the strange standing stones and knew she was going the right way.

Fifteen minutes later she found herself in the glade, with its lush grass and the stump of indigo stone she remembered.

With her chest heaving painfully, she gazed down at the stump. She pressed her hand to its cold surface. It was impenetrable, devoid of magic . . . and she had no *anametris* sphere to open it, wouldn't have known how to use it even if she'd stolen one.

She heard voices. She twisted round to see figures in the forest, some distance away but coming in her direction.

Tanthe plunged back into the edge of the clearing, by the toad-stone, and swung herself up into the branches of a tree. She drew her sword, and waited.

Presently a single Valahyr appeared, walking quite slowly as he looked here and there through the trees. It was Auriel.

'Tanthe?' he called. 'It's only me. Please come back. No one means you any harm. It's all right, I'm on my own.'

So, they'd sent Auriel to lure her out. Smart.

She waited until he passed beneath the branch on which she was sitting. Then she launched herself out of the tree and brought him down from behind.

Auriel hit the grass with Tanthe on top of him. In a flash she twisted his arms up behind his back with one hand, and pressed the blade of her sword to the side of his neck. He cried out in pain.

'So now you can tell me,' she hissed, 'what in the name of Breyid is going on.'

'Tanthe, stop.' He seemed really afraid. 'I can't breathe. What's wrong with you?'

In her normal state of mind she would never have treated someone she loved so viciously. But now the fiery instinct of self-preservation drove her. 'Let me explain. One moment you are fucking me and I'm blissfully happy. The next I wake in a cold sweat, insane with terror and knowing I've been here what seems like forever but unable to remember anything. Wouldn't that upset you, just a little? Come on, Auriel, tell me the truth! I loved you, but I know you're in on this!'

She jerked the blade and he winced. 'I never wanted this to happen!' he said. 'They made me do it, Tanthe. The Valahyr forced me.'

'Forced you – to do what?'

'Let me up and I'll explain. Please, I can't speak. I won't try to run from you.'

'Oh yes, by the gods, you'll explain!' She pressed the edge harder into his throat. A line of bright blood appeared and she stared at it in a mixture of rage and misery that she'd hurt him. 'And you'll help me get back to Earth, or I'll kill you! Tell me, Auriel!'

'Let him up,' said a voice above her.

She looked up and there was Lord Valthiell. He gazed gravely at her, his face stone-hard beneath the badger's mane of his hair. 'There is no need to harm him, Tanthe. We can send you back to Earth, if that's what you truly desire.'

She laughed, incredulous. 'You can? I knew it!'

'I helped you to come through,' said Valthiell. 'You never saw me, but I was there. It was I who created the portal – not Auriel.'

Her mouth opened and tears burned her throat. His words made her feel doubly betrayed.

Valthiell drew from his robe a crystal *anametris* sphere. It seemed alive, as if it had several spheres nested one inside another, each rotating in a different direction. As he moved towards the stump of blue rock, she saw streamers of blue and green light forming above it. Tanthe felt numb with disbelief and fury.

'Come, Tanthe, quickly,' said Lord Valthiell. 'This will not please Falthorn, but he will soon have other matters to concern him. He doesn't need you any more.'

She looked narrowly from him to Auriel, still pinned to the ground, his body hot beneath hers. 'Doesn't need me? For what?'

Auriel began to say, 'Fliyet – forgive me—' but Valthiell cut across him.

'What's done is done, granddaughter. There is no use in crying over it. In these times we must all make sacrifices to aid the greater good, when the survival of Aelyr and human alike is at stake. We are a peace-loving people. All we do – all Falthorn does – is designed to ensure peace in Verdanholm.'

'Unfortunately I don't believe a thing the Valahyr say any more,' she said savagely. 'Auriel's coming to Earth with me, to make sure this portal really leads to Earth and not into a void.'

'No, you ask too much. He must stay here. Falthorn placed restrictions upon him and he could not pass through even if he tried. But the portal is safe, I promise. You should go swiftly, before my son comes.'

Glancing up, she saw that the column of light was strong and bright, and through it she could see the strange perspectives of another world. All she had to do was step through and she would be safe from this madness . . . She got to her feet and let Auriel up on to his knees, still keeping the blade-tip against his throat.

'Trying to get rid of me now?' she said. She looked from Lord Valthiell to Auriel. 'I'm going nowhere until I get the explanation you owe me.'

Auriel stared up at her, his eyes full of regret and misery.

He looked outwardly beautiful but deeply ashamed, and somehow the shame took away from his beauty.

'Fliyet, even when I tell you the truth, you won't believe me. I hoped you'd never find out, that you'd just stay with me here and be happy . . .' Auriel shook his head. 'Once you know, you'll never want me near you again.'

He looked so bleak that she drew the sword back, and sheathed it. 'Try!'

'Tell her,' said Valthiell. 'Quickly.'

It was only when Auriel rose to his feet that she realised, from his expression, that he was frightened of Valthiell. Shivers ran through her.

And Auriel told her, his voice halting, his words stark and blunt.

Tanthe pushed the words out of her head as soon as he'd spoken them. Denial turned her numb. As she stood there, shaking and speechless and beyond reaction, Auriel darted forward and thrust a cool flat object into her hand.

'Take it, Fliy,' he said hoarsely. 'I don't expect you to forgive me.' And he was running away from her, glancing back in fear and misery, as if he could only flee from the pain he'd caused.

He'd given her his *silvenroth* mirror.

'Wait,' she breathed. 'You can't just—' but Valthiell's hands were on her shoulders and he was thrusting her bodily towards the kingfisher light of the portal.

'It is imperative that you go now. For your own safety, granddaughter, forget all you've seen and heard!'

Anguish rose and strangled her. 'Auriel, you liar!' she yelled, struggling against Valthiell. 'You come back!'

Too late.

Valthiell thrust her into the portal. In that moment she twisted and saw Falthorn enter the glade; saw Auriel, who was still looking back at her, run straight into him.

Verdanholm made one of its little time leaps, and froze the moment for her. There was Falthorn, all flowing hair and elemental darkness, grace and power and icy reason, stating calmly, 'You disobeyed me. You let her go.' And there was Auriel, falling to his knees with Falthorn's hands gripping his wrists, collapsing into a pose of degraded worship or of sheer, abject terror.

The void sucked her down and the scene broke up in a whirl of green-blue light.

Chapter Six. Alliances and Secrets

The Sun Chamber shone in golden splendour, dappled with rainbows. Sunlight, blazing through the great stained-glass window that filled the end wall, set afire the clear greens of the Tree of Life, the azurite blue of the sky and the chestnut of the Tree's branches. The graceful figure of Queen Hetys was caught there in glass and lead-lines, offering up a red jewel; the monarch's symbolic offering of her heart, devotion and life to Aventuria.

The Sapphire Throne stood on a dais beneath the window, a tall double chair crusted with lapis and blue spinels and sapphires. The sunlight drew silver-blue fire around it.

Helananthe stood before the throne, waiting for the deputation from Thanmandrathor. Until she was crowned she would not sit on the Sapphire Throne itself; she had no wish to break with royal tradition. Derione was at her right hand side, and at her left, Lord Serpeth, both standing halfway down the nine steps. Dawn and Mirias were on either side of the dais, with a handful of palace guards lining the chamber.

The amber walls and the gilded interlacing of the vaulted ceiling gave back the sunlight in sheets of molten gold. The beauty and warmth of the Sun Chamber filled Helananthe with confidence. The chamber had been designed, she knew, to do just that; to fill everyone who entered with warmth and joyful energy. A free-flowing beneficent *roth*.

Helan hadn't yet reconvened the Council, so the tiers of seats on either side stood empty. In any case, she had wanted to meet the deputation in relative privacy.

Her robes were of stiffly quilted purple and gold satin,

her honey-coloured tangle of hair tamed with clasps, but she wasn't convinced she cut a regal enough figure. She'd spent years of her life roughing it. As rebel leader in the forest, she'd been in her element. Sometimes in the Amber Citadel she felt faintly ridiculous, constantly having to watch herself so she didn't swear, or rest her feet on tables.

'Ma'am,' Serpeth whispered. 'Might I suggest that, whatever their complaint, you use this opportunity to assert your authority over them. Be firm. We may have an age-old friendship with them but they will respect you the more if you don't let yourself be swayed by it!'

That's rich, coming from you, she thought. 'Thank you for that advice, my lord,' she said, grimacing.

Lord Serpeth, Duke of Eisilion, was a smiling, stoat-faced man with flame-red hair. He had entered battle on Garnelys's side only to switch to Helananthe's, effectively ensuring her victory. He was a typical Eisilian, a chamaeleon, whom she could trust only as long as it profited him to support her. As far as she knew, he was unaware that his cousin Lady Nietriya had been sheltering her mother and brother. Serpeth might be on her side now, she reasoned, but the less he knew the better.

'Your majesty,' announced an equerry at the door. 'The representatives of Thanmandrathor request leave to petition you.'

'Show them in,' she said.

The eight men and women who entered were dressed in leather, with leaf-green cloaks thrown over polished breastplates, boots and breeches laced with crossed thongs. They wore their hair in single long plaits. Feathers tipped with bronze beads adorned the shoulders of their cloaks, and they wore the ducal insignia of their country; a bronze clasp in the shape of a triple moon, slashed by a lightning-bolt. As they bowed, the deep brown of their hair glinted richly.

'Lady Branq'elin and Lord Mawrdreth of Thanman-drathor,' the equerry announced.

The man and woman who led the deputation were clearly brother and sister. They were as tall as Helananthe and their faces were proud, with dusky skins and high cheekbones. They regarded her from slanting green eyes.

'Your majesty,' the woman began. 'We are the son and daughter of the Duke and Duchess of Thanmandrathor. Our parents send greetings and the blessings of the Goddess from their house to yours.'

'The greeting is returned.' Helan inclined her head.

'Our Realm has been most grievously served by yours.' The thin skin of Branq'elin's politeness was already breaking. 'Our people are not yours, to be conscripted and dragged from their homes on the King's whim, yet when we objected, the Amber Citadel sent armies against us! We were given no choice but to defend ourselves and we routed Garnelys's force decisively, despite great losses on our own side. Now we come here as victors and to demand redress.'

Helan spoke carefully. 'I understand your rage at my grandfather's behaviour. I share it. As you must have been informed by now, I too raised an army against him and defeated him; in fact I thank you, because without Thanmandrathor to divide his army, I doubt that we could have won.'

'And the army we defeated is now under whose command?'

'Under mine, of course.' Helan was trying to remain friendly. Relations between the two Realms had always been strong, but Branq'elin and Mawrdreth were plainly seething.

'We defeated your army,' said Mawrdreth, 'and yet here you are, a Paranian monarch still claiming sovereignty over us.' Helananthe saw Branq'elin discreetly press her booted foot on to her brother's.

'Now wait,' said Helan. 'I thought you came here to complain against King Garnelys, not against me. We've just fought on the same side, haven't we? You may rest assured that all conscriptions are ended, that Thanmandrathor may continue to order her own affairs as she always has. Any compensation that is due to you, you will receive with all haste.'

'This may not be enough,' said Branq'elin.

'For what?'

'To heal the broken trust between us.'

'Then what will be enough?'

'Relinquishment of the powers you hold over us, that ever allowed such an outrage to occur,' Branq'elin said firmly.

Mawrdreth added, 'We should like our father to bear the title of King, as the rulers of Thanmandrathor did of old, before they were reduced by Queen Hetys to puppet Dukes.'

There was a shocked silence in the Chamber. He seemed to have said more than his sister had meant him to. Helan suddenly appreciated Serpeth's advice.

'What my brother means—'

'No,' said Mawrdreth. 'I've said exactly what I mean. Let's not cloud the issue with diplomacy.'

'Is this true, Lady Branq'elin? Is this what the people of Thanmandrathor want? To break the Nine Realms apart?'

'We want our independence, yes,' she said fiercely. 'We demand it!'

'I see.' Helan paused, thinking, if I grant independence to one Realm, they might all want it. She felt angry. As if I could inherit the throne of Aventuria then immediately give it all away – give away all that Queen Hetys and King Maharoth achieved, and my descendants' legacy!

She was very controlled, authoritative.

'That's impossible,' she said coldly. 'You know full well it's impossible.'

The two glared at her, their fury snake-green in their eyes. 'We have no wish to fight you,' said Branq'elin.

'We have already fought and won,' Mawrdreth added.

'And what did you expect to happen?' Helan said

sarcastically. 'That you would invade Parione and find the Amber Citadel in chaos? That you'd simply take your independence and no one would be here to gainsay you? Clearly you find yourselves thwarted. Aventuria still has a ruler.'

'Then if Paranios insists on ruling us, surely you have a duty to protect us!' Branq'elin blazed.

'But of course. The whole point of the alliance of the Nine Realms is to stand firm against any outside threat. Don't you see that to break away would jeopardise that?'

'But it's already in jeopardy,' said Mawrdreth. 'We are the ones whose country lies next to Vexor. We are the ones who have to live with the Bhahdradomen as neighbours. Where are the royal troops policing the border? Who of your own people have you sent to protect us? No one. It falls to Thanmandrathor to protect herself.'

'But why do you say this?' Helananthe asked, frowning. 'There is a dangerous strait dividing your coast from theirs. They have never dared to cross it. They are not sailors, and their powers to travel by other means were destroyed over two hundred and fifty years ago.'

'There have been rumours,' said Branq'elin, 'of Bhahdradomen activity in Thanmandrathor. When the Duke has dispatched people to investigate, nothing is ever found. But the rumours go on. There are strange storms. Our priests tell us that Q'enartre and Ank'eth are angry.'

'We ignore the warning of the gods at our peril,' Mawrdreth said quietly.

Helan was chilled. She thought of the vanishing Laphaeome . . . Infiltrating her grandfather's court, putting all of Aventuria into chaos . . . so that we were all too busy, she thought, to notice the Bhahdradomen slipping in through the back door?

On an impulse she went down the steps and stood in front of them, reaching out to touch their arms in a gesture of reconciliation that seemed to take them by surprise. 'What you have suggested is very serious,' she said. 'But it is the very reason we must remain friends and allies! Lady Branq'elin, Lord Mawrdreth, you and your retinue are welcome to stay in the palace for as long as you wish. My coronation takes place in a few days' time; I hope you will attend, as representatives of your parents the Duke and Duchess. We'll talk again as a matter of urgency.'

'Very well, ma'am,' said Branq'elin, disarmed. 'Thank you. But we shall not let these matters rest until we receive satisfaction!'

The deputation left, stiff-backed but somewhat pacified – for now. Helananthe let out a deep sigh. 'Gods, this is all I need.'

'You handled it wonderfully, ma'am,' said Serpeth.

As Helan and her attendants left the Sun Chamber, she looked round for Derione, but he hung back because Serpeth had already muscled in beside her. 'You were diplomatic, yet strong; although, forgive me, you could have been just a little less forthcoming with exposition. You are the Queen! You do not need to explain yourself to them!'

Helananthe ground her teeth. 'Thank you for the advice, my lord, but I think that perhaps the monarch should be left to make her own mistakes.'

'Your pardon, ma'am,' Serpeth said contritely. 'Ah, you must think me an impudent fool, trying to tutor you in queen-ship! All I intended was to demonstrate my support for you. I can assure you that Eisilion remains firmly within the Nine Realms, now and forever.' His voice became low and intimate. 'Forgive me, but you seem so alone, with no consort at your side. And there is no need for you to be alone. I am here.'

Helan looked into Serpeth's shrewd eyes, not knowing whether to scream with laughter or punch him. 'I can't rival your facility with words, I must admit.'

'Ma'am?'

'I do believe I just heard you insinuate that you have no wish to be King of Eisilion, when you could be King of all Nine Realms.'

Serpeth didn't miss a beat. 'Well?' he said, looking brazenly into her eyes. 'Am I so repugnant to you? Is it such a bad idea?'

'We approached her as enemies, she welcomed us as friends,' Branq'elin stated. 'This makes things awkward.'

Mawrdreth leaned on the broad golden stone of the battlements, and looked out at the gentle magnificence of Parione; so different from their own home. 'Does it, though, Bran? She could have had us arrested, for what we asked today. Instead she invites us to her coronation!'

His sister's eyes were narrow, and her nails scratched at the stone. 'Trying to sweeten us! We must keep the pressure on her. If we had our independence, this would never have happened.'

'No, but she is never going to grant it to us in a thousand years.'

'Our army is still camped within a few miles of the city.' Branq'elin folded her arms, turning her back on the view.

Mawrdreth sighed. 'I think she would make a very bad enemy. If we start another war, we could lose everything.'

'You seem to have changed your tune, considering your blatant efforts to spell out our ambitions in there!'

'I'm sorry, I was tactless. But now I'm just being realistic. Yes, we negotiate and stand our ground – but this is going to be a compromise, whatever happens.'

'I know. Ank'eth curse it, I know!'

He touched her shoulder. Bran was fiery, but not foolish. 'Would Father truly want the responsibility of kingship, when he has been in such poor health? Would you really want to be queen after him?'

'No, I am perfectly happy with the title of Duchess or no title at all, as long as my country is free and safe. Short of war, we are not giving ground on this, Mawr!'

'Of course not. But she is not Garnelys.'

Branq'elin rubbed her forehead with the heel of her hand, smoothing out the lines of anger. 'The annoying thing is that I almost like her. I didn't want to. She's tough but she's warm-hearted; you can see she's lived in the real world, not been cocooned in the Amber Citadel.'

Mawrdreth clasped her hand. 'She reminds me a bit of you.'

She held his hand tight, raised it to her lips and bowed her head to kiss it. 'I had a terrible dream last night, Mawr. We were separated, and I was going home without you, and the whole world was dark.'

'Bran, it was only a dream,' he said softly. 'We've already come through the worst together.'

'Have we?' she said.

When Jthery came at last to Parione, he found a city sweltering in summer heat, lush and golden and more magnificent than he could have imagined.

It had been a long, arduous journey from Mithrain. Rash of him to undertake it alone, in defiance of his family's concerns. Still, his horse had carried him steadily along the Meiondras Road, and nothing dreadful had befallen them. He was here, breathing the fragrance of unfamiliar flowers, staring up at the Amber Citadel. This was the first time he'd ever left Mithrain and he was full of awe, like a child at Hollynight.

He felt sweat prickling beneath his clothes. His horse, Heron, was tired, with sweat darkening his dappled coat to iron-grey. Jthery dismounted and led him the rest of the way to let him cool off.

Jthery looked around carefully as he walked, taking in everything. The wide boulevards were swarming with people, especially in the mercantile area where the merchants' premises stood open to the street between frontages of marble pillars, displaying silks and rugs from Azura Maroc, food and wine, saddlery, clothes, jewellery. Market stalls were spread beneath tented canopies striped with white and gold. Soon he became aware that folk were watching him as he passed. He wasn't sure why, but their glances were making him uneasy.

Perhaps it was that he looked different, with his Mithrainian clothes of pale watery grey and amethyst, or his rose-gold hair that was as unusual in his own country as here. He wasn't vain, so it didn't occur to him that he drew attention because he looked striking. The attention only made him uncomfortable.

Strange, too, the mixture of people in the streets. Many were obviously citizens of Parione, with their pale pleated robes and auras of relaxed confidence. Yet there were scores of men and women from other realms mingling with the citizens, most in army gear of various styles and different states of wear. Folk dressed like soldiers but wandering the streets like civilians? Others were poorly dressed, thin, out of place.

Suddenly Jthery realised. Some, at least, must have been Garnelys's conscripts. Others, those who had fought at Hethlas Rim and other battles to free those conscripts. On the surface the crowds were benign and friendly, but as they ebbed and flowed like water along the streets, he sensed a seething tension between them. Some had fought against each other. None knew what the future held.

In a moment of fear, he shivered, ice-cold as if an undine had touched him. Heron shied at silk rugs flapping on a stall; Jthery struggled to calm him. He led the horse on swiftly, trying to escape the throng, failing. Half a dozen Parionians cursed as they were forced to jump out of the way. Jthery couldn't fight free.

Lost amidst a thousand strangers, he experienced a moment of pure terror. What in the Nine Realms had possessed him to leave the lakes he loved, to follow phantoms and whispers? *Tread carefully and wisely*, the elemental's warning echoed horribly in his head, *for your choices may save or doom us all!*

'What am I doing here?' he said aloud. He kept one hand firmly on Heron's bridle. The other closed tight, by instinct, around the little carved fish that hung at his throat, the symbol of his Goddess.

Then he sensed Eshte's answer, calm and sure. *Go to Helananthe. She will set you on the path; then it is for you to find your own way.*

Taking a deep breath, Jthery raised his eyes above the crowds and walked steadily towards the Amber Citadel. And soon the fear faded, and there was only the sun-coloured edifice before him, and Heron's solid, sweaty presence beside him.

With a frisson of fear, Saphaeyender entered the prison section of the Amber Citadel. It lay inside the northern quarter of the inner wall, a massive structure that encircled the palace, joined to it at various points by covered bridges. He was expected; a guard saluted him, and let him through two sets of metal doors that thundered shut behind him.

Within, the corridor of bare, sand-coloured stone was dry and well-swept. Most of the cell doors stood open; there had rarely been more than a few wrongdoers in the city. There was a musty smell, an air of drabness and desertion on the place. Saphaeyender thought, presumably Garnelys would have imprisoned me here, if he'd caught me. Could I have borne it?

A female warder met him and led him down the long row of cells. She was austere and straight-faced, but otherwise pleasant enough; prisoners were treated humanely in Parione. Brutality, the saying went, was for the Bhahdradomen. But the idea of being locked up filled Saphaeyender with loathing.

Once he had been so certain of everything, so safe in his world. He had written fluently, been feted and glorified in all he did. But Garnelys had taken it all away. The Old Royal Theatre had been destroyed and now Saphaeyender felt like a king without a throne, while the citizens of Parione had had their lives turned upside down. They had far more important matters to concern them than Saphaeyender's next play. And he – after the Battle of Hethlas Rim, he had little faith left in himself.

But he could still act.

So he approached Ysomir's cell as Tanthe had first seen him; the great poet resplendent in luxurious ivory silk; loose trousers, tunic and a soft coat that hung gracefully on his tall form. Long black hair, in which the wings of silver were growing ever more noticeable, framing a handsome face that was compassionate, but just a little sardonic.

The warder brought him to a door and unlocked it. 'Do you wish me to chaperone you, sir?'

'No, thank you,' said Saphaeyender. 'If she looks like stabbing me, I'll shout for help.'

His attempt at black humour was lost on the warder. She pushed open the door and ushered him through.

The cell, like the corridor, was clean and plain. A shaft of dusty light hung across the room, drawing warmth from the ochre walls. Beneath a high window the prisoner sat at a table, writing. She was dressed in a plain fawn robe gathered at the neck, her golden-brown hair cascading over her shoulders. With a slender hand she dipped the quill in the ink and went on writing, precise and pensive, utterly absorbed.

Her composure startled Saphaeyender. Hard to believe she was only eighteen. He'd expected to find a frightened waif, not a woman.

'Good day, my lady Ysomir,' he said.

She looked up, quickly put down her pen and rose.

'I'm Saphaeyender. I'm a friend of your sister.'

She looked astonished; obviously the warders had not told her he was coming. 'Are you really *the* Saphaeyender – the playwright?'

'The same. Didn't Tanthe mention me?'

'Of course! She never stops talking about you!' Ysomir coloured. 'Just as well she isn't here or she'd berate me for embarrassing her. I can't believe it's you.'

'It is, I'm afraid.' He took her hand and kissed it. She smiled and her face came to life; rosy, dimpled and breathtakingly pretty. Now he could see the country girl in her and – although their colouring was different – something of Tanthe.

'She adores you.'

'I'm greatly fond of her, too,' he said, taking a folded paper from his coat. 'She's given me a letter for you.'

Ysomir read it. Her face clouded. 'I wondered why she hadn't visited me for so long.'

'I'm sorry,' he said. 'It's entirely my fault. I was so wrapped up in my own selfish concerns I forgot to have the letter sent on to you. That's why I brought it myself. You must have been worried sick; I can't apologise enough.'

'Will she come back?'

'I don't know. I hope so.'

He expected Ysomir to be upset, but she looked calmly at him. 'It's all right. If anything dreadful had happened to her I would have known. Won't you sit down?'

'Oh – indeed, thank you.' They sat on opposite sides of her writing table; the chairs were plain and hard. 'You would have known – how?'

'As I knew when Lynden died.'

'Ah, yes. Tanthe showed me the record you kept of your time with King Garnelys. It's a remarkable document. I was with Lynden when he was killed . . . did she tell you that?'

Immediately they were on to precarious ground. Ground that was like human flesh, bruised and sore and jagged.

'Yes,' said Ysomir, 'although I'm sure there were things she didn't tell me, just as there were things I didn't write about.'

Saphaeyender felt tears clawing his throat. Just when he'd been so sure he could talk easily about this. 'Ysomir,

122

I loved Lynden as if he were my brother. He was so easy to love, was he not? An innocent, wounded soul. He died trying to preserve my worthless life.'

'Worthless?' Ysomir said sharply. 'Self-deprecation doesn't suit you.'

He looked at her in surprise. 'You have quite a sting, don't you? But I wanted to talk about Lynden, not myself. If you don't mind, that is.'

'I don't mind. I feel I can talk to you.'

'It was sudden, the arrow that took him. He didn't suffer. It's important you know that.'

'I think you're the one who needs consoling, not me,' said Ysomir, although her eyes shone too bright. 'Lynden is with me. He's inside me. I hear his thoughts in my mind, I talk to him in my dreams.'

Saphaeyender nodded. 'And so do I to my mother.'

'No, you don't understand. It isn't wishful thinking. It first happened with my friend Serenis, who was buried in the mine. Her spirit-*roth* entered me. I began to hear her thoughts and sometimes speak them. "Self-deprecation doesn't suit you", that's the sort of thing Serenis would say.'

Saphaeyender was uneasy, but intrigued. He could put Ysomir in a play . . . if only he could still write without pain, and if only she wasn't so vibrant with life in front of him. 'So you took on some of her attitudes. That isn't strange if you've been close to someone.'

Her golden-green eyes shimmered with light, transfixing him. 'Lynden was well aware that you thought of him as more than a brother, my lord Saphaeyender.'

He held her gaze, trying not to react. 'Tanthe must have told you that.'

'No, of course she didn't. It would have been too hard for her to tell me, and pointless. Anyway, she wouldn't have known that Lynden loved you too, and was on the verge of more, and felt wretched and confused that he had even thought for one second about anyone other than me.'

123

Saphaeyender was nearly speechless. 'Ysomir, I'm sorry. This must have hurt you. It's the last thing I intended.'

'I don't blame Lynden. He'd been alone for so long. And it's better to love than to hate, isn't it?'

He felt his mask slipping. 'But you blame me, and rightly so. I called myself "worthless", not in false modesty, but in mere honesty. I've lived forty-seven years thinking I'm unassailable; practically equal to the gods in my talent and wisdom. It took just a few hours one sunny morning to discover that I am capable not only of the most abject cowardice but of mindless slaughter. I spent half the battle cowering in terror while Lynden tried to protect me; the other half wallowing in blood, trying to avenge his death. Not even knowing what I was doing. Because if I'd stopped to think for one second, the horror of it would have killed me.'

He was shaking. She reached across the table and her fingers were cool and delicate on his hand. 'I killed too, because of Lynden.'

'And you say he's inside you . . .'

'But I can't show him to you. Don't think that.'

'I know. I know. But I want to write about him, if I could only find the right way. Could I come and talk to you again?'

'Yes. I'd like that.'

Saphaeyender clasped her hand in gratitude. 'It's wretched that Helananthe is keeping you here. I for one am glad that Garnelys is dead; who knows how long the war might have continued, if you hadn't ended it? I know the Queen quite well. I could petition her on your behalf . . .'

Dread sprang into her eyes. Her nails dug into him. 'No, don't! I want to stay here!'

'What?'

'I feel safe here. You don't know what it was like in the palace! No one bothers me here, I don't have to see anyone or do anything if I don't want to.'

'I see. And you can write here.'

He felt her hand relax. 'It's all I need. If only I could be sure that Helananthe will not want to interrogate me again, I'd be perfectly content. She hates me.'

'But she's fair, I can't see that she'd deal unjustly with you.'

'She's not unjust. She could have had me executed It's not that, it's question after question that I can't answer.'

Saphaeyender was puzzled. 'What else does she think you can tell her?'

The colour faded from her face. 'Things about Garnelys and Laphaeome. But I don't want her to know . . .'

'What?'

She took a short, painful breath. 'That Garnelys is here inside me too.'

Again he was dumbstruck. He wanted to think she was mad, but had a creeping terror that she was perfectly sane. 'Garnelys?' He swallowed. 'It must be growing quite crowded.'

'Laugh at me if you like.'

'I'm not laughing.'

'The folk in Riverwynde thought I was strange. I could always see dark things happening before they did. I could always feel the Xauroma when other people thought it was just an idea. The Xauroma is more than a promise, Saphaeyender. It's real. I've seen what will happen if it dies.'

'I've upset you,' he said, pulling back uneasily. She took her hand out of his.

'No, I've upset you,' she retorted. 'Can no one bear to face the darkness – not even a writer like you?'

'I'm trying.' He wanted to change the subject. 'What are you writing about?'

'Garnelys. I'm trying to get him out of my head and on to the paper.' Her eyelids fluttered, and when she spoke her voice sounded different, slow and eerie. *I always knew that Laphaeome was not human. From the beginning I knew it but couldn't admit it. His true name was Zhoaah. They promised me – Zhoaah and Gulzhur promised me . . .'*

Saphaeyender's skin crawled. He was aware of a presence, a weird energy emanating from Ysomir. 'What are you doing?' he gasped.

She stopped. Her eyes came open and she stared at him. When she spoke, her voice shook, but it was her own. 'Was it Garnelys again? Oh, no . . .'

'What do you mean – again?'

She took a quick breath. 'It happens to me sometimes.'

'Oh gods,' he murmured. 'You said some names, Bhahdradomen-sounding names. Dear Goddess, what are we going to do?'

'*You* don't have to do anything. It's not your concern, is it?' She reached for a jug of water but her hand trembled and she could barely lift it. Saphaeyender quickly took it from her.

'Here, let me,' he said, pouring her a tumbler of water.

'Thank you.' She sipped the water, and her colour began to return. 'I can't always remember what he said. If I do, I don't know what it means. I just wish he'd go.'

'We are going to have to tell Helananthe about this,' he said heavily.

'No!' Her eyes were wild.

'Why not?'

Ysomir slammed the tumbler down and gripped his wrist, not so much imploring as actually hurting him. 'Because then I'll never be free of her! She will be at me all the time with her questions and threats! I don't want to talk about Garnelys any more. It's over. He's dead. I entreat you, my lord Saphaeyender, as a friend. Please don't tell her!'

He put his head in his hands. 'I came to deliver a letter. I wish I'd left it at that. How will the Queen feel if she finds out that you can channel Garnelys's memories, and we didn't tell her?'

She shook her head stubbornly. 'I don't care. I won't do it.'

'But for the good of Aventuria . . .'

'All the ugly things Garnelys did were for the good of Aventuria, so he said!' she lashed back. 'Do you not think I have been used enough?'

Saphaeyender sat back, trying to think calmly. His fingertips lightly pressed hers. If they hadn't been in a cell, and he hadn't been so plagued by his own demons, and had she not claimed to hold a menagerie of the dead inside her . . . perhaps they would have been close to making love by now. And he knew he shouldn't be thinking that of Tanthe's young sister, but old habits died hard.

'I'm sorry, Ysomir,' he said gently. 'Don't worry, I'll keep your secret. You've already had more distress than anyone should suffer in one lifetime.'

'Almost as much as the characters in your plays,' she said, with the shade of a smile.

The Temple of Nuth was dark, but that suited Rufryd perfectly. There was a rough oval chamber, and at the centre a greasy flame burning in a cauldron, reflecting off the black walls. He sat on a bare stone bench, and the hump-backed priestess sat beside him, leaning on a staff as if it was all that kept her upright. Her name was Rouna.

He poured everything out to her. Lynden's death, Tanthe's desertion, his own rootlessness. The old woman listened without a word, only fixing him with her opaline eyes.

When he'd finished, she said, 'Well, what d'you expect us to do about it?'

'What?' Rufryd couldn't believe her off-hand remark. 'I thought . . .'

'That we'd make it all better?'

'You're a priestess. This is a temple. Isn't that what you're supposed to do?'

'Listen to me, child. You can stay here as long as you want. You will have to sweep the floors and help cook the food, which is no more than any of us are expected to do.

Otherwise stay, and be welcome. But you are full of anger, and none of us can take it away.'

Rufryd glared at her, furious but too nervous of her to show it. Then he slumped, hands dangling between his legs. The idea of staying here made his life seem bearable, just. 'Good mother, I don't expect – I only thought you'd help, when no one else could.'

'Hardest thing is helping yourself,' she said shortly. 'D'you believe in Nuth?'

'Well . . .' He thought quickly. He'd never been respectful of the gods but he had observed the festivals, they had been part of his life. 'Yes. I believe in our gods, Breyid and Anthar, and they're supposed to be aspects of Nuth and Anuth, so yes, I believe in Nuth, of course.'

Rouna hissed through uneven teeth, shaking her head. 'Well, stop,' she said.

'What? You don't want me to believe in the Great Goddess?'

'Lad, it's hard for you to understand and I can't spend all night explaining; I need a beer.'

'Then I'll get you one, good mother, if you tell me where it's kept. But how can you worship Nuth and tell me not to?'

'Because we *don't* worship. We don't believe. Belief is not necessary; Nuth just *is*. She is the darkness; she's the quickening of birth and the emptiness of death. You can always be learning about her, on and on. But believing? No. *Believe* something and you set yourself apart from it. You delude yourself that you know it, you set your relationship to it in concrete, and that's when you stop learning about it.'

Rufryd gasped helplessly. 'You've lost me.'

'Nuth doesn't give a fuck whether we worship her or not,' said the old woman with a chuckle. 'Understand that, do you?'

Rufryd stared at her in astonishment. 'Yeah.'

She pressed her bony fingers into his shoulder. 'What I

read in you is that you want help, but you don't want to hear the truth. You want an easy answer. There isn't one. You're in pain but you'll never get rid of it until you get rid of this anger. Yes, you can stay here, but it won't solve anything.'

'Then what will?'

'Doing what you know you must. You could become a priest of Anuth . . .'

'Could I?' For a moment the idea seemed darkly enticing.

'Oh yes, you could do that, hide yourself here forever,' Rouna said mockingly. 'Or you could go back into the world, face all that you hate. Perhaps go back to Helananthe and serve her, as your friends suggested.'

'You must be joking.' He shook his head grimly. 'Sorry, good mother, but that's the last thing I want to do. She's the same as all the rest, she just uses people!'

'And you don't? All I say to you is this: we all have to hear things we don't want to hear, and do things we don't want to do. Truth's like that. Go through that doorway, along the corridor, to the door at the very end. You'll find it there.'

'The truth?'

'The beer,' said the priestess.

Sometimes life turned up a pleasant surprise. The day before her coronation, Helananthe was walking along a broad amber gallery towards the Sun Chamber when she saw, silhouetted by a window, a familiar graceful figure.

'Jthery?' she said, not quite believing it. She went closer and it was him; Jthery of Mithrain, her cousin.

'Good day, Helan,' he said, smiling. 'Oh, sorry. Your majesty.' He bowed his head.

'None of that nonsense.' They clasped hands, looking at each other. He'd grown into an attractive young man since she'd last seen him. He was dressed in Mithrain's colours, robes of grey, amethyst and watery blue, and his pale reddish-blond hair flowed over his shoulders. His face was a long, pale oval; innocent, serious, introspective. 'How have you got here so quickly? I didn't think there was time for the news of my coronation to have reached your realm.'

'It didn't. I only heard about it when I arrived. I came because I heard about everything that's been happening, and I knew that you needed me.'

'Oh, Jthery.' Touched, she hugged him. 'That is so sweet of you. I don't know that I *need* you, but I am certainly glad to see you. A friendly face!'

She drew him further along the gallery, out of earshot of her retinue. 'Who's been unfriendly?' he asked.

She gave a soft groan. 'Oh . . . politics. I don't even want to think about it. How are you? Did you bring anyone with you? Lady friend, wife?'

Jthery pulled a face. 'You're as bad as my family. I'm on my own.'

She grinned, unable to resist teasing him. 'Not for long, surely. You look like an Aelyr, Jthery, or one of your mythical water spirits. You won't be safe in Parione.'

His pale complexion flushed to a startling rose colour. 'Gods, you always embarrass me, Hel.'

'I'm teasing you, dear. This is beautiful.' She lifted the jewel he wore at his throat and examined it. A carp exquisitely carved in amethyst, suspended from a little sphere of opal, with a teardrop of aquamarine dangling below. 'Where did you get it?'

'You might not believe me.'

'Oh?'

'Never tell a Mithrainian that undines are mythical, Helan.' His voice fell to a whisper. 'I believe the Goddess Eshte gave it to me. It's her symbol. She told me to come here, that you would have a task for me.'

'Oh.' Taken aback, she gazed at him. He had a fey quality about him, her young cousin, but he'd always been quietly level-headed with it. And even Eldareth swore the elementals of Mithrain were real . . . 'Well, except that I would like you to represent your realm at the coronation, I can't think of anything for you to do.'

He folded his hand round the carved fish. 'You will, Helan.'

'You sound very certain. You're making me nervous!'

'You're nervous?' Jthery said softly. 'I'm terrified.'

It wasn't as Helananthe had planned, but still the coronation was glorious.

The Sun Chamber shone in splendour, thronged with officials and citizens as bright as kingfishers in their robes of blue-green, red and gold. All along the tiers they sat, and crowded on foot in every space, leaving a narrow aisle for Helananthe's procession.

Before her moved the priests and priestesses of Nuth; behind, those of Nepheter, and then came the senior officials of the palace, and after them the representatives of the Nine Realms. But Helananthe walked in a space alone. Musicians played harps, drums and horns to herald her arrival. Her robes hung heavy on her in layers of black, indigo and bright gold. With measured steps she ascended the nine steps to the dais and sat, for the first time, on the Sapphire Throne.

The central arm had been removed to make a single seat; it would not be replaced until she took a consort. As her retinue took their places and the traditional hymn of welcome was sung, Helananthe sat trying to calm her rapid heartbeat.

The representatives from each of the realms were gathered in their little groups; Lord Serpeth of Eisilion and his retinue in robes of red and gold, sewn in tiny patch-work like lizard scales that shifted in the light. Lord Mawrdreth and Lady Branq'elin for Thanmandrathor in simple greens and browns, touched with bronze. For Mithrain stood Lord Jthery, dressed in the soft silvery hues of water. Saphaeyender and a handful of his actors, all in white, represented Paranios itself.

There hadn't been time to notify the more distant realms so that their ruling families could send representatives. Ambassadors stood in their place, or even conscripts whom Garnelys had dragged here to work on the Tower. It was a small gesture, Helan thought, to show that all her subjects were equally respected and valuable.

There were Noreyans, yellow-haired, dressed in the dark green of their forests. The party from Torith Mir were harsh-faced and austere in black and grey, but when they moved she saw the flash of amber, jet and diamonds about them. Those from Azura Maroc were flamboyant in red, blue and gold and smiled at everyone. And there were hunters from Deirland, long-limbed and keen-eyed, with cloaks of animal-skin over their tunics of mist-grey and slate-blue.

To represent Sepheret, Helan had wanted Rufryd to do the honour. He'd been hard to find; at first her messengers brought rumours that he'd left Parione, but he'd turned up of all places at the Temple of Nuth. His Sepheran clothes of black breeches and quilted black jacket, heavily embroidered with blue silk, had been restored to their former glory by the palace dressmakers, and he looked extraordinarily handsome, tall and hard-limbed, with his thick chestnut hair just touching his shoulders. His expression, however, was very far from happy. Grim-faced, he headed a group of Sepherans who were thin from labouring on the Tower, uneasy in borrowed robes. But to exclude them would be to deny what Garnelys had done.

Many others were missing. Eldareth and her mother and brother. Her dear friend Rathroem of the Mediators. Tanthe, who should have represented Sepheret beside Rufryd. And there had been no chance to contact the elusive Aelyr and invite them to witness the coronation.

The ceremony was to be compact and brief, at Helananthe's command.

Songs were sung, goddesses and gods invoked.

Saphaeyender stepped up on to the corner of the dais and read a poem he had written to commemorate the occasion. The priestess drew a sacred circle about the Sapphire Throne, using glowing crystals and ceremonial incense. The scent of the sacred smoke would stay with her forever.

Then Ariolne, the high priestess of Nuth, stepped forward and intoned the words of the coronation. Her voice rang powerfully through the Sun Chamber.

'Helananthe Ghiseyma-Galemanth daughter, you are the fruit of the true line of the Amber Citadel; in you resides the seed of the covenant between the monarch and the land. You appear before us the people of Aventuria not as our ruler but as our servant. Do you accept this?'

'I accept it,' said Helananthe.

'On you falls the yoke of the Xauroma; the promise made between the monarch and the land that protects us from all harm. Do you accept this?'

'I accept it.'

'Then make your vow.'

Helan drew a deep breath. It was essential she remembered every word. 'I, Helananthe Ghiseyma-Galemanth-daughter of the Royal House of Silana do vow and swear to serve Aventuria from this day until the end of my days. For Aventuria I lay down my life, my pride and all that I own. I embrace the Xauroma. Until the burden passes to my heir, I *am* the Xauroma.'

Then Ariolne placed on her brow a filet set with a blood-red almandine. Over it she placed the crown of nine jewels. In her hands she laid a long sceptre topped with a crystal sphere, the Orb of Clear Sight. Touching these wondrous artifacts for the first time, Helananthe's heart swelled in awe.

'In the blessed names of Nuth and Anuth, I crown you Queen Helananthe of Aventuria.'

It was done. A great cheer filled the Sun Chamber. As it faded, Helananthe heard the cheering echoed outside the walls of the Amber Citadel, where hundreds had gathered.

She allowed herself to smile, although the true, dark meat of the ceremony still lay ahead.

'I thank you, good citizens,' she said. 'I never expected to take on this role so early; I had thought this day would come some forty years hence, after my father Galemanth had ruled long and wisely. Still, that was not to be. I am well aware of the pain that recent events have wrought upon Aventuria. My avowed intent is to heal all wounds, to restore all that has been taken away. But to this end I need your help. My friends, we have suffered a civil war that has set us against each other! Where hostility lingers we must all work to overcome it, even where it means showing kindness to those whom recently you were required to treat as slaves; and even harder, forgiving those who may have treated you cruelly. Remember we have been friends for far longer than we have been enemies.' They began to applaud, but she went on, fixing Lady Branq'elin and Lord Mawrdreth with her gaze. 'Someone or something, some dreadful force, has tried to divide us. It's more important now than ever that we maintain the unity of the Nine Realms. Our peace and prosperity depend on our combined strength. Aventuria will stand firm; this is my vow.'

Another cheer went up; the Than'drathian party joined in with polite applause. She hadn't quite won them yet. As the musicians struck up a triumphal paean, Helan rose. The priestess Ariolne waited for her, and now she was the only figure Helan could see clearly. Ariolne's face was intent and her black eyes were wells leading down into the secret depths of the earth.

'Now I leave you to your revelry.' Helananthe's mouth was dry, but she mustn't let them see how nervous she was. 'I go into the Underworld, to make my binding covenant with the Earth, the mystery of the Xauroma.'

Once the Queen and her retinue had gone, Lord Poel quietly crept out of the Sun Chamber. He had no desire to join in the feasting. He had no friends left in the Amber Citadel, it seemed; not even Derione, the treacherous rat, who had usurped Poel's high position the moment his back was turned.

The humiliation inflicted on him by Helananthe was worse than if she'd thrown him out of the Amber Citadel once and for all. Instead she'd given him a job as a minor clerk to Derione's aides, hardly more than an errand boy. And for this he was supposed to be grateful! Yet what was he to do?

Everyone in Parione knew him. No one would employ him. They all knew he had ordered the demolition of the Theatre, and despised him for it.

Lord Poel put on a dark, hooded cloak and left the Amber Citadel, passing swiftly along the different levels, through the gates at the inner and the outer walls, emerging finally on to the broad boulevard that skirted the north flank of the edifice. The crowds were concentrated at the magnificent west and south gates of the Citadel, but there were still enough people around to irritate him. He pushed through them, ignoring their indignant shouts.

He despised the city in the glorious golden hues of afternoon, for it no longer belonged to him. He wandered down to the river and stood for some time on the high bank that rose above it, looking down at the wide, slow sheet of gold silk that wound through Parione. Poel was quite seriously considering throwing himself in.

Someone tugged at his sleeve.

He whipped round, coldly angry, to find a peasant there. An artisan, he corrected himself sarcastically. It was a small figure dressed in the grey and purple wool of a stone-mason's apprentice; male or female, he couldn't tell. The figure had a cowl wrapped round its head, hiding most of its face.

'What do you want?' Poel snapped.

'Lord Poel, do you not remember me?'

'I've never seen you in my life before. Leave me alone, or I'll call the city guards.'

The figure didn't move. 'I was there when you demolished the theatre, smiling while the citizens wept and screamed,' it said softly. 'I was there when you stood with sweat running down your face and told Garnelys that his army had lost the war. I was there when sweet Ysomir stabbed him through the heart.'

His heart jolted. 'Who are you?' he hissed.

'Surely you remember. I designed the Tower.'

The figure raised its chin and Poel saw its face down the tunnel of the cowl. An undistinguished face, soft as cheese curds, with shrewd black eyes. The eyes seemed to flow straight into his mind like ink. Terrifying, and then soothing, like a drug.

'Laphaeome?' Poel gasped. 'You look different.'

The figure shrugged. 'Only clothes.'

'Where have you been?' Poel rasped, angry now. 'You deserted Garnelys when he most needed you! The palace was in uproar trying to find you!'

Laphaeome laughed.

'What kind of Mediator are you?'

'Come, now,' said Laphaeome. 'You're not still keeping up that charade, are you? You know full well, and have known for some considerable time, that I am not a Mediator.'

Poel felt sweat dripping down under his heavy robes. 'There have been terrible rumours flying around the palace.'

'Have they been saying dreadful things about me?' His lipless mouth formed a smile. 'Words beginning with B? Why do you think I left?'

'Gods,' Poel groaned.

'Now, my lord, there is no need to sound shocked. You knew, didn't you? You always knew.'

Poel couldn't speak. Laphaeome touched his sleeve. At the palace he had always worn black gloves, but now his hands were bare and his seven spidery fingers pressed into Lord Poel's flesh. 'Forget Laphaeome. He is not me. My true name is Zhoaah. Say it.'

'Zhoaah,' Poel repeated stiffly.

'It means Facilitator. I like to oil the wheels. Were we not always friends? There's no need to be afraid of me. I've come to help you.'

'I'm not afraid of you! How could *you* possibly help *me*?'

'My lord, the time has surely passed and gone when the Bhahdradomen remained in exile, unmentionable like some vile disease. You should get used to seeing us about. We have served our sentence, more than two hundred and fifty years of it. Surely now we are ready to take our place as equal members of Aventurian society?'

'You are joking.'

'Yes,' said Zhoaah. 'And no.'

'Those years may have passed, but no one will ever forget what the Bhahdradomen did in Aventuria,' Poel said without emotion. 'Humans will never countenance such a thing in a million years. Go back to Vexor. I think you have done enough here already.'

'And you helped me. You enjoyed it. How kind have humans been to you? Think of the revenge you could have on all those who have hurt and humiliated you, and I ask so very little in return.'

Poel's words were empty, and Zhoaah plainly knew it. *He knows me too well.* Poel gazed greedily into Zhoaah's soft, sucking eyes. What this creature *was* didn't seem to matter. More importantly, Zhoaah was familiar; he was the only friendly face left from the days of Garnelys's glory. 'What do you want? I can't take you into the palace,' Poel said quickly.

'I don't ask that. Not yet.'

'I don't see what we can do for each other. We're both powerless.'

'Nonsense.' Zhoaah's voice fell to a seductive whisper. 'Trust me, Lord Poel. It's easy. I was there in Garnelys's

137

last, great days, and I am with you now in your darkest hour, and I shall be at your side when you sit on the Sapphire Throne.'

'What?' he said, heart leaping.

'Listen to me, dear friend, and you shall be King of Aventuria. That is our promise.'

Chapter Seven. Touching the Flame

Helananthe walked beside Ariolne down secret passages she'd never seen before, into the windowless heart of the Citadel. The priestess carried a lantern of red glass, Helananthe her sceptre of office, which was long enough to lean on as a staff. Inside the Orb of Clear Sight, fractures in the crystal glittered with moving light.

Before the coronation, a priest of Dyonis, a priestess of Nepheter and a priest of Anuth had come to her in turn. The first two each told her a secret word; the third had given her a strange piece of amethyst, shaped like a mushroom with multiple stalks. Three pieces of the puzzle. The remaining secrets, only Ariolne knew.

Presently they passed along a snaking passage, then down a thin spiral staircase that led deep into the hill itself. Rock strata were heaped massively above them. A stone door slid aside, and they entered a dark round chamber. The space was dominated by a huge sphere of crystal, pale brown in colour with threads of crimson running through it. These threads moved, catching the light. The sphere turned slowly on its curved base, as if it floated on a film of water, giving off a soft, humming vibration. Between the sphere and the chamber wall there was a walkway no more than three feet wide. The domed space thrummed with heavy, rich power.

Ariolne drew an audible breath. They both stood for a moment in respectful awe.

'The *xauroth* sphere,' said Ariolne. '*Xauroth* is the energy of the Xauroma. This great stone was gifted to the humans of Aventuria by the Zampherai seventeen hundred years ago, when the Citadel began to grow from a hill fortress to this . . .' She trailed off, her gaze shifting around the chamber as if she sensed something out of place. 'Forgive me. This is the first time I've seen it. But the colour . . . I was expecting it to be clear.'

Helananthe gazed at the sphere. She reached out, letting her hand hover just above its surface. 'I know why it isn't clear. As I told you, I've been in here before, and not alone.'

Ariolne frowned. 'You did know that only the monarch is meant to come here – and only after her coronation?'

'Yes, I know. But I am afraid that several of us have come here who should not have done.'

'But how did you get in?'

Helananthe walked slowly round to the far side of the sphere, where she found a narrow aperture to another ancient stairway. 'This leads up to an old cell in the fabric of the Citadel, and thence to one of Garnelys's private chambers. He tortured people there. As far as I can tell, he was trying to draw some kind of dark energy from them and direct it into the sphere.'

Ariolne looked from the shadowed archway to Helananthe, her hawkish face half-lit with red. 'That's what I can feel here! *Gauroth*. I knew something was wrong. Why did he do it?'

'I wish I knew. He was frightened and desperate for all the power he could get, no matter how he obtained it. In his madness, he must have thought he was doing the right thing.'

'*Gauroth* is a term for the darkest, most destructive energy of the earth. It may have its uses, but only in the hands of a great *roth*-mage, and there are few, if any, of those left in the world. It's the sort of energy that even the Bhahdradomen hesitate to summon. According to legend, this sphere was as clear as your Orb, full of light. Not this clouded brown.'

'The first time I saw it, it was worse than this, almost purple as if full of blood,' said Helan. 'Ysomir saw it at its

140

worst, wild with pain. I thought it was recovering but now I'm not sure. It seems stagnant, waiting . . .'

'You have empathy with the sphere. That's good.' Ariolne nodded slowly. 'Yet the *gauroth* lingers. This concerns me.'

A shudder ran through Helan. 'Good mother, can my initiation still go ahead?'

The priestess closed her eyes for a moment. Opening them, she said, 'Yes, and it must. Later, this other ingress to the chamber must be sealed off. The bad energies in the torture cell can be channelled away. Rocks and crystals absorb vibrations, though, and I doubt they will ever be wholly free of memory . . . nor will the sphere, perhaps. But initiation includes accepting reality as it is, not as we wish it were.'

'And the fact that I've been here before . . . I haven't somehow initiated myself, have I?'

Ariolne gave a bark of laughter. 'You should have waited, but no harm is done. *This* is not the secret. This is not the Xauroma, only an indicator of its mood or health. It contains light but the light is dim, and there are threads of blood inside. We have other doors to pass through yet. I am only your guide. The truth you learn at the end shall be yours alone.'

Ariolne began to search along the sides of the chamber. Presently she found something in a flagstone of the walkway itself, an arrangement of small holes. She took out a piece of obsidian – shaped like Helan's amethyst mushroom – and pressed it into the holes. A mechanism clicked. Helan helped Ariolne to lift the flagstone, revealing another spiral stair that vanished into the depths of the earth. The perfect treads glinted red in the lamplight. Few feet had ever passed over them.

'Follow me,' said Ariolne. 'I am Nuth, guiding her daughter into the Underworld.'

Down and down the steps led. The stench of earth, mould and stone was overwhelming and the cold seeped

141

dew-heavy through her robes. Fearless on horseback, in battle, even on storm-racked ships, in this place Helan found herself afraid.

The endless spiralling made her dizzy. She helped herself with one hand on the icy wall. By the time they reached the bottom of the long chimney, the thought of ascending again exhausted her. But Ariolne was calm and confident, so Helan tried to match her dignity, trusting her.

They found their way along a short fissure in the rock and into another chamber, whose ceiling pressed almost on their heads. She saw the glint of minerals in the walls and floor. Helananthe hated the feeling of being closed in. It took her all her will to concentrate on Ariolne's words.

'You will have been told a secret name. I do not know it. Call it now.'

Helananthe spoke the first word she had been told. '*Andamanque.*'

Her voice was hoarse. Nothing happened. Drawing breath, she spoke it again, clear and loud, and this time the rocks seemed to tremble. For a moment she feared the roof was about to fall in on them.

A crack appeared in the opposite wall. Through it fell a shaft of lavender light. A tiny figure moved against the light, gnarled as if tree roots had torn themselves from the earth and come to life.

This creature, barely reaching to their knees, shambled forward and stood hunched before them. Then Helananthe saw that it was a wizened Zampherai female. Her head twisted as she looked up at them, her hair hanging like black string around a silver coin of an eye.

'Who disturbs the Keeper?'

'Ariolne of the Temple of Nuth. Queen Helananthe of Aventuria. I bring her to seek union with the Xauroma, that her service to the land may begin.'

'Has she the key?' asked the crone.

Helananthe quickly fumbled for the piece of amethyst.

Its rounded top sat snugly in her palm. 'This?'

'That,' the Keeper said tersely. 'I know where the lock is, but only you can open it.'

The Zampherai crouched down to the floor. At first she seemed to be digging in earth; then Helananthe realised she was actually scooping out the rock itself – breaking it with her bare hands as if it were as friable as cake – to reveal an oblong of smooth creamy marble set in the floor.

The marble block glowed. In its surface were five holes. The two women watched her, saying nothing. Holding her breath, Helananthe slid the amethyst key into place. The five pegs sank home and the lock gave with a crunch.

The oblong was the lid of a chest. It was heavy but she raised it with difficulty and saw what lay inside. Slabs of white and clear quartz, slabs of pale green and red tourmaline and yellow topaz, each one eighteen inches wide and two feet in length, inscribed with faint, flowing runes.

'There is all you need to know,' said Ariolne. 'All the secrets of the Xauroma and of the Basilisks of Calabethron. The Keeper and I cannot read them.'

Helananthe lifted out two or three of the slabs, studying them. Her awe quickly turned to dismay. 'Neither can I,' she said. 'Good mother, this is a language I have never seen before.'

Ariolne didn't react. 'Daughter, from here you must go alone. We shall wait for you.'

'You must go deeper yet,' said Andamanque.

The Keeper pointed to the fissure from which she had emerged. Helananthe placed the slabs back in the chest, gripped her sceptre, and entered the pale violet light.

This space was too small to admit her large frame. She ducked and squeezed between the narrow walls of stone, sweating coldly to think she could be stuck fast here.

Her feet found empty air. She was slipping into a hole in the earth. Slowly at first, but unable to stop.

The light vanished. Helananthe was suddenly alone in

pitch darkness, panic thumping hard in her chest. Sensation left her body; she could no longer feel the sceptre in her hand and she was falling, deep, deep into the earth. She screamed, but her voice made no sound.

She wasn't aware of the fall ending, yet suddenly she was standing in a lightless space; a tunnel or a chamber, she couldn't tell. The smell of earth was thick in her lungs and the air clammy. She sensed the stone moving around her, as if sentient. She felt its vast and terrible power.

'Now what?' she whispered trembling.

A scarlet flame appeared. It was above her, below her, in front of her; yet however hard she tried to draw close to it, it remained the same distance away.

Then she understood. The last stage of her journey was not physical but astral. Unless she could reach and touch the flame, she could not make her connection with the Land, and her promise, however sincerely meant, would have no true power.

The flame was beautiful and dreadful. It swayed like a dancer, ever out of her reach. She stretched her sceptre towards it and it seemed miles away; then right in front of her face, dazzling, choking her with sulphur; but when she put her fingers to it, it was distant again.

Helananthe cursed in frustration. Then inspiration struck. She cried the last secret word and suddenly the flame roared up.

It was inside her, and she inside it.

She was spinning at the core of the earth, arms outstretched. Contained in a sphere of fire, part of it as it was part of her. Aventuria seemed to pour through her in all its beauty and wild raw power. Green and blue and raging scarlet. Energies channelled through her like hot winds and it was too much to bear. She screamed without sound, in anguish and ecstasy.

The land was testing her.

She gave herself up to it. *I am the new queen, the avatar of the goddess, the doe in the thicket, the seed in the winter field, the stream under the stone. I come not as ruler but as handmaiden and guardian. May we nourish you always as you nourish us* . . .

The Xauroma was a web of electric-green light, binding her and the land together so that they exchanged energy in an endless flow. The *roth* of the earth was a force so vast that she could touch only a tiny fragment of it without being destroyed. And she felt the force thundering with anger. There were cracks in it. Cracks Garnelys had made, which were still widening despite all her efforts to heal them.

The force threshed and heaved, crying out. Dreadful revelation came to her. Garnelys had only been a catalyst, a warning, a tiny prelude on a stage while the true dangers loomed like giants outside the theatre. She saw herself starkly as a bridge, holding on to two edges of a fracture, straining with all her strength to hold them together while the chasm groaned and widened beneath her. And from the chasm, billions of insects came teeming to consume the land . . .

With a jolt, she was flung out of the vision.

She was sitting on solid ground, her eyes tight shut. For a few moments she couldn't move. The beauty and terror of it had shaken her to the core.

Slowly she recovered and looked around. Now she was in a small round cave, and on the walls gleamed nine great jewels of different kinds. The same gems that were in her crown, each representing one of the realms. In the centre of the chamber was a red flame burning in a censer. And facing her across the flame was a small slender man dressed in a hooded white robe. A Mediator.

'Rathroem!' she cried. 'Is it really you?'

His voice was deep and eerie. 'You keep my image alive inside you. Ask me what it is that you need to know.'

In her altered state of consciousness, anything seemed possible – even the dead speaking to her. 'Did the land accept my covenant?' Her voice trembled.

'Yes, you do not need to ask me that – but the Xauroma

is fragile. Be warned. It will take all your strength, perhaps even more than you possess, to keep it intact.' He raised a hand to point at her. 'The land cries out in fear that you are not strong enough; that you will break your promise.'

'What?' she cried, horrified, then angry. 'Never!'

'The forces arrayed against you are terrible. Call not upon the Mediators, for this time your enemies will accept no Mediation.'

'You were – you were killed by the Bhahdradomen, weren't you?'

The corners of his mouth turned up wryly. 'That was their way of dropping a hint.' For a moment, in place of this portentous ghost, she caught a glimpse of the gentle, humorous friend he had been in life. She wept.

'What must I do?' she asked.

'The future is not set in stone. You can change it.'

He raised a slim pale hand, making a dipping motion towards the fire. Understanding, Helan copied the motion and plunged the Orb of Clear Sight deep into the scarlet flame.

At once, she found herself back in her physical body, stumbling out of the fissure. She was in the chamber with Ariolne and the Keeper again.

She could imagine what she looked like to them; pallid, dishevelled and wide-eyed as if she'd received a visceral shock. They said nothing, though; only watched her. Their patient dignity helped her to ground herself. After all, who had ever told her that touching the Xauroma would be all sweetness, the news all good, or that her responsibilities would not be formidable? No one.

This was what it meant to be Queen.

The chest still lay open, the crystal slabs shimmering as if lit from beneath. Then Helan noticed that the Orb of Clear Sight now glowed red, as if the flame of the Earth's heart was inside it. She knew what to do as if she'd always known it.

She stood her sceptre upright in a channel cut in the

back of the chest, which fitted it perfectly. She lifted the first slab and held it so that the orb shone through it.

At once the runes shone clearly. The earth-fire brought new, fugitive symbols to life and the lines resolved into a flowing alphabet that she could read.

She gasped. Here were secrets, astonishing secrets that only Garnelys had known. How the War of the Silver Plains had been won, how Aventuria was to be protected . . . but so much information, and none of it easy to understand. The language was archaic, the meaning cryptic. Her heart sank. She picked up the next, and several more; some had strange diagrams on them, but what they were meant to portray, she couldn't tell.

All at once she felt drained. 'Good mother, good Keeper – may I come here again? It will take time to decipher the slabs.'

'You may come whenever you wish it,' said Andamanque. 'I am always here. I saw little of your predecessor; you had better be a keener student, for the Earth is unhappy, and humans have ignored the warnings for too long!'

Ariolne took Helan's hand and placed the obsidian key in her palm. 'The keys are yours now, and shall only be taken back into the safekeeping of the Temple upon your death.'

That's a cheerful prospect, thought Helan. Meticulously she replaced the slabs in the chest, removed her sceptre and lowered the lid. The lock crunched into place, pushing out the amethyst key. The red glow of her Orb bled to clear white, yet she knew it would shine with fire again when she needed it. She felt different; fearful, yes, but strong. Changed forever. Ariolne bowed deeply to her, acknowledging the transformation.

'The circle is unbroken,' said the priestess. 'Nuth's blessings are upon you, Helananthe of the line of Silana, Queen of the Nine Realms, Guardian of the Xauroma.'

*

Rufryd was worried sick about Tanthe. Since he couldn't admit it, though, he only felt rage at her. The Temple of Nuth was like cold black water on his anger, dowsing it to a level that was bearable.

He had been to see Ysomir after the coronation, but the meeting had been brief and awkward. They had never got on well. Just because they both came from Riverwynde, and she had loved his brother, and he her sister, didn't mean they had anything in common. Guilt gnawed at him, both over the way he'd victimised her when they were younger, and over her present, wretched situation. His guilt, too, expressed itself as sullen anger.

So he'd come back to the Temple. He scrubbed floors, washed sheets, made beds, waited on the priests and priestesses – who, to his annoyance, were gracious and told him not to. He wanted to be punished, but they refused to punish him.

Rufryd sat in Nuth's sanctum before the eternal flame, thinking about the Goddess.

'What are you?' he said. 'What do you want from me?'

As always, Nuth steadfastly refused to answer. He sighed. Then someone spoke, causing him to leap almost out of his skin with shock.

'She wants you to know yourself. Without self-knowledge, you are paralysed.'

It was Ariolne, the High Priestess. Before he could get up, she sat cross-legged on the black flagstones beside him. 'Good mother,' he murmured in greeting, feeling awkward.

'Why do you think the Temple of Nepheter is more popular than ours?' she said, looking at the flame.

Some words came into Rufryd's head.

'"Lady, fire of Firethorn, spring of life,
Quicken the molten sap to burn and stiffen
The petals of roses, the loins of lovers and the wings of butterflies
Who dance like us, all unaware

148

That they shall fall in flames, are falling in flames
Into the arms of your dark sister."

'One of Saphaeyender's bloody poems. Thanks to Tanthe I can't get the damned things out of my head. Oh – sorry.'

'I've heard swearwords before. Rouna could teach you some you don't know. Those were lines from *Arkenfell*, actually – but yes, we are here to remind people that they're not immortal. That's why we're not popular.'

'I know the feeling.'

'You can bury yourself here forever if you wish, Rufryd. However, I know that isn't what you want.'

'But this is the first place I've ever been where people just leave me alone. It's amazing.'

'The trouble is that you're hiding in here in order to stay the same. But Nuth is the goddess of transformation. You will only know her when you are willing to change.'

Rufryd glared sideways at Ariolne, annoyed regardless of her position. 'Oh, there's a lot I'd like to change. I'd have to be a *roth*-mage!' He paused. 'Is that something you can train to be?'

Ariolne laughed at him. Rufryd felt stupid, out of his depth. 'Yes, you can train, if you have some aptitude to begin with. I laugh because you asked in such innocence. You have no idea . . . You can never, never do it out of emotions like anger, or desire for control or revenge. All of those passions must be gone first. Acquire perfect self-knowledge, then see if you still want to be a mage; you probably won't.'

'Supposing I did?'

'Then you need the dedication for years of intense study and practise. It's not an art for the impatient or the hot-headed, Rufryd.'

'Right.'

'And which *roth* would you choose to work with? Each has its own resonance, and it's a rare mage who can attune with more than two or three. If you could attune with plants or crystals, you might be a healer, or a gardener or master jeweller. If you can attune with disembodied energies, *ethroth*, then you might be a seer, or a counsellor to the bereaved. You see, it is no easy path to power. There have been only a handful of mages of truly notable skills, who could actually change the fabric of the Earth. Most of them were Aelyr. And some of those destroyed themselves through chancing too much.'

'The flight of the arrow,' he said, 'does that have a *roth* of its own?'

'Well, yes. Everything does, to some extent.'

'I can do that. Use a bow, I mean.'

'Then you are a *roth*-mage of a kind. All of us are. Then again, if you would be a purist and apply the title of mage only to someone like Nilothphon or Theomentis or Calabethron, none of us are.'

'I think I'll stick to sweeping floors.'

Ariolne rose and briefly clasped his shoulder. 'When it's time to leave us, Rufryd, you'll know.'

Parione sweltered in soporific heat and the festival of Midsummer was long past. Helan had still received no news of Eldareth. Her royal duties kept her busy, but each morning she would note the date and recalculate how long it might take Eldareth to travel to Eisilion and back.

He left on the forty-ninth day of Firethorn, she thought, and it is now the forty-second of Midsummer . . . only six weeks, and it will surely take them eight to return. He will have spent some time with Lady Nietriya, surely, so they are unlikely to arrive before Lunagh. I must stop worrying and get ready to welcome them home. Gods, it seems a lifetime since I saw Mother. I can't wait. Veny will have grown so . . . I wonder if he's any less full of himself?

Helan was in the office attached to her private chambers, attending to paperwork as she always did before breakfast. There had hardly been time to sleep since her coronation. Each morning she allowed herself to fret about Eldareth for precisely ten minutes, then she turned all her attention to unravelling the mess left by Garnelys.

Someone rapped impatiently on her door. It wasn't Derione's respectful knock. Dawn and Mirias were supposed to vet her visitors, but now the doors burst open and a rangy figure came striding in. Helananthe's head jerked up. Dawn stuck her coppery head round the door-jamb and said, 'Sorry, ma'am.'

Her mind full of paperwork, Helan didn't take in who it was for a second. Then her jaw dropped and she leapt to her feet.

'Eldareth!'

He looked dreadful. His face was drained, his black hair hanging in limp rats' tails. Several days of beard-growth shadowed his chin. 'Helan, I'm sorry,' he said, out of breath. 'I came back as fast as I could.'

The argument they'd had before he left was forgotten. She rushed from behind her desk and flung her arms round him.

Eldareth, however, was unresponsive. He put his hands on her upper arms and gently pressed her away from him.

'I'd made up my mind you wouldn't be back for another two weeks yet,' she said. 'There was no need for you to run from the stables; a few more minutes wouldn't have hurt. Are you going to tell me what's wrong? They are with you, aren't they?'

Eldareth exhaled, a long groan. 'Helan, I've ridden like a maniac to reach you and now I don't know how to tell you. Your mother and Veny have been kidnapped.'

'I beg your pardon?' She laughed in disbelief. 'Is this a joke?'

'Some might say Veny deserves it,' he said, 'but no, this is not a joke.' He sank into a green velvet chair in front of her desk. Helan poured him some tea from a silver pot on a sideboard. He drained the cup in two gulps then began to explain.

'Lady Nietriya told me it happened just a few days before

151

I arrived. A group of Aelyr entered the house and took them away. There was nothing anyone could do to stop them; they came like ghosts, she said, and you know how terrified Eisilians are of them.'

Helananthe stared at him. 'Did you say Aelyr? *Aelyr* took my mother?'

'So Nietriya says.'

'But why? I've had nothing to do with the Aelyr in my life. Even Garnelys had barely any contact with them. There was an Aelyr once at a state ball when I was no more than seven, they took me away because I wouldn't stop staring at him . . . but these days they stay in Verdanholm and keep apart from humans. What on earth would they suddenly want with my family? Eld, surely Lady N was mistaken.'

His head sank. He looked exhausted. 'Whatever the truth of it is, they were abducted by *someone*. And I believe Nietriya's story because I think I saw the Aelyr party myself.'

'You did?'

'It was some days before I reached Luin Trest; I took shelter in a ruined temple, and in the night I saw a portal open, and a procession of Aelyr passing through from our world to what I assume was their own realm. It was the weirdest thing I've ever seen. And I thought I heard a boy cry out as they went.'

'Why didn't you stop them?' she cried.

'Because it was before I reached Luin Trest. At the time I had no reason to suspect these Aelyr of abduction. Besides, even if I'd wanted to stop them, I couldn't move. Nietriya said they cast a glamour of paralysis. It happened to me, too.'

Helan sat down in her chair, shocked. 'This is unbelievable. Didn't you try to find them?'

'Of course I did, Hel! I scoured the house for clues. I had Nietriya's household searching all over the hills, I sought witnesses; I even returned to the temple on my way back, but the trail was cold. There was nothing to do but come home and break the news.'

'These Aelyr,' she said, 'what did they look like?'

'Their garb was dark, shadowy. Bluish-black. There was nothing about them I recognised.'

'Nothing to do with your friend Elrill, then?'

'I doubt it. He wouldn't do a thing like this. No, they definitely weren't Shaelahyr. Besides, Elrill had no motive.'

'But what Aelyr *would* have a motive? It makes no sense.'

She pressed her fingers to her forehead. Eldareth began to ease off his riding boots. 'I'm so sorry to bring you this news, Helan. The whole journey has been a nightmare. I lost Tanthe to the Aelyr, too, under rather different circumstances, and although she went willingly I am very afraid for her.' He told her what had happened at the Seer's hut. 'I don't suppose she's come back?'

'I've heard nothing of her,' said Helan. 'You'd have to ask Saphaeyender.'

'I'll go and see him later. Damn it. I blame myself for all of this.'

'Don't, Eld.' She went to him and began to rub his shoulders. 'It's not your fault.'

He clasped her hand and kissed her fingers. 'Perhaps not, but I feel responsible. I must make plans to find Ghiseyma.'

'We both must – but not this minute. You need to rest and bathe.'

He gave a twisted grin. 'I'm quite sure I need the latter. I'll strike a bargain with you. I'll bathe, ma'am, if you will send for some breakfast. I'm famished.'

Half an hour later Eldareth reappeared in a blue and silver striped robe, his chin freshly shaven and his straight black hair shining loose on his shoulders. Meanwhile Helananthe had ordered a substantial breakfast of pomegranates, fresh seed-bread, eggs and cold spiced meats and apple-cake. There was Marocian coffee in a tall blue pot. The meal was set on a table by the window, with a glorious view of Parione beyond the Citadel walls.

'I've cancelled all my morning appointments,' she said. 'Come, sit down. No one will disturb us.'

He smiled, his dark eyes shining and melting right to the core of her. More than anything she wanted to hold Eldareth in her arms, feel him inside her again . . . she couldn't imagine loving anyone else. They knew each other too well, and there was no one else she trusted so deeply.

'I don't know why you are being so kind to me,' he said. 'First I refuse to marry you, and now this.'

'I'm just glad to see you.' Eldareth began to eat ravenously, and after a few moments she joined him. She couldn't afford to lose her appetite, even over this news; she had too much to do. 'I've been thinking. Whoever abducted Mother and Veny must have known who they were. They must know that I've taken the crown. Otherwise, why bother? But if the Aelyr want something of me, why not just come and talk to me? This is dreadful. Mother must have been terrified.'

'More likely she terrified them,' Eldareth said drily.

Helan grimaced. 'Something's going on, Eld. It's like listening to people whispering in another room, but as soon as you go in, they all vanish. I can't get to the bottom of it. My lovely cousin Jthery turned up, full of mysterious portents, and scared the hell out of me.'

'Tell me. What's happened while I've been away?'

'Well, you missed my coronation.'

'Gods, I'm sorry.'

'So am I, but it wouldn't wait. After what's happened to Mother, it's just as well I didn't. I've appointed Derione as my Chancellor. Lord Poel is working for him and simply hating it. A very upset deputation is here from Thanmandrathor, demanding their independence.'

He paused, with a yellow peach speared on his knife. 'They're *what*?'

'Because of Garnelys. They want to rule themselves and keep their own army. I don't blame them, but I can't allow it. I've been trying to negotiate a compromise with them for weeks, but they're digging their heels in. That Lady Branq'elin's a little firebrand, and her brother's almost as bad. I could really do without their pig-headedness now.'

'I'm half Than'drathian,' he said, eyebrows raised.

'I rest my case. Eld, the last thing I want is another civil war. But how can I threaten them with the royal army when, as they keep pointing out, they have already defeated it and pursued the stragglers back to the skirts of Parione? I understand their point of view, but I will not be the monarch whose first action was to break up the Nine Realms!'

'Gods, no. That's courting disaster.'

As their conversation went on, she thought how wonderful it was to be able to speak freely at last, to pour out all that was on her mind without fear of it being used against her. She would never have this trust with Lord Serpeth, nor even with Derione. With them she would always have to be guarded, distant. Not herself.

Soon she was telling Eldareth about her coronation and initiation into the Xauroma. By now all the plates were empty, the table a scene of wreckage between them.

'So,' said Eldareth, 'these tablets you saw contain secrets to which only the monarch is privy?'

'Oh yes,' Helan breathed. 'Information that has saved Aventuria in the past, and may save us again, if we should need it. There's only one problem. I can't make sense of it.'

'Even though you could read it?'

'It was like being handed sheets of music. All the information is there in front of you, but unless you can read music and play an instrument, it's useless. The language is archaic. *Parts* of it made sense, but that could be even more dangerous. What if I acted on what I thought I understood, but got it wrong?' She expelled a breath of frustration. 'If Galemanth had succeeded to the throne, he would have taught me all this. Even Garnelys might have helped, if that woman hadn't killed him! But the natural order of things was hacked to pieces, so here I am in the dark.'

'Perhaps I could help.'

'I doubt it, Eld. I am very much on my own in this. Only my eventual husband will be allowed to see the contents of the chest.'

Their eyes met, and tension crackled between them. Helan said lightly, 'I suppose you haven't changed your mind?'

He was the first to break the contact, and his face was troubled. 'I'm sorry, Helan. I love you, but I cannot be king. I'd be wholly unfitted to the task.'

She held herself steady against the rush of disappointment, which came anyway. 'It's all right,' she said, managing to keep her tone free of emotion. 'Besides, I've had an offer from Lord Serpeth.'

He sat bolt upright. 'An offer of what?' he said in disgust.

'Marriage, among other things.' Helananthe's smile was grim. 'Imagine that, King Serpeth of Aventuria.'

Eldareth looked horrified. 'You are not seriously considering it? The man switches sides at the drop of a hat!'

Helan was grave. She'd wanted to torment Eldareth a little, but the news about her mother put her in no mood for teasing. 'Now I realise it was for the best that you refused me. I shall have to marry Serpeth, or someone like him.'

'But it's not compulsory for the monarch to marry.'

'No, but I have to think of the politics. I must cement the union of the Realms.'

'That's not a good enough reason. Helan, you can't mean to marry someone else.'

'I shall, eventually. I've now embarrassed myself by asking you and being rejected twice; I shan't do it a third time.'

Eldareth groaned. 'You don't understand. I'm not

rejecting you. I can't be king, but that doesn't mean I don't still love you. I want to be at your side and help you in everything. We can remain as lovers. Nothing in protocol rules it out.'

She chewed her lower lip until it hurt, cursing herself for giving him the chance to humiliate her again. 'Well, we can do that if you wish,' she said harshly. 'Only how are we going to explain to our future children why their father refused to join their mother on the Sapphire Throne?'

He looked down in shame. All she wanted – all he wanted, too, she knew – was for them to leap joyously on each other and make love, as they often had in the past. But now his refusal stood like an ugly wall between them.

She said in a low voice, 'It was fun, wasn't it, when I was only the king's granddaughter and we could both be wanderers and adventurers without responsibility? Racing our horses, exploring, sleeping together in forests. But those days are over. I have Nine Realms to watch over. If you will not give your whole self to me, then don't blame me if I look for someone who will.'

They glared at each other, unrelenting. Pain was beginning to crack their hearts but neither would give in to it.

A tap at the door made them both start. Dawn came in and announced. 'Your majesty, Lord Serpeth is here to see you.'

Helan whipped round angrily. 'Dawn, I cancelled all my appointments until noon!'

'Ma'am, it *is* noon,' Dawn said simply.

'It's all right,' said Eldareth. He rose, throwing a crumpled napkin on to the table. 'I'll leave you to your suitor. I'm sure he's as eager to place his arse on the Sapphire Throne as I am to rescue your mother.'

Chapter Eight. Confession

Tanthe walked. One foot in front of the other, on and on, until the ache of exhaustion ran all through her and congealed as raw fire in her feet. But as long as she kept walking, the pain kept its distance.

Her eyes were glazed. The green mountains slipped past her in a blur, like stage sets. When the nights came she went on until she tripped over rocks or tree-roots in the dark, slept fitfully where she had fallen. At dawn, she sucked dew from the grass to moisten her mouth and stumbled onwards.

She could not think of the Aelyr. Dared not think of anything.

She'd fallen through the portal on to a hillside somewhere near the Seer's hut, disorientated, shocked, frightened. There was nothing to do but go home, like an animal running to ground. As long as she kept her mind empty and her feet moving she was safe. The Valahyr would not catch her.

Tanthe hallucinated. She thought she was back in Sepheret, then couldn't understand why the foliage was different, moist ferns and thorned plants with flowers like exotic genitalia. Strange birds like white arrows, others that were bright red or blue. She tried to recall their names. Pointers, pipers, blue-doves . . . yes, this was Paranios. Not Sepheret.

There were shadows walking alongside her. Sometimes she thought it was Lynden and Rufryd there; at others, that Auriel and Falthorn were following, trying to persuade her back into their honeyed webs. The shadows came and went, making her catch her breath in fear as she strode on through endless steep-sided valleys.

Once she saw the shadows moving in front of her; three of them, slipping softly through a stand of hazel trees in the dusk. The landscape looked false to her, everything too sharp and edged with light, but she saw the figures clearly. Shepherds, perhaps, camouflaged in drab greens and greys . . . but when they turned to speak to one another, she saw their faces and her heart froze.

Long gaunt faces, staring skulls smeared over with mottled, translucent flesh. Terrible eyes, like dark ponds filled with primeval spined creatures lurking deep and luminous in the silt. As she watched she saw one of these faces suddenly growing longer, arching into the long blade-like skull of a wolf, and this creature dropping on to all fours.

The sight horrified her. *Shapechangers*. She felt wildly for her *mnelir*, the Aelyr knife that had saved her from the Bhahdradomen in the past – but of course, Falthorn had taken it back. Tanthe dropped down behind a boulder and crouched there, breathing fast and shallow like a hare. When she dared to look out, the three figures had melted away.

Another hallucination.

Setting her jaw, she rose to her feet and went on. As long as she could keep her eyes open and her feet moving, nothing would touch her. Home. She must head for home.

Eldareth hadn't meant to stay with his old friend Saphaeyender for long, but the poet's villa was so relaxing with its cool marble rooms, sunny porches and moist green ferns that he found himself still there several days later. He felt little inclination to return to the Amber Citadel. Helan was frosty and preoccupied; Eldareth felt guilty for letting her down, horrified at the prospect of her marrying Serpeth – but the simple fact remained. He could not in a thousand years see himself as King of Aventuria.

Saphaeyender seemed melancholy, and glad of his

company. He had begun to rehearse a classic play, *Arkenfell*, and each day the actors would come to his villa to read their lines; but Saphaeyender would listen to them in suppressed irritation, sometimes interrupting every other line, at others drifting off into a reverie in which he was plainly not listening at all. Eldareth began avoiding these sessions. The tension between Ashtar, Saliole, Sharm, Evender and the other actors was tangible. But whether Eldareth remained in the house or wandered the streets, the cause of Saphaeyender's depression loomed constantly. The bulk of the half-built Tower, where their beloved theatre had once stood.

It was afternoon, and Saphaeyender had sent the actors away early, claiming tiredness. Eldareth joined him in the living area, bringing a large carafe of Marocian wine, red as garnets.

'Vintage of '45, from the southern slopes of Lapiszul,' Eldareth said, seating himself on a couch between two tall ferns. 'Rehearsals not going so well?'

Saphaeyender sighed. He rose, padded around the room, took the goblet Eldareth handed to him, and sat down again. 'Hopeless. Did the Battle of Hethlas Rim make them all forget how to act? No, it's not them. It's the play. I should rewrite it.'

'Nonsense. It's too well-known!'

'The venue, then. That poxy little theatre at the bottom of Amber Street!' He shook his head vigorously. 'Everything's wrong. Eld, I wish you would direct it for me, or even take the lead role, like in the old days. Put some fire back into it.'

'I can't, my friend. I have to mount a search for Princess Ghiseyma and her son. I would dearly have liked Rufryd to go with me but I can't find him.'

Saphaeyender shrugged. 'He was at the coronation. He's still in the city somewhere. The last time I spoke to him, he gave me a black eye, so he's rather less than welcome here . . . but still, I don't blame him.'

'Over Tanthe, I take it.'

'More about Lynden than Tanthe,' Saphaeyender muttered. 'Anyway, when will you go?'

'Soon. I'm making some enquiries first. Searching out those who might have some knowledge of the Aelyr.'

'But why do this for Helananthe, if she's planning on marrying weasel-features?'

Eldareth spluttered on his wine. 'Because I still love her. I'm not going to punish her for my failings.'

'You have a fine sense of loyalty.'

'I'd do anything for her, anything – except that one thing. But she's so like me; her forte is action, not politics. Her judgement . . .' he shook his head. 'Her new Chancellor, Derione, hardly inspires confidence. She's seriously thinking of marrying a man she loathes. And she still has Poel working for her.'

'Poel?' Saphaeyender hissed through his teeth. 'Now, that bastard I wish I *had* met on the battlefield. How could she?'

'Either she's floundering, or she's playing a game too subtle for me to follow. Time will tell.'

Saphaeyender took a long draught of wine. 'It's not the play, nor the actors,' he said quietly. 'It's me. I fought to get my old life back, but it's not the same. I can't turn back time. I can't rebuild the Old Royal, can't bring Lynden back to life, can't wipe out what happened on Hethlas Rim. It just won't go away.'

'You had better not let this stop you writing,' Eldareth said sternly.

'Oh, I've never been busier. It's given me a cycle of three plays and an epic poem, at the least. But, gods, does anyone really care? I've found a writer younger and fresher than me, who writes from her heart as I never did. Ysomir. I'd rather be her mentor, and never write another word, than carry on like this.'

'Saph, if I didn't know you better, I'd accuse you of self-pity. Another thing; don't you dare try to seduce her! I think you've left quite enough wreckage behind you as it is.'

Saphaeyender laughed. 'Dyon's balls, how could I seduce her? She's in prison. Apart from that, she scares the life out of me.'

Eldareth leaned forward, intrigued. 'Really?'

'Did you know, she actually doesn't want to be released? Says she feels safe there. She's another play in herself . . . but I don't think I can use her like that . . .'

Both men were quiet for a few minutes. In the silence, a voice called urgently from the courtyard, 'Saphaeyender!'

'That's Dawn,' said the poet, sitting up.

Dawn and Mirias, both smart in royal livery, appeared in the doorway from the courtyard, supporting a woman who swayed between them. For a moment Eldareth didn't recognise the tall slim figure; her clothes were grimy and grass-stained, her hair hanging in a black tangle over her drooping head. Then he and Saphaeyender both rose to their feet in amazement.

'Tanthe!' cried Eldareth. 'Thank the gods!'

'Let's get her to a seat,' said Dawn. Eldareth rushed forward to help and together they eased Tanthe on to the couch he'd just vacated. She collapsed with a long, deep breath of relief, eyes closed. Her riding boots were worn and split. As Dawn eased them off in order to lift her feet on to the couch, they all saw in horror that her feet were swollen and bleeding with blisters.

'First she needs some hot tea, with plenty of honey,' Dawn said briskly.

'I'll get it,' said Saphaeyender. He went to an inner doorway and called for his staff. Tanthe lay with her head lolling back on the rolled arm of the couch, her eyes fluttering. She seemed unaware of her surroundings.

'Where did you find her?' asked Eldareth

Mirias answered, 'We were on the Serpentine Road, north of the city, delivering messages for Helananthe. I suddenly saw her walking – or limping – towards me. We

163

knew she'd been missing so we went to meet her. She didn't seem to know us at first. She just kept going, like she was walking in her sleep. Finally we got it out of her that she's trudged non-stop for four or five days, all the way from the Seer's hut. I don't think she's eaten in that time.'

'She more or less collapsed on us, so we brought her straight here,' said Dawn.

Eldareth shook his head. While he was overwhelmed with relief to see her, he was horrified at her gaunt appearance.

Saphaeyender came to her side and knelt down, cautiously taking her hands. 'Tanthe?'

'Gods, my feet,' Tanthe groaned. 'They're on fire. I didn't realise how much they hurt until I sat down.'

'It's all right. We'll get them bathed and bandaged. Have you really walked for five days?'

'I must have done.' She frowned. 'It's hard to remember. All I wanted was to find you, Saph.'

'Well, you're here. You're home. I've missed you.'

'Have you?' She raised her head and looked at him, her eyes glittering with raw pain and hope. 'I'm so sorry, Saph. If I'd known . . .'

The tea came and she clasped the cup, breathing the steam, taking grateful sips.

'What happened?' Eldareth said gently. 'Did you go into Verdanholm?'

She was silent for a few seconds. 'Yes, I was in Verdanholm.'

'What happened there?'

'Nothing. Are you all well? Have you been writing, Saph?'

'Copiously,' Saphaeyender said, 'but never mind that. Tell us about Verdanholm.'

'There's nothing to tell, really.' Her tone was flat.

'How did you come back?' asked Eldareth.

She shrugged. 'I just did. They let me go and there I was

164

'on the cold lonely hillside.' She gave a short laugh.

'But did you find out what you needed to know about your mysterious Aelyr?' asked Saphaeyender.

Tanthe rolled the cup between her fingertips. 'You know, I'm really tired. I don't want to be any trouble. I'm sorry to impose but could I stay here tonight?'

Saphaeyender gaped at her. 'Tanthe, you live here. You don't have to ask. You're exhausted; would you like to eat first, or bathe, or sleep? Anything you want.'

She seemed to shrink back a little from his kindness. Eldareth was gravely worried. This was not the vibrant, stroppy woman he had guided to the Seer's hut some eight weeks ago.

'Tanthe,' he began gently, 'it's obvious something painful has happened to you, or you would not have set out to walk all that way without resting or eating. What is it?'

A spark flared in her eyes and was gone. 'Nothing's happened. I'm perfectly all right.' Eldareth glanced at Dawn, but she only shrugged as if to say, *she wouldn't tell me anything either*.

'We've been worried sick about you! I lost not only you, but Helananthe's mother and brother, and I was the one who had to come back and break the news.'

Tanthe looked down. 'I'm sorry. I didn't mean to cause you any trouble, Eld. What happened?'

'I'll tell you later.'

Suddenly agitated, she struggled to sit upright. 'My mare – Redbird – where is she?'

'Redbird is perfectly fit and happy in the Citadel stables. She came to Eisilion and back with me.'

'Oh, thank Breyid. And Ysomir – has anyone been to see her?'

'I have,' said Saphaeyender. 'She's well, but worried about you. As we all were.'

She relaxed with a long exhalation. 'Well, I'm back and I'm absolutely fine, no harm done. I'm just tired.'

'Of course. You should get some rest.'

'Saphaeyender,' Tanthe said with sudden brightness, 'there are still theatres in Parione, aren't there?'

'Oh yes.' He grimaced. 'No great theatre, but several lesser ones that escaped Lord Poel's attention.'

'What I should really like is to go to the theatre. To do all the things I dreamed of doing before I came to Parione. Plays and music recitals and receptions . . .'

The others looked at her in surprise, but Tanthe smiled dreamily, seeming not to notice.

'Then I will take you, and with the greatest pleasure,' Saphaeyender said, kissing her grimy hand. 'You can be *in* a play, if you so desire. Anything you want, my dear. I've missed you.'

'I don't deserve this,' Tanthe murmured. 'I really don't deserve it.'

The favour Zhoaah asked of Lord Poel was simple.

A house.

Poel wasn't wealthy, but he had been prudent and made the best of his time in Garnelys's favour. It was easy for him to purchase a property on the eastern fringes of the city, a plain but sprawling villa of grey-white granite hidden in a cool valley. Pines, ashes and limes veiled the low ridges of its roof. This area had never quite become fashionable. There were only a few other houses dotted about, the dwellings of less well off merchants and river traders.

'This house is under your protection,' Zhoaah told him. 'You will come here only when we summon you; you will allow no other citizens to come here, nor will you ever question who comes and goes and dwells here.'

Poel looked at the figure of Zhoaah, pallid against the dark, dusty interior of the house. He felt slightly sick. 'Since you are my tenant, is it not my right to enquire whom you plan to have living here with you?'

Zhoaah only gave his sugar-soft smile. 'Friends, who –

when the time comes – shall be only too willing to bow to you and call you their King. That's all you need to know.'

Poel turned to leave. He wanted to scrub his hands of the matter.

'One thing,' Zhoaah said softly.

'Yes?'

'You have been thinking of leaving your post at the palace.'

Lord Poel stopped. How had Zhoaah worked that out? 'For some time. It's demeaning.'

'Well, don't. I need you in the palace. The humiliation is a small price to pay, is it not?'

Saphaeyender was in bed, Tanthe sitting on the edge in a fine white shift that was almost transparent. He lay gazing at the high, neat globes of her breasts gleaming through the silk, the way the material fell between her thighs, delineating their lovely contours and the dark triangle between them. The gleam of Rose Moon fell through the lattice shutters, dappling her body. Her face was half-hidden by her dark hair. 'Ysomir likes you,' she said.

'I like her, too.'

'Pretty, isn't she?'

'Very.'

'And she writes well. Better than I ever could.'

'Well, she has time,' Saphaeyender said with a touch of irony. Not enough to upset her.

'And she's very nearly thirty years younger than you.'

'What is this?'

'This is me being jealous and suspicious,' Tanthe said bluntly. She had been back for ten days but this was the first time she'd come into his chamber. Although he'd been aching with desire for that time, he'd left her to make the first move.

'Why?'

She folded her arms. 'Your record hasn't been too

167

wonderful, has it? I was scared there might be someone else when I got back.'

'Well, there isn't,' he sighed. 'I have no designs on your little sister. I've treated you like a princess since you've come back. Would you please tell me what I've done wrong?'

'Nothing. I'm sorry. You've been wonderful. And all I've done is kept you from your writing.'

Tanthe had recovered too fast from her journey, almost overnight. Her feet had healed quickly; she ate ravenously and was full of energy. 'I want to do everything I always dreamed of doing in Parione,' she'd said, and he had obliged, taking her to art galleries and theatres, to poetry readings and gatherings at the mansions of renowned artists, writers and musicians. They attended devotions at the Temple of Nepheter, and afterwards walked in beautiful lush parks where fountains danced and bright green, feathery arkh-woods clasped the hems of wide lawns. Everywhere they went they were treated as celebrities. Everyone wanted to know Saphaeyender's latest lover. But Tanthe insisted they were told as little as possible. 'I don't want all your gifted, generous friends knowing I'm a peasant from Riverwynde,' she'd said.

'It's nothing to be ashamed of,' Saphaeyender had replied.

'Still. I'll just be a woman of mystery, if you don't mind.'

She made him laugh when she said things like that. She basked in the attention and that pleased him; but she was too bright and vivacious, hiding her real self behind a mask.

He waited for her to tell him about Verdanholm. She didn't. The longer she stayed silent, the less able he felt to ask. Instead he gladly indulged her wish to dress in elegant pleated robes and jewellery of white gold and opal that were the current fashion in high society. She looked exquisite, but it wasn't the Tanthe he knew. She was a walking shell.

The truth was that he didn't question her, so that she wouldn't question him. Neither of them were being honest. Their life seemed to have become a smiling simulacrum.

'Are you going to come to bed with me?' he said.

Only the briefest pause. 'Yes.' She rose, pulled the shift over her head, and stood naked and gleaming in the lattice-light. She slid between the cool sheets – and soon, he slid inside her.

It seemed to be love he felt for her, through the dead wood of numbed emotions. Yes, love, which could express itself in embraces and thrusts and cries, better than any words. When they lay back on the pillows, drained and entwined, Tanthe smiled and said softly, 'Thank the Goddess for the gift of arkh-wood.'

He didn't have to ask what she meant. The feathery tree that gave its rubbery substance to prevent conception, its juices to ease all female pains, was a blessing. Yet he suddenly felt sad.

'Shouldn't you like a child, one day?'

'No,' she said fiercely. 'Not yet. Not for a very long time. Probably never.'

'Oh. I think I might.'

'You probably have several children already, that you don't even know about.'

Saphaeyender propped himself on one elbow, shocked. 'No, I haven't. Every female lover I've had, I am still friends with, and I can assure you that none of them has a child by me. Now I think that I have lived this ridiculous life long enough and perhaps it would be nice, for a change, to share my life with a wife and family.'

Tanthe looked, for half a second, completely terrified.

'What have I said?'

Her face relaxed and she stroked his cheek. 'I'm sorry. I thought for a moment you meant me.'

'I did.'

This time she hid her reaction. She grimaced and said,

169

'You could invite your boyfriends to live with us.'

'Yes, and you could invite yours,' he said through gritted teeth.

She smiled, looking at his shoulder, not his face. 'I don't know. I can't think about this.' He remembered that last time he'd broached the subject, she'd fled to Verdanholm.

'Why not?'

'Because you – you're *Saphaeyender*, and I'm just me. I do stupid things, too many really stupid things. It wouldn't last. It wouldn't be real.'

'Not real?' He frowned. 'I'm just a man, Tanthe. I hate to break the habit of a lifetime, but I seem to be in love with you.'

She stroked his arm, but didn't reply. He lay back, holding her. Quite soon she fell asleep, but he lay awake. Eventually he got up, slipped into a gown, and went to his study.

He must have fallen asleep over his desk. The next he knew, sunlight was spilling golden-white through the shutters, dazzling him, and Tanthe was standing beside him with a sheaf of paper in her hand. She'd dressed in her favourite robe of embroidered white satin with a boned bodice, with opals at her throat and in her hair, but she seemed to have put her hair up rather hurriedly and it looked charmingly dishevelled. She was staring at the paper she held.

'What time is it?' he groaned, trying to shake off the daze of uncomfortable sleep. 'What are you doing in here?'

'I came to find you,' she said tonelessly.

He felt annoyed, defensive. 'You know I prefer no one come into my work room. Put that manuscript back where you found it. I don't ask much of you, Tanthe, but until my work is finished, it's private.'

She turned to him, her face pale, eyes glassy with distress. 'What work?' she said quietly. She shook the sheets of paper at him, then put them down. 'This is dated

170

fourteen days after Hethlas Rim. Three titles, all crossed out. One and a half pages of writing, mostly crossed out. And that—' she pointed to another sheet on the corner of the marble surface. 'Your epic poem about Lynden? A title and five lines, all scribbled out. Stacks of paper here, and most of it is blank. I daren't even look in your waste-basket!'

Saphaeyender groaned. 'Why don't you go through the drawers, while you're at it?'

'I looked in the top one. Just old plays. Nothing new. Where is all this work you said you were doing?'

He rubbed his forehead. An ache pierced his right eye. 'Tanthe, this is rather like a visit from my old schoolmaster Aenander. Desist.'

'What *have* you written lately?'

'Nothing,' he admitted painfully. 'Nothing. I can't do it.'

When he looked at her he saw, to his shock, that her eyes were full of tears. She was trembling. Her face was rigid and she didn't sob, but the tears spilled and rolled down her waxen cheeks. 'Why didn't you tell me?'

'I couldn't,' he murmured.

'This is terrible.'

'Yes, it's terrible for *me*, but not for you. No need for you to cry. Maybe it's over. I've done my best work. It's not the end of the world.'

'But it is,' she said. 'Saph, I only have to look at you to see you're in agony over it! This is my fault.'

'What?' He turned in his chair and put his arm round her. 'No, it isn't.'

'It is. It's my fault. Ever since we met, you've written nothing. I've distracted you. This is the last thing I wanted. I wanted to love Saphaeyender, and instead I've destroyed him.'

'Tanthe, you're talking rubbish. You were expecting a legend and instead you find a rather failed human being? Well, I'm sorry. But if it's anyone's fault, it's Garnelys's and Poel's, not yours.'

171

'No, it's mine. It's mine.' She kept saying it, even when he took her into the living area and sat her down; wouldn't listen to him, only sat there rigid and glassy-eyed, saying, 'My fault.'

That was when Saphaeyender grew really alarmed, and shouted to Eldareth to fetch help.

Rufryd was at work in the sanctum, polishing the candle sconces of dark metal, filling the censers with fresh incense, tending the eternal flame. He was absorbed, but something made him look up. In the doorway, silhouetted against the red glow from the outer temple, he saw a lean, unmistakable figure.

'Rufryd?' the man said softly. 'So you are here! It's taken me days to find you. I heard rumours you were here, but I didn't quite believe it.'

Rufryd went to him, but offered no physical greeting. 'Eldareth. It's good to see you, but you needn't have bothered. I'm living here now.'

'So I heard. I don't want to disturb you . . .'

'Don't, then.' Rufryd folded his arms. 'I'm happy here. I want nothing to do with my old life. Whatever you want, you're wasting your time.'

Eldareth took a sharp breath. 'If that's the case, I'll trouble you no more. However, there's something I thought you'd like to know. Tanthe's back.'

Rufryd hesitated. He chewed at his lip, tasting blood. 'And?'

'She seems to be unwell. If it's not too much trouble, perhaps you could find a priestess to come and look at her?'

Tanthe sat on the couch, her arms clasped across her waist, staring out at the courtyard. The room was beautiful with its pale marble, its screens and alcoves and ferns and cool shadows, so tranquil. It was perfect, her life for the past ten days had been perfect. She didn't know what was wrong

172

with her. There shouldn't be anything wrong. But all she could think was that Saphaeyender couldn't write, and it was her fault.

She was glad when he stopped trying to reassure her, because she was too lost in shame to respond. Now he moved slowly round the room, occasionally pausing to look out at the courtyard, as if waiting for something. She wanted to tell him she was fine – to ignore her and try to work – but she couldn't speak.

There was movement on the terrace.

'I found him,' Eldareth announced, appearing in the open doorway from the courtyard. 'Here we are, Rufe. Tanthe, in one piece.'

Tanthe was jolted out of her reverie. She and Rufryd stared at each other.

Saphaeyender cleared his throat and withdrew to a safe distance. Tanthe had forgotten that Rufryd had attacked him, and hardly noticed. Rufe looked as if he'd been sleeping rough; he was wearing a plain dark robe, his chestnut hair had grown long and he hadn't bothered to shave for a couple of days. She felt like an iced confection in contrast.

'Gods, look at you,' he said.

'Ashtar withdrawn your clothes allowance, has she?' said Tanthe. She didn't mean to be vindictive, but it was a reflex. She didn't know what to say to him.

'I left Ashtar weeks ago,' he retorted.

'Where have you been?'

'Living at the Temple of Nuth.'

She frowned. 'Why?'

'I like it there.'

'Well, I'm glad to see you,' she said, pulling the cotton-wool arms of numbness around herself again. 'Really glad.'

Rufryd stared at her incredulously. He came closer, looking into her eyes until his face was only inches from hers. Then he drew back and said, 'What's wrong with you?'

'Nothing. I'm fine.'

'Come off it. You look like you've seen a Bhahdradomen. I've seen dead fish with more life in their eyes.'

She began to feel irritated. 'I'm worried about something. Is that allowed?'

Saphaeyender said, 'I've got this unfortunate condition called writers' block. Tanthe seems to think it's her fault. I can't persuade her that it isn't.'

Straightening up, Rufryd gave the poet a look of disgust. Saphaeyender came towards them and added, 'However, I have a strong feeling that that isn't what's really upsetting her. I think it's something else entirely.'

'How long has she been like this?' said Rufryd.

'Since she came back from Verdanholm.'

Tanthe looked up, indignant. 'Like what? I'm fine.'

Eldareth shook his head. 'You've been like a maniacally happy marionette – not like Tanthe. I think it's time you told us what happened in Verdanholm, don't you?'

'Nothing happened!' Tanthe snapped. She saw another figure moving against the green glimmer of the courtyard. An old woman in the black, white and red of Nuth, so hump-backed she was almost spherical. A priestess. Sensing conspiracy, she began to panic. 'What's going on?'

'We thought that if you wouldn't speak to us, you might speak to a priestess,' said Eldareth.

'You bastards!' she cried. 'Leave me alone! It's Saph who needs help, not me. Saph, tell them!'

He didn't answer. Her interrogators were unmoved, serious. The priestess came towards her with painful slowness, leaning on a staff, yet Tanthe couldn't seem to move out of her path.

'This is Good Mother Rouna, a priestess of Nuth,' said Rufryd. 'Rouna, this is Tanthe, a bloody nuisance.'

The priestess fixed Tanthe with a piercing grey eye. Fear thrust metal fingers through her numbness, which wasn't lack of feeling but a coiled mass of terror she daren't unleash. 'I don't need to talk to anyone. I've nothing to say, damn it!'

'Hush, dear,' said the old woman, leaning on her shoulder and sitting down heavily beside her. 'D'you want this lot to leave? Talk to me alone?'

She hesitated. 'No, they can stay. Since I've nothing to tell you, anyway.'

'Well, it's up to you. Don't have to tell me anything.' The priestess looked up with difficulty, leaning on her staff and angling her whole torso. 'What does a woman have to do to get a drink round here?'

Saphaeyender hurried to pour a goblet of wine, handed it to her. Rouna sniffed. 'Hmph. No beer?'

'No, I'm sorry, good mother. It is vintage Marocian.'

'Oh well, it'll do.'

'Can I have one too, please?' said Tanthe.

'We'll all have one,' said Eldareth.

The passing round of drinks eased the tension a little, but Tanthe felt they were all watching her, waiting. She began to breathe too fast. Saphaeyender was right. Her distress at his problem was only the symptom of a deeper misery, one she'd tried frantically to deny.

'Y'don't have to tell us,' said Rouna. 'It's your business. It might help, that's all. How bad can it be, after all? Did you kill someone?'

'No!'

'Well then.'

'It's just . . . I can't . . .'

'Was it so terrible?'

She gave a quick nod. 'I can't even remember it properly. That's what made it such a nightmare.'

'Can't remember? Or don't want to?'

'I'm frightened to,' she whispered.

The men were silent. All she could hear was her own blood rushing in her ears. The priestess looked into her eyes, shrewd and compassionate.

'I know, child,' she said. Tanthe felt the woman was

175

hypnotising her, in a gentle way. 'What I see in you is that this knowledge must come out, or it will poison you from the inside. That no one can help you, until you tell it. That you are ashamed; but Nuth knows all and will not judge you. You can speak without fear to us, for we'll protect you.'

Tanthe began to shudder. She took a gulp of wine then shoved the goblet on to a table, nearly dropping it. The floodgates of memory were opening, coaxed by Rouna's power. Losing control, she drew her knees up and clawed at her hair.

'This is too much for her,' Saphaeyender said, distressed. 'Perhaps we shouldn't . . .'

'No,' said the priestess. 'Let the pain come.'

Tanthe remained like that for a few moments, convulsed with the misery she'd been suppressing for days. Only the priestess's eyes held her steady. After a while her limbs relaxed, and she felt Rouna's hand on her shoulder, and she was able to unfold. She sat forward, her forearms resting on her thighs and her head bowed.

Then the words began to emerge, controlled but flat with pain.

'I'm only ashamed of getting tricked and used,' she said. 'You warned me the Aelyr were tricksters, Eldareth, and I didn't listen to you. Gods, I wish I had! They lied to me, all of them, from start to finish. Even Auriel. Especially Auriel.'

She told them of her arrival in Verdanholm, how Auriel had taken her to the forest hall to meet his family. How kind they'd been. How it seemed the most natural thing in the world for her and Auriel to make love . . . She didn't look at Saphaeyender or Rufryd as she said it, didn't want to see their expressions.

And then the nightmare that followed, her loss of time and memory. How she'd returned to clarity, fought her way out and persuaded Lord Valthiell to help her return to Earth.

'Just before I stepped through the portal,' she said, 'I made Auriel tell me what they'd done to me. I still can't believe what he said. Or the blunt way he said it, as if it happened because Falthorn willed it and that's all there was to it.'

The priestess gave her a drink of wine. She felt Saphaeyender's hand on her back. She couldn't look at any of them but she sensed their grim, complete attention.

'I didn't believe him, but when I went through the portal I began to remember flashes of it. It was as if it happened to someone else . . . and yet, I know that person was me.' She swallowed hard. 'Auriel and I conceived a child, which was what Falthorn had planned. Then they drugged me with honeyed potions and Valahyr magic, so that I wouldn't know what was happening. They kept me in that state until I gave birth to the baby, and then they took it away from me.'

'Oh, gods,' Eldareth breathed. The others said nothing; she could have cut their silence with a sword. She glanced up and saw their faces frozen in various expressions of disbelief; but she didn't want their shock or their sympathy.

'Too late, I found out that Auriel wasn't with the Valahyr of his own free will. Falthorn and his brother Talthaliorn – our father, supposedly – are enemies. When Talthaliorn and Fiomir fled, they weren't fleeing from outside enemies, but from the Valahyr. Auriel isn't sure what started the dispute, but part of it seems to be that Fiomir was Fhelethyr. Both *eretrue* disapproved of their union. There was a dreadful quarrel. Talthaliorn and Fiomir fled in fear of their lives, hiding me and Auriel as they went.

'Auriel was left with the Fhelethyr, but Falthorn tracked him down and captured him. Then the Valahyr used him to try and lure our parents back, but it didn't work. However, when they discovered Auriel was secretly trying to contact me, they decided this was a great idea. They would use him as bait to trap me.'

Her listeners expelled sighs of dismay. Eldareth said, 'Tanthe, I'm so sorry. I knew something wasn't right! I should have done more to save you.'

'You couldn't have known, Eld,' she said. 'It was something I had to find out for myself. *Auriel is their prisoner*. That's what I didn't realise. He's in thrall to Falthorn. When Auriel used to appear to me in visions, frightened because someone was coming after him, it wasn't some awful pursuer like the Bhahdradomen he feared. It was the Valahyr. His own family.'

Tanthe smeared a tear off her cheek and went on, 'They needed both of us as levers against our parents. I don't understand it all yet. But this is the important part. I suppose you know that the Aelyr believe their souls pre-exist, and come into the flesh when they're ready to be born?' The others nodded. 'Somehow, Falthorn discovered that there was a potential child, a soul that would be of particular worth or use to him, that could only come into being through Auriel and me. I don't know why he needed this being, but gods, he was determined to have it. So he commanded Auriel to impregnate me.

'Auriel lied.' Her voice was rough. 'He told me that we couldn't be fertile together because my body was human and his was Aelyr. And all the time he knew what he was doing. Falthorn told him to seduce me and, gods! how Falthorn must have been laughing, when it was virtually the other way round! I was drunk on their wine and affection. I thought I had entered the summer-lands of the gods, and all the time they were tricking me, using me! I hate Auriel for lying, for being so weak.'

She broke off, heat burning her cheeks. There were murmurs, uneasy hands on her shoulders. They were devastated, and didn't know how to comfort her. Eldareth said. 'Are you sure that you actually gave birth – if you can't remember?'

'Yes. I'm sure. Why else was I sore and bleeding when I woke? I've been trying to deny it but there are too many fragments of memory. The pregnancy was very short, as Aelyr gestations are; less than seven months, they told me. I felt pain when it was born, but it wasn't bad; not enough to rouse me out of the trance I was in. I can see them now, like shadows all standing around me, and the baby being lifted up and taken away . . .'

Saphaeyender interrupted reasonably, 'Tanthe, this can't have happened. You were only away for eight weeks or so.'

'Eight weeks here,' she said fiercely. 'But time passes differently there! They measure their time by ours, but still theirs can pass quicker or slower, as if they bend it along loops. And I was there, out of my mind, for nearly seven months.'

'All right. We believe you.'

Tanthe was shaking, but she went on. 'I caught a glimpse of it. It was very small, very white. When they wiped the blood off, it shone like mother-of-pearl. Not a human baby. I never saw it again, never heard it crying. What they did with it, I don't know. After that, I suppose my task was done and they forgot about me. Either their potions lost effect or they forgot to keep me enchanted. That was when I came round and I knew something terrible had happened.' Her mouth flickered in a smile. 'I don't think they expected me to be so angry about it.'

'So Auriel didn't know why they wanted this child?' asked Eldareth.

'He said he didn't. Of course, he might have been lying. Eld, I'm sure Falthorn is a *roth*-mage, a powerful one. He had occult knowledge that this child would have special powers. That's why he went to such lengths to get it.'

No one spoke. Even the priestess seemed dumbstruck.

'But that was my baby,' Tanthe said. 'They forced it on me, then they took it away from me. I loved Auriel but now I despise him. He did nothing to help me, just sucked me into the trap and all the time he was telling me he loved me, all the time he was fucking me, he was lying.'

179

Tanthe was trembling violently now, caught between tears and fury. The others seemed lost for words. It was Saphaeyender who came and caught her hand, holding her steady while the storm of anguish shook her.

'There's no need to comfort me,' she said, when she could finally speak. 'You must hate me for leaving you when you gave me so much. For being such an idiot!'

'No, no,' said Saphaeyender. 'I don't care what you've done, or whose fault it was. You've had a dreadful experience. What was done to you was an outrage against the Goddess.'

'He's right,' said Eldareth. 'I'm so sorry, Tanthe. You could only find out for yourself what the Aelyr can be like, but I wish you hadn't had to find out like this. This is the worst I've ever heard of them.'

Their response calmed her. What a relief to have told them, and still feel she was safe among loving friends. The priestess rested a hand on her shoulder and said, 'Pour her some more of that wine. Pour me another, too, while you're at it.'

Eldareth said, 'Helananthe should be told of this. It might have some bearing on what happened to Ghiseyma.'

Tanthe sagged, wiping her nose on the back of her hand. All her tension was gone now. 'The worst thing is that I used to think the Aelyr were so mysterious, so wonderful. Now I'm just terrified of them. Completely terrified.'

Someone moved in front of her. She looked up; Rufryd was there, but there was no sympathy on his face. His hands were on his hips, his face hard with the anger she'd seen there so often. 'You are absolutely unbelievable, Tanthe,' he said.

'What?' She felt distraught and vulnerable, not prepared for an attack.

His eyes glittered with pain, fury, jealousy – whatever twisted emotion it was that fired him. 'You are the most selfish little drama-queen in Aventuria, and that is really saying something in this city. You're never satisfied, are you? You fantasise about Parione, but once you get here it's suddenly not enough. You get Saphaeyender on a plate and even he isn't enough; you're off again, looking for something different and better. Anthar's prick, I never thought I'd feel sorry for him, but I do now. Humans not good enough, it's got to be the Aelyr now. What next, the fucking gods themselves?'

She gasped, incredulous. 'Haven't you got any idea what I went through?'

'You took stupid risks, Tan! Unbelievably stupid risks. So you got your fingers burned. About bloody time too. Next time you have some fantastic sob-story about sex with your brother and stolen babies, don't come whingeing to me about it.'

Eldareth caught his arm. 'Rufryd, that's enough!'

'Yeah, you're damned right it's enough.' He jerked himself free and turned towards the door. 'She'll do anything to be the centre of attention. She's always been the same. Maybe when you know her as well as I do, you'll see through the act and just leave her to dig her own grave!'

He stormed out, slamming the door dramatically behind him. Tanthe stared after him, open-mouthed.

'Bastard!' she cried.

'Now he's gone too far,' Saphaeyender said quietly. 'He can attack me all he likes, but not Tanthe.'

Eldareth turned to her as if mortified on Rufryd's behalf. 'He's angry because he was afraid for you. He overreacted. He can't have meant it.'

'Oh, can't he?' she snapped. 'I know how his mind works! Everyone is sympathetic to me, so he has to be different. Has to prove he's more hurt than I am. I know his stupid games and I've had enough. I'll never forgive him for this.'

The others' hands were on her, soothing, but she shook them off and leapt up.

'Bastard!'

She dragged off the opal necklace she wore and the hair

181

clasps, throwing them on to the couch. She headed towards the inner passageways that led to the bed-chambers, pulling at the laces of her robe as she went.

'Tanthe, what are you doing?' Saphaeyender said, following her.

'Changing,' she said.

'Why?'

'These clothes aren't me! I want my travelling gear on. I want to be myself again.'

'But where are you going?'

He caught her arm. His big dark eyes were anxious; and Tanthe loved him, but she knew that the love between them wasn't enough. Her dream of being with Saphaeyender was only a painted canvas. The more she tried to possess it, the more she destroyed it.

'I'm going to see Helananthe,' she said. 'I refuse to be frightened of the Valahyr. I'm not going to let them get away with this. If I didn't dream that child, I'm going to get it back – and Auriel, too. They tried to scare me? Well, all they've done – all Rufryd's done – is make me bloody angry!'

Behind her, the priestess Rouna of Nuth shook her head knowingly.

Lord Elrill of the Shaelahyr rode hard across the slopes of the Whiteveil Mountains, along ravines, down through the foothills towards the lakes of Mithrain. His mount was a tall showy stallion, white as ice. Its mane and tail and its rider's hair made triple flowing banners the colour of sunlight on snow. Elrill's garments were pearly grey, his cloak the glacial blue of the high peaks, his long sword bright as a mirror.

He was riding towards Paranios to deliver a warning. First time he had left Silverholm in years, but his message was too important to entrust to anyone else. If there was a life to be risked, it would be his own.

Making camp below a great hanging rock where the

foothills flowed into Mithrain, Elrill was approached by two small shadowy figures. In the twilight they seemed to emerge from the rock itself. Zampherai. They saluted him, and he bowed in return.

One was a thin fierce warrior, with bright blue streaks in his black hair, his only garments a loin cloth and a pectoral hung with crystals. The other was a gentler figure in a grey tunic, with great black eyes. These two had once been enemies and fought nearly to the death, but since honour was satisfied they had become allies.

'Vranof, Orque,' said Elrill. 'Shadowing me again?'

'Where you and Lord Eldareth are, things change,' said Vranof, the warrior. 'We have been, and shall be, your eyes underground.'

Elrill smiled. 'I'm glad of that. It's good to see you. What news?'

'The earth is disturbed,' said Orque. 'The crystals deep in the earth sing so painfully that it is hard for us to bear it.'

'Some power is trying to leech the *roth* from the earth,' added Vranof.

Elrill released a long, sad breath. 'Ah, this is grave news,' he said, 'but not unexpected. The surface also is wrought with disturbance. We have seen alarming signs in the Whiteveils. That's why I'm making this journey.'

'Where are you riding to, so urgently?'

'To Parione. To the Queen, to warn her of the danger before it reaches her.'

Chapter Nine. In the Mirror

Tanthe walked through the lofty, curving corridors of the Amber Citadel with her heart lodged in her throat. She was hardly aware of Saphaeyender and the priestess walking with her. They were on their way to an urgent meeting convened by Helananthe, and Tanthe wasn't looking forward to it. The Queen had changed since her coronation, Tanthe reflected, exchanging her informal, comradely approach for one of fierce authority. Inevitable, perhaps, but the result was unnerving.

Several days had passed since she'd told Helananthe about her experience in Verdanholm. The encounter had been taxing. Tanthe had told the story freely, gratified that the Queen took her seriously – until Helananthe had begun to pace the chamber, bombarding her with questions that she couldn't answer. 'Did this Falthorn mention my family, drop any hint that he had designs against us or against humans in general? Is he the leader of the Valahyr, or only of a splinter group? In what way is your child valuable to him?' On and on. By the time the session ended, Tanthe was ready to drop with tiredness and frustration.

Afterwards, Rouna had taken her to a drawing-room of gold leaf and red velvet, where she was able to rest and eat. Presently the hawk-faced Ariolne had joined them, and asked Tanthe if she might examine her physically. Like most priestesses, she was a midwife.

Past caring, Tanthe had agreed. She had lain on a velvet couch and closed her eyes while Ariolne gently pressed and prodded around her pelvis.

'It seems that your experience was real,' Ariolne said

when it was over. 'You have had a child, albeit a very premature one in human terms.'

Tanthe had sat rigid between the two women, staring at her hands as she flexed them. Ariolne's words made it all too real. 'I know,' she said, 'but it's as if it happened to someone else. I don't feel anything for the infant. I don't even know that I want it. I'm just so furious that they could do that to me, then take the child and throw me away!'

Rouna held her hand. Ariolne listened patiently. Tanthe was glad of their company, feeling she could say anything to them. 'Maybe Rufryd's right about me,' she sighed. 'I never am satisfied. I blame myself for what happened.'

'Why?' asked Ariolne.

'I was over-confident. So sure of myself. I thought I'd go storming in and rescue Auriel, find out the truth, take my rightful place among the Aelyr; oh, I assumed nothing bad could happen to me and everything would be perfect.'

'Instead, a hard lesson.'

Tanthe pulled a face. 'Am I really this dreadful person Rufryd thinks I am? I'm beginning to think so. I know I shouldn't have had sex with Auriel, but I was so drunk on my own cleverness and this happy delusion that I couldn't do anything wrong. When I want someone, I just leap on them. Not that Rufryd's any better, but still, he feels he can say, "I told you so," and I start hating myself.'

Rouna said, 'Don't be daft, girl. You made a mistake; no reason to punish yourself for it. There are times for lust and times to hold back; y'need a bit more practise discerning between the two.'

'Thanks, good mother,' Tanthe said, darkly amused. 'It's just that . . . well, it felt so right. At the time.'

'Desire is sacred to the Goddess. That living creatures can come together and create ecstasy – if not life itself – is that not miraculous?' One eyelid veiled the old priestess's iris; Tanthe wasn't sure whether it was a twitch or a wink. 'It's the very fire of life, and therefore to be exercised with reverence.'

'Oh, we were reverent. I truly think Auriel loved me, in his way. But if I ever see him again, I'll hit him so hard . . .'

'What if the Aelyr were right, that this child was *meant* to be?' Ariolne said. 'Then what you both did wasn't wrong. Only the circumstances that were inflicted on you.'

Tanthe gave a tired laugh and rubbed her forehead. 'That's a good one to tell Rufryd. "Oh, it was my destiny". I don't know why I still care what he thinks!'

All the same, Ariolne's words had given her pause for thought afterwards.

It was Auriel's child too, she thought now as they walked the amber galleries towards the Sun Chamber. It wasn't born for Falthorn's use.

Tanthe's story, apparently, had been important enough for the Queen to call this meeting. But Tanthe was dreading another interrogation, and beginning to understand why Ysomir shrank from Helananthe's relentless questioning.

As she and her companions entered the ante-chamber of the throne room, they found several others already waiting. To her surprise, Rufryd was there with Dawn and Mirias. Tanthe cursed inwardly. It struck her how similar Mirias and Rufryd were; two leanly built, handsome young men with strong limbs and lovely faces; Mirias slightly darker-haired, Rufryd slightly taller. They could be brothers, she thought, but only physically. One was decent, kind and valiant, the other a miserable bastard.

Turning her back on them, Tanthe saw a slim figure in white entering the ante-room behind her. She caught her breath in astonishment.

'Lord Elrill?' she said.

She stared at the familiar form, so strange in this new setting. She took in the ice-blond fall of his hair, the blue eyes burning in the long marble mask of his face. Even the shadows were blue as snow in the folds of his clothing; a soft white tunic over loose trousers, with patterns of leaves shining in the weave.

'Tanthe,' he said. Unsmiling, he came towards her and kissed her hand, his lips barely brushing the skin. She saw the same guarded coolness that she remembered in his eyes, when he had inexplicably withdrawn his friendship from her. Just after one of her visions of Auriel, in fact. 'You are well, I hope?'

'Fine. What are you doing here?' she asked.

'If the Queen has summoned you, you'll know soon enough,' said Elrill. He inclined his head to Ariolne, Rouna and Saphaeyender. 'Greetings, good mothers, good sir.'

'Can I talk to you for a moment?' Tanthe said. Her simmering anger was making her even more impulsive than usual. She lacked the patience to show respect to anyone, even to Aelyr lords.

Elrill hesitated. 'Of course.' He said to the others, 'You will excuse us?'

He let Tanthe take him to a corner of the antechamber, where portraits of Queen Hetys and King Maharoth gazed impassively over their heads. 'Why didn't you tell me?' she whispered.

'Tell you what?' His composure cracked a little.

'That I am, according to pernicious rumour, an Aelyr. Half Valahyr and half Fhelethyr, to be precise. You knew, didn't you?'

'Tanthe . . .' his gaze drifted away from her, then snapped back, concerned and wary. 'I suspected.'

'No, you knew! You even told Eldareth! Why didn't you say something to *me*?'

'Because it seemed best that you continued thinking you were human.'

Rage coursed through her; she held on to it, with effort. 'But how did you know? Did you see it in my eyes, read my subconscious?'

'In a manner of speaking. I saw it quite suddenly. There is an aura that only the Aelyr have. It's veiled in you, because you appear human, yet it is still there.'

Her throat tightened. She was determined not to cry in

front of him. 'You should have told me, instead of cold-shouldering me. I know you have some quarrel with the Aelyr of Verdanholm, but that's not my fault! I knew nothing about it! I'm none too happy with the Valahyr myself now.'

Elrill's eyes were frozen glass; then his demeanour softened by a degree. 'I'm sorry, Tanthe. You are right. But I didn't know how you would react, nor what you might start to remember, if I told you. If I seemed hostile to you, I apologise.'

'You did. I suppose you had no choice, though. I don't know how I would have reacted, either. You'll be happy to hear I haven't managed to remember anything yet.'

He was still looking cautiously at her, trying to weigh her up. 'How did you find out?'

'If the Queen has summoned you, you'll know soon enough,' Tanthe said thinly.

'We're glad you've come back,' said Mirias.

'Really?' Rufryd said, unconvinced. He glanced at the amber walls and the portraits of monarchs gazing down at him. 'I don't know what I'm doing here.'

'I think you do,' said Dawn. 'We've got work to do, and your heart led you back.' They smiled at him, but their warmth didn't move him.

Rufryd shrugged. 'I sometimes wonder why we even bother. I'll probably give the Queen a hearing, then go back to the temple.'

'Why?' said Dawn. 'What do you mean?'

'Come on, Dawn. Secret meetings, strapping swords on, rushing about the countryside. What's it all for?'

Mirias looked shocked. 'To protect Aventuria, of course.'

'Is it even worth it?' Rufryd was trying not to think about Tanthe but couldn't stop. If she asked why he'd attacked her with such vicious words, what would he tell her? That he'd been trying to hurt her so that she would hurt him back, because he deserved it. That he was so horrified at the risks she'd taken, he could only express it as anger. That he was jealous of her other lovers. That she needed shaking out of self-pity and back to her normal self. And that he'd wanted to hug her but couldn't, because his anger and bitterness always won. Without her, his life was pointless, but she couldn't see it and because of that, he was in no heart to forgive her. 'Pointless,' he murmured.

'I can't believe you said that!' Mirias spoke in a whisper, still loud enough to be overheard. 'Not worth protecting Aventuria? Rufe, what has got into you? I would lay down my life for the Nine Realms and so would Dawn! How can you stand there saying, "Oh, maybe it's not worth it"?'

Dawn pressed a hand on each of their shoulders, to ease them apart. 'Hush,' she said, frowning. 'There's no need for this.'

'Sorry,' Rufryd said flatly. 'You're right, Mirias. It's easy to be brave and clear-sighted when everything's so black and white. I should try to be more like you. You and Dawn don't even know how lucky you are.'

Helananthe convened the meeting in the Serpentine Chamber, a smaller council room that nestled alongside the Sun Chamber. Tanthe tried not to stare at her surroundings, but couldn't help it. The walls were panelled in flakes of olive-green amber that sparkled with little sunbursts. Three round windows in the outer wall represented the three moons in delicate glass hues. White and clear for Lily Moon, pale greens for Leaf Moon, blush-pink for Rose Moon. In the centre stood a large oval table of blonde marble, inlaid with a swirling mosaic border of green serpentine and bloodstone. The chairs were high backed, burnished with greenish gold leaf and studded with malachite, emerald, moss agate and tourmaline.

'Sit down,' Helananthe said brusquely. 'Most of us know each other so there'll be no standing on ceremony. There is wine, water, cakes; if anyone requires any other refreshment, speak now, for I want no interruptions. Lord Derione shall introduce everyone.'

The Queen wore a robe of dark blue figured satin, with a high stiff collar framing the coiled honey of her hair. Her strong face was serious. She sat in the centre on the long side of the oval directly under the Leaf Moon window, with Lord Derione on her right, Lord Serpeth on her left. Tanthe took her seat around the curve from Derione, which meant she wasn't facing the Queen, to her relief. Ariolne and Rouna were on Tanthe's left, Saphaeyender on her right. He touched her knee beneath the table. Further round sat Eldareth and Elrill, and on the far side from Tanthe were Dawn, Mirias and Rufryd.

Rufe looked tired and grim. Tanthe avoided his eye, as he seemed to be avoiding hers. She couldn't forgive his outburst, and so far he'd offered no apology. She set her jaw, determined to prove that she, at least, could control her emotions.

There were fifteen people around the table. The other three were two men and a woman she didn't know. When Derione rose to announce everyone, she attended carefully.

'Lady Branq'elin and Lord Mawrdreth of Thanmandrathor, heirs to Duke Tasq. Lord Jthery of Mithrian.'

Tanthe looked at them with interest. Two proud figures in rich earth colours, with glossy umber plaits hanging down their erect backs. They looked intimidating, like tribal leaders from an older time. Jthery, though, looked a personable young man. He had a lot of pale red-gold hair, tied back at the nape of his neck, and he appeared earnest, determined, yet innocent.

'Thank you for coming,' Helananthe began. 'I wanted all of you here who were with me at Enhavaneya; Eldareth and Saphaeyender, Dawn and Mirias, Rufryd and Tanthe. Many of us thought that the Battle of Hethlas Rim was an end to our troubles. However, since I took the throne I have been receiving a stream of disturbing news, disturbing signs. Now I must admit to a suspicion so appalling that I can hardly bring myself to express it. Which is, that the civil war was deliberately engineered by factions intending to destabilise the Nine Realms. That we didn't so much win a victory, as fall into a trap.'

The silence in the chamber was stone-heavy. The Queen was a powerful presence, her strong hands clasped motionless on the table. If she seemed overbearing, Tanthe admitted, it was because she couldn't afford to be otherwise.

'I had assumed those factions to be Bhahdradomen infiltrators who took advantage of my grandfather's weakness. The truth may be more complicated. I believe that the Aelyr may also be involved.'

There were soft indrawn breaths.

'My mother, Princess Ghiseyma, is alleged to have been kidnapped by Aelyr. So has my brother Veny – who would become King, should I die without issue. There has grown up in the Nine Realms a sentimental attachment to the Aelyr, a belief that they are a benevolent and god-like race. Admittedly they fought on our side in the War of the Silver Plains, but we must never forget that we've had quarrels with them in the past, nor that there are different factions within the Aelyr, some of whom are less well-intentioned than others. Tanthe has a tale to relate which demonstrates that the Aelyr' – she glanced at Elrill – 'or, I should say, *some* of the Aelyr are not to be trusted. Tanthe?'

Tanthe cleared her throat and told her story again. She was growing quite practised at it now. Almost as if it had happened to someone else.

She tried to ignore the mixed expressions of shock and sympathy that greeted her tale. She didn't want sympathy, had no use for their opinions. Lord Serpeth said acidly, 'If you'd wanted advice on whether or not to trust the Aelyr, my lady, you should have come to me, not Eldareth.'

'Thank you, my lord, but I prefer to learn by my own mistakes,' Tanthe retorted.

'But what *are* the Valahyr's intentions?' said Helananthe. 'It's essential we find out.'

Serpeth's voice was a soft razor. 'Perhaps Lord Elrill can shed light on the matter.'

The Shaelahyr lord said evenly, 'I take into account that you are Eisilian, my lord, and that your irrational hatred of us is inborn.' Serpeth shook his head, grinning ferally as if to intimate that Elrill was making shallow assumptions. Elrill continued, 'I can't comment on the motives of the Valahyr. I am here only to represent my own people, the Shaelahyr, and to assure you that we are still friends to the human race. We quarrelled with the other Aelyr *eretrue* centuries ago about the value of the Earth to us – for we believe that Verdanholm is a reflection of Earth, without which we couldn't exist – and since we decided to dwell here, Aventuria has made us welcome. We may have had our quarrels with humans, but our loyalty lies with you.'

Saphaeyender said, 'Don't you have *any* idea of what the Valahyr are up to?'

'My people no longer have contact with them. The Fhelethyr are a peaceful people, but secretive and clannish. The Valahyr are vibrant, outgoing and brave, but they can also be vain and self-serving – as can we all, no doubt. You must remember that Verdanholm itself came under attack from the Eaters in the past. If it happens again, the Valahyr will take measures to defend themselves. That's all I can say. I don't know this Falthorn. Tanthe says he acts as their leader – yet we have no leaders, although one will sometimes arise to whom other Aelyr look for unity. I hold that honour in Silverholm, yet it doesn't mean I hold power over my *eretru*. Only an obligation to speak for them.

'I come here as Silverholm's representative. I came to deliver a warning. There has been Bhahdradomen activity in the Whiteveil Mountains.'

There were gasps of concern, but the Queen didn't react. Elrill must have told her in private, Tanthe thought.

'These Eaters did not appear to be armed,' Elrill went on. 'They had the appearance of peasants, and they offered no threat. I believe they have come from hidden pockets in Sepheret, Deirland and Noreya where they have been permitted to live in secret since the War of the Silver Plains. But there are a great many of them, and they are heading towards Paranios.

'When we challenged them, they refused to tell us why they had left their permitted areas, or where they intend to go. They said that they would speak only to the Queen herself. Therefore I rode here with all haste to warn her of their approach. The Zampherai, too, have told me of disturbances in the depths of the earth. These are matters of great concern, thus it was my clear duty to deliver this information.'

When Elrill finished, everyone began to speak at once. Derione called for order, but they didn't subside until the Queen spoke.

'Please! Listen to what Lady Branq'elin has to say.'

The Than'drathian woman had an accent that Tanthe found hard to follow at first, but she soon caught its rhythm and fluid beauty. 'My brother and I have spent many days in negotiations with the Queen regarding the future status of our realm. I can't divulge the result of those discussions, except to say that we have reached a compromise that will suffice for now. It is time for my brother and I to return to our father, Duke Tasq, and put the Queen's proposals to him. The one thing we're agreed on is that we must remain friends and allies.

'There have been perplexing signs in Thanmandrathor too, strange storms and rumours of Bhahdradomen activity. As part of our conditions for dropping our immediate claim for independence, we have made a special request of her majesty; that she send a deputation into Vexor itself, to communicate directly with the Bhahdradomen.'

There were a few gasps, but Tanthe guessed that some of the people around the table already knew.

'It's the only way to be certain of what's going on there,' said Helananthe. 'Lady Branq'elin is right. Perhaps if Garnelys had done this years ago, we would not be having trouble with the Bhahdradomen now. So, I am proposing two expeditions. One to Verdanholm, to discover the Aelyr's intentions and – I hope with all my heart – to find my mother and brother. The second, to Vexor. Each party will be small, in order to travel swiftly, attract minimal attention and not be seen as threatening.'

Tanthe already knew about the Verdanholm quest. It had been her idea.

Ariolne said, 'How do they propose to reach Verdanholm? Only Aelyr can create and open portals.'

Elrill said, 'Good mother, I shall be going with the party.' He produced a quartz ball, like the one Tanthe had seen Valthiell and Auriel using. 'This *anametris* sphere has not been used for some centuries, but I trust it still contains the *roth* for our purposes. In the past, portals have been most common in Sepheret, Torith Mir and Eisilion. We shall endeavour to find one of those portals, and reopen it.'

Eldareth said, 'We aren't going to Torith Mir, and Sepheret is too far. So we'll try our luck in Eisilion.'

Lord Serpeth shook his head. 'You're insane. Trying to deal with the Aelyr is madness. They're not human.'

Elrill gave him an icy look, but didn't retaliate, to Serpeth's obvious irritation.

'Who else is going?' Rufryd asked.

'In addition to Eldareth and Elrill,' said Helananthe, 'my intrepid cousin Jthery has volunteered. I have no idea why.'

'That's not true, Hel,' Jthery said quietly. 'I love Ghiseyma and I want to find her. I said you would need me for something. As soon as you mentioned it, I knew this was what I'm meant to do.'

'Yes, thank you, cousin,' Helananthe said, smiling. 'And the fourth member of the party shall be Tanthe.'

Saphaeyender said nothing. He'd already offered his

arguments against her going, and had to surrender.

'You're joking,' Rufryd exclaimed. 'That's an insane idea! You can't send her!'

'No one's sending me,' Tanthe snapped. 'I volunteered.'

'What? You've already got roasted in the cauldron, why d'you want to go and jump into the fire?'

Whether he spoke in contempt or concern, Tanthe couldn't tell, but her blood rose. 'I must go,' she hissed. 'They can't do this to me and not expect consequences.'

'That proves my point,' he said, folding his arms. 'You're too involved. You're nuts, you'll get yourself killed!'

'Stop it. This isn't the place for an argument,' Helananthe said stonily. 'It's decided. Tanthe at least has some idea of what she's dealing with.'

Rufryd subsided, shaking his head in a gesture of contemptuous despair that made Tanthe want to punch him.

'The second expedition,' said Helananthe, 'is going to be a long and perilous journey, with an unknown end. Mistakes were made after the Silver Plains. I am sure King Maharoth believed that with the head, Ghaurthror, cut off, the body would be harmless.' The tension turned thick as rain-clouds as she spoke. 'When the Bhahdradomen were exiled, Vexor should have been policed. But since humans find it intolerable to be near them, they were left to their own devices; the only condition being that they should never set foot off the island. The result is that we have only the most shadowy knowledge of what goes on in Vexor. They are obliged to tell us nothing. The last message was received from them some fifty years ago, when the leader Aazhoth reassured Garnelys of his full cooperation. All the Bhahdradomen wanted, so Aazhoth said, was the continuance of their peaceful existence.

'However, recent events have hinted at something rather more ominous. I already have two volunteers, and although I am deeply loath to lose them, I know that I could find no more trustworthy ambassadors anywhere. Dawn and Mirias.'

'What?' said Saphaeyender, sitting up and glaring at them. 'Is it not enough that I lose my two best actors – now you want to go and kill yourselves? Wonderful. Go, throw your lives away. I'm beyond caring.'

'Saph, shut up,' Dawn said, reddening. 'I actually prefer real life to playing at it.'

'We play at it in order to understand it,' he said tartly, folding his arms. 'It's the only way we cast light into the shadows. Don't go, Dawn.'

She didn't answer. Helananthe said, 'If you are going to bicker about these decisions, would you please save it until after the meeting? Now, Branq'elin and Mawrdreth have decided that Mawrdreth shall also go into Vexor. With characteristic bravery they both wished to go, but since it would be foolish to risk both heirs to the Dukedom, Branq'elin – being the immediate heir – shall return to her parents' hall. So I should like another volunteer, to make the party up to four.'

'I'll go,' Rufryd said without hesitation.

Now it was Tanthe's turn to be horrified. 'Rufe, you can't!'

He looked coldly at her. 'There is absolutely fuck-all reason for me to stay in Parione.' Derione and Serpeth both stirred in outrage at his language, but no one took any notice of them. 'I have no desire to help you chase after your Aelyr lover. Vexor sounds far preferable to me. Ariolne told me I'd know when it was time to leave – and she was right.'

Ariolne and Rouna said nothing. Tanthe was devastated. If she'd harboured any faint hope he might forgive her and travel with her, he'd killed it. 'But it's thousands of miles away. Rufe, you mustn't. You don't know how dangerous it might be.'

He shrugged. 'How could the Bhahdradomen be any more scary and vicious than you are?'

A furious breath shot out of her, but Helananthe spoke over them, cutting their argument dead. 'Thank you,

Rufryd. Do you and Tanthe wish to discuss this outside?'

'No. Nothing to discuss. I'm going.'

'Good,' she breathed. 'It's settled. Elrill, Eldareth, Jthery and Tanthe are going to Verdanholm. Mawrdreth, Dawn, Mirias and Rufryd to Vexor.'

Saphaeyender said, 'And what if they find the worst? That the Bhahdradomen are preparing to make war?'

The Queen was silent a moment, looking around at their faces. Her eyes were troubled. Tanthe had never seen her look so worried, nor so obviously not telling the whole truth. 'The War of the Silver Plains was won with the help of certain, specially made *roth*-weapons that were hidden afterwards. They were known as the Basilisks of Calabethron, after the mage who made them. Now that I have taken the covenant of the Xauroma, I shall soon have access to these weapons – just in case the very worst should happen. Let's hope it won't come to that. Diplomacy first!'

Everyone murmured agreement. 'Right, I'm calling this meeting to a close,' Helananthe added in a brisk tone. 'The fifteen people in this chamber are the only ones who know about these expeditions. Let's keep it that way, shall we? My thanks to all of you.' As she rose, all the others shot to their feet in respect. It might have been all right to sit while the Queen was standing not so long ago, but no more. Leaning on the table, she looked meaningfully at Eldareth, then at Mawrdreth and Branq'elin. 'Although some of us have had our differences in recent days, I trust you all the more for being unafraid to speak your minds to me. We are all on the same side and the love between us, which is strong enough to withstand argument and disagreement, is the bedrock of Aventuria's strength. Goddess and God go with you.'

Tanthe found Ysomir as she always did; dignified, poised, solemn. Still with a warm smile for her older sister; but she'd changed so much since the days in Riverwynde. It struck Tanthe now that their roles had reversed, that she was the fearful one while Ysomir was strong and protective.

They sat on the edge of Ysomir's low plain bed, holding hands. 'I have to go away again, dear,' Tanthe said.

Ysomir frowned slightly. 'Where?'

On a previous visit, Tanthe had told her about her stay with the Valahyr. Ysomir had been shocked, yet she'd believed Tanthe immediately. Once, Tanthe would have thought this was because Ymmi was gullible, superstitious; now, though, her belief seemed to stem from an eerily mature intuition.

'I have to go into Verdanholm again.'

'On your own?'

'Not this time, no. Last time I went as a stupidly trusting friend. This time I'm going as a royal official. You understand, don't you?'

Ysomir nodded, but gripped her hands tighter. 'But how will you find a way into Verdanholm? Only the Aelyr can open portals, I heard.'

'Elrill's coming with us. He reckons we'll find a portal in Eisilion.'

Ysomir shut her eyes. Her face seemed luminous. '*No. Go to Torith Mir,*' she said in a strange voice.

'What?'

'It's in Torith Mir.' Her eyes came open again; she looked startled.

'Gods, Ymmi,' Tanthe said, her mouth turning dry. 'I wish you wouldn't do that. That was someone else speaking. Who . . .?'

Ysomir looked down at their joined hands. 'It was Garnelys,' she whispered.

It took all Tanthe's will power not to break away from her in fright. She took a long, shaky breath. 'You know, I think Auriel and Falthorn have made a mistake. If there was an Aelyr cuckoo placed in our family, it must have been you, not me.'

She meant it as a joke – a bad one, admittedly – but Ysomir looked alarmed. 'What do you mean?'

'You're the ethereal one. It was always you who had the strange intuitions and premonitions.'

'That doesn't prove anything! Can't humans have those feelings?'

'Yes, of course. Don't get upset, Ymmi. I don't mean it, I'm just trying to understand what's happening.'

'I know.' Ysomir looked up, her eyes bright. 'Perhaps there is a way to find out.'

'How?'

'You said that Auriel gave you a little *silvenroth* mirror as you left. And there's another one at home, isn't there?'

'Which I lost,' Tanthe sighed. 'Hid it under my bed, never saw it again. Auriel was pretty annoyed about that.'

'Maybe it's still there.'

'No. I did sweep our floor occasionally! I consciously looked for it a couple of years ago but there was no sign.'

'Perhaps Mum moved it. Show me the one Auriel gave you.'

Tanthe took the *silvenroth* mirror from her pocket and cupped it in her hands. It shimmered like snow under moonlight. She looked at her reflection, which was blurred by the imperfections in the crystal. 'I don't know how to use it. I wish I'd asked him.'

'You must have some instinct about it.'

'Why? Because I'm supposed to be Aelyr?' Tanthe felt frustration rising, and subdued it. 'Ymmi, do you really believe what they told me?'

'I don't know.' She touched Tanthe's wrist. 'You're still my sister, still Tanthe. If it's true, I think your knowledge of it is very heavily veiled. That's why I can't see it, either. Try staring into the mirror. Concentrate.'

Tanthe settled herself, cradling the mirror with her hands resting on her thighs. She felt foolish, staring at herself. She tried to relax, to let her eyes go out of focus until she was gazing, not at the mirror, but through it.

'*Can anyone hear me* – oh, this is stupid. I can't feel anything.'

'Hush! Keep trying!'

Tanthe sighed. She steadied her breathing, tried not to think how ridiculous this was. Her image blurred again; she stared through it, past it until she could no longer see it. The rock crackled palely across her vision, expanding, scintillating. And then she felt something. Her mind was slipping down into the infinite depths of the mirror, the *silvenroth* of the stone entering her as a rhythmic pulse of white light.

Tanthe was somewhere else. A paper-thin plane between worlds. Her own voice sounded strange, like rushing water as she spoke, 'Is anyone there? Can you see me in the mirror? If you can hear me, if you know where the mirror is, pick it up!'

Part of her was still insisting that this was hopeless, and doubt nearly flicked her out of the trance. She concentrated harder, kept herself floating in the pale layer of *silvenroth*. It was weird, exhilarating and confusing, like floating beneath the foam of a waterfall. She kept talking, 'This is Tanthe. Mother, Grandmother, whoever is there, look at the mirror.'

She had a vision of the first mirror, lying buried in leaf-mould under a hedge somewhere, talking to itself.

Then a face appeared. She blinked. At first she thought it was her own reflection again, that she was losing the trance. But when it came into focus it was the face of a fair-haired boy, about ten years old.

'Feryn!' she gasped. 'Ymmi, I can see Feryn!'

Their little brother. How much older he looked than when Tanthe had last seen him. His brown eyes were wide with wonder.

'Feryn, can you see me?'

'You're blurred,' he said. His voice was faint, but she heard him clearly. 'You look like Tanthe.'

'Yes, it's me, Tanthe! The little mirror you've got – where was it?'

'In my room. I've had it years. I found it,' he added, a bit defensively.

The little sod, Tanthe thought. So it was Feryn who'd taken the mirror! Yet she couldn't really blame him, for he must have done it almost as soon as he could walk. She was more relieved than annoyed. 'Feryn, I'm a long way away from you. I've got another mirror like yours, that we can talk through.'

He nodded, staring in wonderment but accepting the idea without question as only a child could. She said, 'Is Mum in the cottage? I want you to take the mirror to her. I must speak to her.'

'All right.'

There was movement and the image broke up. Tanthe felt her concentration wavering. A headache began behind her eyes; using the *silvenroth* energy was hard work. No wonder Auriel had found it so hard to maintain contact with her, especially from another realm. She couldn't keep this going much longer.

Aynie's pert face swam into the mirror, surrounded by sun-streaked hair that dissolved into pure light at the edges. Tanthe caught her breath and tears filled her eyes.

'Mum, it's Tanthe.'

Aynie cried out, and must have dropped the mirror. Tanthe saw the cottage ceiling swing across her field of vision, and she was so deeply into the image that it made her dizzy. A second later, her mother's face reappeared. 'Tanthe? How is this possible? Where are you?'

'In Parione. We don't have much time, I can't maintain this much longer. Is everyone well?'

'Yes – yes – but we miss you. What's happened to you?'

'Everything,' Tanthe breathed. 'We found Ymmi, she's here with me. She's well. Rufryd's here too. But Lynden died. There was a battle, the king's dead, there's a new queen. I can't tell you it all.'

Tears were running down Aynie's face. 'It's all right. Just to know you and Ymmi are alive. But poor Lynden . . . And you, how are you?'

'Fine. But Mum, there's something I must know. About when I was born.'

Aynie's face lengthened; becoming guarded. She seemed to be shooing Feryn out of the room. 'What is it?'

'It has something to do with this *silvenroth* mirror, doesn't it? This came to you with me, an Aelyr gift. Will you please tell me the truth? Am I really yours, or was I a baby abandoned by the Aelyr?'

Her mother's expression confirmed her fears. Tanthe groaned. Now Aynie hardly had to say anything; Tanthe's throat closed up with tears, and she had to struggle to maintain the link.

'Oh, Tanthe, I wish we could talk properly. I can't tell you like this.'

'Try! Mum, you've got to. I'm a big girl now. My life might depend on it.'

Aynie's sweet face was pale with shock. 'It's not what you think. Your Aelyr parents didn't abandon you. They gave you to us for safe-keeping, but Tanthe, it's complicated. You asked me once if I'd ever seen the Aelyr and the truth is, I often used to go in the woods looking for them – and sometimes, yes, I saw them and I must have drawn their attention to me. They came to me out of the trees, one day when Eodwyth and I had not been hand-fasted long; a male and a female, dressed in the colours of twilight.'

'What were their names?'

'The man was called Talthaliorn. The woman, Fiomir.'

Tanthe sobbed openly, soundlessly as her mother went on, 'They followed me home and I was afraid; but as we spoke I saw that they were more afraid than I was. They were fleeing from something. Eodwyth and me took them in and they stayed the night, talking to us, asking questions. They said that an Aelyr soul was ready to come to them – they meant a child – and they couldn't deny her, because if they didn't conceive her then, she might never be born at all. I don't know how to explain. It's not random as it is with humans.'

'It's all right, I understand. Go on.'

'Well, they *couldn't* have this baby, because they were fleeing from their enemies. But if they didn't, she would be lost to them forever. So they asked me – they asked me to bear the child for them.'

'They *what?*' Tanthe whispered.

'I gave birth to you, love, just as if you were really mine. As far as I'm concerned, you are mine and your dad's.'

'How was it done?' Tanthe didn't want to know, but couldn't help herself. 'Did Talthaliorn make love to you?'

Aynie coloured. 'Tanthe, please . . .' She glanced away, as if to be certain Feryn wasn't listening. 'I don't want to tell you. You'll see us differently, and I don't want that.'

'I've got to know!'

'We all made love. All four of us. But this was sorcery as well as sex. Somehow Talthaliorn put his essence into me and into Eodwyth, and Fiomir put hers into Eodwyth and me. We all loved each other. So really, you were part of all four of us. I don't know how it worked, love. It was a magical force that created you. Don't be angry with us.'

'I'm not.' Tanthe tried not to be shocked, but she was. Now the image of her human parents and her Aelyr parents entwined in passion would never go away.

'They left. Seven months later, you were born.'

Tanthe took a quick breath. 'But why did you agree to it?'

'Why not? They were beautiful, loving people and they were in desperate need. How could we not help them?'

'And Ymmi – and Feryn?'

'Just mine and your father's. We never saw Talthaliorn and Fiomir again. The mirror was so that they could some day speak to you and tell you what had happened. But when you said you'd lost it, I was glad. I thought it was better you didn't know.'

'Mum, I'm going to find them. I've got to.'

'Love, why?'

'Something's happening, with the Aelyr and the Bha—' she stopped herself, recalling Riverwynders' aversion to the word. 'Something huge. It's not just about me. It's about Aventuria.'

Aynie's image was breaking up, her voice becoming hard to hear. Tanthe was seeing stars with the effort of sustaining the *silvenroth* link. 'Tanthe, will you ever come home?'

'I hope so, Mum. I'm losing the image, I must go. Love to everyone.'

A sharp pain shot through her skull. She seemed to be thrown back into the real world, the mirror shrinking back into sharp focus and lying inert in her hands. Her reflection showed a forehead lined with concentration, red-rimmed eyes, face puffy with tears.

Tanthe slumped, rubbing her aching eyes. 'That was hard,' she said.

'Are you all right?' Ymmi asked, putting her fingers to her sister's cheek.

'Yes. Did you hear anything?'

Ysomir nodded. 'All of it.'

Tanthe cried again with a mixture of shock and relief. She and Ysomir held each other. 'It was so good to know Mum's all right.'

'It's made me homesick.'

'And me, but we can't go back yet.'

'We've both got a long way to go,' Ymmi said softly.

'So Auriel and Falthorn told me the truth, after all. I really am part of their family. But I'm part of Mum and Dad's too. I'm still your sister.'

'So are you human, or Aelyr?'

'I don't think I'll ever be Aelyr unless I break through to that part of myself. And I can't. It's too frightening.'

The warder tapped on the door. 'Visiting time is over,' she said.

'I must go,' Tanthe said quickly. On impulse she pressed the mirror into her sister's hand. 'I want you to keep this. They won't take it off you, will they?'

'No, they let me have personal possessions,' Ysomir said, startled. 'But why? You might need it.'

'Who knows? I can probably get another, where I'm going. But if you have it, and learn to use it, at least you can speak to Mum sometimes.'

Ysomir looked stunned, but accepted it. 'Thank you, Tan. I don't know what to say now.'

She smiled wanly. As always, it nearly broke Tanthe's heart to leave. It seemed so wrong that Ysomir should be locked up. But since she refused to appeal against Helananthe's decision, there was nothing Tanthe could do.

She embraced her sister. 'At least I know you'll be safe here,' she said.

'Go, quickly, or we'll be sobbing on each other all night,' Ysomir said, giving her a last hug. 'Goddess go with you, Tan.'

Chapter Ten. Quest and Revelation

The late summer sky brooded over Parione, heavy with thunder. Early sunlight washed the hillside mansions, the Temple of Nepheter and the Heliodor Tower with palest gold, so they stood luminous against the blue-black rage of the clouds.

The two parties were ready to leave. They were in a courtyard between the inner and outer walls of the Citadel, making last-minute checks on their horses, weapons and provisions, saying their farewells. Rufryd stood at Halcyon's head, impatient to be off so he didn't have to speak to Tanthe. What could he say to her, anyway? Half of him wanted to seize her and kiss her; the other half would gladly have left her with barely a backward sneer.

Helananthe was there with Lord Derione and the priestess Ariolne at her side, waiting sombrely to see them off. Eldareth's party would be the first to leave. Eldareth was already on his stocky, flaxen-tailed horse Gany, leaning down to exchange a few last words with the Queen. The affection between them was obvious, even though (so Rufryd had heard) they were no longer a couple. Rufryd pressed his lips together, wondering how they could both be so forgiving.

Lord Elrill and Jthery of Mithrain were also on horseback. Elrill's horse was pure white, Jthery's dappled grey, both like ghosts against the sandy gold walls of the courtyard. The horses and their cloaked riders looked magnificent. Rufryd felt an unexpected thrill of excitement, suddenly proud to be part of this. He glanced round for Tanthe, saw her on foot beside Redbird, saying goodbye to Saphaeyender.

The poet had his arms around her and they both seemed close to tears. Rufryd looked away in disgust. Then he changed his mind and went towards them, leading Halcyon. 'Why don't you go with her, if you're so devoted?' he said.

The two broke apart. He hated the superior way they looked at him. Saphaeyender gave a ghostly smile. 'I hardly think I'd be of any help to her. I'm unfit, I hate the rain, I'm not used to horses. And of course, we all know that I'm not the bravest person in the world.'

Confronted with the self-effacing honesty in the poet's eyes, Rufryd looked away. 'Well, good luck, Tan,' he muttered.

'Oh . . . thanks. And you.' She looked coolly at him, without rancour or warmth. She'd had her hair cut to collar-length and it suited her that way. She looked as lovable to him as she ever had, her dark hair falling around the blue-green jewels of her eyes. But she was distant, self-contained, as if she'd moved beyond her fury at him. She clearly wasn't going to give him another chance to hurt her.

Confronted with Tanthe's dignity, Rufryd felt ashamed of his outburst. He'd meant it at the time, all his reasons had been fierce and genuine . . . but looking back, he saw it as mere petulance, self-indulgence. Not that his hurts hadn't been real. Pain that even though she'd left Saphaeyender, she hadn't come back to him but found someone else, as if *anyone* was preferable to him. Outrage that she'd risked her life. Misery, knowing that even if he showed her the love and sympathy she wanted, she would only reject him again. Yes, pain . . . but hers had been worse. All he'd been was ungracious. Now, realising the genuine anguish she'd been in, he was on the verge of forgiving her. He just couldn't bring himself actually to say it.

'Are you all right?' was the best he could manage.

'Well, I know what I'm doing, and why. I hope you do, too.'

He shrugged. 'I've made my choice.'

'Yes, you have,' she said lightly. 'It's a shame we couldn't have stayed friends, but there it is.'

'Look, Tanthe . . .' His voice was gruff. He cleared his throat. 'I don't wish you any . . . I don't want . . . We might not see each other again.'

'It's all right,' she said. 'No hard feelings at all. Hope you find what you want.'

Without waiting for his response, she turned away and rose lightly on to Redbird's back. Rufryd dropped back, helpless. The mare arched her neck, chewing at the bit with an eager and somewhat comical expression, dripping white foam on to the flags. Saphaeyender gave Tanthe's hand a last touch, then slipped away through a gate in the inner wall.

'All set?' said Eldareth. 'Then we'll be away. Fare you all well and may we meet again before the fires of next Firethorn are lit!'

'The blessings of Nuth and Anuth be upon this party,' said Ariolne, drawing a circle on the air with her staff. The inner gates swung open, then the tall outer gates of filigree and jewels, and the first party was riding under the arch; Elrill and Jthery in the lead, Eldareth and Tanthe following.

They passed out of sight, but Rufryd stood gazing after them. He couldn't believe Tanthe had gone, that they might never meet again. Couldn't believe that, knowing it, she'd still been so cold. Not upset, not even furious at him. Just indifferent.

For a moment he considered galloping after them. Then Mirias slapped his shoulder and said, 'Come on. Looks like Aventuria called you in opposite directions this time.'

'No,' Rufryd said under his breath. 'Just sheer bloody-mindedness.' He checked his saddlebags were secure, and swung on to Halcyon's back.

The second party was bigger. In addition to Rufryd, Dawn and Mirias, Branq'elin and Mawrdreth had a retinue of eight Than'drathian riders who would go with them to the Hall of Duke Tasq. Their dun horses were impressive; muscular, athletic and showy, with thick necks, long straight heads and fine muzzles, a high-stepping gait. They were all different shades of gold, with dark dappling on their rumps, rippling black manes and tails, black shading on their legs. Halcyon was small and delicate in comparison, though Rufryd had no doubt he was at least their equal in stamina, and greater in speed.

Dawn and Mirias had stocky Paranian horses, like Eldareth's, dark chestnut with flaxen manes. Secured to her saddle, Dawn was carrying a basket containing four blue-doves, with which they would send messages back to Parione. Rufryd could hear the doves cooing softly, a fluid purr.

'Convey my greetings to your mother and father,' Helananthe was saying to the Than'drathian nobles. 'Our realms stand firm together. I thank you for your bravery in undertaking this journey on my behalf.'

'We do this as much for our parents' sake as for your majesty's,' Branq'elin said stiffly. 'In respect of all you have said, the friendship you have shown us and the undying bond between us, we pledge our loyalty. But still the question of Thanmandrathor's sovereignty will rise again.'

'And when it does, we shall discuss it again,' said Helananthe, laying a hand on Branq'elin's. 'Go swiftly, return safely.'

The party began to make their way towards the gates. Four riders of the retinue went in front and four at the rear, with Rufryd, Mirias and Dawn in the middle, just behind Branq'elin and her brother.

Again Ariolne said, 'The blessings of Nuth and Anuth be upon—'

As she spoke, three bright red piper-birds came tumbling over the walls, squawking loudly as they squabbled. Two swooped low over Mawrdreth's head, tumbled to the courtyard flags and rose again in a flurry of scarlet feathers. The third skimmed his horse's ears as it wheeled past, screeching. Spooked, the horse crouched on its hindquarters and reared.

Taken unawares, the young lord tumbled backwards out of the saddle. Rufryd heard the crack of bone as he fell. Halcyon shied. All around him, horses danced and riders cursed as they tried to bring the startled animals under control. Branq'elin leapt to the ground and knelt down at her brother's side.

'Mawrdreth? Oh gods, get a healer!'

His face was grey, his mouth a square of agony. When he tried to speak, all that came out was a hiss.

'Fetch the physicians!' Helananthe barked at Lord Derione. 'Have a stretcher brought at once!'

Derione rushed to obey. Ariolne was bending over Mawrdreth, running gentle hands over his body. The priestess seemed unmoved by his gasps of pain or by Branq'elin's distress. 'He has broken his left leg halfway down the thigh,' she said presently. 'Alas, Lord Mawrdreth, you are going nowhere now.'

'But I must!' he rasped. 'I can't let my sister go alone. Bind up this leg, give me milk of poppies!'

Ariolne shook her head patiently. 'It will take more than bandages and medicines to make you fit to travel. You will be spending at least the next six weeks in the palace. I am sure your sister can stay with you; but you cannot travel.'

He groaned. He appeared to lose consciousness, while Branq'elin knelt, anxiously squeezing his hands and calling to him until his eyes fluttered open again.

Rufryd, still in the saddle, watched the scene with a sense of doom. He wasn't superstitious but it seemed the most horrible omen, the blood-red pipers squalling over the wall, halting their expedition before it had even begun. He, Dawn and Mirias exchanged looks. They waited as brother and sister whispered to each other, while the palace physicians and stretcher-bearers appeared from the inner circles of the Citadel.

Presently Mirias said, 'Well, the three of us can still go alone, if it comes to it.'

'I'd rather, if anything,' said Rufryd. 'We'd travel faster.'

'It's up to the Queen, though,' said Dawn.

Mawrdreth's leg was splinted and his tall body eased on to the canvas. Spots of warm rain began to fall. Halcyon, never happy with rain, shook his head and snorted emphatically.

Lady Branq'elin leaned over the stretcher, kissing her brother. He was borne away but she remained in the courtyard, watching forlornly as he vanished through the gate of the inner wall. Then she and Helananthe turned and came towards Rufryd and his companions, with Derione following them.

Branq'elin's dark skin was drained, her eyes bruised, but she still looked very striking. Her face with its strong cheekbones was neat and powerful, her slanted eyes as green as her cloak. Rufryd had never looked at her so closely before, nor realised how attractive she was. Her rich brown hair hung forward over her shoulder, strands of it escaping from the loose plait. She pressed her gloved hands to Halcyon's neck as she spoke.

'My brother and I have decided that I must go back to Thanmandrathor – and thence, albeit against his wishes, to Vexor,' she said. She had a natural dignity, yet her manner was down-to-earth.

Rufryd was lost for words. 'But I thought your brother didn't want you to go without him, my lady.'

'He doesn't. But neither does he want me nursing him, when I have so much to do. I know he is in good hands here and I must make this journey.'

Rufryd leaned down towards her, curious. 'Why?'

Perhaps the question was over-familiar, but she held his gaze and answered simply, 'If the Bhahdradomen break out of Vexor, my country will be the first to suffer. Since the Queen is sending her people into danger, I cannot do

212

otherwise than go with you on Thanmandrathor's behalf.'

'Here is your horse, Lady Branq'elin,' Helananthe said, gentle and sombre. A stable-hand offered her the reins of the golden mare. 'Now go, my dear friends, before I have second thoughts about this journey. Nuth and Nepheter keep you. Your bravery shall not go unsung, nor unrewarded.'

Subdued, the second party moved off at last, out through the gates, into the streets of Parione where rain dampened the dust of summer, and a fork of jade lightning caressed the horizon.

Five days out of Parione, Tanthe was beginning to feel she had spent her whole life in the Serpentine Mountains. Their steep green sides were so familiar, the deep valleys strewn with huge grey boulders, the streams and the valleys folding away endlessly in silvery-blue mists. The Serpentines were imbued with both ecstasy and nightmare. She loved them passionately . . . and wondered for the twentieth time how she had brought herself to leave Saphaeyender again.

She felt calmer now they were on the move. She was glad of Eldareth's amiable company, for the other two were habitually quiet. Elrill was self-contained and saw no need to talk for the sake of it. He was a magnificent sight on his white horse Nefri, his hair a fall of ice against his silvery-blue cloak, his long pale Aelyr sword a twin to the one she carried.

Jthery was quiet too, but more through inexperience than aloofness. He was like a shadow of Elrill on his slender dapple-grey gelding, Heron. With his grey and amethyst garments and sunset hair, he was ethereal enough to be taken for an Aelyr, Tanthe thought. She could well believe he had risen from the mists of Mithrain's lakes to take the shape of a sprite who might well seduce an unsuspecting young woman into the water . . . Except that he'd caught a summer cold, and his coughing and sneezing rather spoiled the effect.

Eldareth and Tanthe wore plain travelling gear of black, rust and green, with changes of clothes in their saddlebags, towels, basic first aid kits and provisions to last three or four days. It felt familiar, like being on her first journey to rescue Ysomir. Sometimes she could almost feel Lynden and Rufryd riding alongside her, and it gave her a jolt to know that Rufryd was hundreds of miles away by now. That she might never see him again.

She bit her lip. She would have done anything to hug him, to say goodbye properly with kisses and tears . . . but he'd hurt her too badly this time. She couldn't have softened towards him even if she'd wanted to. The strange thing was that she'd risen above it, genuinely no longer cared what he thought of her. That was why she'd been able to say, 'No hard feelings', and mean it.

It had been different with Saphaeyender. He had always been so kind to her, endlessly patient with her hero-worship, her impertinence and her wayward behaviour. Unlike Rufryd, he'd never judged her. No, she'd judged herself.

The morning they had parted, she'd tried to explain to him that it was the fact she adored him that meant she had to leave. 'I don't want you to be different, because of me,' she'd said. 'I want you to be the Saphaeyender you would have been, if we'd never met. I don't know how to explain. It's as if someone gave me the most sublime painting in the world, and I added my own daubs to it . . . I'm not making any sense, am I?'

'No, I understand you,' he'd said tiredly. 'It's just that you're talking nonsense. It's not your fault I can't write. You haven't changed me; you're not that powerful, my love, but neither are you some kind of pollutant in a pure spring of water! Gods, if I have changed, it's because I needed to. Just a shame, isn't it, that I am old enough to be your father; that I want to get married and you want something else entirely?'

'You only think you want to marry because you're depressed,' she retorted.

'Well, that could be true, as well,' he sighed.

'And I'm not helping you. I just remind you of the battle and Lynden all the time. You will be better without me, Saph. And this quest isn't yours.'

It hadn't been a quarrel. They'd both spoken gently, embraced and wept. And he hadn't argued with her any more, because he knew she spoke the truth, and that made her sadder than ever.

Suddenly Tanthe felt piercingly lonely. She'd loved them all, Rufe and Saphaeyender and Auriel, and she'd lost them all.

She took a quick hard breath. Her self-pity never lasted long. This journey was all that mattered now.

Their first attempt to enter Verdanholm had already failed. They'd returned to the Seer's hut and tried to recreate Tanthe's entry into the other-realm through the well. It had taken persuasion and many gifts before the Seer even let them try; then, as Elrill had predicted, no portal had appeared.

Now they were making for Eisilion, first to try the temple where Eldareth had seen the Aelyr. Tanthe, though, was thinking of what Ysomir had said to her.

'Eld,' she said, trotting Redbird alongside Gany, 'I think we could be wasting time going to Eisilion.'

'Really? How d'you make that out?'

'I think we should go straight to Torith Mir.'

Eldareth stared at her, looking uncharacteristically angry. 'Do you, Tan? Why?'

'I know you'll think it's ridiculous, but it was something Ysomir said. Sometimes she . . . she seems to channel other people's thoughts or knowledge.' Her voice fell, though she suspected Elrill and Jthery – riding ahead – could still hear her. 'People who are dead.'

He frowned. 'That's quite a claim. Do you think it's true?'

'Yes,' said Tanthe. 'Thing is, Ymmi's never made things up. She's always been transparent – so transparent she can't even protect herself very well – and completely honest. And I've seen her do it. She said it came from Garnelys. The best place to find a portal to Verdanholm is in Torith Mir.'

Eldareth was silent for a while. Then he set his teeth, and shook his head vigorously. 'We won't have to travel as far as Torith Mir. We will find a portal in Eisilion!'

'I'm sorry,' said Tanthe, startled. 'I just thought I should tell you what she said.'

'I hate to say this, Eldareth,' Elrill added, turning in the saddle, 'but she is probably right. There were more portals in Torith Mir, and more frequently used. Their *roth*-energy is more likely to be active and accessible.'

Eldareth said nothing, but his expression would have cracked stone.

'What's wrong?' said Tanthe.

'It's simple,' said Eldareth. 'We're not going to Torith Mir. I *cannot* go to Torith Mir.'

Helananthe rode for half a day west of Parione, along the Meiondras Road and into the Hethlas hills where, a bare few moons ago, her army had defeated that of Garnelys. Purple clouds rolled over Hethlas Rim, edged with gold. How strange to pass the site of battle, to see the hillsides lying silent and drenched in summer rain.

She pulled the hood of her cloak deep over her face. With her rode Derione and Serpeth, and a retinue of armed riders in their uniforms of green and violet. Perhaps she would have the various uniforms changed, when time allowed, to distance her own administration from that of her grandfather's. For she felt that the people of Aventuria no longer trusted the monarchy as they once had, with unquestioning love. Garnelys had destroyed their innocence.

It was a shame no one liked Lord Serpeth, she thought.

He was clever and indefatigable, and the fact that he'd changed sides in battle showed shrewd judgement as much as opportunism . . . she was as certain as she could be of his loyalty. But what sort of king would he make? She grimaced. She must make a decision soon, but every day it seemed easier to put it off until tomorrow.

The rain was easing off as they came to the meeting place on the Meiondras Road. A long, flat valley curved back into the hills. Moving along it came a mass of figures; strange hunched beings cloaked in dull browns and whites and lichen-greens. For a moment she thought of toadstools, of strange woodland growths that had torn themselves from the wild-wood and come crawling to life.

The royal party reined in. Helananthe's stomach kicked in apprehension. Ridiculous to be afraid, nothing to fear . . . Serpeth cleared his throat and said quietly, 'Your majesty, I think it was inadvisable for you to come. Derione and I could have handled this matter alone.'

'Come on, Serpeth, you know me. I can't bear to miss anything,' she said, grinning. 'They don't have to know who I am. As far as they're concerned, I'm Lady Vyne, the Queen's representative.'

With the straggling mass of figures came cattle, the like of which she'd never seen before. It was the cattle, more than anything, that seized her attention. Ghastly-looking things, thickset and bloated, with fungus-white skin and staring eyes. She felt dizzy suddenly, shook it off.

'Gods,' Derione said suddenly. 'Ma'am, we should retreat.'

'Why?' She saw how pale he was.

'If we stay here, they'll be all around us in a few minutes!'

She imagined it; the gnomish figures and their ugly cattle flowing around her and her guards, surrounding them, trapping them . . . She felt a touch of Derione's panic but suppressed it.

'Hold your ground,' she said firmly. 'Nepheter's braids, Derione, if you panic at the sight of a few cattle-herders, what would you be like in a battle like the Silver Plains?'

At once she regretted her sharp words, for Derione looked horrorstruck. She wondered if it would be better to ride up the hillside, get above them. But when the first of the herders came within ten yards of her, they stopped, and the whole ragged mass shambled to a halt. Many pairs of eyes stared at her from beneath cowls or scarves. Some of the eyes were the green of stagnant ponds, others ochre or black or blood-pink. Their skin was pallid, tinged with pale brown or green like the bark of trees. They were silent.

As they halted, their cattle began to graze the hillside, tearing out grass by the roots and leaving raw earth; patches of darkness that spread and joined rapidly even as Helananthe watched.

'I am Lady Vyne, representative of her majesty Queen Helananthe,' she called out. 'Who is your spokesman?'

One of the Bhahdradomen came forward. Superficially there was nothing to distinguish him from the rest, but as she saw him more closely she saw that he had eyes black as berries with green sparks in the centre, cheeks so hollow that the shadows were like brushstrokes beneath his cheekbones. The rest waited, downcast and watchful.

Helananthe dismounted. Serpeth and Derione did the same, and stood on either side of her; behind her, she heard the soft sounds of her guards placing their hands on their sword-hilts. But these people seemed passive, as if they were sunk in starvation. They certainly had no weapons visible.

'I am Tzumezht,' said the spokesman. Was it a man? She'd heard that the Bhahdradomen were neither male nor female, or both. For the sake of simplicity, she decided to think of the speaker as 'he'.

His voice went right through her, and seemed to buzz in the centre of her skull. She breathed the smell that wreathed like steam from the group, a smell of sour earth, of dead wood split open by fungi.

'Greetings to you, Tzumezht,' she said, inclining her head in wary courtesy. He echoed the gesture. He was shorter than her, perhaps five foot six, and he had less a presence than an *absence* that made her feel disoriented, as if she had accidentally touched a deadly poison to her tongue and could only stand aghast, waiting for it to work.

Again she pushed the feeling away. She went on, 'It was reported to us that groups of Bhahdradomen were on the move across the Whiteveil Mountains, making for Paranios. When you were challenged, your response was that you would explain yourselves only to the highest authority in Aventuria. Well, we are here. I must tell you that we, too, are more than eager to hear your explanation.'

'Madam, we are utterly at your mercy.' Tzumezht opened long, spidery hands. 'We have been driven from our homes by humans and by hunger.'

'Your home, strictly speaking, is Vexor.'

'Untrue,' he replied. 'These people have never lived in Vexor. If you are close to the Queen, then you must know that we are here legally. We were allowed to stay in Aventuria, as part of the peace treaty after our . . . our surrender.'

'I do know that,' Helananthe answered, trying to remain impartial although she was privately amazed her ancestors had agreed to this deal. 'However, it was part of the agreement that the Bhahdradomen remain in strictly defined areas, and never stray beyond those boundaries.'

'And we have abided by those conditions for over two hundred and fifty years,' said Tzumezht, softly reasonable. 'We have lived in peace, silent, invisible, masquerading as peasants in remote places such as Ardharkria, Sarmest, Imnion. But those areas are exhausted; there is nothing left for our flesh-animals to eat. We were forced to go beyond our boundaries or die. Our numbers have increased, humans have become aware of us. When we have tried to find new territories they have driven us away. So now we wander, homeless.'

'Tzumezht, good sir.' Helananthe clasped her elbows, took a breath. 'Have you no concept of land management? Grass grows again. There was no reason for your – your flesh-animals to go hungry.'

Tzumezht simply looked at her. An involuntary shudder went through her from head to foot. She remembered Tanthe and Rufryd's story of the forest of Ardharkria; how the Bhahdradomen colony there had stripped their territory bare, stripping even the bark from the trees, sucking the sap, sucking all life out of the soil until not even fungus would grow. She saw the hillside turning from green to black under the cattle's attention even as she watched. They consumed, and moved on.

'No reason for them to go hungry, indeed,' he said at last, 'if we were allowed enough room.'

'You were given enough room. Now you have broken two tenets of the treaty at least; you've gone beyond your allocated boundaries, and you have allowed your populations to increase – both of yourselves and of your animals.'

'After two hundred years and more, this was inevitable.'

'Not necessarily.'

'The clauses by which we have been forced to exist were completely unreasonable! We protest.'

'Your protest is noted,' Helananthe said carefully. 'I must remind you, however, that you were free, in the aftermath of the War, to join your countrymen in Vexor. That you are still free to do so.'

Tzumezht radiated anger, but it was a helpless, passive rage. 'Such a thing would have been utterly impractical. How could we have crossed thousands of miles of hostile territory? We were trapped in our pockets of land, and there we remained. It must seem very far in the past to you, my lady, for humans rarely live past one hundred and ten years. For us, though, our exile was a living memory of our hosts and grand-hosts. We have suffered dreadful indignities.'

220

Helananthe sensed Serpeth at her elbow, willing her to give these people no quarter. He was beginning to annoy her. She wished with all her heart that Eldareth was there instead; Eldareth had always trusted her instincts. He hadn't kept telling her what to say and do.

'Yet you were allowed to live, despite the fact that the Bhahdradomen were the aggressors in that War. Tzumezht, I appreciate your difficulty, but you cannot stay here. Nor can you wander at will across Aventuria.'

Serpeth put in, 'The Queen may view it as an act of aggression if you persist.'

Tzumezht turned his face up to her, his cheeks lined with pain, his eyes imploring, his mouth showing long yellow teeth. 'Then tell us what we are to do! We are not fell warriors under a dread and glorious leader such as Ghaurthror of the Flies. We are peasants. Look at us; we have nothing, we are less than peasants in a hostile land! Sirs, madam, we throw ourselves utterly on your mercy. We are refugees!'

Helananthe, Serpeth and Derione all looked at each other. The mass of Bhahdradomen looked pitiful indeed. On a visceral level, something about them repulsed her, and perhaps they felt the same about humans; but on a rational level, they offered no threat. Helananthe hated being cruel. If they begged for mercy, what could she do but help them?

She and her companions withdrew and talked softly for a few minutes. Then Helananthe went back to Tzumezht.

'Tell me the truth,' she said. 'Have you had recent contact with anyone from Vexor? Has something happened to cause this exodus?'

Tzumezht shook his head, a slow, insectile swaying motion. 'Those of us who remained in Aventuria were severed from all contact with the exiles, as well you must know.'

'No messages from Vexor? Are you sure?'

'I have told you our reasons for moving.'

'H'm. Well, since you have begged for refuge, and you are the crown's responsibility, we have no choice but to grant it. I will arrange a holding area for you, well away from human habitation, on certain conditions.'

'We shall do our utmost to fulfil them, my lady.'

'These flesh-animals of yours,' she said. 'Are they all you can eat?'

Filmy eyelids flicked over his wet black eyes. 'No, my lady. We can eat certain fruits and grains, and some of your fish, although it disagrees with us. The *graukhim* are what we prefer to eat, for the benefit of our health and that of our hatchlings.'

A less healthy bunch she had never seen, Helananthe noted. She swallowed hard. 'When you slaughter one, can you salt or preserve the flesh in some way?'

Tzumezht hesitated. The Bhahdradomen behind him stirred and murmured. 'We can, but . . .'

'Good, because you will have to do without them from now on.'

A resonance of shock came from them. Tiny pulses of anger rained on her from their sullen, luminescent eyes and the stench of sour earth nearly choked her. She went on, 'Your *graukhim* are the problem. They don't merely graze the grass and foliage, they kill it. They make whole tracts of land sterile, unusable. This can't be allowed to continue.'

Tzumezht looked distraught, as far as she could read his alien emotions. 'My lady. I beg you. They are our staple diet. Without them, our existence, our culture will not be the same.'

'That's unfortunate, but you give us no choice. You've failed to keep your herds within the prescribed areas. Your herd must all be slaughtered. The preserved meat will last you some time; after that, we will provide your food.'

'No.' Tzumezht shook his head stubbornly. 'This is unacceptable!'

222

Helananthe turned away, and signalled to her soldiers. Pallid and sour-mouthed, they set bolts to their crossbows and rode forwards.

The *graukhim* died hard, bellowing and raging. Only a shot through the eye, direct into the brain, could still them. One charged a young soldier, gouging its horn into her side before her comrades could slay the beast. As they helped the wounded woman away, Helananthe's heart was in her mouth and she prayed to all the gods and goddesses that her injury was not fatal.

The massacre was far from quick and clean. The stench that rose from the animals' torn guts was abominable and their screams sounded almost human. Helananthe looked away, shuddering.

At last it was over. The last of the flesh-animals fell heavily on to its flank and lay motionless, its body steaming. The Bhahdradomen were like statues.

Trying to steady herself, Helananthe turned to the spokesman again. 'I want you to move north and east of here. Beyond that chain of hills—' she pointed, and all the refugees turned to look – 'there is a good wide valley with fresh streams, the Danen Valley. That will be your holding area for the time being. If any more of your people come from different areas, they can live there too; but if they bring *graukhim* with them, save yourselves another visit from the army and slaughter them. If you need help salting and storing the meat, you have only to let us know. You can keep ordinary cows and sheep, anything but those – anything but *graukhim*.'

For a horrible moment she thought the Bhahdradomen were going to do something unexpected; rush her party, unfurl weapons from nowhere, change shape into something dark and ravening. She felt a flash of vile emotion from them, bitter-black hatred. But the feeling vaporised. They were already turning and moving away as she had directed, downcast and passive.

'We thank you, my lady,' said Tzumezht, with a deep

bow. 'My people thank you deeply for your mercy and munificence.'

As soon as the royal party dwindled into the distance, one of the quiet Bhahdradomen peasants stepped to Tzumezht's side. He put back his hood, revealing a bald skull on which veins snaked and throbbed inside the translucent flesh.

'That was no Lady Vyne,' he said. 'That was the Queen herself.'

'I know, Enabler. I know.' In the background, the mass of Bhahdradomen was trudging away, leaving the two alone.

Enabler Gulzhur touched his companion's arm. 'You did well, Tzumezht.'

Tzumezht spat yellow venom on to the grass. 'She has committed an act of outrageous brutality against these wretched *domenim*! This will not be forgotten. I could forget my instructions and pursue her now—'

Gulzhur gripped his thin arm. 'But you will not, because like me you are well trained in patience. Don't let the humans make you angry. Just add it to the reckoning. You handled her well.'

'Did I? I felt that she must see straight through me.'

'No. All she saw was a wretched refugee like the rest.'

Tzumezht, the watchful clear-sighted one, chewed at the grey flesh of his lower lip. 'Vaurgroth has sent us and others like us to lead our poor countrymen out of their incarceration and back into the light. It pains me to enact this charade, to stand passively by while she destroys our flesh-animals. Even more it pains me to see how downtrodden our own *domenim* are, that they lack even the will to protest!'

Gulzhur sighed. 'But that's why we're here. They are only *domenim*, they are helpless without adepts like ourselves to save them. Have they hatchlings among them, still young enough to imprint?'

'A few.'

'Then *graukhim* can be made again. Anything can be made.'

Tzumezht gave a long, soft groan. 'This has been a bad day.'

'No, this has been a good day. At some cost, we have what we want; a legitimate hold only half a day from Parione itself. And Zhoaah is already at work in the city. He has a safe house there, and a palace official in his pocket.'

'Surely I don't have to caution you, Enabler, against over-confidence.'

Gulzhur chuckled. 'It's called optimism, my dear friend. Come, let us tell Vaurgroth what has transpired today.' From a pocket in the dappled green-brown fabric of his robe he drew a lump of oily grey stone, a haematite that would help channel their astral forms into the higher dimension, the *ezht*. Gulzhur rubbed the shiny surface with his sleeve, then paused. He grinned, and touched his companion on the shoulder with his spiny fingers. 'You know, you are well-titled, Tzumezht, Prefigurer; a harbinger of what is to come.'

Returning to the palace late at night and exhausted, Helananthe found herself too tired and preoccupied to sleep. She'd had enough of Serpeth's sharp wit and endless advice, even of Derione's patient good sense. At least with Dawn and Mirias she could have unwound, had a drink and been herself – the self she used to be before responsibility descended on her like a gem-heavy robe. But they were far away, facing Goddess-knew-what dangers on her behalf.

Instead she found herself drifting towards the royal guest quarters. Light was still glowing under Mawrdreth's door.

She knocked gently. Heard him call, 'Come in,' and entered to find him lying on top of his luxurious canopied

225

bed, the thick cast of his leg making an odd cylindrical shape beneath his robe, his naked toes poking comically from below the hem.

'Lord Mawrdreth?' she said. 'Excuse me, I have had a very long day and I came to see how you are before I retire. I hope I'm not disturbing you.'

'Of course not, your majesty.' He put the book aside. A standard history of the Nine Realms with a jewelled cover. The lamp beside his bed flooded his deep brown hair with gleams of gold; his green eyes were startlingly clear, limpid as springs, so different to the muddied eyes of the Bhahdradomen.

'How's the leg?' she asked, sitting in a chair beside him.

'Healing well, they tell me. The pain is less. I hope I shall not impose on you for long, ma'am.'

'You are no imposition, sir, believe me. Can I talk to you as a friend?'

He looked startled. 'My sister and I came here hardly as friends. That is, our countries are friends, of course, but . . .'

'Please. I don't want to talk politics. I simply want to have a good moan about the dreadful day I've had and here; I've brought whisky, the very best, from the Serpent Isles no less, to ease the process along for both of us.'

His mouth twitched in a quick, uncertain smile. 'I'm sorry, ma'am. If we might set aside who we are for now, then I would be more than happy to talk and share a drink with you.'

'Call me Helan. For tonight, at least. I'll pour.'

Since Mawrdreth had been a guest in the palace, she had visited him every day. Up to now they had been slightly awkward, diplomatic meetings, as she had to be the face of Aventuria maintaining kind but firm authority over Thanmandrathor. The more she saw of Mawrdreth, the more she was beginning to like him. Under his reserved exterior she glimpsed an intelligent and thoughtful young man.

226

'One of the monarchy's most shameful secrets,' she said, splashing whisky into tumblers and handing one to him. 'Bhahdradomen allowed to remain on the mainland, because it was too problematic to move them, and their leadership made it a term of their surrender.'

Mawrdreth showed no surprise. 'One of their worst-kept secrets. It's long been suspected there are nests of them still in Thanmandrathor, though they are never seen.'

'Well, they're visible now. Pouring into Paranios, insisting they've been forced to leave their territories and begging me for refuge.'

Two neat lines indented his high, smooth brow. 'Do you think they are dangerous?'

Helananthe sighed and took a mouthful of whisky, a sunburst in her throat. 'Hardly, from the look of them.' She told him everything that had happened; Mawrdreth listened calmly and his responses were measured.

Helananthe was impressed; at least he wasn't one of those who panicked at very mention of the Eaters' name. 'To be honest,' she said at length, 'I felt sorry for them. They aren't warriors; they have nothing, not even a homeland. How must it feel, to have even your own animals slaughtered and be forced to eat your enemies' food instead?'

'Don't show them too much sympathy,' said Mawrdreth. 'Remember how they savaged Aventuria in the past!'

'Oh, I have not forgotten my history. But these refugees were not responsible for the crimes of their elite, several hundred years ago. And it's not their fault that their way of life is utterly inimical to ours. Oh, my first concern is Aventuria's welfare; it's only that they looked so pathetic . . .'

'You're strong, Helan,' he said quietly, 'yet you have a kind heart.'

Shaking her head, Helananthe poured more whisky and

began to enjoy its glow. She and Mawrdreth talked and talked, but when there was a lull in the conversation it was not uncomfortable. He was very handsome, she observed, although that meant nothing to her; they were not the kind of looks that particularly appealed to her and she had no feelings for him, and yet . . . the idea that now unfurled in her head and stood there fully formed was so simple, so obvious, that she felt it must have been ordained from the beginning.

'You don't have to love me,' she said, drunk but still clear-minded.

His beautifully slanting eyes opened wide. 'I beg your pardon?'

'You don't even have to find me attractive, although it would help.'

'What . . . why?'

The expression on his face made her want to laugh. 'I need a king, Mawrdreth. Not because I can't manage without one, but because I would like heirs some day, and this marriage could be so very useful, politically speaking.'

'I thought we weren't talking politics,' he gasped.

'You look dumbstruck. I hope it's with excitement rather than horror.'

Mawrdreth took a gulp of his drink, went on staring at her. 'You're not asking me to—?'

'To be my husband? Yes, I am. Your argument about Thanmandrathor wishing to govern herself would then become redundant, wouldn't it? For you would be King of your own country, my dear. You would be King of Aventuria.'

Chapter Eleven. Gem Harthnir

The leaves were turning colour, a light autumn drizzle making the air sparkle around Tanthe and Eldareth's party as they sat despondent under the edge of the trees. The dark, gnarled branches of hard-oaks leaned over the bubbling spring beside which they'd made camp. Beyond their refuge, sharp hills with high, narrow valleys stood against the dusk.

The weather was turning colder the further north they travelled. Tanthe missed Parione's melting warmth. Still, she liked Eisilion, with its heathery hills and patchwork landscapes. It reminded her a little of Sepheret. The people, though, she was less sure of. At the village inns where they'd stayed, they had been friendly enough – until they'd seen Elrill. Then their fear and hostility towards the Aelyr lord had shocked her. Although, after her experience with Falthorn, she began to think that Eisilians might have some justification for their feelings.

Elrill had been unmoved and polite, generally managing to mollify the situation so that they were not deprived of food and rest. He was the one who'd told Tanthe that, in ancient times, the Eisilians had worshipped the Aelyr as gods. But the Aelyr, philosophically advanced and disdainful of human worship, had descended furiously to destroy the temples. Unfortunately, their action had not had the desired effect. Instead of making them see the folly of worship, it had only caused the Eisilians to regard the Aelyr as demonic.

Now, in a long trail across Eisilion, Eldareth and Elrill had tried to find the sites of those ancient *rothanamir* portals and create an opening to Verdanholm. After their first failure at the Seer's hut, they'd gone to the ruined temple where Eldareth had seen Aelyr using a portal. All four of them, trying to channel every mote of their will and energy through Elrill's *anametris* stone, had failed to stir even a ripple in the veil between worlds.

'When they passed through they must have sealed it well,' Elrill said at last when they gave up in exhaustion. The altar-stone lay cold and impenetrable under Tanthe's hands and she was half relieved, half dismayed. 'Every portal is different and in some the *roth* is deeply unreactive. It will only awaken in the response to the very specific vibration of the Aelyr who created it.'

'What do we do now?' Tanthe had asked, suddenly uneasy in the vine-wreathed silence of the ruin.

'We go on, and try to find the next site. But I fear that all the *rothanamir* in Eisilion may be as well-sealed as this, precisely because of the ill-feeling between human and Aelyr in this realm.'

So they had travelled on, zig-zagging northwards in search of places where energy lingered. Ruined temples where nothing remained but their overgrown foundations; strange stone circles that reminded Tanthe of Verdanholm; springs and wells where elementals were reputed to live. But no door would open to them.

Now their travels had brought them to this valley in the Emment Hills, twenty miles from the border of Torith Mir and twenty miles from the sea. Tanthe had never seen the sea, but imagined she could hear the waves crashing if she listened hard enough.

'I hate to say it, Eld,' Elrill began, 'but it is looking more every day as if Tanthe was right. We shall have to go into Torith Mir.'

Eldareth was sitting on a rock, his hands dangling between his long legs. He expelled a grim breath. 'It's not a good idea. Not for me, at least.'

'My friend, since you will furnish no explanation for your reluctance, what are we to do? The *rothanamir* in that land were always more numerous and freely used. We might almost step through one by mistake, without needing the *anametris* to open it. It's the only way, unless you're planning to wander about in Aventuria for ever more.'

'Then perhaps you should go without me.'

'Eldareth!' said Tanthe. 'This isn't like you. I thought you'd been everywhere and done everything and nothing frightens you—'

'Well, my heroic status seems to be slipping in all directions, doesn't it?'

'But why? I know you're a man of mystery and all that, but we are your friends. What's the problem with Torith Mir? Let me think; that General Grannen came from there, didn't he, and you killed him in battle. Are you afraid his family will come after you?'

'Tanthe, shut up.' Eldareth spoke quietly but his voice was dangerous. 'You have no idea what you're talking about.' He rose to his feet and strode away into the trees, his face lined with anger.

Tanthe stared after him. 'Eldareth!'

'Leave him be,' said Elrill, rising from the grass and going to groom Nefri – to avoid talking to her, she thought. 'Whatever his reasons, he has not told me. But I'm sure they are good ones.'

Annoyed, Tanthe went to the edge of the pool, where Jthery was filling their leather flasks with water. He did this slowly, his slim form folded in a crouch and his pale apricot hair floating down to the surface. He tended to avoid arguments. His graceful quality reminded her of the Aelyr, and once she might have been attracted to him. Since Auriel, though, she'd brought down firm barriers to protect her life from becoming any more complicated.

'How's your cold?' she said.

'Better, thanks. Glad it wasn't bad enough to stop me coming with you.'

'And why are you with us?' she asked brusquely. 'You never say anything.'

Jthery pushed his hair behind his ears, and looked sideways at her.

'All sorts of reasons.'

His face was a long oval, his features slender but with a masculine firmness to them. His eyes were violet, their colour all the more startling against the soft hues of his clothes. She began to realise he was not merely shy but introspective, even troubled.

'Don't you start being cryptic too. I've had enough from Eldareth. You're Helan's cousin from Mithrain – that's about as much as I know about you.'

He smiled. 'It's worse than that. I'm heir to the Dukedom.'

'I didn't realise.'

'Don't worry about it. I shall be ninety-seven before I ever take the seat.'

'Your family let you come on this mad journey, though.'

'They had no choice. I simply left. Something called me, if you like. You may not realise it, but Helananthe has more Mithrainian than Paranian blood. Her grandmother Mabriahna was my great-aunt. She was a magnificent woman, a great queen. But she died of a broken heart, caused by Garnelys. I'd like to know what lies behind it all.'

Tanthe sat down on the damp grass, wrapping her arms round her knees. The air smelled of rain and compost, with a trace of woodsmoke from some distant dwelling. 'Are you looking in the right place?'

'The water?' He sat back on his heels. Was he being sardonic? He was so straight-faced it was hard to tell.

'No, I meant in Verdanholm. You might have got more answers about Garnelys by going with Rufryd's party. Or even by talking to my sister.'

'It's not that simple,' he said. 'Helan's mother Ghiseyma is another of our cousins. I love her too. I want to find her. And there's something that I feel I'm looking for. I don't know what it is yet.' He touched the carved amethyst fish

232

he wore round his neck. 'I had a sort of message . . . you wouldn't believe me.'

'I might. I've travelled through Mithrain.'

His eyes widened, as if he didn't quite believe her. 'You have?'

'Well, of course. It's right between Deirland and Paranios, I could hardly avoid it, could I? Sorry, I don't mean to be sarcastic. I'm just in one of those moods. Anyway, I love Mithrain. My companions thought it was scary, but I didn't. The silver lakes and the way the mists rolled up and turned everything a beautiful lavender colour. I think I saw the water elementals. They might have been just shapes in the mist, of course, but since when does mist have eyes?'

Jthery was staring at her with a mixture of amazement and pleasure. 'You have seen them! You're making me homesick.'

'According to Eldareth, you either love Mithrain or hate it. Perhaps there are spirits in the water who drag unsuspecting young men and women to their deaths, but I'm sure it would be a delicious way to go.'

Jthery laughed. 'Stories.'

'Don't take the romance out of it.'

'Oh, it's not romantic, Tanthe. The elementals are real, and they can be dangerous . . . but only to those who anger them. You see, they—'

He stopped, dipping his fingers into the pool. Tanthe said, 'You know when you thought I was asking you if you were looking for answers in the water? You weren't joking, were you?'

'No, I wasn't.'

'What did you mean?'

'Do you always ask so many questions?'

'I do now,' she said fiercely. 'Keep on asking one question after another, until people stop offering me crap and finally come out with the truth.'

Jthery seemed startled by her forthright attitude.

Perhaps he was more used to people like Eldareth and Elrill, who kept their secrets and politely did not probe into other people's. 'Understand, Tanthe, that I was born among the lakes of Mithrain and what I do is not that rare in my realm. I've always had an affinity with water. An undine appeared to me and warned me . . .' He paused.

'What?'

'Water runs over stone and earth. When the *roth* of one form of crystal is disturbed, all others are disturbed in the same way, and the water-*roths* pick it up and transmit it to those of us who can hear. There's a terrible disturbance building in the earth. Garnelys was only the first sign, and Mabriahna only one of the first victims.'

'What sort of disturbance?'

'Huge quantities of *gauroth* energy on the move.'

'Meaning what?'

'Either that someone, somewhere, is gathering great and destructive energies to themselves, or that some terrible force of nature is about to erupt.'

'Can you tell?'

'It's not easy.' He lifted a handful of water to his mouth and sipped it with intense concentration, as if it was giving him far more than its taste or coldness. He shook his head. 'I believe the undine who appeared to me was Eshte herself.'

'Your goddess?'

'You don't believe me.'

'No, I've seen too many strange things myself to disbelieve you. Never seen a goddess, mind, but that doesn't mean you haven't.'

'Thanks.' He looked pleased. 'I've told hardly anyone. It's a relief to talk to you. I can feel the distress of the elementals; that's real. It must be the Bhahdradomen causing this trouble, mustn't it? For the Aelyr never touch *gauroth* energy, and yet . . .'

'I wouldn't put anything past Falthorn,' said Tanthe, shivering. Jthery might be a bit strange, but she liked him.

He was trustworthy, she sensed, a little like Lynden but without Lynden's impetuous naivety.

'Eshte told me to go and seek something,' he said. 'To follow my instinct, but to be careful, because I would be acting for her in everything I did. I don't know what I'm looking for yet, but I'll know it when I find it.'

'How exciting,' said Tanthe. 'I rather envy you.'

She heard movement, Elrill's voice. Looking round, she saw that Eldareth had come back, and was standing with his hands braced on his hips and a familiar, grave expression on his face, a mixture of resignation and self-mockery.

'You're right, I can't let age-old wounds prevent me travelling wherever the need takes me. Very well, against my better judgement – we'll go to Torith Mir.'

Torith Mir. The name gave Tanthe a frisson of excitement; all she had heard and read of it described a wild country populated by a proud, aggressive people who had only been brought to heel by the need to unite against the Bhahdradomen. Garnelys had appointed the general of his army from Torith Mir, and the vicious self-seeking Grannen had been far more deeply hated than Garnelys, blamed for all the acts of which people could not believe Garnelys was capable.

They gathered amid a stand of trees on a hillside, looking down a long stony valley at a great wall of stone, topped with wooden stakes. The horses shifted and pawed at the ground. A mist of drizzle fell, but Tanthe was growing hardened to the discomforts of being constantly damp and tired.

'There it is,' said Eldareth. 'The border of Torith Mir.'

An astonished breath shot out of her. 'You mean there's a wall round it?'

'Most of the way round, yes.'

'So we can't just walk in?'

'Alas, no.' Eldareth's tone was weary. 'The Torish have

235

always made a fuss about protecting their borders, despite the fact that they were historically the aggressors in most disputes.'

'I suppose we might be able to climb it, but we'd never get the horses over.'

'Indeed, but you can't see the moats and ditches from here, nor the unpleasant creatures that live in them.'

Tanthe was indignant. 'They've got no right to do this. The Nine Realms are meant to be united as friends! Who do they think they are?'

'Tanthe, getting angry will not make the wall go away.'

'But how does anyone get in or out?'

'There are gates, of course. The main gate is a massive one, about thirty miles west of here. They were allowed to keep their wall but not to restrict access to their realm, nor to keep an army – in theory. In practice, they get round it by pretending the army are civilian officers of law. And while they don't actually stop anyone entering Torith Mir, those who do are thoroughly questioned. They'll want to know all our business.'

'There must be some way through,' said Jthery. 'A place where the wall has broken down, or where there is a river, or the coast itself . . .'

'I've been thinking about that,' said Eldareth. 'There is such a place, where the wall had collapsed and not been repaired. It's a short way east of here; the trick is to reach it without any Torish guards seeing us.'

He turned Gany and began to ride off, but Tanthe said, 'Hang on. We haven't done anything wrong. We're travelling with the authority of the Queen and we have her seal to prove it. They'll just let us through, won't they?'

'They may let you three through. But what will happen if they recognise me . . .'

'Why?' she said. Eldareth didn't answer. 'You don't seem to think much of them. I thought your father was from Torith Mir.'

'He was. That doesn't mean I have to like them, does it?'
Eldareth urged Gany into a canter and the others followed.
They swung lightly over the hillsides, riding parallel to the
wall but keeping out of direct sight of it. Tanthe's heart
was pounding. So far this journey had consisted of one
frustration after another.

Presently they entered a stony valley that brought them
the closest they'd been to the wall. It towered above them
in forbidding blocks of granite, far bigger than it had
seemed from a distance. A moat ran along its base, filled
with sluggish green water. The landscape was bleak and
deserted, with no sign of habitation nearby. Tanthe
glimpsed what appeared to be a gap in the wall – but it
wasn't empty. It had been bridged by a huge gate, with
wooden watchtowers on either side.

Eldareth groaned. 'Damnation. They've made a new
guard post there.'

'Easier than rebuilding it,' Elrill sighed.

They reined in, gazing at the bright new wood of the
watchtowers and the handful of guards who stood about
on either side, looking bored. Their uniform was black and
grey, their colouring like Eldareth's; fair skin and black
hair. Men and women alike had a tough, grim demeanour,
like the hated Grannen, yet they also had a certain proud
grace, like Eldareth.

'We'd best move on, and try to cross at the coast,' said
Eldareth.

'Alas, I fear they have seen us,' Elrill said matter-of-
factly. Tanthe saw the glint of spy-glasses. The border
guards were blatantly staring in their direction. 'What will
you do, Eldareth? Stay here while we three go on without
you?'

'No, of course not.'

'How great is the chance that they will recognise you?
Call yourself by a false name, and they'll be none the
wiser.'

Tanthe put in, 'Elrill will scare them to death, anyway,'

only to receive a disdainful look from the Shaelahyr lord.

'The risk must be taken,' Eldareth said under his breath, urging Gany into a trot towards the gap. He laughed. 'I'll tell them I'm Serpeth.' As they came down on to the gravel area that lay before the gates, the stench of stagnant water rose to meet them and three dra'a'ks soared high over the wall, black and straight as spears.

A stockily-built guard stepped out to meet them. 'Good morning and blessings on you. What brings you to Torith Mir?' he said, unexpectedly friendly. He pronounced it, 'Torit' Mirr', rolling the R.

'We're travelling on Queen Helananthe's business,' said Tanthe, smiling back. 'Look, we have her seal to prove it.' She showed the guard the big disk of emerald rimmed in gold, rather like an oversized rald coin with an image of the Amber Citadel, attached to her belt with an ornate gold ribbon. They each had one.

The guard pursed his lips and whistled. 'What business is that?'

'Now, come on,' Tanthe said, leaning down and blatantly flirting with him. 'It was worth a try but you know we can't tell you.'

A smile tugged at the guard's mouth. His eyes moved over her companions; Elrill's pale radiance, Jthery's stillness, Eldareth's rough but powerful presence. He looked awed, clearly aware that these were not ordinary travellers. 'All right, but you have to tell me your names.'

'Tanthe Aynie-daughter of Sepheret. This is Lord Jthery of Mithrain, Lord Elrill of the Shaelahyr, and, er, Lord Serpeth of Eisilion.'

'That's fine, Lady Tanthe. As representatives of the Queen you may pass freely over our borders. It's an honour for us.' He waved a signal, and the huge gates began to open, the green timbers shrieking. 'I'm Manaken Erit-son.' He said the name again, as if to impress it on her memory. 'Welcome to our beautiful realm of Torith Mir.'

They were through, trotting down a long gravel path

and then on to the short tough grass of the valley-floor beyond. Tanthe was smiling to herself. 'Why did he tell me his name?' she said. 'Hoping I'd put a good word in for him with Helananthe?'

'Without a doubt,' said Jthery, laughing. Eldareth was silent, his face colourless.

The landscape here was bleaker than that of Eisilion, the hills of black peat patched with wiry heathers and boulders. No trees. The sky was high and ashen, threatening rain. A chill breeze blew, and Tanthe had a feeling they were coming to the edge of the world.

'I hope we don't have far to go through this,' she said. 'What's their Duke called?'

'They don't have a Duke, they have a Viceroy,' said Eldareth. 'Thanks to their belligerence in the past, they weren't allowed to keep a noble family. The Viceroy used to be appointed from Parione, but nowadays they're allowed to appoint their own.' There was distaste in his voice. 'I think the man in question is still Viceroy Drathnen.'

More dra'a'ks flew over. The sight of them always made her uneasy. She saw a faint flickering of greenish light in the east, and thought she was imagining things.

They had ridden for only fifteen minutes when they heard galloping hooves behind them, voices shouting at them to halt. Eight guards were in pursuit, mounted on fast, skinny horses of chestnut and black. These horses came swerving and snorting around them, forcing them to stop.

'Hold!' shouted the leader. He was a man of about sixty with close-cropped steely hair that emphasised the fleshiness of his face. On his shoulder was the royal sigil; the eight-spoked gold wheel with the Tree of Life superimposed. He looked straight at Eldareth. 'Wait, I'm afraid there has been a misunderstanding. My colleague failed to make a sufficient check on your identity, my lord. You are not Serpeth, are you?'

Eldareth's face was still but grim as stone. Elrill said, 'Why do you make this assertion?'

'The Queen is going to be furious if you delay us!' Tanthe added.

The officer was unmoved. 'I have met Lord Serpeth. I remember him well enough to know that this man is not him. For I know this man's face; there's hardly a creature in Torith Mir doesn't know it, since his portrait has been posted all over the realm in connection with the most heinous crimes. You are Mordraken Mordraken-son of Gem Tarken, are you not? Also called Eldareth the Wanderer.'

They were all silent. Tanthe stared horrified at Eldareth, who only raised his face to the clouds in dismay. Elrill's hand lighted on his sword-hilt, and so did hers, only for Eldareth to shake his head vigorously. 'Don't!' he hissed. 'There is no point in all of us getting into trouble!' He exhaled wearily. 'Yes, I am Mordraken-son.'

The mounted guards were manoeuvring their horses to surround him. Tanthe looked on in accelerating panic. They'd lost their only chance to run for it, and she saw how fast those lean horses were, how well-armed their riders.

'The rest of you are free to go,' the officer said heavily. 'But you are under arrest, Mordraken Mordraken-son. By the authority of Viceroy Drathnen of Torith Mir and the laws of the Nine Realms, I am detaining you for the murders of your father, your mother and your brother.'

The town was called Gem Harthnir – or Hart'nir, as the locals pronounced it – a mass of stern, high dwellings clustered on a steep hillside above the river Harth. Dominating the town on the north side stood the fortress Arabeth, a square edifice of ash-grey stone and black tiles and tiny slitted windows. Here the Torish brought Eldareth; and although Tanthe, Elrill and Jthery followed the mounted guards closely, they were stopped at the gate

240

and ordered to remain outside.

'But we are on the Queen's business!' Tanthe kept insisting, to whoever would listen. 'You can't do this!'

'Then let the Queen take the matter up with our Viceroy,' was the bland reply. 'Eldareth is wanted for serious crimes and we have no choice but to detain him.'

Everything in Gem Harthnir seemed to tower over her, Tanthe felt. Buildings reared up on rocky outcrops. The streets wound upwards in gullies between great boulders and bluffs of rock. The roofs, rain-drenched, shone black against the luminous grey of the sky. Suddenly she hated Torith Mir.

'I feel that this is my fault,' said Elrill. 'I was the one who persuaded him, against his better judgement, that the risk was worth taking.'

'Did he really do it?' Tanthe said. She hadn't spoken for a time, out of shock; now her voice nearly failed. 'Did he kill his family?'

'I don't know.' Elrill shook his head. 'I knew something terrible had happened in his past, but truly, he never told me of it.'

'I don't believe it,' said Tanthe. 'He's a good man. Helananthe loves him, for the gods' sake. We've trusted him with our lives and he's never let us down!'

'What are we going to do?' said Jthery.

Elrill responded with a long, grave sigh. 'We have a choice. We can go on alone and seek a portal to Verdanholm, or we can stay and try to secure Eldareth's release.'

The Shaelahyr's cool tone shocked her. 'We can't even think of leaving without him.'

'It could delay us by days, weeks.'

'At least we must try!'

'Jthery, what do you say?' asked Elrill.

'I agree with Tanthe,' he said. 'I wouldn't abandon any of you in that situation. I hope that you would not abandon me.'

241

It had taken them most of the day to reach the town. Night was falling. The fortress stood closed before them. 'I'm tired,' said Tanthe. 'I suggest we find lodgings for the night and come back first thing in the morning.'

The others agreed and they wound their disconsolate way towards the heart of the town. Tanthe was leading Gany; at least the officials hadn't confiscated Eldareth's horse. They found an inn, a narrow grey house that looked as unwelcoming as the rest despite the yellow light glowing in its windows. The innkeepers came into the porch to meet them, a couple who were short and stocky, with soot-black hair and harsh expressions.

'Yes?' said the man, his voice gruff and accented.

'We need three rooms for the night,' said Tanthe. 'Perhaps for several days.'

'Of course. Come in, be welcome; let me take your horses to the stable while my wife shows you the rooms.'

To her surprise, the man came bustling out to take charge of the horses, while the woman was drawing them in, placing warm plump hands on their arms. Their expressions were suddenly warm, transformed from winter to summer. They smiled more with their eyes than with their mouths, but their friendliness was genuine and unforced.

Inside, the inn's stone walls were softened by tapestries and the glow from a fire blazing in a huge black grate. The ceilings were high but filled with light from candles massed on chandeliers. The heads of strange creatures adorned the walls. A jet-black stag with branching antlers, a narrow-skulled ram with huge carved horns, a strange mammal she didn't even recognise with greenish fur, tiny ears and long fangs like a wolf. There were only a handful of other guests seated at the long table but they greeted the newcomers with raised glasses.

'That's a greenwolf,' Jthery said in her ear, seeing her staring at the trophy.

'Never seen one before.'

'It's not really a wolf. They live in the water. Some say they are more akin to rats. There aren't many left in Mithrain. They're dangerous, so they got hunted.'

Tanthe smiled warmly. 'Consider me impressed by your store of useless knowledge, Jthery.'

'I think it's despicable that they're hunted,' he said, and she realised he was angry. 'They harm no one if they're left alone.'

Elrill, Tanthe and Jthery seated themselves, and the food began to arrive. There were slabs of meat coated in fiery spices, fresh bread and a dozen different vegetables each in its own, piquant sauce. It was delicious. When Elrill offered a handful of spinels to pay, the innkeeper waved his money away. 'Oh, never mind that now. We'll settle up when you're ready to leave. Meanwhile, make yourselves at home and anything you need, good lady and sirs, just ask.'

The three looked at each other in complete amazement. 'I always heard the people of Torith Mir were vile,' Tanthe whispered. 'Maybe they're not so bad after all.'

Jthery smiled. He was less reticent now they knew each other better. 'Have you never heard of Torish hospitality? It's legendary.'

'Actually, Eld did mention it once,' Tanthe said, taking a mouthful of ruby-red ale. 'I didn't believe him.'

'It's true, they have their reputation as fierce fighters,' said Elrill, 'but on their home territory – so Eldareth has told me – you couldn't hope to find a more welcoming people. The rumour appears to be true – of ordinary folk, if not of officials.'

A draught of cold air surged in as the front door was thrown open, bringing with it the sound of rain, horses' hooves and carts rattling along the cobbles outside. The tapestries lifted, the fire wavered. Striding in came the officer who had arrested Eldareth, with a handful of his guards.

The officer's party caught sight of Tanthe's. The two

243

groups stared at each other in mutual shock. 'At ease,' said the officer. 'We're off-duty. Only came in for a few beers.'

Elrill rose and bowed gracefully to them. 'We have no quarrel with you, sir,' he said quietly. 'Come, sit with us. Allow me to purchase your drinks.'

The guards seemed transfixed by Elrill, so obviously unhuman. Tanthe bristled a little, wondering how it would be if they could see that she, too, was Aelyr, but secretly she was glad that they took no special notice of her.

'No, no,' said the officer. 'You're in our land now. Let me.'

'We take turns in Sepheret,' Tanthe said primly. Presently, when drinks had been brought, she asked, 'Do you really know if our friend is guilty?'

With a jar of red ale in his fist, the officer was considerably more forthcoming than he'd been earlier. 'Guilty as Ghaurthror of the Flies,' he spat. 'There's a streak of madness in Mordraken-son. Must have turned even madder, to come back.'

'But what did he do?'

'Slaughtered his mother, his brother and his father. Caught very nearly in the act, the sword still dripping blood in his hand. A great man, his father.'

Tanthe thought of Ysomir, and shuddered. 'When did this happen?'

'Oh . . . twenty-five years ago, or more. His father Mordraken was a jewel-mage in the employ of Viceroy Drathnen; very clever man.'

'But you don't think Eldareth really did it, do you?' she said. The officer looked narrowly at her. 'He's our friend, the Queen's friend! If you knew him, you wouldn't believe it.'

'Since when have people been the same underneath as they seem on the surface?' He leaned towards her. 'You think I'm a Goddess-forsaken, hard bastard. I can see it in your eyes, lady. But my grandchildren love me well enough. They don't see an officer in the uniform of Torith Mir. They see their granddad.'

'Yes,' said Tanthe, embarrassed. 'And whatever you think about us probably isn't true, either. But if he's guilty – why did he do it?'

'You'd have to ask him.'

'Then tell us how to get into the fortress.' She turned the sea-coloured beams of her eyes upon him. 'It must be possible for us to visit him, or to petition someone on his behalf. Please. Tell us how to get in.'

The officer exhaled through his teeth. 'Write a letter. A really polite letter. I mean, a sickeningly, humiliatingly, grovellingly polite letter. Believe me, you can't overdo it. And I'll take it to the fortress governor Ordrai for you.'

Inside, the walls of Fortress Arabeth were glossy black, and torchlight danced like oil on the surface. Guards led Tanthe and Elrill along high, narrow corridors that all looked the same; a labyrinth of basalt. The prisoner was allowed only two visitors at a time, they'd been told, so Jthery was waiting for them outside.

They'd left their weapons with Jthery, rather than risk them being confiscated; Tanthe felt naked without her Shaelahyr sword.

Even with the officer's help and the lever of their royal connections, it had taken ten days to gain access to the prison. It hardly seemed to matter that Tanthe was in Torith Mir on the Queen's behalf, nor that Elrill was a Lord of the Shaelahyr, nor that Jthery was the Queen's cousin and heir to Mithrain; there was still endless bureaucracy to grind through before they finally received grudging permission to enter the fortress.

Before they were allowed to visit their friend, though, they must undergo an interview with the governor. They were taken to his office, which lay behind huge ebony doors in the stately, outer part of Arabeth. The guards ushered them into a large dark-panelled chamber that was austere in colour but richly furnished with what she recognised as silk rugs and hangings from Azura Maroc; black and silver with touches of white and sparks of colour. On the governor's desk stood large, perfect mineral specimens; spheres of obsidian and onyx, a replica of Arabeth carved from one huge piece of amber. And behind these treasures sat Governor Ordrai himself, a big man with a powerful, hungry face, the head broad and thick-necked as if squashed directly on his shoulders. He gazed impassively at them, his hands folded over his belly.

'I gather you've come to see the prisoner, Mordraken-son,' said Ordrai.

'Yes, sir,' said Tanthe and Elrill. They'd been warned to be excruciatingly polite.

'Why?'

'Because we are friends of his, sir,' said Tanthe.

'You claim to be travelling on behalf of the Queen?'

'We are, sir.' She started to show him the seal, but he waved it away.

'I've seen one. It means little in this realm. Where are you going?'

Tanthe hesitated, not knowing how much to tell him. Elrill said, 'We are on an urgent mission to convey messages from the Queen to the Aelyr. We're here to find a *rothanamir* into Verdanholm. That is all.'

Ordrai stared at them in bemusement for several seconds. Tanthe held her breath, certain he was going to find some pretext to lock them up. But, apparently, he had no idea what to make of this information, so decided to overlook it. He didn't even comment on it.

'You're aware of Eldareth's crime? I prefer to call him Eldareth, since he is unworthy of his given name.'

'We are now,' she said. 'We weren't before. Sir.'

'There's something you should know,' the governor drawled. 'The Viceroy and I are very close. Mordraken Senior was a very dear friend of ours and one of Torith Mir's greatest assets. In a slight lapse of judgement he

246

married a foreigner, which we forgave – even though it proved the death of him. You must understand that I took Mordraken's death very personally. It is a known fact that Eldareth killed him. There were witnesses. He made a confession. He is not here "under suspicion"; he is guilty.'

Tanthe felt her blood rising, couldn't help it. 'But—'

She felt Elrill gripping her elbow in warning.

'One more thing,' said Ordrai. 'You are here to visit the prisoner. You are not here to protest his innocence. If either of you utters one word of petition on his behalf, you will be expelled instantly and not allowed back in. Is that understood?'

'Yes sir,' said Tanthe and Elrill.

'Good. Go, say your goodbyes. Guard!'

They were escorted out and the ebony doors slammed shut. Tanthe was shaking from head to foot as the guards led them on a long, confusing trek into the heart of Arabeth. 'What a horrible man!' she whispered, and her voice seemed to reverberate all through the labyrinth of dark tunnels.

'Well done for waiting until you could get a good echo,' said Elrill. The guards laughed out loud. Tanthe felt herself flushing bright red.

The guards brought them to a high, dark passage that seemed to stretch the length of the fortress. A door of black iron screeched open to reveal a long narrow cell. 'Half-hour,' said one of the guards.

Eldareth was sitting at a table, a silhouette against the grey light that sifted in through a skylight. His face was like the light; ashen, thin, gaunt. Seeing his visitors he rose shakily, as if he'd aged twenty years since they'd last seen him.

'Greetings to you, dear friend,' said Elrill. He seemed close to weeping; she'd never seen him upset before, and it shook her.

'Hello, Eld, how are you?' Tanthe said, her voice loud to her own ears. 'We've tried every day to see you.'

'Ahh,' Eldareth groaned. 'I wish you hadn't.' He waved at the two hard-oak chairs opposite him. 'But since you're here, sit down.'

Tanthe and Elrill sat, poised on the edge of the hard seats. Two warders stood unsmiling, one on each side of the door.

'Is this your cell?' Tanthe asked. Elrill was white and silent beside her.

'No, this is the visiting room,' Eldareth said heavily. 'My cell is rather smaller than this, but reasonably comfortable. I'm used to sleeping on the ground so the floor doesn't trouble me.'

'You look dreadful,' she said. She shook her head, suddenly frightened. 'We've spent every day at the gate of the fortress, trying to get you released. We've written letters, been shunted from one official to another, kept waiting in horrible offices for hours on end, but no one would listen to us. Ordrai was vile. At least he let us see you – but – I got the feeling he'd love an excuse to arrest us too.'

Eldareth reached across the table and took her hand in his bony one. 'Tanthe, dear, I'm sorry. You look as tired as I feel, and I had no wish to drag you into this. All I can tell you is forget me; go on with your journey.'

'We can't,' Tanthe said, glaring at him. 'Apart from anything else, Helananthe would kill us if we left you here.'

'You don't understand. They aren't going to release me, ever.' He closed his eyes. His eyelids were hooded with peaks of exhaustion. 'This is my fault. I knew it was too much of a risk to come here.'

'No, it's mine,' said Elrill. 'I am the one who persuaded you that the worst would not happen.'

'But I didn't have to listen to you, my friend.'

'Oh, stop it!' Tanthe exclaimed. 'Never mind whose fault it was. Eld, they're saying that you killed your family.'

The words rang into silence and hung on the air, resonating. Eldareth drove the tips of his fingers into his eyes and rubbed until his eyelids turned red and she felt like dashing his hand away before he drew blood. Finally he looked up. 'So you know.'

She felt the cell tilting, tears and panic rising in her chest. 'You didn't really, did you?'

'No, of course not.' He closed and unclosed his hands. 'And yes. I killed my father.'

Both Tanthe and Elrill stared at him. 'Why?' she asked faintly. He didn't reply. 'Eld, for the gods' sake, tell us!'

His face twisted with pain. Tanthe was desperate to comfort him, but he seemed untouchable, far beyond her comfort. Elrill simply waited. Finally Eldareth seemed to come to a decision, and began to speak.

'I told the story once, and wasn't believed, and I swore I'd never tell it again. It's anguish even to think of it . . . yet what's the point in staying silent any longer? All right.' He cleared his throat gruffly. 'The most I've ever told you both is that my mother was from Thanmandrathor, my father from Torith Mir. They were both *roth*-mages who worked with the energies of stones; my father with jet and metal ores, my mother with amber. She was a healer; my father a craftsman and trader who worked for Viceroy Drathnen. They met, so my mother Elq'esq told me, at one of Torith Mir's great jewel fairs, where traders come from all over Aventuria to buy jet, amber and diamonds. My father was a clever trader. He controlled the market and was responsible for making Drathnen one of the richest men in Aventuria.'

'No wonder Drathnen's so sore at losing him,' Tanthe murmured.

'Mordraken and Elq'esq fell in love and they worked together at Drathnen's court at Gem Tarken for a time. But my father had a flaw in his character. He was a jealous man – so my mother told us – jealous to the point of obsession. He envied her *roth* gifts, which were greater than his; once when she healed Drathnen's brother of pneumonia, he convinced himself that she and her patient

249

were lovers. It wasn't true, but truth meant nothing to Mordraken. He saw that Elq'esq was finer, wilder in spirit, more gifted than ever he could hope to be, and the knowledge twisted some proud fault in his soul.

'I can recall, when I was a small child and my brother Aidren an infant, several occasions when he threatened her and struck her. Terrible, unforgivable violence against she who never harmed a soul, as if he'd struck the Goddess herself, violated life itself! She forgave him for a time, she told us afterwards. Tried to understand and heal him, but in the end it was too much. His jealous rages became life-threatening. I tried to protect her, and he hated me for that. So she fled, and we lived in hiding in Thanmandrathor and Eisilion while my brother and I grew up. But he came after us. He was a terrifying man. Even now I can't think of him without fear. Like a thunderstorm, like everything that is rotten in Torith Mir with none of its redeeming features.

'I trained to ride and handle the sword and bow, because of him. Well, there came a time when he seemed to have given up; we'd heard nothing of him for several years and my mother thought we were safe.

'The trouble was, she loved Torith Mir. She missed the bleakness of its landscape and the richness of its amber. So she took a great risk. She brought us home. I was seventeen, Aidren thirteen. We took a little croft on the cliffs of the northern ocean, and I was training as a farrier and swordsmith in the village nearby. That's where I was, away at the smithy, when my father found our dwelling at last.'

Eldareth's voice grew strained. 'He came with armed men – and permission from Drathnen – to carry my mother and brother away with him. She, though, persuaded his companions to leave the house so she could talk to Mordraken alone. She thought that if she could only reason with him, she would persuade him to leave us in peace.

'When I came home, I knew something was wrong. I saw the Torish soldiers, sitting about on the cliff, sharing a flask of liquor. I heard voices inside the cottage. It was a modest place, not much bigger than the Seer's but with a good thatched roof and whitewashed walls. And in the dim light I saw my father shouting at my mother, and Aidren trying to protect her. I drew my sword and went in.'

Eldareth rested his head on his hand, pushing thin fingers through the silver-threaded black tangle of his hair. 'So was it my fault? If I had not come then, would they have lived? When my father saw me, he went mad. He seized my mother and put his sword to her throat, swearing that she would go back to him or we'd all die. His face . . . his eyes were mad, his black hair shaking in curved strands over his forehead, his mouth an oblong of hatred with foam at its corners . . . I can't get his face out of my mind. But she – she cried out that we would *never* go back. And at that, he gave a howl of rage and drew the sword across her throat, and she fell.

'My brother screamed and flung himself at my father. He was unarmed; he virtually impaled himself on my father's sword. I can still see him sliding off the blade; it seemed to take forever . . . Then there were only the two of us left. We fought. Mordraken was more experienced, but I had youth and blinding passion to aid me. It was over quickly; I ran him through. Then his men came running in – I thought they had heard the shouts, but it turned out that Aidren had crawled a little way before he died, and they had seen him, lying over the threshold of the cottage in a pool of blood.' Eldareth took a shuddering breath. 'So the men came in, and found my family dead, and me standing over them with the sword dripping red in my hand.'

Eldareth sat back and ran his hands over his face. The skin glistened with sweat and tears; his hair was damp. He exhaled noisily. 'I swear, Saphaeyender never wrote a

251

story so tragic, so ludicrously melodramatic even in the wildest of his plays. I tried to tell them what had happened but they wouldn't believe me. Mordraken had instilled it into everyone he knew that I was the unstable one, the evil influence on my mother. They arrested me. But once we got out on to the cliff-top I broke loose, and made a run for it, and escaped by throwing myself into the sea.'

'Off a cliff?' Tanthe gasped.

'Unfortunately, the tide was in.' Eldareth grimaced. 'I would have been quite happy to dash myself on the rocks. However, I lived, and swam around the wall to Eisilion, and dragged myself on to the shore to seek a new life. I forsook my father's name, of course. To be called Mordraken? I couldn't stomach it. I made a new identity, with some success, for twenty-seven years. The trouble is, for the whole of that time I have been fleeing. I had to come back and face it in the end.'

Tanthe and Elrill sat in shocked silence. She reached out and gripped his hand; and presently, Elrill's pallid hand slid over the table and clasped Eldareth's other wrist. Even the Shaelahyr had nothing to say.

'You could have told us,' Tanthe said eventually.

'No. I couldn't.'

'But you're innocent! You were trying to save your mother and brother.'

Eldareth raised his red eyes to the ceiling. 'Innocent? If not for me, they might have lived. I shall never know, and so I have to bear the guilt.'

'You have got to tell the authorities!'

'They know my story. They don't believe it. My father was a highly respected man with powerful friends. I found out more . . . My father brought more than riches to Drathnen. He was using his *roth*-skills to fashion weapons; deadlier arrows, sharper swords, spears with *roth*-fire in their tips. That's what some of my mother and father's quarrels were about. Elq'esq was horrified, of course. Drathnen and his cronies were planning to seize independence from Paranios, but Mordraken's death brought a halt to their plans. And I killed him; that's all they care about.'

'But you were a boy.'

He shook his head. 'A grown man, in their eyes.'

'You've got to appeal!'

'It will make no difference.'

Tanthe leapt up, her chair scraping on the stone floor. 'I can't believe you're just giving in to this! If you won't make Ordrai accept your story, I will!'

'Tanthe!'

He reached out after her but she was already up and striding out of the cell.

Flustered guards followed her but she gave them the slip; managed not to lose her way – even at a run – and found herself outside Ordrai's massive ebony doors.

The guards came round the corner, with Elrill following.

Catching her breath, she thrust the doors open and flung herself through into the dark office. Behind the gleam of onyx and obsidian spheres, Ordrai looked up.

'You again,' he said. 'Don't you ever knock, in whatever realm you are from?'

She launched into full flow, imagining in her desperate naivety that once the story was properly understood, everything would change. But the governor only listened with a weary contempt that made her, at last, talk herself to a standstill.

By then, the guards were standing on either side of her, but he didn't signal them to seize her. Picking up a quill-pen, he scratched on a piece of paper. 'You seem to think this is news to me. However, I have heard it all before. Eldareth made a statement.'

She gasped. 'Then why won't you listen? He's innocent!'

'He killed his father, who was the best *roth*-mage this realm has ever known. Mordraken's death deprived Torith Mir of much wealth, good fortune and strength. It also deprived me of a friend.'

'What about Elq'esq and Aidren? Don't they matter? Don't you care why he did it?'

The governor leaned forward, folding his big pale hands on the desktop. 'No. And furthermore, I don't believe him. We only have his word that he didn't kill them himself, to spite his father. Excuses, excuses. I think guilt got to him in the end, and forced him to give himself up. Don't you think it's best to accept it?'

In his eyes she saw absolute intransigence, and a trace of sorrow. Ordrai had lost a friend, and was bent on vengeance. That was all.

'What's going to happen to him?' she said faintly.

'He is going to stand trial, and be found guilty. Then, by the law of Torith Mir, he shall be executed by the sword. Now go.' He flicked a hand at the door, and a female guard grasped her arm.

'I want to talk to Eldareth again.'

Ordrai's small eyes hardened in his over-fleshed face. 'Were you not warned that you were here only to visit – not to petition? Be thankful I am doing no more than expelling you.'

'Tanthe,' Elrill said behind her. She ignored him.

'You don't frighten me,' she said thinly. 'I shouldn't like to be in your place when the Queen hears about this!'

'The Queen's feelings on the matter are of no interest to us. If she wishes to send an outraged deputation, let her; it will all be over by then. Let her prove that we broke any laws. Now go! I've no more time for this.'

She stood seething, helpless. Elrill said gently, 'Tanthe, come on.'

The governor's face and voice were iron. 'You may stay in Gem Harthnir until the execution, if you so desire, but after that you and your friends must leave. And if you try this again, so help me, I shall have you all arrested and you'll never see the light of day again!'

Jthery waited outside Arabeth while Tanthe and Elrill

were inside, wondering if they would ever come out. They'd left the horses stabled at the inn, so he was on foot, walking slowly around the high bleak skirts of the fortress. He wondered what he'd do if he were left to carry on the journey alone. Or if they were all imprisoned, and left to rot? Well, it hadn't come to that yet. A deeper part of him was calm, knowing that he'd been guided here for a reason. One day the reason might even become clear.

A chilly rain was falling, but he didn't mind that. It connected him to his element. The back wall of the fortress marked the end of the town; downhill in the distance, veiled by a stand of hard-oaks, he saw a lake. Its surface was still, but to his enhanced senses the underwater world writhed with life. The impressions was so vivid he recoiled and shut it out.

Walking down from the fortress, he crossed the street and stood looking down at the river that ran below the embankment. Its colour was unexpected in the monotone surroundings; rich dark blue. The surface was wide and flat and rapid, running in wide, shimmering arrow-shapes over unseen stones. He felt a tugging of empathy that was almost sexual.

The rush of water seemed loud to his ears. It was all he could hear. He wanted to touch the water, but it was too far below, and he was divided from it by a low stone wall topped with a rail. He gripped the rail, feeling its coldness, smelling the complex odours of the water.

The rushing sound became Eshte's whispering. *The creatures in the water are friends to you and always were, from the days of your childhood. Wherever you are they lift their heads to you and listen. Was it not always so?*

Yes, he thought with a thrill. Fishes had always shoaled around him, otters swam joyously alongside him.

And so it will be always . . . for as long as you make the right choices.

Cold amazement. 'Eshte,' he whispered into the murmur of rain, reflexively touching the amethyst carp, feeling its little cold, hard scales. 'How am I supposed to know what is right?'

You may not. That is the danger. Beware . . . for you are moving closer . . .

Chapter Twelve. The Road to Vexor

By the time they were halfway to Tasqabad – the Hall of Branq'elin's father, Duke Tasq – Rufryd felt he had been travelling all his life.

It was a companionable enough journey, with Branq'elin's retinue of eight men and women riding alongside them. The bulk of the Than'drathian army were returning home behind them, but Rufryd's party had swiftly outpaced them. He liked the steady rhythm of travelling; for as long as it went on, he didn't have to think.

He'd been unable to tell, in the first weeks of the journey, where the realm of Paranios ended and that of Thanmandrathor began. First they passed through the lush farmland and vineyards that lay to the east of Parione; then came the towns and villages that lay along the great Atasq'eth Road, beautiful towns of cream or pale gold stone like modest echoes of the capital. The hills were green and gentle, the woods verdant with beech and birch, arkh-woods and ferns. He saw the season change by a tiny but perceptible degree each day, autumn beginning to edge the leaves with red.

The clusters of obviously Paranian towns ended, and the landscape was suddenly on a grander scale. Here, somewhere among these green escarpments, one realm ended and another began, but there was no definite boundary. The road wound on through steep hills and thick forests, through sunshine and rain and ever-changing light. Suddenly the villages where the party found rest some nights were of a different character. Tall, crooked houses with teetering slate roofs, beamed walls painted ochre, wooden shutters at the windows.

Rufryd had never seen villages of such character before. He thought of the stone cottages back in Riverwynde; the brown brick and thatch houses of drab Havereyn; the austere grey stone of Sepheret's main town, Skald. They had nothing to compare with this. These communities were filled with tall Than'drathians, with their long brown or corn-coloured hair, their watchful green eyes. Proud and suspicious at first, then warm and gracious to their guests – especially when they found out who Branq'elin was. Then the travellers would be treated like royalty.

To Rufryd, Thanmandrathor felt eerily like home. He tried to suppress all such warm emotions, though; they were traitors. Once, Tanthe had felt eerily like someone with whom he was meant to spend his life.

'All seems so peaceful, doesn't it?' said Dawn, riding alongside him.

'Until you actually listen to them talking,' said Rufryd.

'That's what I meant,' Dawn said grimly. 'You can't see the harm that Garnelys did on the surface. It's only when you talk to Than'drathians that you realise how many people they've lost, how much grief he caused.'

'His memory lives on, all right,' said Mirias, shaking his head.

'You can't blame Branq'elin's folks for wanting their independence, can you?' Rufryd said drily.

The party travelled for many days with a chain of mountains on their left; Seat of Ank'eth, the range was called. Several rivers surged down from the peaks, spanned by great stone bridges. The hills grew steeper and their valleys were dark with firs. There were many birds of prey, Rufryd noticed, and dra'a'ks of kinds he'd never seen before. He would watch them wheeling in the air currents above the heights, and shiver with cold excitement. They reminded him of home. A place he doubted he'd ever return to.

Rufryd had little to do with Lady Branq'elin, only on the most practical level; he found her aloof, rather intimidating. Dawn seemed to strike up an easy rapport with her, but then Dawn could get along with anyone. Even me, thought Rufryd.

It was afternoon and they were heading for a village called Fveybad, intending to reach it by dusk. The weather had been strange all day; too still and humid for the time of year, the blue sky suffused with a haze. All day Rufryd had noticed birds streaming across the sky from the east. The horses were skittish, especially Halcyon, who was nervous at the best of times. Rufryd couldn't manage him as delicately as Lynden had done, and eventually Halcyon barged forward, causing Branq'elin's mare to kick out in irritation.

'Would you like to ride in front?' Branq'elin said sharply, turning in the saddle.

'Sorry, my lady.' The blue stallion arched his neck and chewed at the bit as Rufryd tried to rein him in. 'Something's upsetting him. If I went in front, you probably wouldn't see us for dust.'

'This weather,' Branq'elin said more forgivingly. She faced forward again, presenting him with the thick silken plait that hung between her resolute shoulder-blades. 'It isn't what we expect at this time of year.' As she looked up, a drop or two of rain fell and there was a sudden gust of wind. 'I think it's breaking.'

Dawn, riding alongside Branq'elin, caught her arm. 'Look!'

It began on the eastern skyline; the distant flicker of sheet lightning, it seemed. But gradually the flickering grew more insistent, a vivid glow growing and spreading towards them.

All the riders reined in and stared at the sky.

The glow was green, and it was not lightning. It was more a throb of radiance that came streaming towards them, gathering speed as it came. Winds surged with it. Halcyon half-reared and spun in a circle, but throughout his antics Rufryd didn't once take his eyes off the sky.

259

He thought the end of the world was coming. The closer the radiance came the faster it travelled and suddenly it was rushing, racing overhead. The whole sky was suffused by a rippling green wave of light. It shimmered and trembled with spurts of red and blue, tiny forks of electricity dancing between the ripples.

Rufryd forgot himself. It was the most awesome sight. Weird, heart-stopping, terrible – yet beautiful.

The wave passed, surging westwards. Behind it came a boom of thunder, and a hard, hot wind that made the horses turn on their haunches and their riders crouch miserably on their necks until it had gone.

When it was over, there was silence. Rufryd took a breath that went to the roots of his lungs, and scratched Halcyon's neck in reassurance. No one asked, 'What was that?' They were all in shock.

'We should be in Fveybad within the hour,' said Branq'elin, quite calmly. 'I don't know about all of you, but I need a drink.'

It was a tall inn they stayed at that night, with crooked, dark rooms. They'd had supper in the taproom, where all the talk was of the strange weather. The mood had become increasingly festive, but Rufryd was exhausted, and left them to it. He was sitting on the edge of his bed, pulling his boots off, when there was a knock on his door.

It was Branq'elin who came in, to his astonishment. 'Rufryd, can I talk to you?' she said.

'Er . . . yes, of course, my lady.' He moved up to make room for her, but she sat down almost touching him. She was wearing a simple fawn robe with bronze embroidery on the neck and cuffs, and her hair was loose. He'd never seen her hair unplaited before, nor realised there was quite so much of it. He watched candlelight weaving gold spindles amid the brown waves.

'I hope you don't mind. It's very noisy down there. Dawn and Mirias are acting some scene from a play.

They're very good, I'm sure, but I've had enough for one day. I can't stop thinking about what we saw.'

'I take it that . . .' he cleared his throat. 'That sort of phenomenon doesn't happen all the time in this realm?'

She breathed out, half-way between a groan and a sigh. 'Never used to,' she said. 'But of late, it has been happening more and more. A few strange little storms at first. Now these weird fires in the sky, more powerful each time. I was hoping that when I returned this way, it would have ceased. But people tell me it's growing worse.'

'What do you think it is?'

'The wrath of our gods. Q'enartre of lightning and Ank'eth of thunder. That's what people are saying. But I don't know. What have we done to anger them?'

She gave a half-smile, but he could see she was deeply upset. 'No good asking me,' he said. 'I don't believe in gods. Well, I do in a way, but I don't believe they sit in the heavens throwing bolts of lightning around. Bit childish, really, isn't it? I'm sure they've got better things to do.'

She laughed. 'Gods, Rufryd, don't say things like that at my father's house. You're quite refreshing, though.'

'Really? I'm just a peasant. You're nearly a duchess.'

'Oh, don't remind me of that.' She tightened her hands, digging her fingertips into her knees. 'If anything happens to my father, I shall be Duchess of Thanmandrathor, and then all of this realm is my responsibility. And if these lights and storms destroy us, it will be my fault!'

There was a long silence. 'I didn't mean to sound flippant,' he said.

'It's all right.' She was so close now her thigh was pressing against his, her warm scent filling him. 'I want to forget about it tonight.'

She put her hand on his leg. Rufryd froze. He wanted to put his arms around her but for some reason he couldn't move.

'It's been so long since I had a lover, and I can't bear to

spend another night alone,' she said; not seductively but in real need. 'I think you are lonely too. Well?'

At that point, he needn't have said anything. To slip his arm across her back and his other hand into her hair and press his mouth to hers . . . that was all that was required. He felt his prick stiffening, his heart accelerating. And yet . . .

'I'm sorry, my lady. It's not that I don't think you're beautiful, but . . .'

'You are beautiful too, Rufryd. But?'

'I don't think it would be a good idea.'

She paused. She went on touching him for a few moments, while he remained unresponsive in her embrace. Presently she withdrew her hand and sat away from him.

'I see,' she said, and rose slowly. 'Actually, I don't see. I thought we should both enjoy it.'

'I'm sure we would,' he said. 'It's just . . .' He couldn't explain. Once he would have leapt at the chance, but now he felt cold, inside and out. He didn't want to fall in love with her. He felt too remote even to indulge in sex without love; simply didn't want anyone that close to him. Couldn't stand any more of the emptiness Ashtar had brought him. It felt weird and deadly not to care, but he couldn't help it.

'You're a peasant and I'm a duchess?' she said sharply. 'As if that matters!'

'No, it's not that. I just can't. I'm sorry.'

She lowered her head, the rich brown skeins half-hiding her face. 'Well, I'm sorry too,' she said, her voice low. 'I didn't mean to embarrass you. Please forget this ever happened. Goodnight.'

She was Lady Branq'elin again, cool and aloof. Turning, she placed her hand on the door handle, then looked back at him. 'You must love her very much, whoever she is.'

Rufryd said nothing. When she was gone he fell back on the bed, cursing himself. 'What the fuck did I do that for?'

he murmured, clutching his head. 'Tanthe doesn't want me, has never really wanted me. Why the hell can't I leave it behind?'

In the morning, as he was on his way to breakfast through the dark, creaking corridors, he saw her coming out of another room with one of the soldiers from her retinue, a tall and extremely handsome young man who looked, frankly, exhausted. Branq'elin caught Rufryd's eye and gazed straight at him; no sadness, no apology, just a clear direct look. *I found someone else.*

He was half glad for her, and half angry. But the anger was directed at himself.

Conawr clung to his friend Noal, terrified and exalted.

As the green wave passed over Tasqabad Hall, everyone in the stable-yard stopped working and stared up at the sky. Some ran for cover, others were rooted to the flag-stones and stood gaping as the spreading ripples raced overhead, just as if someone had thrown a stone into a pond. The hot wind whipped straw around their feet; horses screamed and pawed in their stables.

The two boys had been crossing the yard on their way from the kitchen to the hen-house when the storm came. By reflex they'd dropped their baskets and grabbed each other. It was the most terrifying thing Con had ever seen.

'What is it?' he gasped.

Noal's eyes were rapt, mesmerised. 'It's coming,' he said.

The gale buffeted them. The boom of thunder deafened them. They huddled together, eyes shut against the whirling splinters of straw.

It passed suddenly and they straightened up, looking around with blinking, reddened eyes. Grooms were running to calm the horses. Servants and cooks had come rushing out of the kitchen and everyone was talking and pointing.

'What did you mean, "it's coming"?' said Con. 'What's coming, Noli?'

'I don't know.' His friend shrugged awkwardly. 'Something important, but . . . I don't know what it is.'

Noli sometimes went a bit strange in bad weather. Con didn't like it, wanted to joke him out of it. 'That was a hell of a storm,' said Con. 'Or whatever it was. I wasn't scared, though.'

'Yes you were!'

'No, *you* were!'

Con began to chase Noli, hurling handfuls of straw at him. At fifteen they were too old for such childish behaviour, but the electric atmosphere had woken wildness in them. The two lads weren't related but could have been taken for brothers, slim and dark. They'd grown up together in the Duke's household, Noal like Con's younger shadow. Shrieking, they ran through a flock of chickens and there were feathers everywhere, and leaping, squawking hens scattering across the yard.

'Get back to work!' bellowed the head cook from the kitchen doorway. 'The show's over! I need those eggs *now*!'

They stopped in their tracks, ran back to seize their fallen baskets, then scooted round the corner of the stables towards the hen-house. The moment they were out of sight, though, they leaned back against the wall, breathless and laughing.

'I'm not going to spend my whole life here,' Con said suddenly. 'I want to know what's sending these storms. I want to go somewhere wild, and meet Aelyr and *roth*-mages.' Noli said nothing, only gazed at him with wide eyes. 'What about you?'

'I shall go wherever you go, Con,' he said.

It was close to Hollynight when they came to Tasqabad Hall.

Winter was setting in, mild and damp rather than bitter-cold. They didn't get the harsh winters of the north, Branq'elin said, but normally it was colder than this. She

264

seemed disturbed by it. There had been more of the strange green storms, not as severe as the first, but eerie enough. Rufryd thought of Tanthe and wondered where she was. In Eisilion, in Torith Mir . . . in Verdanholm? Did they have winter in the realm of the Aelyr?

Since the night in Fveybad, Branq'elin had been civil but ice-cool to Rufryd. She never gave him a second chance, but even if she had, it would have had the same outcome. He felt vaguely saddened by this, but there was nothing he could do, or even wanted to do. In another life they might have been happy together, but he had no love to give her. He was heading towards Vexor as if hoping to be swallowed up by death.

The scale of the landscape became grander, with wide valleys pushing between sheer hills as if gigantic rivers had once flowed along them; dark volcanic mountains in the far distance; an endless sweep of great hills filled with forests and rivers. They rounded a bend in the road and there stood a beautiful town with cobbled streets, houses painted white and yellow and blue that stood five storeys high with windows peeping from between brightly-painted shutters. Wet snow was pattering in the streets, but the sun glowed luminous through bars of black cloud, splashing light on the cobbles, drenching the houses.

'This is Tasqabad,' said Branq'elin. 'In a few moments we shall see my parents' hall . . . There!'

The seat of the Dukes of Thanmandrathor was a magnificent hall of stone and timber set on a wooded hill, with the town falling away around its flanks. It looked rough-hewn and cold, compared to the buildings of Parione, yet it had a raw majesty that appealed to Rufryd. Sunlight spilled over its shining slate roof and gilded its timber pillars. Orchards and meadows lay around it, blending raggedly into the town itself.

'It's splendid,' said Dawn.

Branq'elin smiled proudly. 'I wish Mawrdreth were with me, but alas . . . I shall have to go and tell my parents what befell him, and everything else that has happened.'

She led them to the flanks of the hall and into a huge courtyard. Grooms came to take their horses, but Rufryd insisted on stabling Halcyon himself. He was tired; he needed some time alone before he must steel himself to meet yet more nobles. Once the stallion was settled, with his nose thrust happily into a bucket of grain, Rufryd wandered outside and found two lads hovering, one with a pitcher of beer and the other offering bread and apples. They approached him nervously, smiling.

'Sir, our lord and lady asked us to offer you refreshment,' said one. He was a tall thin youth of sixteen at most, with brown-black hair in a plait, very white teeth and bright green eyes. The other was shorter but similar-looking, with an air of intense shyness about him. They both seemed so innocently friendly that Rufryd felt somehow shocked; aware of how he must look to them, unkempt and bearded, and disturbed to find he couldn't return their smile. He couldn't even remember how it felt to smile.

'Thanks,' he said, accepting a glass of beer from the taller boy.

'I'm Conawr, sir. I work in the kitchens.'

'I'm Rufryd. I work as little as possible.'

The boy laughed awkwardly, unsure whether he was supposed to find this funny or not. 'Where are you from?'

'Sepheret.'

'Sepheret? But that's—'

'A long way away, I know. Who's your friend?'

'I'm Noal,' said the smaller boy, smiling up at Rufryd. His voice was very quiet.

'Everyone calls us Con and Noli. We work together. He's my best friend. Do everything together, don't we, Noli?'

'That must be fun,' Rufryd said caustically, beginning to wish they'd leave him alone. He took a piece of bread, found it dense with rye and molasses.

'Is there anything else we can get for you, sir?' said Noli.

'I'd quite like to shave,' Rufryd said. 'If I can remember how.'

'Lady Branq'elin told us to show you to your rooms . . .'

Rufryd shook his head. 'I'll just wash wherever you do. I feel more at home around stables and kitchens than I do around great halls.'

Thrilled to keep their new friend, the two boys took him to a small room off the kitchen and brought him a bowl of hot water, soap, a long sharp razor. They hung around chattering while he slowly scraped the beard from his chin. They'd been very excited by the unnatural weather. They seemed so young, and they were full of curiosity to the point of irritating him – Noli an eager echo of Con – but he let them stay. He dried his chin on a towel and looked at his reflection in the mirror they'd provided. He'd left Riverwynde at twenty-two and now he was twenty-four, but he felt older. Looked older, definitely. His hair had grown long and hung in ragged chestnut skeins over his eyes. Women might still see beauty in his strong features and his brown eyes – they told him so, occasionally – but he only saw pain.

'Did *you* see the green storms?' asked Noli. 'Do you know what they are?'

'Yes I did, and no I don't.'

'Why are you travelling with the Lady Branq'elin?' asked Con. 'What's happened? There's been a war, hasn't there? Who won?'

'Did Lady Branq'elin give you permission to interrogate her guests?'

Con reddened. 'Sorry, sir. No one tells us anything.'

'I know that feeling. All right, I'll tell you – if, for Anthar's sake, you'll stop calling me "sir".'

'Who's Anthar?'

'Our name for the Goddess's consort.'

'You mean Ank'eth.'

'All right, only our boy doesn't throw thunder around, he just lives in the greenwood and keeps Breyid happy.'

'Who's Breyid?'

'Give me strength. You call her Q'enartre. Now, where shall I start?'

Although winter was imminent, the day was fine and not too cold. Rufryd sat on a bench in the courtyard with the boys on either side of him, their backs against the kitchen wall, soaking up the last of the weak sunlight. He told them all about King Garnelys, the civil war, Thanmandrathor's petition for independence; almost everything, except Lynden's hopeless quest and death. The boys were spellbound. He found himself enjoying their attention.

'Rufryd, what are you doing?'

Dawn was standing over him, hands on hips.

'Sitting and gossiping. What does it look like?'

'Well, you'd better come inside and get washed and changed if you want to be in time for supper.'

'Think I'll give it a miss. I'll sleep with Halcyon.'

She pressed her lips together. 'Oh no, you won't. The Duke and Duchess want to meet all of us tonight. We're meant to be on a quest on their behalf, not to mention the Queen's – remember?'

The Great Hall, set ready for the evening meal, was breathtaking. Even Rufryd's determination to be contrary evaporated as he entered with Dawn and Mirias.

Tall golden pillars soared up, lost in the vault of the roof; fires blazed in vast grates of yellow stone. The pungency of smoke blew back into the room, and they were assaulted by sudden draughts of cold or scorching air as they walked towards the long table. There was an ancient and stark quality to this place, after the luxury of Parione; bare stone walls adorned with simple banners and flaming torches; straw mats on the floor; big lanky hounds wandering loose, even a couple of hairy pigs chasing each other around the arches in a far corner. Through the smoky golden light and the plain grandeur of the hall, the

Than'drathians moved; upright and graceful in green and bronze. Their long thick plaits gleamed the colour of ripe chestnuts, brooches shone on the shoulders of their cloaks. Despite himself, Rufryd was captivated.

Branq'elin was there with her parents to welcome them, standing at the top of the hall beside the huge blazing arch of the main fireplace.

Duke Tasq was a slim quiet man, with iron-grey braids hanging over his shoulders and a circlet of bronze set on his head. He looked strong-willed but physically frail, Rufryd thought. Branq'elin's mother Annuin appeared younger; she was a large, rosy woman who smiled and spoke to everyone. They were kind people, noble people, Rufryd thought, rather shamed at his own evident lack of either quality. He could see why even their youngest servants were so open and good-natured. Yet these folk had put up the fiercest resistance to Garnelys, when other realms had simply given in to his cruel demands.

Branq'elin introduced Dawn, Mirias and Rufryd to her parents; obviously she had already explained the reason for her brother's absence. The Duchess led them to a round table that was placed away from the communal ones, so they could talk without being overheard. The food that the servants placed in front of them was typical of this realm; spiced meats and sausages, pickled red cabbage, heavy breads, drinks made with spiced yogurt. Rufryd had thought the fare strange at the start of the journey, but he was used to it now and ate hungrily.

As the conversation progressed, he noticed that the subject of Thanmandrathor's independence was carefully not mentioned.

'So, you mean to go into Vexor?' said the Duke. His voice was deep and hoarse, as if he'd been ill.

'A cross between a diplomatic visit and spying,' said Mirias. 'In theory, the Queen's representatives can enter Vexor at any time, but in practice no one has ever been there. Not in living memory, at least.'

'No surprise,' said Tasq. 'No one in their right mind wants to be anywhere near the Bhahdradomen. But we have known for a long time, and have been trying to warn those in Parione, that the Bhahdradomen will rise again.'

The Duke's forthright manner and the glint of his olivine eyes sent a spasm down Rufryd's spine.

'Well, the Queen has listened to you,' said Dawn. 'She's sent us. I wonder what we'll find?'

The Duke pushed his food around his plate. He had only eaten a few mouthfuls. 'I can only imagine, from what history tells us. A few thousand years ago, in the glory days of Azura Maroc, the inhabitants of Lapiszul and Parione imagined they had reached the very peak of civilisation, while Thanmandrathor was still overrun with tribes. But we had our own way of life that was no less than theirs; we were closer to Q'enartre of the Lightning, we hadn't forgotten how to read portents in the weather, and the Aelyr dwelled among us just as freely as they did among the citizens of Lapiszul. The Marocians never thought they'd fall – but along came the Grey Death to take them down.

'After the plague had wreaked its havoc, the Aelyr began to quarrel with humans and eventually withdrew to their own realm, rather than patch up their differences. At some time within that period, the Bhahdradomen began to appear. Alas, the good folk of Azura Maroc and Paranios were too embroiled with their Aelyr troubles to notice what was happening in Thanmandrathor.'

'So the Bhahdradomen made their first appearance in this realm?' Dawn asked quietly. Her freckled face was colourless.

'So it's believed,' said the Duke. 'Whether they landed on the shore in ships from some land of their own, or stepped through a portal from another realm, it's never really been known.'

'Hellaxis,' said Rufryd. 'The blackened land.'

'But where is that?' said the Duke, pointing his fork at Rufryd. 'Can you draw it on a map? No. They appeared

270

with their dreadful flesh-animals that consumed every-thing in their path and they spread, devouring the land, leaving sterile earth behind. Their eyes contained no souls and their hearts no feeling. They were hard to kill and yet their mere presence could turn humans mad, their fingers can cut through human flesh and bone like knives. Can you imagine the terror they spread in the early days, when our settlements saw them coming and could do nothing to defend themselves? We had no help from Parione in those days. It was centuries before the Nine Realms were united against them.

'Humans challenged the Eaters, of course, but we couldn't hold them back. It was like trying to stop the wind. We made war upon them and drove them back several times, but each time they came again, or spread into different places, like a stream seeping through a dam to find a new course. We believed they were disorganised.' The Duke gave a sharp laugh. 'Our mistake. You've heard the name Ghaurthror, which is still used to frighten naughty children in this realm? Just as humans thought the Bhahdradomen might be defeated, they produced a great and fell leader who led them to victory. Ghaurthror the Dreaded, Ghaurthror of the Flies, they called him. He ruled most of Aventuria for two hundred years. He never took Parione itself, but he pushed humans further and further back into the heart of Aventuria while his legions ate up the land around it; Deirland, Sepheret, parts of Mithrain. Can you imagine it? I have nightmares about it. Our beautiful land, black and ruined. Dra'a'ks and vultures circling to pluck at the remains.'

The Duke paused, studying his wine glass. He looked weary, as if his passion on the subject had worn him out. His wife and daughter looked concernedly at him as if they'd heard this a dozen times before, but still shared his feelings. Rufryd, against his will, felt drawn to Duke Tasq. He seemed to be everything that his own father, Arthryn, was not . . .

271

'Still, they never reached Parione, never conquered the Amber Citadel. That saved us in the end, for without that place of freedom, that rallying point, I doubt that the Nine Realms could ever have conjoined and struck back. Ah, but times have changed. The King abuses our friendship, the Paranians attack those who were their friends.'

'That's over now, Father,' said Branq'elin.

Everyone at the table seemed to be waiting with held breath for Tasq to speak again. His eyes were heavy-lidded; Rufryd wondered for a moment if he was losing his faculties, dwelling too much in the past. Then the Duke's eyes opened wide and they were as bright as new leaves. He looked straight at Rufryd. 'Many disturbing signs have reached us, great storms and earth tremors, emanating from the mountains that lie between here and the Silver Plains. Farmers and villagers are fleeing from the skirts of the greatest peak, Q'enartre's Throne. It's no coincidence, it seems to me, that there were once many Aelyr in that area; that the mountain was considered theirs, and no one dared to venture upon it.'

Branq'elin took his hand. 'We've experienced strange weather on our way here, Father. What do you think it means?'

'Q'enartre and Ank'eth are angry. Humans have become blind to the changes under their very noses, so the gods are trying to warn us! These are terrible omens. Something is disturbing the energies of the Earth – or the Earth herself is disturbed by changes we don't understand. This feels to me like the breakdown of the Xauroma.'

'I don't think that's fair,' said Rufryd, meeting Tasq's gaze. 'Helananthe has only just remade the covenant. She wouldn't break it.'

'She may have no choice. If Garnelys has damaged it beyond repair, it may simply fragment like eggshell in her hands. I sent someone to Q'enartre's Throne in the hopes that they'd find the source of these storms, but they have not returned. I'm loath to send anyone else. Where are the

Aelyr, who might have helped us? Gone! Turned their backs upon us.'

Rufryd asked, 'My lord, do you think the Aelyr have something to do with these disturbances?'

For a moment he thought that the Duke hadn't heard or understood his question. He said slowly, 'There is a stone there. It points at the mountain. Its name is Nilothphon's Finger. No doubt this means nothing to you.'

'I've heard of Nilothphon,' said Rufryd. 'A great Aelyr mage, who was supposed to have tamed the energies of the Earth, whatever that means.'

'Ah. You can make a deduction then.' The Duke shifted in his seat, as if to ease a painful back.

'It was an Aelyr place of power?'

'Exactly! So we have the lunacy of Garnelys, we have civil war, we have mysterious storms and disturbances. Are they caused by Aelyr, Bhahdradomen, Q'enartre? We don't know. The point is this. *They are all distractions.* One event follows another to divert our attention from what is happening underneath. Shall we allow ourselves to be distracted?'

Along the other tables, the murmur of voices went on, but those at the Duke's table were transfixed. Despite his fragile appearance, Tasq had the fire of prophecy within him.

'No, we shall learn from history. What preceded the last Bhahdradomen invasion? Plague. Foolish quarrels between humans and Aelyr. *Distractions.* But Q'enartre illuminates everything in a sharp clear light. Nothing can be hidden from Her.'

Tasq stopped. He coughed, dabbed at his mouth with a napkin. The silence was doom-laden. Eventually Rufryd said, 'Well, that's why we're going to Vexor, my lord. To discover if there's any foundation for our fears. We'll look at this mountain, too, if it lies on our way.'

The Duke shook his head, more in sadness than refusal of the offer. 'Ah, this is brave of you, young man.'

Rufryd shrugged. 'Someone's got to go, or we'll never learn anything.'

Tasq placed his hand on Rufryd's arm, seeming to rest his whole weight on him, as if he were close to collapse. 'Indeed, and I wish you the protection of Q'enartre and Ank'eth on your journey. Who's going with you into Vexor?'

'The four of us, father,' Branq'elin said quietly. 'Mirias, Dawn, Rufryd and myself.'

The Duke put down his fork. Sweat made a greyish sheen on his forehead; he took a quick mouthful of water. 'No, Branq'elin. There is no need for you to go.'

'But I want to.'

He began to breathe hard. 'Why?'

'Because if someone must go, why not me? Our family leads Thanmandrathor, the least I can do is to show that I am not afraid to undertake the worst and most dangerous tasks on this realm's behalf.'

'Well, that's very finely spoken, but you are not going. You are my heir.'

'What sort of Duchess will I be, if I don't prove my worth?'

'You have led our army to Parione. Freed us from Garnelys. You have nothing more to prove.' He coughed, a hoarse gasp of pain. 'You're not going.'

'You can't stop me, father,' Branq'elin said. 'Please, calm yourself.'

'I forbid it. Not to show my authority over you – for that vanished a long time since – but because you are my child and I don't want to lose you.'

Branq'elin stood leaning on the edge of the table, taut with passion. 'I know, father. But still, I have to go.'

She straightened up, as if to leave. Her father reached out to her, crying, 'No!'

His face was white. He tried to rise but collapsed back into his chair, one hand gripping the table's edge, the other clutching his abdomen. His cry turned to a strangled gasp of pain; everyone was on their feet, Duchess Annuin leaning over him in alarm.

'What is it?' she said. 'The pains again?'

'Yes – but worse. Worse!' The Duke bent double, his face screwed up and his voice fading from an agonised rasp to silence. He slumped in his chair and his lips were blue.

'Father!' Branq'elin cried. Then to the servants at the edge of the hall, 'Quickly, send for the healer. Carry the Duke to his room.'

Lord Poel climbed Theatre Hill in the twilight, lifting the hem of his robe to pick his way over the flagstones. He had donned a plain cloak of nondescript grey-brown, with a deep hood. He had always cut a distinctive figure in Parione and this was a two-edged sword. Once he had been respected as Garnelys's chancellor, but for implementing the demolition of the theatre he was universally loathed, and his statuesque build and bearing made him all too easily seen and reviled. So he'd taken to creeping round in this nondescript guise, which he hated, and still, sometimes, he was recognised.

Tonight, though, he passed no one on the hill. There had been some improvements since Garnelys had wreaked devastation on the site. The silt and debris of the building work had been swept away; new trees had been planted; the gardens ruined by constant traffic and the dragging of stone blocks up the hill had been replanted. The gate to the underground network, where the conscripts had been billeted, was sealed off with stone. All seemed peaceful.

But there was one thing that Helananthe had been unable to do, and that was to demolish the unfinished Tower and rebuild the theatre. Too much labour, too expensive, too dangerous; perhaps even impossible to take down such an edifice. Poel smiled. His reasons for hating the theatre were so deeply buried now that he hardly thought of them; all he knew was that it was a small secret victory, that the Heliodor Tower remained.

His victory, and the key to his future power.

He stepped at last on to the broad crown of the hill and glanced over the scene. He had not been here since before Garnelys's death so he could see how the site had changed. No longer a mass of conscripts labouring, no creak of rope nor ring of chisel on stone. All was deserted. Grass had grown over the mud, even pushed up through cracks in the broad flagged area that surrounded the base of the Tower. The sky was soft grey silk; he had a clear view of Temple Hill, and of Citadel Hill with its golden-amber diadem. He'd seen it all before; and in his own way he loved it, and wanted it all to be his. But as Poel raised his eyes, the sight of the Tower amazed him.

Two hundred feet in diameter, great buttresses supporting its curved walls, a huge solid column soaring up against the sky. It rose for a dizzying three hundred feet and ended suddenly in a gap-toothed row of blocks; a great monument unfinished, not the slender finger it should have been but something baser, a stump. Yet, still impressive. When we are all dust, Poel wondered, what will future ages make of it? In the gloom it was not sun-yellow but luminous white as limestone; a monument at once as dense and heavy as a mountain, yet crisp and ethereal.

Shadows lay deep in the unfinished inscriptions high on its sides. He could tell what the half-words said, though; had he not helped Garnelys to plan them? *Garnelys, King of Light, raised this Tower of the Sun to the glory of Nuth and Anuth in the year 1751 Of Silana. Blessed be the Great Mother of Life Unending.*

The truth was, the Tower was not meant to be finished. Garnelys had planned to go on building it forever, believing that for as long as he worked on it, he would never die. And perhaps there had been some arcane power behind his belief. Poel was ready to believe almost anything.

Poel stepped towards the Tower. There were ways

inside, tall apertures that were dwarfed to mere slits by the bulk of the walls. He found one; a long, high corridor through the thickness of the wall. The damp odour of stone wrapped around him, laced with something sweet, organic.

Inside, Garnelys had meant to make a simple temple, with stairs winding round and round so that the devoted could make pilgrimages to the top – but never quite to the top, since it was meant to grow forever. But that work had not been done. Instead Poel stepped into emptiness, a great cold chimney with a coin of sky far above him, and on the ground rough earth on which rain and leaves and dead birds had fallen. A sharp, cold shiver went through him. Never in his life had he possessed a shred of the sensitivity or intuition that made writers or priests or seers of others; but here, even the pragmatic Poel felt the weight of something dark creeping round and round the walls.

The Bhahdradomen were already waiting for him.

They came out of the twilight, making him jump. Their cloaks blended with the surroundings, shadow-dappled stone. The grinning skull-face of Gulzhur; Zhoaah – once called Laphaeome – soft and pale; and a third he did not recognise. There were others, but they stayed back where he could barely see them. It was growing darker, and although the Bhahdradomen seemed faintly luminescent, they kept the light to themselves.

'It's not bad, is it?' said Zhoaah.

Poel was confused. 'What?'

'The Tower. It's not bad, though I say so myself. I was a good architect.'

'Unquestionably.' Lord Poel cleared his throat, composing himself. 'A shame it was not finished.'

Zhoaah shrugged. He had a charm about him, when he chose. 'Well, there's enough of it to serve our purpose. That was the point. Not to finish it, for it was never going to be finished, but to build enough.'

Poel waited. He had no idea why they'd asked him to

meet them here, but he suddenly felt alone and vulnerable, like a child. The smell . . . the feeling that something was crawling around behind him . . .

'We would like you to meet Tzumezht. He is sent from Vaurgroth to aid our cause. This is the man I have told you about, Lord Poel, once a close associate of our late friend Garnelys, and now invaluable in helping our *domenim*. Our people.'

Tzumezht's face was grey and hollow-cheeked, his teeth overlong like those of an ancient horse, but his eyes were black jewels, on fire with energy. Intelligence, excitement? Poel rarely noticed such things but now he wished he could read their minds as they seemed to read his.

'I am delighted to meet you,' said Tzumezht, in what seemed a mockery of a Parionian drawl. He stretched out a hand. Poel never knew whether or not to shake hands with these creatures, but they seemed happy to ape human customs. So he took the proffered hand, and felt multiple bony fingers close drily around his like the legs of a huge scorpion. He flinched, trying to hide his revulsion. Tzumezht smiled.

'You find yourself in illustrious company,' Zhoaah told Poel. 'These are some of the most talented Bhahdradomen you will meet. We all have our own skills; Enabler Gulzhur commands his *ghelim* and calls them across time. Prefigurer Tzumezht here is a mage, a manipulator of *gauroth*. My own talents as Facilitator, diplomat and architect are insignificant by comparison but I like to think—'

Tzumezht cut across him. 'Zhoaah is too modest. We need your help, Lord Poel. We want to test the Tower's true function, to channel *gauroth* energy, and this is more easily done with humans, so . . .'

Poel heard a voice among the other group of Bhahdradomen; a human voice, whimpering in fear. 'What's that?' he said.

'You will know, in a moment. As I was saying—'

'What do you mean, the true function of the Tower?'

Poel frowned. 'It was meant to be a monument to Garnelys. True function, what is that?'

'I thought I had just explained,' Tzumezht said, his voice dangerously low.

'Zhoaah never mentioned this to me before. A monument!'

The pale Bhahdradomen insinuated his hand through Poel's arm. 'It must have slipped my mind. But come, you are an intelligent man; you must have known there was more to it than met the eye. Forgive me for assuming that a great man like yourself would not need every subtlety explained to him.'

Lord Poel was momentarily paralysed. His vanity would not let him admit his ignorance. 'Indeed, but . . . but go on, Lord Tzumezht.'

'As I was saying, we intend to raise *gauroth*, to open the *ezht*.'

He had no idea what the grey one was talking about, but dared not admit it. The human cries grew louder. Poel looked over to the other hooded creatures, and saw in their midst a human boy, perhaps thirteen years old and terrified.

'Why is that lad here?' Poel asked warily.

Gulzhur replied, 'We need pain, to raise *gauroth*. There are other ways but they are longer and more difficult. With human pain, it is quick and easy – at least for a mage of Tzumezht's abilities. Gods, even Garnelys could do it!'

He laughed; his laughter was grossly inappropriate, for the boy was staring helplessly straight at Poel, obviously aware that he was in mortal danger. 'Help me, my lord!' he called weakly, struggling in the hands of his captors. 'Please help me!'

Even Poel was shaken. 'You can't mean to . . . Let him go!'

Zhoaah sighed. 'Well, we could. It's your choice. If you don't want us to torture the boy, we'll have to torture you instead.'

Poel's head snapped to left and right. There were Bhahdradomen all around him, quiet and soft as spectres, with hungry eyes fastened on him. A feeling of nightmare madness swept through him; he was unarmed but it didn't matter, they could take him to pieces with their eyes without even touching him. He wanted to flee but there was no escape route; he felt sweat pooling in his armpits, oozing across his wide shoulders.

'Whose pain is it to be, Lord Poel? Yours or the boy's?'

'Gods,' gasped Poel, shaking. 'I can't . . .'

'Please make up your mind quickly.' Tzumezht's eyes bored into him like pins. 'I would like to start.'

'The boy.' Poel pointed at the youth with a wavering hand. The words exploded like spit from his lips. 'Don't hurt me. Use him!'

Zhoaah grinned. 'So be it, but you must be the one to wield the knife.'

'What?'

Zhoaah pulled a very human, wry face and shook his head. 'We get more power if humans hurt each other. I don't know why. Twice as much pain, I suppose. It's especially efficacious if the one doing the hurting is reluctant; Garnelys was perfect because he so hated what he was doing. So if you find it difficult, don't feel inadequate to the task; it actually makes it better for us.'

He placed a big, curved knife in Lord Poel's hand.

The others brought the boy before him. Poel stared into the young, desperate face. He trembled, and his bowels cramped with horror. In his everyday dealings he was stiff, cold, sometimes cruel; but even he drew the line at inflicting physical pain. But the Bhahdradomen were all around him, eager, dangerous. The boy whimpered, wetting himself in terror. Poel closed his eyes, and plunged the knife forward.

The youth dropped to his knees, emitting terrible, tearing groans. Poel jumped back in panic; his aim had been poor and he had wounded him in the abdomen.

Blood poured out through the boy's fingers as he clutched at the wound, staring up at his attacker with uncomprehending, pleading eyes. His pain and fear were so intense that even Poel felt them.

At once the whole Tower seemed to throb.

Tzumezht's arms were raised and his lips moved soundlessly. Between his hands he held a lump of rock, some mineral that reflected dull liverish light from its facets. Poel, watching dizzily, had the impression that the boy's pain was being dragged into the crystal, focussed, and sent spinning out around the walls. The very fabric of the Tower itself seemed to absorb the stark energy, vibrating with it.

A column of dark purple light appeared in the centre of the chamber. It stood there, growing brighter and brighter, until Lord Poel shrank back, dazzled. Thunderous power emanated from it and he seemed to be looking into another world, a black world that was no more than a path crossing a plain under a dark sky. Yet the sight of it filled him with irrational terror.

'What is it?' he mouthed, but no sound came out.

A figure appeared in the centre of the column. His robe swirled black and purple like a storm but his face was white, blue-white as a cave of ice, the high, domed skull tattooed with red web, eyes that could swallow galaxies; and then the tattooed web vanished as the face and skull flushed crimson and the dreadful eyes tipped back in their sockets, and hands with too many writhing fingers were stretched out towards Poel.

'It is Vaurgroth of the Fire,' said Gulzhur. 'Chosen of the Ancestor, our leader. He sees you. Bow down to the Master of Light!'

Terror exploded through Poel. Losing control and reason he sprawled on the ground and soiled himself. *Vaurgroth saw him.*

'He's pleased with you,' Zhoaah said gently. 'He asks not that you worship him, but that you worship the Ancestor,

281

the only true creator of life. Give yourself up to him, and you will be King.'

Poel clawed at the earth, and a wild ecstasy filled him. It was easy. All he had to do was give up his humanity, follow the Ancestor, and all Vaurgroth's terrible power would fill him. 'Yes,' he rasped. 'I give myself to you, I accept the Ancestor!'

A strange deep noise rang like a bell. A laugh of satisfaction.

Gulzhur said, 'You see, with a human king on the throne it will all be so much easier.'

Poel neither knew nor cared what he meant. He outstretched his arms to the dreadful figure of Vaurgroth and gave himself up, lost in the bliss of surrender, felt the leader's eyes filling him with a new, savage strength; collapsed back on to the earth, losing consciousness for a moment.

There was a cry. He came back to himself to find the vision gone, the Tower dark again. And Gulzhur was standing over the boy, plunging bare fingers straight into his breastbone, killing him instantly. Poel shivered, suddenly feeling sick and drained. He didn't know what had happened but it seemed something depraved. A swamp into which he had now sunk so deep there was no hope of rescue.

'You should go home now, and rest.' Zhoaah sat on the ground beside him, his legs bending at strange angles more like a reptile's than a human's. 'You have helped us immeasurably tonight. We have awoken the Tower to its true function, which has proved to my cynical friends that when I designed it, I knew what I was doing. We have used the power to manifest Vaurgroth, and see! We have shown him our work, and he has seen and approved of you.'

Poel groaned.

'Is something wrong?' asked Zhoaah.

He managed to sit up, brushing the earth from his robes

and feeling humiliated at his loss of control. He could smell his own excrement. His mouth curled in distaste. 'Nothing.'

'Don't think of telling your human friends. Don't think of backing out; it's too late. You've sworn yourself to the Ancestor now, and Vaurgroth has seen you. If you want to be King, stay with us.'

The last words brought Poel back to his senses. He remembered how it had felt to taste the Bhahdradomen leader's power. His will hardened, and he sloughed off his feelings of disgust along with the remains of his conscience. From this loathsome nadir, he could go nowhere but upwards.

'I have no human friends,' he said. 'And I shall be King, whatever the cost.'

'Has he been ill before?' Rufryd asked.

He stood in the doorway of the Duke's chamber, while the Duchess, Branq'elin, a priestess-healer and several others fussed around his bed. The Duke was conscious but silent, with no energy for anything but fighting the pain. Branq'elin and her mother were distraught.

'Several times, over the past few months,' said the Duchess, her voice shaky. 'Always after eating.'

'Has anyone else been ill?'

She shook her head. 'He thinks that his digestion has become poor with age, but I think it's more than that. His chest pains him, and he complains that his hands tingle and his head spins . . . This is the worst he's been, though. I have never had to call the healer before.'

The priestess, a young sharp-faced woman, looked hard at Rufryd. 'Thank you for your help, but I should be asking these questions, not you. These herbs will ease his pain, then perhaps we can find out what the trouble is.'

'What do you think it is?' Branq'elin asked anxiously.

'It might be his heart. Or indeed, something he has eaten.'

'Hope you don't take too long to work it out,' Rufryd

said sourly. He pulled away from the doorframe and went down the stairs, back into the dining hall. He had the strangest feeling . . . perhaps it was something quite obvious, but the others were too busy fussing over the Duke to think about it.

There were still a lot of people in the hall, some finishing their meal and others milling about, waiting for news of the Duke. Servants were beginning to clear the long tables, but on the round table where Tasq's party had been sitting, the half-laden plates were still there. Rufryd watched wryly as a couple of hounds came sniffing their way towards the table, one of them raising its long head to wolf down what was left of Branq'elin's meal. The plate fell on the floor, and the food was gone in a couple of mouthfuls.

The hound glanced around furtively, as if it knew it was taking a chance. Reaching the Duke's place it dipped its head sideways, lapping the rim of the plate until its teeth closed on a solid morsel. Rufryd watched. To his curiosity, the dog pulled away from the table and dropped its head to the floor, its face a picture of revulsion. Its jaws opened and it pushed the mouthful out with its tongue in a taut bow of disgust. Then the hound shook itself and trotted away, uttering deep retching coughs of disgust.

Rufryd went to the table and looked at the food on the plate, sniffed it cautiously. There seemed nothing wrong with it, nor with the sour yogurt they had been drinking. Some bitterness only dogs could taste?

Rufryd went down to the kitchen, and pushed his way through the men and women working there until he found Con. The boy looked delighted to see him, until Rufryd pulled him into a dark recess where bins of flour were stored.

'The Duke is ill,' Rufryd said.

'Yes, we heard,' said Con. 'Is he bad?'

'Bit soon to tell. Do you know of anyone who works for him who might want to harm him?'

'No, of course not!' The lad looked horrified. 'What do

you mean? Everyone loves him!'

'You can't think of anyone, then, who might want to poison his food?'

Con gaped at him. He seemed so utterly dumbfounded that Rufryd felt almost sorry for him. 'No! That's impossible!'

'I hope so. But think about it, Con. The Duke has been ill before; yet he suffers this pain only after he has eaten. Tonight the pain is bad enough to make him collapse.'

'I know he's been ill, but it could be anything. No one else has been affected. It can't be the food.'

'Strange, then, that I watched a hound happily eating everyone else's leftovers, but spitting out the Duke's . . . isn't it? Perhaps it's something that humans can't taste, I don't know. Strange, that.'

'No, it's nothing we've done, I swear!'

'I'm not accusing you of anything, but think. Is there anyone who is alone with the food before it reaches the Duke?'

'Lots of people. Someone wheels the food on trolleys to the end of the corridor, then the waiting staff take it to the Great Hall.'

'Who did it tonight?' Con's eyes were wide. He shook his head. Rufryd gripped the edges of his shirt and thrust him into the corner, just hard enough to frighten him. 'Think.'

'Noli.'

'And the other times Noli was on trolley duty – did they coincide with the Duke being ill?'

Con's colour drained away. He was scared, but defiant. 'A few times. I don't remember. The upstairs staff don't tell us everything!'

'They obviously tell you enough.'

'Noli's my best friend. I know him. He has no family, this has always been his home. He wouldn't do anything like that!'

'We'll see, shall we? Go and make a hot drink.'

'What sort?'

'A posset for bad stomachs, with whisky and ginger root in it, or whatever you use here. Then send Noli to take it to the Duke.'

'How d'you know *I* won't poison it?'

'I don't – but I don't think you're likely to do it with me watching, are you? Go on.'

Trembling, Con did as Rufryd asked. No one asked Con why he was heating milk on the huge black stove. From the recess, Rufryd watched as he made the drink and gave it to Noli. The shorter boy took the steaming glass, carefully wrapped a napkin round it and placed it on a tray. Nothing untoward.

Noli set off into the dimly-lit corridor that led from the kitchen to the stairs. Rufryd followed at a distance, aware that Con was a couple of yards behind him. The lad carried the tray with great care, one hand holding the glass steady; innocent, eager to do his job well.

Noli didn't have a free hand to put anything into the drink. Rufryd began to feel his suspicion was wrong. Then, on the bend of the stairs, Noli stopped and looked around. Rufryd pressed back in the stairwell so the boy wouldn't see him. And in horror, he saw Noli spit a clear yellowish liquid into the milk.

Rufryd's stomach lurched. Beside him, Con's eyes were huge in the faint lamplight. Swallowing hard, Rufryd mounted the stairs softly after the boy.

Noli walked into the Duke's room and eased himself between the onlookers to offer the posset to the Duke.

'Ah, that's thoughtful of you, lad,' the Duke said weakly. He was resting back against the pillows, whey-faced but looking better than he had. 'Smells wonderful.'

'What's in it?' the priestess said suspiciously.

'Whisky and ginger root, for his lordship's stomach,' said Noli. 'As you requested, good mother.'

'I don't know who sent for it,' said the priestess, 'but I suppose it will do no harm.'

'All the same, I suggest you don't drink it,' Rufryd said, walking forward.

Everyone looked at him. 'What?' said the Duke.

'I was following him. I saw him spit in it.'

Branq'elin, Annuin, all the others around the bed stared at Rufryd, their mouths crimping in distaste. 'What?' said the Duchess. 'Dear goddess, you didn't, did you, Noal?'

Noli shook his head. He began to look unreal to Rufryd. His eyes were odd, the pupils filling too much of the space between the lids. His hair clasped his head strangely, more like a lank wig than his own hair. Something about his skin . . . a translucency, an odd texture . . .

Rufryd's heart began to beat hard. His head swam. Gods, was this what Lynden had experienced when he sensed things that others couldn't see? He'd never felt anything so horrible before. Never had any sensitivity to the unseen . . . had Lynden passed some of the *ethroth* to him when he'd died, or was it a sense you picked up by chance, with experience or trauma?

Rufryd fought hard to keep his voice calm. 'Either this child has spit the colour of piss, or he had put something in his mouth that he knew would not harm him.'

Noli glanced around him. Then he dropped the tray, splashing hot milk everywhere, and tried to run. Rufryd caught him and held him halfway to the door. The boy struggled briefly then was still, but Rufryd felt a strange wiry strength in his thin limbs. 'How long has this boy worked in your household?'

A long pause. 'All his life,' said the Duchess at last. 'He was an orphan. Con's family, who work for us, took him in. He's always been here.'

'And you trust him?'

'Naturally. He's a good young lad.' She looked at the other boy, who was at Rufryd's side. 'He's a good friend of yours, isn't he, Con?'

Con nodded, then frowned.

'But hasn't anyone ever really looked at him?' said

Rufryd.

Everyone stared at the boy, uncomprehending. 'What is this?' said Branq'elin.

Rufryd felt his arms going numb from holding the boy. A horrible, white sensation was creeping up his chest like visceral fear. 'Something strange happened in the Amber Citadel. The King had an advisor he trusted, who turned out to be . . . not human. An almost but not quite perfect copy of a human. I just think . . . are you absolutely sure . . .'

Now the captive was glaring back at Rufryd, his head twisted, and Rufryd was beginning to see more and more clearly. He felt a thrill of terror go through him as if the whole world had turned inside out. Yet, because he knew what was happening, he kept control. 'If you look closely at his hands you'll probably see that he has odd growths there, like extra fingers that haven't grown properly. His joints aren't quite in the right place. His eyes have barely any white to them. He doesn't smell of good honest sweat, but of something strange, a bit like mushrooms that have rotted.'

No one spoke. Dawn gasped, but none of the others seemed to *see*. And then one of them shouted.

'Bhahdradomen!'

It was Con who'd seen. And Rufryd nearly wept, because he saw the horror of revelation tear through the boy's soul, saw it spread through the others. But it was worst for Con because this had been his friend.

Someone was yelling for the guards. Men and women came running with their round shields held ready and their short swords drawn. Somehow Noli writhed out of Rufryd's grasp and fell to his knees, raising his pale face to plead with them. Bhahdradomen or not, he was transfixed with terror.

'I'm not Bhahdradomen! I'm human!' he cried. 'Human!'

Rufryd stepped away from him. He expected them to lift

him up and take him away to be questioned.

What happened instead left him boneless with disbelief. For the guards made no attempt to arrest Noli. They simply attacked him. Uttering hoarse cries they set on him with swords, battered their shields into his head. Rufryd saw the boy flat on his back, trying to crawl away. His eyes were blind with incomprehension, his fingers grasping the air. Terrified and in agony, but not dying . . .

'Stop it!' Rufryd yelled hoarsely.

No one seemed to hear him. Then almost everyone in the room was joining in, using pots or fruit knives or bare hands, as if in the phobic frenzy of one who sees a spider in the room and cannot rest until it is dead. Even the Duchess, even Mirias and Branq'elin took part; only Rufryd and the priestess, Dawn and Con stood aside in amazed horror.

Rufryd and the priestess both lunged forward, trying to pull the attackers off, but it was hopeless. Rufryd got a bruised jaw, the priestess was thrown across the room. Dawn held Con, trying to hide his eyes from the slaughter.

They did not stop until Noli lay dead; his head nearly severed, his body covered in wounds that did not bleed but oozed a pinkish-yellow plasma. Someone retched.

A horrible, crawling silence descended on the room.

Very soft, the priestess said, 'The Duke. His heart has stopped.'

Branq'elin's father was dead. His face hung in a rictus of dismay. It was clear to Rufryd, without the healer saying anything, that the shock had caused his heart to fail. The shock of knowing what he had harboured in his household . . . and the shock of watching the wretched creature dismembered in front of him.

'Oh, fuck,' Rufryd breathed between his teeth. 'Fucking hell. What have you done?' Shaking, he went forward and caught his friend's arm. 'Mirias? Is this what you call doing anything to protect Aventuria, you bastard?'

Mirias snatched his arm free angrily. 'You were the one

who showed us what he was!'

'Yes, I did,' Rufryd panted. 'But I didn't mean this to happen. *I didn't know this would happen!*' Suddenly he couldn't breathe.

Everyone stood like statues, blinking as if coming out of a trance. People started to sob and exclaim; some ran out of the room. Branq'elin looked at Rufryd with clear, fiery, uncompromising eyes.

'He was Bhahdradomen. He was poisoning my father. He had to die.'

'He was a boy! He didn't even seem to know what he was! Hasn't it occurred to you that you've destroyed your only chance of knowing if he was following orders, or trying to kill the Duke because that's what his kind do by instinct – or what?'

No one answered him. Con was shaking, sobbing so hard that he couldn't even make any sound. Dawn held him close.

Rufryd had to get out before he screamed or broke down himself. He strode out, pushing savagely past anyone who got in his way.

'You fucking barbarians! Goddess help the Bhahdradomen if ever they do come back!'

Rufryd stood outside in the darkness, leaning on the wall of the stables, with only the clucking of hens and the faint, indefinable noises of the night for company. Sunrise found him still there. He watched the slow fingers of sunlight creeping over the landscape, suffusing it with dramatic winter colour; lemon yellow, silver, misty blue, black. The town slumbered peacefully, but the steep forests and distant mountains beyond looked ineffably sombre, regal, enduring.

Mirias was right. Of course this land was worth protecting, of course it was. But at what cost?

Rufryd rubbed moisture out of his eyes. He was numb, exhausted, wretched. It had been his fault. He'd wanted to help . . . more than that, he'd wanted to prove himself cleverer than them, to off-handedly draw their attention to what had been under their noses all the time. Arrogant. Childishly, unforgivably arrogant.

Yet he'd never dreamed they would react like that.

Where had that frenzy come from? He didn't think any of them had even seen a Bhahdradomen before. Fear? Some primal reflex that they couldn't even control? He couldn't bear to think about it.

There was a movement beside him. Branq'elin was there. She moved softly to his side and leaned against the wall beside him. Her hair hung free on her shoulders and she'd changed into a plain gown of green velvet.

She had bathed since the killing; Rufryd could smell the freshness of soap and perfumed oils on her. He said nothing. After a few seconds, she spoke. 'I can't go to Vexor with you now.'

'I'm sure the Bhahdradomen will be relieved to hear that.'

He felt her stiffen with anger beside him. 'This is not a matter for jokes. I can't go because I am now Duchess of Thanmandrathor. And my mother needs me, I can't leave her.'

'That's all right,' he said coldly. 'We'll manage.'

'Perhaps you will not want to go either, after tonight. I shouldn't blame you. I relieve you of any obligation to continue the quest.'

He folded his arms. 'Why?'

Branq'elin said stiffly, 'You called us barbarians. Fucking barbarians, to be accurate. I cannot allow my countrymen to be insulted like that.'

'Why not? You deserved it. I don't want any Than'drathians coming to Vexor with us. I don't want you anywhere near me.'

'And you are so pure-hearted?' she hissed. 'Never had revealed to you a monster who was cold-bloodedly killing a loved one of yours?'

'Yes, and I revealed it!' he lashed back at her. 'It's my

fault. Goddess help me, I wish I'd left well alone!'

A long, angry pause. Her eyes shone with green fire. 'No, you did the right thing. But if you can't see it, and since we are so loathsome to you – just go!'

'I shall!' Rufryd pulled away from the wall and stood glaring at her. 'Why are you angry with me? I've done nothing. Oh no, hang on – I refused to sleep with you, that must be it.'

'You think that's why I'm angry?' she said incredulously. 'How dare you? Dear Ank'eth, how arrogant are you, to think that you are so special? I'd forgotten about it.'

'Really?'

She lunged at him, digging her fingers into his arms so hard he gasped with pain. 'My father died last night. The last thing he saw was his daughter murdering a serving boy! Do you think that I enjoyed what happened in that room? This has made it quite hard for me to think clearly, let alone not to be angry with everything and everyone.'

Somehow he got his hands twisted on to her forearms, trying to prise her off. The struggle mutated; his hands were moving over her shoulders and hers round his waist until suddenly she was leaning hard against him, sobbing in his arms.

'Gods, don't,' he said. 'Don't.'

He found her mouth. The kiss was hot and hard with anguish, slippery with the salt of tears. Then she looked at him, her lips still parted, her slanting eyes brilliant with moisture, and the scent of her hair wreathing all around him.

'Come in the stable,' she said. She took his hand and this time he went with her like a fish slipping through water; no resistance, no thought.

They went into the nearest stall, bolted the door behind them and lay down on the warm, pungent straw. Branq'elin wore nothing under her robe; Rufryd slid his hand over her naked thighs and between them, into her wondrous softness, thinking that this was hurried and desperate but it didn't matter. With strong quick fingers she was unlacing his breeches, easing his prick into her palm, gasping with pleasure to find him already hard.

'Quickly,' she said. She pulled him down to her, as eager to guide him as he was to be inside her. Still dressed they coupled fiercely, Branq'elin pulsing like a drumbeat beneath him, sweet fires washing over his skin and arrowing through his loins.

Through it all, the horse in the stall slept; his spine facing them, black mane and tail spread on the straw, the golden-yellow mound of his belly rising and falling.

Branq'elin cried out. Then she was weeping and laughing at the same time, very soft, before subsiding into drained stillness beneath him.

Rufryd didn't even touch her breasts until after he'd come. Then he stroked her nipples through the soft velvet, and kissed her mouth. He wanted to smile and say something affectionate, but it didn't seem appropriate, somehow. She looked at him from under half-lowered eyelids, calm and melancholy.

'Well, we didn't wake the horse,' he said. He withdrew from her and decorously rearranged her robe.

'No.' She nearly smiled, not quite. After a while she said, 'Now it's no longer my father's decision, whether or not to go on petitioning Helananthe for our independence. It's mine.'

'What? I can't believe you're talking about politics!'

He made to sit up, but she held him. 'I need to talk about this.'

'Well, what do you think you should do?'

'My heart tells me we should rule ourselves. My head tells me that Helananthe is right; we are stronger together.'

'So be independent and make an alliance, or something. Gods, I don't know.'

'I don't think you care, either, Rufryd.'

'Not particularly, no.'

'But you care enough to go into Vexor.'

'Yeah, well, if I say I'm going to do something, I do it.'

'And sometimes, if you say you are *not* going to do something, you do it.' He didn't answer. She said, 'You don't regret it, do you?'

'No, Branq'elin, I don't regret it.'

'Would you just call me Bran?'

'Bran. Whatever.' He sat up, fastening his clothes. 'Gods, I've just made love to the Duchess of Thanmandrathor. I wonder how much stranger my life can get.'

She frowned. 'Do you find me strange?'

'I didn't mean that, but yes, you're one of the strangest people I've ever met. I don't like you very much.'

She sat up behind him, stroking his back. 'And you, Rufryd, are conceited, miserable and ill-tempered. I don't like you either. All the same, I keep feeling drawn to you, I almost . . .'

He turned convulsively, and put his arms round her. 'Gods,' he said into her neck. 'I can't do this. I can't afford to be in love with anyone.'

'I'm not asking you to,' she said softly. 'But why?'

'Because . . . because of Vexor.'

She held on to him hard. She was crying again, he could feel her tears running on to his neck, the controlled, tiny spasms of her body as she tried to suppress it. He thought she was going to ask him not to go; then she said, 'Go as my champion, Rufryd.'

When they came out into the dawn, a solitary stable-boy was filling buckets at the pump on the far side of the yard. He didn't see them.

Five days passed. Tasqabad Hall had settled to a grim quiescence, but the atmosphere – so warm and vivid when they'd arrived – was vile. Rufryd felt he couldn't stand it a day longer. It was not only the Duke's death or the murder of Noli, but the dreadful suspicions aroused by the exposure of a Bhahdradomen. Everyone looked at everyone else with cold, wary eyes, uncertain whether their friends or family were truly human or not. If it could happen once . . .

Now he and Dawn and Mirias were on horseback, their saddlebags stuffed with fresh clothes and provisions, their weapons sharpened and oiled. A few specks of snow were falling from a grumbling sky. He couldn't wait to be on his way.

On his saddle he carried the basket with four little blue-doves inside. Once they were in Vexor, they would be released to carry messages back to Parione. But Vexor still seemed impossibly far away, so far in the future that he couldn't imagine it.

All the household were assembled before the Hall to see them off. Branq'elin was there with her mother Annuin; the older woman's rosy colour had fled and her eyes were sad, gazing off into the distance where once she had looked with keen warmth at everyone. Branq'elin looked sombre and splendid in a bronze-coloured gown with a green cloak thrown over it, bronze jewellery shining at her throat and wrists, a circlet on her forehead. Now she was saying her goodbyes to Dawn; the two women clasping hands, looking warmly into each other's eyes, Dawn leaning down in the saddle to kiss her. It crossed Rufryd's mind that there was more between them than friendship, although when they'd found the time to do anything about it, he didn't know.

Rufryd had slept with Branq'elin every night, against his better judgement. Twice he'd tried to refuse, only to be at her door five minutes later, giving in.

Unlike Ashtar, she didn't leave him feeling empty. That was the frightening thing. He couldn't forget that she'd helped to kill Noli. He found her abrasive, intolerant, and preoccupied. Yet when they were together there was a warmth . . . a comfortable feeling, as if they understood each other as he and Tanthe had never done. And it scared the hell out of him.

'Dawn, come on,' he said.

'I'm ready,' said Dawn. She turned her chestnut gelding towards Rufryd and Mirias, urging him into a brisk walk. 'My Lady Branq'elin, Lady Annuin, we shall see you again when we pass back this way from our journey. Our thanks for your hospitality.'

'Fare you well,' Branq'elin said formally. 'Blessings of Q'enartre and Ank'eth upon you.'

Her gaze met Rufryd's for the briefest moment, a spurt of leaf-green fire. Then the three were riding away, the Hall dwindling . . . the town itself dwindling . . . until they were out in the open countryside, with Tasqabad no longer even in sight.

'You all right, Rufe?' said Dawn eventually.

'Fine. "We shall see you again when we pass back this way." I admire your blithe confidence.'

'We will come back,' she said, frowning. 'It's no good not believing it.'

'Take no notice of him,' said Mirias. 'Gods, if you get any more cheerful, Rufe, I'll have to shoot you.'

'Shut the fuck up.'

'It just amazes me that you can spend all week pleasuring the lady of the house and still be so miserable.'

Mirias sounded archly Parionian. Rufryd turned in the saddle and said quietly, 'It amazes me that you can join in hacking Noli to pieces and still be so cheerful.'

'Stop it!' Dawn barked. That night had caused some friction between her and Mirias, Rufryd knew, and it was evil of him to stir it up again. 'If you two are going to carry on like this, I'd rather go to Vexor on my own!'

Mirias had gone white, to Rufryd's satisfaction.

'I shan't say another word,' he said.

Two days passed. The road became narrower and wound through dark forests. Rufryd began to get the vague but persistent feeling that they were being followed. He hated it. This was another of Lynden's characteristics, that he'd never possessed before. He hoped it was his

296

imagination, not Duchess Branq'elin riding after them with a change of heart.

They were in a damp-wreathed forest on the second evening, preparing to make camp, when a figure came riding up out of the mist. A small horse, brownish-dun rather than the prized golden colour, but with the distinctive arched neck and high gait of the Than'drathian breed. On its back was a lanky silhouette, who looked less than comfortable in the saddle.

They all stood up from tending the fire and stared. As the rider came closer, Rufryd saw that it was Con.

'Great,' he said. 'What the hell's he doing here?'

Con reached their camp and reined in. He looked travel-worn and fraught. Before any of them could speak, he looked straight at Rufryd and said, 'I want to come with you.'

'You what?' said Rufryd, placing a hand on the dun horse's neck. 'I don't think you do. D'you know where we're going?'

'I don't care. I've ridden two days to find you. Don't send me back!'

'Where did you get this horse?' asked Dawn.

'I took it from the stables.'

'Stole it,' said Rufryd.

'I know her ladyship will understand. I want to go with you, Rufryd. I must.'

The youth looked nothing like Lynden; he was taller and thinner, gawky and almost feminine in his youth, and his hair in its long braid was dark as umber. Yet there was something of Lynden in his eyes, that same haunted innocence.

'How old are you?' Rufryd asked.

'Fifteen,' Con answered.

Even younger than he'd thought. 'Anthar's balls, you had better go home. I can't look after you.'

'I don't need looking after!' Con said fiercely.

'Oh, right,' Rufryd snarled. 'Until you break your ankle,

catch a fever or decide to rush off and do something heroic on your own. Well, when that happens, you needn't come crying to me for help. Go home!'

'I have no home!' Con cried fervently. 'Don't you understand? If not for me, Noli would still be alive. I betrayed him!'

'But you had to. You didn't know what they were going to do. Neither did I.'

The boy shook his head, tears rolling down his face. 'I don't care what he was. I'd rather never have known. He was my friend. How the hell do you think I *can* go home, after what I've done? *You* did this, Rufryd. Now I don't care where you're going, I'm coming with you!'

Chapter Thirteen. Valley of Stone

The fortress gate clanged shut behind Tanthe and Elrill, black iron forming a seamless barrier with the rugged ashen rock of the walls. Her desperate appeal to the governor had failed; if even the threat of the Queen's wrath failed to move him, there was no recourse.

Outside, the day was gloomy; black clouds wreathed across a stone-grey sky, and the wind blew flurries of rain into their faces. Tanthe looked about for Jthery, saw him across the street on the paved bank of the river, his cloak pulled tight around him, the hem fluttering. She and Elrill began to walk disconsolately towards him over the shining cobbles.

'Gods, I hate this,' Tanthe growled.

'What is it that you hate?' Elrill asked evenly.

'Feeling powerless! I can't bear to think that there's nothing we can do to get Eldareth out of there. I can shout until I'm purple in the face and they won't listen to me. I can't fight my way in and rescue him, I can't direct a huge bolt of lightning to break the walls down. What use am I? I've probably just made things worse for him.'

'At least you tried.' Elrill's perpetual calmness was partly aggravating, partly reassuring. 'You have courage, and that's to be admired. Eldareth knows, at least, that his friends are around him.'

She turned on Elrill in accusation. 'Isn't there something you can do? Haven't you any *roth*-power? Can't you rescue him with Shaelahyr sorcery, or something?'

Elrill stared hard at her. He looked angry. 'I am not a sorcerer, nor have I ever claimed any such skills. Any

299

ability with *roth* energies that I do possess will not break down fortress walls.'

'What about putting the guards in a trance, or something? I know the Aelyr can do that, they did it when they kidnapped Helananthe's mother.'

He sighed. 'It's a possibility, but it would be unreliable. Such things are done by the Aelyr spinning webs of energy between them that affect—' he stopped, as if he'd begun to tell her too much. 'Alone, I could not make an effective web. I have never even tried. I've never had cause.'

'There would be two of us,' Tanthe said fiercely. 'I've never tried it either, but . . .'

'You have no access to your Aelyr nature,' Elrill said dismissively.

'I've used a *silvenroth* mirror,' she retorted.

'Almost anyone can do that, if they can attune to it. Tanthe, there is no easy answer. There's no great act of heroism or sorcery that can solve this problem. There never has been.'

'We must appeal to the Queen, then! They'll have to halt the trial until she responds. She will never let this happen.'

'We could send a message, but as Ordrai warned, they will have tried and executed him before the news even reaches her.'

She groaned. 'The folk tales where people storm citadels and rescue prisoners – they make it sound so easy!'

'That's why they are only folk tales,' Elrill said wearily. 'There are three of us, not an army. Although . . .' As he looked up at the sky, his eyes caught the light and shone brilliantly blue violet. 'That does not make us powerless. The Shaelahyr move quietly, and we do not give up easily, and we have friends who will swim through the very rock itself to aid us.'

Tanthe's eyes widened. She caught a brief memory-image; a huge creature of stone, forming itself and tearing itself from the very fabric of a cave wall. She said, 'Are you thinking what I'm thinking?'

Eldareth waited. He sat on the floor with his forehead propped on one hand, trying to compose a letter to Helananthe; but he was no Saphaeyender, and the words wouldn't come. In the light of a lone candle the paper gleamed dully on the dark flagstones.

The cell walls were dark as coal and they were all he had seen for the past thirty days. Often an hallucination gripped him; he was not in a cell in Gem Harthnir but in a cave, deep under the earth, cut off from all life. The regime was austere but not brutal; the guards kept him slightly cold, slightly hungry, but not enough to cause him deep distress. He was used to austerity. His discomfort came not from his imprisonment, but from its cause.

Tomorrow they would try him in front of a court that already knew he was guilty. Immediately afterwards they would take him to a small round chamber with a floor sloping down to a central drain. There they would bind him and blindfold him and run him through with swords. A guard had described it to him in vivid detail, but he still couldn't imagine it.

His pen began to move again, splattering black ink on the rough paper.

'I can't find the words for this,' he wrote. 'So I shall stop trying and instead write what is in my mind, Helan. All my life I've been a man of action, forever travelling, wandering, seeking new experiences as if I can never rest. I am strong – that's how everyone sees me. Or am I? This is the truth; I was not adventuring but fleeing. Always fleeing from the shadows, from the justice of Torith Mir. Justice I eluded, but the shadows came with me.

'I still see my mother's face, and my brother's, as I failed to save them. Helan, I have never stopped seeing them; even while I was with you, even while we made love or fought side-by-side at Hethlas Rim. That is why I cannot be

King. I cannot watch over Aventuria while my loved ones' faces hang in the way, screaming and dying in front of me. Even my father's. For I loved my father, too, despite all he did. Hated him, yet loved him.

'A violation of the Goddess's own being, is it not, to take life when the death is undeserved? But if I am not a violator, I am the son of one and I can't feel the *roth* of the Horned God running through me, whole and vigorous; I can only feel this darkness, this trickle of black madness from my father.

'That's why I never wanted to come back here, and yet, that is why I'm glad I did. I have lost you and now I don't want to fight my fate. I'm guilty. Let them punish me and then it will be over, all debts paid. Strong? No, I am not strong. I'm simply resigned.

'Helan, I wish you all the love and strength and good fortune in the world. All the love I gave you will stay with you always, and . . .'

He stopped writing and raised his head. A sound disturbed him, a weird scratching, slithering noise. Rats? At first he thought he imagined it. Then it grew louder, oddly piercing, irritating, like something sharp moving inside the rock itself.

He had heard that sound before.

Eldareth put down his pen and stood up. The bottom row of stones around the walls jutted out, so he could find a toehold on them and raise himself up to look through the tiny window. There was little to be seen; just sky. Now it was dark so all he could see was blackness, while chill air and raindrops blew on to his cheeks. The ground lay three storeys below.

The sound was outside and yet also inside. Crawling, scratching. Right by his ear and yet no sign of what could be causing it . . .

A face was suddenly thrust into his, making him bite back a shout of terror. He lost his footing and stumbled down on to the floor. The dim light of the candle glanced on a small face with silver-grey skin, black eyes, a fall of black hair standing stiffly from its skull with blue streaks in the blackness.

Eldareth was violently wrenched out of reverie.

'Vranof?' he gasped.

The Zampherai warrior squeezed through the window and clung to the sill, his hands appearing to sink into the stone rather than rest on it. A wiry figure no more than two feet tall, flesh the colour of pewter, blue crystals dangling over his loins and chest. His demeanour was fierce, but he was a friend of sorts.

'Hush,' said the Zampherai. 'We're here to get you out.'

'How . . .?'

Another Subterranean face appeared in the embrasure. This one was rounder, gentler, the black eyes deep as caves, the hair soft as sable with no bright colours in it. A Zampherai of a different tribe.

'Orque!' said Eldareth. 'What is this?'

'Elrill called us.' Orque answered. He and Vranof had once been enemies, but Eldareth wasn't wholly surprised to see them together.

'Fortunately for him, we were not far away,' Vranof added.

Eldareth put his hands to his head in disbelief. 'Still following us?'

'Always. Where you go, things change. We feel the echoes of it in the crystals of the earth. Now, your friends are waiting below and we are here to take you to them. Be ready!'

Vranof and Orque worked at the window-ledge with bare hands, driving their fingers into cracks between the blocks of stone as if into cheese, sending pressure waves along the lines of tension deep inside the rock. Eldareth stared.

'Wait!' he hissed. 'I don't know that I want this.'

Vranof paused, frowning. 'You don't want to be free?'

'What good would it do? They will only pursue me and

bring me back, and then my friends will be in trouble for helping me. I've resigned myself to my punishment; I can't change the course of it now.'

The Zampherai warrior looked disgusted. 'Can't change your course?' he said. 'You're resigned to giving up, to dying? Then you do not deserve your friends' loyalty!'

'Look at these walls,' Orque added. 'They have soaked up centuries of dark *roths*, floating *gauroth* energies of pain and despair that emanated from all the prisoners who have been incarcerated here. You are soaking them up. That's why you are paralysed to the point of death!'

'No. This is my own pain.'

'Soaking them up, and adding to them,' Vranof said acidly. 'You're coming with us, even if you force us to bind you hand and foot! Think of your friends. If you delay, they will be caught.'

Eldareth knew that he was right, yet the situation still didn't seem real. He took a deep breath of the cold, damp air. Then there was a resounding crack, and the stones began to split.

'Stand back!' said Vranof.

He'd seen the Zampherai do this before, destroying a section of wall at the outer gate of the Amber Citadel so Helananthe and her troops could enter. Eldareth stepped back quickly. The edge of the embrasure began to sway and then a whole section of the wall fell suddenly inwards, narrowly missing his legs. The noise was tremendous; a ragged hole yawned open on to the rainy night. There were three seconds of taut, echoing silence; then he heard the shouts of other prisoners, guards' booted feet pounding along the corridor.

'Quickly!' said Orque from the ruined wall, holding out a hand.

The shock of the crash and the blades of cold air piercing his lungs brought Eldareth suddenly back to life. In this moment his own fate didn't matter, but that of his friends did. Scrambling over the fallen stones into the gap, he saw

304

the firefly glint of lanterns far below. Curtains of rain swept past. He saw a pale line of rope, looped around a jutting block of stone on the outside wall and vanishing down the flank of the fortress.

Setting his teeth, Eldareth gripped the rope, swung out of the gap and began to descend hand over hand, his feet braced against the wall and his arms straining. The wind buffeted him. For several minutes he moved in pitch darkness. At first he was aware that the two Zampherai were descending the wall unaided alongside him, but he couldn't hear or see them and he felt utterly alone, in a void. Eldareth began to sweat, despite the cold.

'Keep going,' whispered Orque. 'They're waiting for you. As soon as you are on the ground, go!'

'What about you two?'

'We're in no danger. We'll vanish into rock, into the deep places of the earth.'

Faint lights began to sway around him, and he suddenly felt the ground beneath his feet. With relief he stood up and released the rope from his sore palms.

'Eldareth, it's us!' said Elrill's voice. The Shaelahyr was waiting there in the shadow of the fortress, with Nefri and Gany; Jthery and Tanthe were behind him, already on horseback. Their faces shone white and anxious in the lantern-light.

Rain lashed down; the fortress stood bleak above them. High in the wall, Eldareth saw light swaying dimly in the hole he had just left; the guards knew he was gone. He put his foot in Gany's stirrup and swung into the saddle, shocked at how weak he'd become during his incarceration. But he felt the Torith Mir wind cutting into his lungs, searing away the inertia and doom that had gripped him. Gods, there was surely more to his life than an age-old guilt. Perhaps the Zampherai had been right, the collected anguish of the cell had affected him.

'I'm ready,' said Eldareth. 'Lead on.'

Even as the party began to move off, a troop of mounted

guards appeared round the corner of the fortress, clearly visible since they carried a small forest of lanterns. They were a hundred yards away but they saw Eldareth's party at once. A shout went up.

'Halt! You're under arrest!'

'Run!' cried Eldareth. 'Put these lanterns out, just throw them down!'

Hurriedly, Tanthe and Jthery obeyed; then their horses were plunging into darkness, across the street that wound round the fortress, down a steep wooded slope, crossing the street again where it snaked around on itself, and then a grassy slope that led out into the open countryside. The horses ran wildly, hardly able to see where they were placing their hooves, stumbling and righting themselves and galloping on.

Arrows rained around them, but none met its mark. Redbird, the swiftest, ran in the lead and they were making good ground; then the mare suddenly propped to a violent halt, nearly pitching Tanthe over her head. 'Shit!' Tanthe gasped, clinging on and managing to right herself. The other horses milled to a halt beside her.

'What is it?' Eldareth panted.

'The lake,' said Jthery.

They were on a slick, grassy bank that tilted down into a swathe of reeds; beyond lay a black stretch of water, sluggish and stagnant. A fork of lightning flickered, illuminating the scene starkly for a second or two. Against the background patter of rain, the water uttered sounds, *glop, sloop*, as if something were moving about in it.

'Oh, fuck,' Tanthe breathed. 'It's a good job Redbird can see better than I can. I nearly went straight into that.'

'Which way now?' said Eldareth.

Elrill looked side to side, listening. 'To the left,' he said.

They turned in that direction, but at once they saw the lanterns of guards heading towards them. 'Other way!'

They wheeled round, heading to their right along the edge of the lake; but within moments, they saw another party from the fortress closing on them. At least twenty armed men were coming from both directions, and their only escape route was blocked by the lake.

'This is hopeless,' said Tanthe. 'We'll have to go through the lake itself. Swim for it.'

'No,' Jthery said sharply. 'There are greenwolves in there.'

'What? How d'you know?'

'I . . . I can sense them. Too dangerous.'

'We might just get past the guards before they cut us off,' said Eldareth, booting Gany's sides. 'If not, we shall have to stand and fight.'

He felt alive again, with the breath rasping through his throat, his lungs burning and back aching. He felt alive. Gods, how much better to be cut down trying to escape than to die passively like a slaughtered pig.

The horses ran flat out, but they were not going to outrun the guards, who had already reached the edge of the lake. Now the guards were fanning out, and the other group were riding hard behind them to cut off any hope of retreat. Eldareth's party came to a sharp, skidding halt.

'Throw down your weapons!' yelled the guards' leader, a squat dark-haired woman. 'Give yourselves up or we'll cut you down where you stand!'

Jthery whispered, 'Stall them for five minutes. That's all I need.'

Eldareth had no idea what he meant; but when he glanced at Jthery, the young man's eyes were shining like eerie torch-beams. Eldareth rode Gany in front of him, half-shielding him from view, and in the same moment he came alongside Redbird, seized Tanthe and put his sword across her throat. Taken by surprise, she gasped convincingly.

'Who is under arrest here?' Eldareth barked.

The leader looked taken aback by his action. 'All of you,' she said.

'No. I am the only one the governor wants. These others

307

can't legally be put to death simply for aiding me. This woman is the Queen's representative; if anything happens to her, have you any idea how much trouble you'll find yourselves in?'

The leader clearly had no idea. 'Give yourself up, Mordraken-son.'

'Stay back,' shouted Eldareth. 'Come any closer and I'll kill her. The Queen may not care for my life, but she'll send armies to avenge this one. Is that what you want?'

Tanthe struggled, muttering, 'Eld, that hurts!'

'Sorry.' He eased his grip; the leader was whispering with her colleagues, planning their next move.

'Right,' called the leader at last. 'This is obviously a bluff. You have ten seconds to let her go and drop your weapons; after that . . .' she drew herself up and hefted an axe in her fat right hand – 'you're all dead.'

From the angle at which Eldareth held her, Tanthe could see Jthery, and with her breath dry in her throat, she watched him closely.

The young man was silent; his head tipped back, mouth open, rain-soaked hair lashing round his face. His hands hovered above the surface of the lake; Tanthe thought it a trick of the light at first, skeins of water not falling into the surface but rising from it, wrapping themselves around his fingers. His form was suffused in a silver, rainy nimbus.

The surface of the water began to heave. Shapes were rising; humped backs covered in fur that hung like heavy rope with the weight of the water. But as they emerged, the water rolled away and their fur rose, shimmering, each hair tipped with light. Their heads came up, long noses with high nostrils snuffing at the air. Their small ears lay flat against their skulls and their lips rose to show sharp carnivorous teeth. She recognised them from the trophy head on the wall at the inn; deadly, savage greenwolves.

The greenwolves came snaking through the water towards the bank, straight towards Tanthe and her companions. For a moment she was transfixed, horrified. They snarled and chattered as they came, their eyes bright beads, their teeth bared like rows of Aelyr swords. Their fur was dull green, she saw in a burst of lightning, like the pondweed beneath which they lurked. When they rose on to their hindlegs – hunched on massive haunches, but moving easily with the counterbalance of thick tails – they were huge, their arms thickly muscled and their fingers terminating in great black claws.

For a few seconds she thought they would attack; caught between the guards and the greenwolves, she and her friends were lost. But Jthery's mouth was moving in a soundless language and the creatures were obeying him, surging past him, smearing water and silt on to his clothes as they passed. Then the creatures were running – some on all fours, some on their hindlegs – out into the path of the fortress guards.

'We've nothing to fear from them,' Jthery said faintly, his voice a gasp of effort. 'I called them. They will only attack our enemies.'

'You are amazing, Jthery!' said Eldareth.

'Here the lake is only a narrow arm. We can reach the far bank.'

'What?' said Tanthe, disgusted at the thought of entering the turbid water.

'We must. There's no other way.'

Their horses plunged into the water, kicking up foam, lurching as the silt sucked at their hooves. But Jthery was right; the lake here was only thirty yards wide. Soon they were surging up on to the far bank. The horses shook themselves almost hard enough to unseat their riders, then plunged at a frantic gallop into the night.

Tanthe heard ghastly sounds behind her. The snarling of the greenwolves; the cries of the Torish guards, the screaming of their horses. She shuddered, and swallowed her horror, and tried to close her mind against it until the sounds faded and were lost in the night.

This time, no one followed. They were free.

After a time, Eldareth said flatly, 'Now all we have to worry about is coming back and crossing the border again.'

For days they rode under clouds that massed over the northern ocean and rolled inland to create spectacular skies. No one pursued them, but Tanthe knew that the trouble they were in had increased tenfold and she didn't see how they could travel south again without being captured . . . Still, there was no point in worrying about it. After a time she put it to the back of her mind, as Eldareth seemed to have done.

Most days it was gloomy, but there were mornings of icy sunlight and mist that reminded Tanthe of autumn in Sepheret. Sometimes, as they wound their way through the steep valleys, they would come upon a stand of birch trees that glittered green and gold against the dark rock, or a waterfall foaming white into a sapphire pool. Torith Mir held such jewels and she grew to understand why Eldareth had such strong feelings for this realm.

'I used to think Parione was the centre of the world, and if I could only get there everything would make sense and life would be perfect,' she told Jthery as they rested one evening. 'I don't know how I could have been so naive. There's so much more to Aventuria than Parione. I feel as if I'm only just starting to realise it.'

'Really?' said Jthery, who looked cold and miserable. 'I'd do anything to be back in Mithrain, swimming in a warm lake on a summer's day. I hate this place.'

Tanthe was startled. 'You can't hate the landscape, it would be like hating the earth itself, the Goddess. I hate the way they treated Eldareth, that's all. If not for that, I could almost grow to love Torith Mir.'

'You're a very idealistic person, Tanthe,' he said.

She pulled a face. 'Rufryd used to say things like that about me, only not in such a polite tone of voice.'

'But I like idealistic people,' Jthery said, realising she

thought he was criticising her. 'I feel drawn to them, somehow.'

'Why?'

'I don't know.' He smiled, picking at grass blades. 'Perhaps because I try to be idealistic but I'm not very good at it.'

They were riding onto a high plateau country, where slabs of black stone jutted from the ground and the trees were sparse and tough. The weather was cold, the wind wild. They were tiny figures under a vast sky that was filled with an ever-changing display of clouds. The days shortened. The sinking or rising sun flooded the clouds with brilliant gold light, with flushes of red and violet. At night the three moons sailed impassively above them, changing their positions and their phases in untouchable serenity.

Elrill seemed to be watching the skies constantly. Distant storms raged, shattering the sky with sound and light. Once the whole sky was lit with wavering curtains of colour, through which brilliant beams of white and red light danced and flashed. The world seemed full of static, of unfettered *ethroth* energy; Tanthe had never felt anything so eldritch before. It made her skin prickle, her hair float and crackle. Everything seemed to glow.

'This weather isn't natural,' Elrill said uneasily. Eldareth nodded, but Tanthe had lost patience with such cryptic remarks.

'What do you mean?' she demanded.

He turned his bright eyes upon her and for once he didn't mock her need to know everything. 'I can't be sure, but I fear there is a disturbance in the Aelyr realm that is affecting the Earth. Displacement of great energies. This is not good.'

Not good, Tanthe said to herself with a sigh. She felt apprehensive but filled with excitement, ready to shake off all her set ideas about the world and step into chaos.

By morning, the weird storm had settled but left the

311

earth reeking of electricity and ozone. The plateau came to an abrupt end and they began to descend the steep chalky slope of its northern flank. The valley that lay below them was wide and filled with trees; the strangest forest Tanthe had ever seen. Even for a forest in early winter, there was an eerie stillness and coldness upon it.

As Eldareth led them down the slope, she realised the vast scale of the forest. The trees were monumental, with rough grey trunks and white branches stretched against the sky. Some had fallen, blocking their path or leaning against their neighbours to form arches. Then she realised why the forest was so strange; there were no fallen leaves around them, only dark silt. These trees had unfurled no leaves for many seasons; they looked long-dead, and there were no animals nesting in their hollows, no birds on the branches nor insects crawling under the bark.

Touching a trunk as she passed, she found it ice-cold.

'Gods!' she muttered, snatching her hand away in surprise.

'What is it?' Eldareth said with a wry smile.

'It felt like—' she placed her hand to the trunk again and the granite texture flooded coldness into her palm. 'Anthar's horns, it's stone. These trees are made of stone!'

They stopped and looked around in awe at these monoliths that had once lived and swayed in the wind. She wondered how long it must have taken for the living tissue to petrify.

'Did I never tell you of the stone forests of Torith Mir?' Eldareth said quietly. There was a mixture of bitterness and pride in his voice. 'This is Elta Arta, Valley of Black Stone.'

'I think you mentioned them,' said Tanthe. 'And I must have read about them. But couldn't picture them. I never imagined anything like this. But how could this happen? How long has it been like this?'

'I expect the Aelyr would have more idea than humans,' said Eldareth.

'Millions of years,' Elrill answered. His voice rang off the hard trunks.

They rode on, slipping like shadows between the great columns. There was nothing but black and white and shades of grey in this ancient world; but here and there Tanthe saw colour. Floods of amber clustered on the trunks.

She stopped and plucked at a mass that was like fossilised sunlight, with tiny insects trapped inside. She couldn't dislodge it.

'This must be valuable,' she said. 'Why hasn't it been taken?'

'Much of it has,' Eldareth replied, 'but Torith Mir is full of amber and precious stones, so few risk their lives coming this far to find it.'

'What do you mean, risk their lives?'

'There are a lot of wild animals on the fringes of Elta Arta,' Eldareth said. 'Dra'a'ks, mountain lions, snakes, greenwolves.'

'Oh, thanks,' said Tanthe, giving the sparkling mass of amber a rueful backward glance. 'Now there's something you didn't mention!'

Eldareth grinned with a touch of his old fire. 'Come on, Tanthe, you surely didn't expect an easy ride? We have our weapons, and it's no worse than anything else we've faced so far. We may see nothing, anyway; most wild creatures are shy and only attack if they're provoked.'

'Not where I come from,' she murmured.

Tanthe was silent for a time, but her senses were magnified to every tiny sound. Above the petrified branches she saw tiny winged silhouettes floating on the wind currents; eagles, she thought. Dra'a'ks don't fly like that. But then she saw three tiny black shapes like arrows, a snake-like quality about them, an unmistakable straight flight; and then one of them peeling off and descending in a series of loops to drop on to its prey out of her sight.

Dra'a'ks at home had been a danger to lambs and even,

occasionally, to children. Were there greater dra'a'ks here who would swoop on adults? A shiver went through her but she wasn't really afraid, only uneasy. Eager to reach the end of the journey.

'Elrill, have you any idea when we might find this portal?'

The Shaelahyr gave her the icy look that she'd learned to ignore. 'Before dark, I hope. There's a *rothanamir* in this area, but it may not be easily recognisable. If it gives out no vibration, or one so subtle that the *anametris* cannot easily attune with it, it could take days. Let us hope for the best, shall we?'

'"Shut up and be patient, Tanthe,"' she said drily. Elrill actually smiled.

They stopped to rest and eat, sitting on the knuckles of a tree's tangled stone roots. The sky was still bright. As they moved on, Elrill dismounted from his horse and began to cast about with the *anametris* sphere. Their progress was slow and Tanthe wished there was some way she could help.

'What are you looking for?' she said at last.

'Energy,' he said. '*Roth*.'

'I know, but what might it physically look like?'

'Perhaps a clearing with a mass of stone in the centre. Perhaps a cave or a spring. It might not look like anything, Tanthe, so there is no point in guessing.'

She bit her lip. As time went on the afternoon darkened, and a chill wind cut through the branches.

All the forest began to sigh with eldritch music. A thin, icy sleet sifted down, turning rapidly to hail. They pulled up their hoods, but there was nowhere to shelter. The horses shook and stamped, hating it. Tanthe looked up and saw an infinity of whirling white particles against the heavy glow of the sky, gasped at the weird sound of hail rattling through the petrified branches; then a hailstone caught her in the eye and she ducked her head, swearing, caught for a few moments in agony.

Unable to see properly, she was confused. Other sounds rose through the whining of the wind and the hammer of hail; an ominous, bubbling growl, Jthery shouting.

She blinked the pain away. Jthery was suddenly beside her and this time she heard him clearly. 'Greenwolves!'

'Where?' said Eldareth.

'They're coming through the forest behind us. I should have sensed them, I don't know why I didn't. There are lakes to the east and the north of us, but I never thought the greenwolves would come this far from the water. I'm sorry.'

'Don't start apologising, it's not your fault,' Eldareth said gruffly. 'Are they far off? Hungry?'

Jthery pointed. Tanthe saw at least seven hunched figures, trotting on their hindlegs with their tails stiffly curved for balance and their clawed hands held in front. They were several hundred yards away and tiny between the trees, but gaining on the party. The hailstorm made her shiver and gasp for breath.

'I'm trying to sense their mood. I don't know,' Jthery said.

'Let's keep moving,' said Eldareth.

They went on at a brisk walk, Elrill casting round intently with his gaze fixed on the vibrant orb in his palm. Tanthe strung her bow; it wasn't easy on horseback, but she managed it. Jthery went on anxiously, 'I can't understand why I wasn't aware of them. I'm trying to communicate with them. Once I can reach them, they'll know we are friends and they'll leave us alone.'

Well, stop talking and get on with it, Tanthe thought, but didn't say it aloud. She tried not to think about the beasts rising from the lake under Fortress Arabeth, the shrieks of the guards and their horses. She had faith in Jthery. She was more taxed by the hailstorm that whipped viciously around them, upsetting Redbird. She tried to calm the mare, talking gently to her.

'They're catching up. Keep moving!' Eldareth said as Elrill slowed down.

'It's here somewhere,' said Elrill. 'There's a flicker . . .'

'Well, never mind it until we've got these creatures off our backs.'

'Let Jthery deal with them,' Elrill said with a touch of imperious anger. 'If we go on now it might take me days to find the *roth* trace again!'

'Then how quickly can you open the portal?' Eldareth demanded.

'A few seconds, a few minutes . . .'

Elrill dismounted and began to cast around a wide clearing, the *anametris* gleaming like ice in his palm. Eldareth and Tanthe had no choice but to stop and hope to fend off their pursuers while he worked. Glancing at each other, they swung their bows off their shoulder and set arrows to the strings. Redbird and Gany wouldn't stand still but fidgeted and sidestepped in fear.

Jthery halted his horse between two huge stone trunks on their left, his eyes closed and his hands pressing on the air. Tanthe watched the greenwolves intently, but there was no change in their pace. They were approaching fast.

'It's no good,' Jthery panted, hail dashing his face. 'I can't make them hear me. I can't feel anything from them . . . nothing of the water . . . it's like reaching out to touch fur but finding bone.'

Tanthe's chest tightened with foreboding.

'Elrill, we'll have to run for it,' Eldareth said through his teeth.

'No,' said the Shaelahyr. 'The *rothanamir* is here. Give me a minute more to open it!'

Tanthe glanced back and saw a fallen tree in the centre of the clearing. The trunk, which must have been blown down countless centuries ago, lay like a fallen column across the clearing, but the root system was raised up in the air like a strange round mouth, twelve feet high, carved of basalt and ringed with stone tendrils. She saw Elrill moving back and forth in front of it, twisting the sphere as she'd seen him do many times before with no result. This time, though, she saw a light gathering in the heart of the root system. The hail turned to mad fireflies in the glow.

'Then hurry!' Eldareth gasped. 'Jthery, are you communicating with them?'

Jthery shook his head, his hair whipping in wet skeins. 'I can't stop them,' he said. 'They're not greenwolves.'

'What?' Tanthe cried. 'Then what are they?'

'I don't know, but they won't listen to me.' Breathing fast, Jthery gathered his horse's reins. He was white with disbelief. 'I don't know what they are!'

They came crashing through the thin undergrowth, their fur rippling like pond-weed over their haunches, tiny ears pressed back, jaws gaping to show thick yellow fangs. Their clawed hands grasped at the air. With a curse Eldareth let fly his first arrow, missed, shot again and felled the leader. Tanthe joined in, unleashing three arrows. Only one struck, landing in a greenwolf's shoulder, but the creature hardly seemed to feel it. It reached up, wrenched out the arrow and threw it down without breaking stride.

'Time to retreat,' said Eldareth, turning Gany on his haunches and trotting towards the fallen tree.

Catching her breath, she rode after him towards Elrill, turned again, let fly another useless arrow. She wished she was as good as Rufryd, who could turn in mid-flight and hit the tiniest moving targets without even appearing to aim properly. She wished Rufryd was with them.

The portal was glowing strongly now. The root-mouth was lost to sight in a haze of sparkling lilac and silver light, shot through with green and rainbow colours. Tanthe glimpsed another world inside the glow, but it wavered like a theatre set painted on silk. Dread gripped her as she remembered the portal that had led her to Auriel . . . Elrill was working frantically, weaving the *anametris* in and out of the light as if to pour more energy into the portal. The glade hummed with energy; the great trees all around lit up with ghostly blue fire.

'Can we go through?' Eldareth shouted.

'It's ancient,' Elrill said. 'Hard to open. I'm trying.'

'If we don't go through now, they'll be coming with us!' cried Tanthe.

The portal flared, dazzling.

'Come!' Elrill beckoned frantically. 'It's the best I can do! Quickly, before it begins to close again!'

The greenwolves were less than ten yards away now. For a moment Tanthe was hypnotised by them, as if she'd slipped into another level of perception. She saw beyond their clashing fangs and long horny claws to something worse . . .

It was Redbird who saved her, leaping forwards after the others. Eldareth and Jthery were urging their horses towards the centre of the clearing. Tanthe heard one of the creatures give a loud bubbling growl, turned to see it nearly on Redbird's heels and slashing out at her hind-quarters.

By reflex she swung the mare in a tight circle and slashed out with her sword. The keen Aelyr blade cut through the creature's neck and it fell, the head nearly severed. No blood spurted out, only some kind of ooze. And Tanthe knew.

Something about them . . . so nearly perfect in their savage greenwolf form, yet so barely perceptibly *wrong* . . .

'Bhahdradomen,' she panted. 'Jthery, you saw. They're shape-changers, *ghelim*!'

She couldn't tell if the others had heard her. Behind her the monstrous animals came striding on through the ice-storm, snarling their hunger. Before her, the disc of light shimmered and the prospect of leaping into it was as terrifying as throwing herself off a cliff – but there was no choice. She saw Jthery's horse jump into the light and vanish, Gany following with Eldareth looking back over his shoulder, shouting at her to hurry. Elrill was waiting, with one hand outstretched as if to usher her through.

Redbird sprang. Tanthe caught a huge breath and held it

as the world vanished and her stomach thrilled with the shock of falling. For a few moments she seemed to be out of her body and still watching the glade, Elrill dragging his horse into the portal, the shape-changers leaping after them, the light vanishing like an extinguished flame. The *ghelim* falling back as if they had hit a closed door.

The tunnel between realms swirled and cast them down into a place where the landscape and all the colours and scents were different. The horses stumbled and found their feet; Eldareth and Jthery looked disorientated, but this time Tanthe – like Elrill – was immediately alert and aware of her surroundings. She raised her head and took in everything.

The biting ice of hail, the sounds of wind and snarling *ghelim* were gone. In place of the petrified forest was a wide curving plain that was silver and rainbow-coloured like dew. She heard the faint background music of stars and against it, voices shouting in the distance. Strange and terrible sounds pierced the air, like the ringing of glass, and figures were running all around them; Aelyr in spider-silk grey with long shining swords in their hands. There were cries, the clash of weapons, the shudder of unseen energies . . .

They had stepped into the midst of a battle.

Chapter Fourteen. Akarata

Rufryd rode east with Con, Dawn and Mirias, some fifteen hundred miles still to cover before they reached the Vexat Straits. The countryside here was rough and hilly, but even in the fringes of winter intensely verdant; dark evergreens against emerald grass. The weather worsened as they travelled. There were wild, deafening storms, lukewarm winds, torrential downpours of rain that sent them rushing for the cover of trees or overhanging rocks. At other times, dry storms would rage high in the heavens, filling the sky with lightning and strange waves of light. Clouds writhed and flickered and the whole atmosphere crackled with unspent power; but no rain fell.

'Is Thanmandrathor always like this in winter?' Rufryd asked as they sat in the mouth of a shallow cave, waiting for the lightning to die down.

Con shook his head. 'We usually get storms in late summer, not at this time of year. And I've never seen storms like this, never.'

He seemed nervous, starting at every roll of thunder. Dawn put her hand on his arm. It was Rufryd from whom Con continually sought guidance and reassurance, but Dawn was the one who always ended up giving it. Rufryd seemed to spend the whole time wishing they could shake the boy off, leave him at some farm and forget him.

'We saw some strange things in the sky on our way to Tasqabad,' she said. 'Frightening, but beautiful, too.'

'It turned strange many months before you arrived at Tasqbad,' said Con, 'but it's getting worse every day now. Noli used to—' He stopped.

'What?' Dawn said gently.

Con's voice cracked. 'He always acted strangely in a storm.'

'Frightened?'

'Yes, but excited as well, as if he sensed something in it I didn't. But when I asked him about it afterwards, he didn't seem to know what I was talking about.'

The last word was lost in a violent crack of thunder, a spear of lightning turning the world white. They all ducked by reflex.

'Sounds like the god and goddess arguing,' Mirias said as it died down. His tone was light-hearted, but Con looked shocked.

'You don't make jokes about Q'enartre and Ank'eth!'

'What are they going to do about it?' Rufryd said flatly. 'In Sepheret we make jokes about anything we want, even gods. Maybe it isn't the weather getting worse.'

'How d'you mean?' said Mirias, folding his arms on his drawn-up knees.

'Maybe it's that we're travelling towards the centre of whatever's causing it.'

Rufryd had no idea what had made him say that. Duke Tasq had been vague, citing the gods, a mountain, a standing stone, forces unknown . . . Yet now, Rufryd had the clear intimation that there had been a lot in what Tasq had said. It was a feeling . . . like the sensation he'd had when he'd recognised Noli for what he was. He shuddered inwardly. He didn't want to be fey like Lynden and Ysomir, he wanted simple, solid reality. Rain, earth, the grassy, sweaty scent of horses, his bow and arrow.

Later, as they rode through a long, wooded valley – the sky now white and silent above them – Rufryd said to Con,

'Do you know what we're actually going into?'

'Yes, we're going to Vexor.'

'Vexor. The land of the Bhahdradomen,' Rufryd said grimly. 'You can't come with us, Con. It will be dangerous, worse than dangerous. I've seen people completely lose

322

their reason, faced with them. So have you, for the gods' sake.'

'I'm not frightened.'

'You should be.'

'Why?' His young face was pallid. 'I had one as my best friend. Why should I be frightened of them?'

'Because—' Rufryd didn't know what to say. 'They'll probably kill us as soon as look at us. I can't be responsible for you!'

'I'm not asking you to be responsible for me,' Con said waspishly. 'I'm not a child. I just want to help you, Rufryd. Wherever you go, I'm going.'

'My brother—' Rufryd began, and stopped.

'Go on. Your brother, what about him?'

'Nothing. He was older than you. I still couldn't save him.'

He urged Halcyon into a trot to catch up with Dawn and Mirias, hoping Con would just vanish. But when he looked back, the boy was still riding along behind him, fixing him with dogged, inescapable eyes.

There were days of torrential rain, making their journey unbearable. At last they took refuge in Q'alathbad, a village of tall, timbered houses painted a dusky red. Here they rested for a few days, while their clothes dried out and the horses recovered. While they were there it snowed and they woke to a world of wondrous glittering whiteness. Within a day, though, the snow had melted under another downpour, swelling the rivers, bringing news of destroyed bridges and flooded paths. As soon as the water subsided, Rufryd and his party set out again along muddy tracks that sucked at the horses' hooves.

They were following an ancient road but the travellers upon it all seemed to be coming towards them, seeking refuge in Q'alathbad. Some of them stopped Rufryd's party, speaking anxiously in a thick dialect that he could barely understand. Sheep and goats trotted with them, frequently blocking the road.

'What is it?' said Rufryd, trying to make a black joke of the very worse possibility. 'Bhahdradomen invasion?'

Con shook his head. 'They're escaping from the storms. They tell us not to go on any further.'

'But they're scared peasants, whereas we have a special dispensation from Queen Helananthe to be heroic.'

Rufryd was being sarcastic, but his companions all seemed to have lost their sense of humour. 'We can't let this weather stop us,' said Mirias, deadly serious.

'I agree,' said Dawn. 'There's no telling when there'll be a lull, and I don't think we should waste any more time. You can turn back if you want, Rufe, but Mirias and I—'

'For gods' sake, of course I'm going on,' Rufryd growled. 'All I'm saying is, don't let's kid ourselves we're in any less danger than these folks who are very sensibly running away. Con, if you want to go after them, that's fine. I think you should.'

'Well, I don't,' Con said stubbornly. 'I'm coming with you.'

What worried him more than the human migration was that of the birds skimming overhead; hawks, geese, herons, pointers, all fleeing west. Sometimes he saw dra'a'ks hunting among them, picking off stragglers in midair.

The rain ceased as they went on, leaving the road coated in stiff mud rather than running water. They rode for days under a vast, restless sky. Clouds rolled layer upon layer above them; wisps sped like black smoke on the wind beneath looming masses of slate-grey and green. Sometimes these higher banks of cloud would break, revealing strange lights that flickered and crackled in the upper atmosphere. The whole landscape was bruised with purple and black.

The hills on their left became low mountains with a single great peak thrusting up on the eastern horizon. Its head was lost in clouds that flickered pale green, as if lightning danced inside them.

'What's that mountain?' Rufryd asked.

'That's Q'enartre's Throne,' said Con, his voice low with reverence. 'I've only ever seen it from a great distance. You can't mistake it, though.'

Each day the peak drew nearer, and the air thickened with static that gave everything a spectral glow. Six days out of Q'alathbad, they came in sight of a high, broad hill about half a mile off the road. It was distinctive, rising like a dome above the surrounding grassland. Its broad summit was crowned by a tall menhir, tilted off the vertical as if yearning towards the mountain.

'This must be Nilothphon's Finger!' said Rufryd. 'Duke Tasq spoke about it. A standing stone named for the legendary Aelyr mage.'

'I suppose you want to take a closer look?' said Mirias.

'I'm going to,' said Rufryd. 'I don't care what the rest of you do.'

Rufryd rode ahead and the others followed. The slope was steep, the air fragrant with wet grass. The horses were blowing hard by the time they reached the broad curve of the summit, so they reined in and let them rest. The standing stone reared above them, sublime and immovable.

Its size and colour amazed them. It was a good twenty feet high, and it did indeed resemble a rough finger, pointing meaningfully at Q'enartre's Throne. To their surprise it was blue, rich and glowing and gold-flecked like lapis lazuli. A circle of smaller stones surrounded it, half buried in the earth.

There was a sense of power on the place that made them fall quiet. Their exertion was rewarded by a spectacular view of the surrounding landscape. Open countryside fell away on the southern flank, brooding under the unnatural storm-light. To the north were mountains, and a river surging eastwards below them until it vanished into a gully. After that, Rufryd couldn't see which way the river ran. If it bent across their path, he hoped the bridge that spanned it was still intact.

He let his gaze follow the tilt of the finger to the towering peak of Q'enartre's Throne. Its flanks were sheathed in green light. Faint crackles of lightning danced around it. Rufryd felt a great pressure emanating from the mountain, like the tension of imminent thunder on his skull. There was a vortex of cloud swirling about the peak, as if all the storms and cloud-layers and mysterious lights were birthed there and came streaming outwards on electric winds. He saw the tiny silhouettes of dra'a'ks, black scraps buffeted by the currents.

They stood in silence for a while, looking from the mysterious pointing stone to the distant mountain. The unfettered *roth* in the air was so strong that even Rufryd felt it, and it filled him with intense foreboding.

'The mountain is the heart of the strange weather,' Dawn said eventually. 'It must be. I wonder what's there?'

'It's at times like this we need Eldareth with us,' said Rufryd. 'He'd know all about it, I expect.'

Con said hesitantly, 'It was said to be an Aelyr place. Humans were afraid to go there.'

'And now?' said Mirias.

'Aelyr are rarely seen these days. But the mountain still has a reputation . . . a forbidden, fearsome place.'

'It's obvious, isn't it?' said Rufryd. 'It must have been an Aelyr portal. I'd put ralds on it. Maybe they guarded it jealously to stop humans going through. What happened when they stopped using it?'

'I don't know,' said Con. 'They say the mountain's been quiet for centuries. It's only in the last year or so we started hearing rumours about it, and then the storms . . .'

'Maybe the portal's opened up again, for some reason,' said Rufryd. He thought grimly of Tanthe.

'Could we go through it?' Con said, in sudden excitement.

'Are you out of your mind?' snapped Rufryd. He seized every chance he could to put Con down, couldn't seem to help himself. 'The Aelyr aren't a gentle, sweet race who float about on dragonfly wings and grant you wishes. They're like us, only worse. In fact they're every bit as nasty as the Bhahdradomen, just better-looking.'

'Rufryd, for Nepheter's sake,' said Dawn, sounding thoroughly disgusted with him. 'That's unfair.'

'Really? Have you forgotten the state they left Tanthe in?'

She looked away, and didn't reply. Mirias said, 'Something's happening in Aventuria. Something we don't understand, that most people haven't even noticed yet. It's going to take us all by stealth, before we even see it coming.'

They fell silent. Q'enartre's Throne quivered with distant thunder.

Rufryd had once envied Mirias's simple idealism, his easy knowledge that Aventuria was perfect and must be defended at all costs. Now he felt vaguely sickened by it. He couldn't forget how the folk of Tasqabad Hall had killed Noli, as someone might stamp on a spider in a mindless reflex of disgust.

'Well, we'd better decide what to do,' Dawn said at last. 'Should we risk actually riding to the mountain itself, or head straight on?'

'Head on, I reckon,' said Rufryd. 'We've seen it. If we go closer, there might not be any more to see, but it could be dangerous.'

'I agree with Rufe,' said Mirias, leaning on the pommel of his saddle. 'We could waste a lot of time.'

'Con?' said Dawn, ever democratic.

The boy shrugged. 'I don't want to go to the mountain. I'd only go if Rufryd went.'

'Right, we're agreed,' she said. 'On to Vexor. But I think Helananthe should know what we've seen here. And we should tell her about the Duke; Mawrdreth especially will want to know that. Rufe, have you got one of those doves we can send to her?'

'Yeah, whatever,' said Rufryd. They dismounted, letting

327

the horses graze around the standing stone. He took one of the blue-doves from the wicker cage, holding her carefully in both hands. Her heartbeat was rapid against his fingers.

Dawn took ink, pen and paper from her pack and wrote a message. When she had finished, Rufryd folded and rolled the piece of paper, slipped it into a metal cylinder which he then clasped to the bird's leg. Then, with an odd pang of regret, he launched the dove into the sky, watched her flutter against the clouds and skim away to the west. Breyid go with you, he thought. The remaining three birds cooed loudly and fluttered in the cage.

As they watched the messenger, Dawn pulled at Rufryd's arm and said softly to his ear, 'What is wrong with you? You've been vile to Con and not much more civil to the rest of us, and you seem to get worse-tempered every day. I'm starting to wish you'd stayed in Parione. I wish you'd talk to me, instead of taking it out on everyone. What is it?'

'Don't you know, Dawn?' Rufryd said bitterly. 'Do you really not know?'

'Lynden. Tanthe. But—'

'And the rest,' he said.

'Noli.' She looked gravely at him. 'Was it serious, between you and Lady Branq'elin?'

'How come everyone knows about that?' he growled.

'Oh, come on. It only took one or two people to notice you going into her room and it was all over the house. Not to mention the way the two of you kept looking at each other. Well?'

'I don't think it's really any of your business, is it?'

'No,' she said, annoyed. 'It's just that I'm concerned about you, and rather more concerned about Con. Were you in love with her?'

'No, Dawn, I wasn't in love with her,' he said savagely. 'We were both desperate about something or other. Now will you shut the fuck up about it?'

He started to turn away but she grabbed his arm, her

eyes burning. 'Look, Rufe, all I'm saying is don't take it out on Con! We've all had bad things happen and we don't all—'

Her words were swamped as a fork of lightning lashed down and struck the stone. The crack of thunder that came with it was so loud it seemed to split the very earth asunder. The horses screamed in terror and Rufryd nearly lost hold of Halcyon. The stallion reared, plunging in circles as Rufryd hung on to his reins. His hair crackled and the atmosphere thickened with electricity.

The stone shone with sea-green fire yet, amazingly, it was undamaged. Rather it seemed to reach up and beckon the lightning, drinking it greedily.

'Let's get out!' Rufryd yelled.

He wondered if it was worse to mount again and make lightning-conductors of themselves, or to stay on foot and keep low? Wrongly or not, all four of them opted as one for speed and leapt on to their horses' backs, bending flat over their necks as they galloped down from the hilltop. The storm chased them and the horses bolted, weaving through a web of dancing lightning forks.

Rufryd caught a glimpse of Con's face, sickly white with terror. Again he felt no sympathy, only irritation. Mirias was ahead, struggling to angle his horse north-eastwards, down towards the gully where the swift river ran.

'Find some kind of shelter down there!' Mirias shouted back over his shoulder.

The gully was steep-walled and the horses were forced to slow down as they picked a diagonal path down the slope. Below them, the river ran fast and wild, swollen with flood-water. Above, the sky swirled with curtains of coloured light that were repeatedly stitched and torn by spears of lightning. Rufryd's shirt was plastered to him with sweat. He'd never have admitted it, but he was terrified for his life. Some part of him knew that this storm was far from natural, that it was caused not by thunder-clouds or quarrelling gods but by the displacement of vast energies. And if there was a portal and this energy was emanating from Verdanholm . . . was Tanthe there, in the midst of it?

The path they were on brought them to a bridge. There was nowhere else to go.

'We'll have to cross,' said Mirias. 'Look, we can get to lower ground on the other side, find a cave or something.'

'Lead on, then!' Rufryd shouted over a rumble of thunder. 'We can look at the map later, find out which bank we should be on.'

The bridge was a spidery thing that arched low over the torrent, its planks narrow and slick with moisture. They had to dismount and lead the horses in single file; Mirias and Dawn went first, with Con following and Rufryd at the rear. Their progress was slow; the bridge trembled and the horses hated it, hooves skidding on the planks. Rufryd had one hand on Halcyon's reins, coaxing him, the other grasping a thin rusted handrail.

A deep roaring noise began, somewhere upriver, surging rapidly in volume. A roar much deeper than the crack of thunder, a rumbling that seemed to come from the roots of the earth itself . . .

Rufryd glanced upriver and it was already too late. A wall of water was surging along the gully towards them. A flash-flood.

All the rain that had been pouring on to the mountains for days had met the snow-melt, gathering and swelling, breaking the banks of lakes and tiny streams, its weight and volume swelling until nothing could contain it. Now it came surging into the gulley below, a foaming weight of water as high as Tasqabad Hall, filled with mud and branches.

They were lost. He shouted and the others seemed to react in slow motion, crawling and slipping on the surface of the bridge at the pace of snails while the water raged towards them. Even if they could have reached the far bank it wouldn't have helped; the flood was too fast, too deep. Rufryd stood paralysed for three seconds, his mouth open in utter despair. Then the avalanche of water hit.

The bridge broke up in the onslaught. Briefly he saw his companions falling, swept away like twigs. Rufryd and Halcyon were thrown off their feet. He was under the surface with water bubbling wildly around him, the deathly shock of coldness. Debris bumped against him. He couldn't tell which way was up but through his straining chest and clamouring ears he felt the black certainty of death.

Then his head broke the surface and he saw Dawn's head bobbing above the flow, her red hair turned black by water. He thought he saw Mirias too but both of them were flailing helplessly, being borne away from him. He glimpsed the horses struggling to swim. Rufryd was choking on water and couldn't shout to them, couldn't make a sound. He spotted Con floating away, thrashing, going under . . .

Lightning flickered on the surface of the flood. Halcyon was trying to swim next to him, mouth open, ears plastered back. The birdcage still attached to his saddle was half afloat, the doves pressing themselves into the air gap at the top.

Rufryd managed to reach out and throw his arm over Halcyon's withers, so he could get his head clear of the icy current; but the stallion was being carried helplessly downstream. Dawn and Mirias seemed to be caught in a faster part of the flow; they were vanishing, and in the deceptive light he no longer knew whether he was seeing them or debris bobbing on the surface. He did his best to push the cage up and keep it on top of the saddle, so that the poor captives at least could breathe. He fumbled to open the wicker door but couldn't.

Con's head suddenly reappeared thirty feet in front of Rufryd, one hand thrashing at the water. Rufryd tried to call his name but it came out a choked whisper. He couldn't see Con's horse, only the boy's head and the helplessly grasping hands. Con was drowning.

Rufryd's soul was overwhelmed by the wave of horror. Unbearable. Another young man dying pointlessly in front of him and again nothing he could do to save him . . .

And then something happened that Rufryd couldn't believe.

A huge dra'a'k, bigger than any he'd ever seen, came gliding over the torrent. Between the spokes of its wings, the stretched skin gleamed with scales and rudimentary feathers; its great clawed legs swayed in the air beneath it. The sheer size of the creature made him forget his plight for a moment. Its wingspan must be thirty feet, at least . . . a great black silhouette sailing over his head, plunging for a second into the current, rising again with something grasped in its claws.

Con. Anthar's prick and horns, the dra'a'k had seized Con.

Halcyon seemed to have got into a part of the current that was carrying him in towards the bank. Rufryd found himself being carried towards a thick branch that was wedged in the flow. He seized it, got a good purchase, then felt he was being torn apart as he tried to hang on to his horse but couldn't.

The branch broke. Rufryd was swept on again. All was dark, he couldn't breathe . . .

Sudden collision. He'd hit Halcyon's shoulder. Flailing, he painfully found rocks beneath him. His knees and legs were bruised, but he managed to scramble and find a tenuous purchase. He and Halcyon had been swept into a shelf of rock that was just submerged under the flood's edge. With the last flare of his strength he grabbed the stallion's reins.

Breathless and choking, he saw a tough little tree leaning over the water. He seized its lowest branch. Inch by inch he pulled himself out of the flow and on to a ragged shelf that could hardly be called a bank, dragging Halcyon after him. The horse's legs were trembling and his hooves skidded on the slick stones, seeming unable to take the last step out of the fast-flowing water. Rufryd groaned with the effort of holding on to him. Then with a rush the stallion came springing up out of the foam and stood shivering on the bank, legs splayed and head drooping.

Rufryd wept with relief; the sound that came out was halfway between a cough and a sob. There was no sign of Con's horse. No sign of Dawn or Mirias. How could there be? He'd seen them slipping away from him, carried swift as mercury into the darkness. The storm had subsided but now rain began to lash down and he could see nothing beyond the bedraggled figure of Halcyon.

Halcyon coughed then shook himself violently, spraying Rufryd with water. Rufryd was caught between cursing and crying. How could that still feel cold, after what he'd been through? He led Halcyon a few steps further up the stony bank and looked around, called out, but there was nothing around him but water, darkness, absence.

He was alone.

Dawn and Mirias might well have drowned by now; but if they hadn't – and he entreated Nuth with all his soul that they hadn't – he knew they could look after themselves. But Con . . .

Rufryd stared up at the darkening sky, but all he could see was cloud. He could still hear distant thunder but the lightning was no more than a faint flicker above him. If he hadn't imagined the giant dra'a'k, where was the boy now? Unbearable to think of it, he wouldn't think of it. He cursed, to stop himself weeping. Exhaustion overwhelmed him. He leaned on Halcyon and somehow the two of them struggled up the steep, mud-thick incline until they came to a patch of flatter ground. Dragging up a last faint wisp of energy Rufryd removed the saddle and saddlebags from his horse's back, did his best to dry him with handfuls of leaves. Then, regardless of mud and rain, Rufryd collapsed and slept.

*

A sound woke him. A long, metallic, un-human squawk.

Rufryd opened his eyes to bright daylight. For a moment he had no recollection of where he was or what had happened; then it came back, and he groaned.

'No,' he moaned, his head in his hands. 'Breyid, please tell me it wasn't real. Or Q'enartre, whatever they call you here. Please.'

He was so cold he could hardly move. Halcyon was nearby, nibbling disconsolately at a tussock of grass he'd managed to find. He didn't seem too distressed by his ordeal, but Rufryd knew he must get the stallion properly dry before he caught cold – if he hadn't already. The saddle lay on the ground, the leather drying stiffly. The saddle-bags were soaked of course, their contents ruined. Rufryd forced himself to his feet. His body was chilled through and felt like lead.

That was when he noticed that the bird-basket was open, and two of the three remaining doves were missing. They'd either drowned or taken flight; the latter, he hoped. He must have unlatched the door after all, or it had burst open and they'd made their escape. But the last one was sitting dazed on the rung of the open door, thinking about it. Rufryd managed to catch her quickly and put her back inside, latching the door with a sigh of grim relief. The bird cooed and fluffed her feathers.

'Daft little thing, you don't even know what's happened, do you? I'll have to call you Survivor. We'll find you some seed or nuts in a bit, eh, Su?'

He sat down to examine his weapons. The Shaelahyr sword and his belt knife were fine. His bow was the thing he feared for . . . but it was stoutly made, and its layered components of wood and bone were still firmly bonded and flexible. The string was ruined, but he had spare strings, stored in a little leather container that had been made waterproof with waxes and resins. The arrows, though; sighing, he turned them between his fingers and knew that they were going to dry warped. A few might still be okay, or maybe he could shoot to compensate for the curve until he acquired new ones.

As he tried to dry everything and polish the saddle and bridle, he thought of his companions. Another wave of despair rolled through him. How far downstream had they been swept? Could they have survived?

Below him ran the flood, not as high as it had been the night before but still flowing fast and wild. Above him was a thin belt of rowan trees, and then a steep, pale mountain. Gods, he was right on the hem of Q'enartre's Throne!

The mountain seemed quiescent today. From this angle he couldn't see the summit, and there was only the faintest aquamarine shimmer against the sky; none of last night's wild lightning and eerie lights. Still, he wanted to get away from the place.

He could see no way to follow the course of the river; the bank had all but gone. How was he to find Dawn and Mirias? And Con? Sighing, Rufryd pulled a shirt from a rucksack, squeezed it out as dry as he could, then began to rub Halcyon's coat with it.

The truth was, Rufryd was not by nature a rescuer. He'd only gone with Lynden, on their ill-fated attempt to rescue Ysomir, in order to protect his younger brother. In both tasks he'd failed miserably. He set his teeth.

'What do we do now, lad?' he said. 'Waste days trying to find the others, or go on alone?'

Halcyon snorted and flicked his ears. At least Rufryd's money pouch was still safely on his belt, with a handful of ralds and spinels that with any luck would buy him a passage across the Vexat Straits. Rufryd already knew the answer. 'We'll go into Vexor on our own. It'll be better that way.'

He looked up and saw the shadow of a huge dra'a'k flying into what looked like a ledge, high on the mountainside. Hard to make out the height, but if the creature was as far up as it seemed, it must be huge. Had it really taken Con up there?

Rufryd cursed. Surely Con was dead . . . but what if he wasn't, what if he was still alive up there and waiting to be fed to the dra'a'k's young? I can't help that, he thought. He'll have to take his chances. I'm not climbing that bloody mountain on his behalf. I never wanted him with us, I can't look after him. He is not my fucking brother!

'Con!' he shouted, but his voice was hoarse. He waited a few seconds; there was no answer. No way was he going to climb that slope without any certainty that the boy was even there.

'Come on, lad,' he said, slapping Halcyon's neck. The stallion was as dry as Rufryd could make him, and he'd oiled the saddle before he put it back on. 'Let's find our way down from here, and be on our way.'

Two hours later, Rufryd was climbing Q'enartre's Throne.

He'd walked a short way over its flank, and noticed a farm cottage nestled in a valley on the other side. Smoke rose from the chimney. Halcyon was coughing; it was plain he couldn't go on, that if he didn't have food and a rest he was going to be very ill and probably die. The same went for Rufryd.

So he had gone to the cottage and knocked and been greeted by a very startled old couple. Both had their hair plaited in the Than'drathian style; the woman's was pure white, the man's silver. They reminded him a little of Tanthe's grandparents, Helwyn and Osforn; they had that strange wisdom and passivity that came from being at peace with the earth in a way he didn't understand. They wore loose white garments with panels of stiff embroidery over them, as rich as anything he'd seen in the Amber Citadel.

He was so startled to find them still here, at the very foot of Q'enartre's Throne, when so many others had fled, that the first thing he said was, 'Why haven't you gone?'

They stared at him; an exhausted half-drowned wreck on their threshold. Yet the woman seemed to know what he meant. 'This is our home,' she said. Her accent was strong, much stronger than Con's or Branq'elin's, but he understood her.

'I was in a . . . in a flood.' He hardly had the strength to speak, let alone string his thoughts together. 'Have you a stable where I could leave my horse? He's been wet through and chilled. He needs somewhere warm to rest, and I have to go and look for my friend . . . I've got money.'

He took a coin out of his pouch; one rald, a grass-green disc of emerald rimmed with gold, carved with Garnelys's insignia. The couple stared at it as if they'd never seen a coin greater in value than a cateye before.

'Too much,' said the woman.

'Take it. I don't care, as long as Halcyon is looked after.'

'We don't want money from you,' she said. 'Come in, poor child.'

'I've no time. Just look after my horse, please. Oh, and if you've some seed for my blue-dove . . .'

'But you are cold and tired. You need to eat.'

'I can do that later.'

'Where are you going?'

He pointed at the mountain. 'I saw a dra'a'k take my friend. He's up there somewhere, if he's still alive.'

The woman was shaking her head vigorously. 'No, you can't climb Her Throne!'

'I've seen the storms. I've seen the dra'a'ks. Is there anything else I should know about?'

The woman put a hand on her hip and said sharply, 'They have put fences around the mountain, to stop fools like you trying to climb up there!'

Rufryd was taken aback. Then he shrugged. 'So I'll cut through them, or climb over. Thank you, good mother, good father.' Instinctively he addressed them as priestess and priest; they didn't object. 'If I don't come back, you can keep my horse. He's a good horse.'

Leaving Halcyon, he began to walk away. After a minute or so, the woman came hurrying after him and thrust a package at him. It smelled of onions and herbs.

'At least take food with you,' she said.

Thanking her, Rufryd thrust it into a pocket and went on.

And now he was climbing the mysterious Throne of the Goddess, cursing his own conscience for forcing him to do this. If he got to the top and found Con not there . . .

The wind had dried his clothes and the exertion had warmed him. Now the going was so steep he could no longer walk but had to seek hand and footholds. He was quite good at this, for he had always been strong and he had sometimes climbed in the mountains at home. Even the height did not worry him unduly. But his head span with hunger and tiredness, and he was all too aware of dra'a'ks circling close by. They weren't as big as the monster he'd seen, but big enough. In this position, he couldn't get hold of his bow.

On the mountain, the green glow that had appeared to sheath it from a distance wasn't visible. But he felt a subtle vibration in the rock, and there was a metallic taste on his tongue. Only the faintest swirling in the clouds above, but it hurt his eyes and made him dizzy to look, so he kept all his attention on the climb.

Dra'a'ks were squawking, flying in and out of the mountainside in agitation. They were above him. Rufryd took a breath, reminded himself that they did not attack human adults – usually – and went on climbing towards them.

The dra'a'ks spiralled away into the air as he approached. He exhaled in relief. Now they were a hundred feet above him, circling, but keeping their distance. Yet he could still hear one shrieking, louder and louder, as if it were directly ahead.

The slope flattened out, giving him respite. And here he found the fence; a tangle of wire and wooden spikes, with a few crystals knotted into the wire as if that could fend off the Aelyr *roth*. It was nasty, but he was sure he could climb through it. Except that there was a large dra'a'k trapped in the wire, flapping and squawking, tearing its wings as it struggled.

Rufryd stopped. He eyed the dra'a'k and it glared furiously at him, clashing its long, toothed jaws. It was the first time he'd seen one so close – alive, at least. Different to the ones he'd seen in Sepheret, with a long bony crest on its head. Very dark, almost black, scales shining bronze, eyes tiny red dots of fire.

He reached for his bow, strung it and began to draw out an arrow, hoping to find one still straight enough to use . . . but something stopped him. The dra'a'k was in pain and distress. Difficult for a human to get himself out of such a tangle, impossible for an animal. He edged closer. All he had to do was part a few strands of wire, ease its wings free, and the creature would be loose.

The dra'a'k froze, and stared belligerently at him as he drew close to it. Would talking to it help? They were only reptiles, they had less intelligence than birds, but Rufryd murmured, 'Hush. Be still. I'm going to help you. Never thought I'd help one of your kind, but . . .'

He lifted the first strand of wire. The dra'a'k lunged at him, grazing his skin with its vicious teeth as he snatched his hand away.

'Bastard!' Rufryd snapped. He tried again, this time freeing its left wing while trying to keep out of reach of its teeth. The moment the wing was loose, the dra'a'k threshed and caught him a muscular blow across the thigh.

Rufryd jumped back with a cry and glared at the beast; knowing then that it couldn't understand what he was doing, that he couldn't rescue it without being savaged.

Seeing that its right wing was torn to shreds, broken and covered in blood.

As he saw this, a shadow swept over him, growing suddenly immense. He jerked round in alarm, saw a massive dra'a'k diving straight towards him; wings folded, long jaws open, claws poised to rend him.

With a yell he dived out of the way. The monster balked, veered off, came round for another attack. The air whirled with the flapping of its great dark wings. This time he just managed to set an arrow to the bow, but the shaft he had was warped and it flew wide without even grazing the creature's wing.

Rufryd was half-lying on the wire, tangled and in pain. He thought it was the end of him. But the arrow had been enough to startle the giant dra'a'k and again it swerved away in a surge of displaced air. This time it flew a long way out from the mountainside. He saw it wheeling on the wind, gliding in a slow turn to make another attack. Pushing himself up into a crouch, he drew out a second arrow and found it more or less unwarped.

The dra'a'k trapped in the wire was threshing and screaming. Its good wing caught him on the shoulder and he yelped with pain, backing out of its way. He saw there was only one way to get across this damned fence and that was by climbing over the entangled dra'a'k itself – if there was the faintest chance he could do it before its giant guardian came back.

Rufryd straightened up, set the arrow to the string, and shot.

The arrow took the wounded dra'a'k in the chest, killing it instantly.

Rufryd wheeled round, ready with a third arrow to aim at the huge attacker, sensing its great shadow almost upon him.

To his astonishment, the sky was empty.

He lowered his bow and stood sweating as he scanned the sky; but all the other dra'a'ks were gone. They could still be heard shrieking, somewhere on the mountain. Looking at the dead dra'a'k, he felt none of the sense of triumph he used to have at home when he'd saved lambs, even once saved a couple of children by killing dra'a'ks; all he felt was that Lynden and Tanthe would not have been pleased with his actions. They would have wanted him to save the injured raptor – even though it couldn't be saved.

He shouldered the bow and climbed on, using the creature's leathery body to help him over the worst of the wire tangle.

Beyond, the climb rose almost to the vertical. Panting for breath, Rufryd struggled on, trying to plan his next move. It hadn't looked so steep from below, and now the clouds were rolling in again, turning the light to an eerie luminous blue that made everything shadowless, so he couldn't see the contours of the rocks.

He was spreadeagled on the rock face, toes on precarious holds, hands reaching up for the next ledge, when his head began to spin. This couldn't be happening. More than vertigo; he felt sick and his sight was turning black and he couldn't feel the rock under his fingers . . . then Rufryd knew he'd made the mistake of thinking he was invincible, but this was the worst place to find out his body's limits. The shock of the flood, exertion and sheer hunger overcame him.

He fainted. He fell.

He gave himself up to the almost sensual relief of falling – until there was a horrible midair jerk. It was as if someone had thrown ropes around him and yanked them tight. Half-conscious, he felt something close to resentment at the discomfort, but then it all vanished into blackness again.

When he came round, he was lying on bare rock.

A wide silver-white shelf, striated with grooves; above and in front of him, a steep slope curving up to the narrow pyramid of the peak, with the sky an intense dark blue behind it. The blue of stormclouds, not clear sky. Rufryd was lying in a hollow in this shelf. His head throbbed, his chest ached. Dragging himself on to one elbow, he saw Con.

The boy was lying a couple of yards from him. His back was turned to Rufryd and his head, resting on one outstretched arm, was jet against the silver rock. Beyond him, a couple of goats and a sheep lay dead, heaped together.

'Con?' Rufryd said.

The lad stirred, turning his head. His young face distorted with pain. 'Rufe? You weren't there before, were you? How did you get here?'

'I climbed up after you, you stupid sod.' He hadn't the energy to tell the rest. He edged himself closer, noticing the long drop that lay beyond their eyrie. 'Are you hurt?'

Con nodded. 'My back. I can't move.'

'Oh, hell. What have you done, broken it?'

'I don't know.'

'Well, can you move at all?'

Con flexed his arms, gingerly moved his toes in still-sodden boots. He tried to sit up, but flinched in agony and fell back.

'It can't be broken,' Rufryd said brusquely. 'You must have torn the muscles or something. I'm no physician, but if you'd broken it you'd be paralysed.'

The effort of trying to move had rendered Con speechless with pain. Rufryd shivered, suddenly wishing he had fallen to his death so that he would not be facing the dilemma of how to get Con down off the mountain, let alone find somewhere for him to rest and be healed . . .

'We need to eat,' Rufryd said. He remembered, suddenly, the pack that the white-haired woman had given him. He took it out and found flat cakes made of potato and onion, pieces of cooked lamb tender with spices, rye bread. There was also a small leather flask full of a fiery white liquor. They shared the food and drink, eating ravenously.

They'd barely finished when the air shook. A shadow came down, great wings snapping on the wind, bringing with it a blast of musty, gamey odour that made Rufryd gag. Adrenalin surged through him. It was the immense dragon-hawk that had attacked him at the fence, trying to protect the wounded one.

His hand was on his sword-hilt, dragging the Aelyr sword from the water-stiffened sheath. The dra'a'k landed in front of them, claws skidding on the shiny rock. Rufryd rose into a crouched position, determined to protect Con or die in the attempt.

The dra'a'k was huge. He couldn't believe his eyes. The ones he'd shot at home had been big enough, bigger than eagles sometimes, but this was monstrous. It towered at least eight feet over him, its scaled head nearly five feet in length, its wings trailing on the ground like two dark tents.

Single-minded, pitiless hunters, dragon-hawks. Rufryd never had qualms about killing them. They killed to survive? Well, so did he.

It was too close for him to draw his bow and shoot it. He could only hope to defend himself with the sword, but he feared even the Aelyr blade might break on its tough hide and bony tendons. The dra'a'k reared above him and he saw it in all its magnificent detail. Its scales shone dark bronze, with purple skeins of iridescence flowing where the light caught them. On its flanks these fugitive colours brightened to sapphire blue and gold; the feathery tufts on its neck were red as fire, and the stretched skin of its wings like dark purple velvet mapped with pulsing veins. Reptilian, alien, magnificent. He almost expected it to breathe fire. Instead a cloud of rank carnivore breath issued from between the rows of tiny sharp teeth. Its great claws were big enough to grasp a man.

It raised its head to strike.

Rufryd drew his arms back, ready to swing his sword two-handed to meet the attack. With luck he'd sever its head in one blow. The dra'a'k hissed—

Con shouted, 'No!' And he grabbed at Rufryd's arm, causing him to topple backwards.

'You fucking idiot!' Rufryd cried. 'What are you doing?'

'You don't understand!' said Con. 'It saved me from the flood.'

'No, it was hunting! It's got a nest somewhere!'

'There's no nest,' said Con. His eyes were wide, desperate. 'It saved me. It told me. Ask it!'

'You're out of your head!' Rufryd snapped, struggling to right himself. 'Great, so you've damaged your skull as well as your back!'

'No,' Con whispered.

'Con, what d'you think those sheep and goats are doing here? We're in its larder!'

Rufryd faced the dra'a'k. His arms had lost their strength and he knew he couldn't land a good blow now if he tried. And the dra'a'k was furious. Its jaws parted and it uttered a metallic shriek that nearly made him drop the sword and cover his ears.

A picture flashed into his mind. Not his own thoughts, but an image from outside.

The dra'a'k caught in the fence.

'Oh, shit,' he whispered, suddenly terrified. 'It knows I killed it.'

'Killed what?' said Con.

'A dra'a'k I found caught in some wire. I couldn't free it and it was injured so I shot it.'

'It's all right,' said Con. 'She knows.'

'She? Con, she attacked me down there.'

'No.'

Rufryd went on staring at the dra'a'k. The image was repeated, and this time there seemed to be an emotion attached to it. If not emotion, at least a feeling. Gratitude. *Gratitude. How dare he attack her while she was trying to show him?*

'Gods,' he whispered.

'She's thanking you,' said Con.

'Why?'

At once an answer came, in another powerful image that was so bright and real it hurt Rufryd's eyes. This great dra'a'k, this empress of dragon-hawks, was thanking him because she knew Rufryd had done the right thing. He couldn't have saved the wounded one. He'd put it out of its misery. Done the only correct thing.

'She wasn't attacking you,' Con said, very soft. 'She was trying to kill the injured dra'a'k herself.'

Her pragmatism shook Rufryd to the core. And far greater than the shock of thinking he was about to die – he'd grown quite used to that – was the shock of realising that this creature had intelligence.

Her thoughts were cold and proud; she had no sentiment, no sympathy with humans; but she did have a sense of justice. A knowledge of what needed to be done that was like prescience.

Something Rouna had taught him. Tried to teach him, at least; he hadn't wanted anyone's lessons at the time, but something of it must have seeped in. To make his mind go absolutely quiet, to open himself to whatever images came. He made himself do it.

The dra'a'k drew back her head and made a rumbling noise, almost a purr, deep in her chest. He saw a shower of falling stones, but they made a specific sound. A-ka-ra-ta.

Con said, 'Her name is Akarata.'

Rufryd turned on him. 'How did you know that?'

Con frowned. 'I don't know! She showed it to me.'

'So you're seeing this too, right?'

The dra'a'k rose on her legs and flapped her wings, making a violent draught. Forks of yellow lightning danced behind her. Then she settled again, and seemed to be waiting for Rufryd to speak.

'Did you save Con?'

He knew at once that she didn't understand speech. He made an effort to concentrate, to show her a mental picture. Her answer came at once.

She'd taken Con for meat, yes. But she had seen something in him, more important than mere food. Decided to spare him.

Rufryd sent the image back to her, as a question. 'Why?'

An image of Con as a shepherd; but his herd contained

all kinds of animals, goats and lynxes and foxes and birds. *Con will help to save the animals.*

That immediately made him think of Lynden, and he felt a stab of pain. 'How touching,' he muttered, but Akarata hadn't finished. She showed him a shocking image of Bhahdradomen flesh animals. *These we cannot eat. In the chaos that is to come, Con will help to save the animals. Our prey.*

Your prey?

Your prey, also. All that lives, preys on others.

'She has a point,' Rufryd said. 'Con is special?' He didn't know how to show her 'special'; he began to imagine Con with a sword in his hand, fighting. No, that could merely imply 'violent'. Instead he showed her Con standing out in a crowd, colourful where they were drab.

Yes. She added Rufryd to the image. *You also.*

He felt uneasy, rather than flattered. *How?*

He'd got it wrong again. It was a question. She was asking *him* how he would be special, what he intended to do. He was stumped for a moment; then he showed himself going into Vexor. Only he couldn't picture it, so it was only a vague plain with a few Bhahdradomen and flesh-cattle on it; but she understood.

Balancing on one scaly leg, Akarata reached out with the other and closed her huge black claws on his shoulder.

Rufryd froze; he was convinced she was about to attack him and he daren't move. The reek of blood and meat on her was overpowering, yet she was magnificent, fiery bronze against the sky, like some fantastical feathered serpent from one of Tanthe's books come to life.

Her claws, though, were gentle. She was telling him something. She wanted him to go with her.

Rufryd looked round at Con, who said, 'Where's she taking you?'

He lifted his hands in bemusement. 'I don't know. I'll come back as quick as I can.'

Akarata walked with a ponderous, swaying gait that teetered between dignified and comical. Rufryd followed her, over steep curved shoulders of rock, clinging on with his hands and feet and trying not to look down. They were climbing higher, with the summit of Q'enartre's Throne soaring directly above them. There was a disturbing noise that grew louder, a crackling and tearing of the atmosphere. He saw webs of light shimmering against the sky, red like watered blood against the fungal green of the clouds, and his skin burned with its power. Akarata brought him to a hollow in the mountainside and he found himself staring into a whirling vortex of green and blue light that seemed to be more than a hole in the mountain. It was a tornado raging in another world. He couldn't reconcile the sight; it made his eyes hurt and his head spin.

A portal? He asked, though he'd never seen one.

No more. None pass through, though some have fallen in and died. She showed him a couple of young people passing into the wild storm; spat out again with great force like arrows into the clouds, and falling to their deaths. Rufryd clung to the rock, teetering towards the vortex as if being drawn in. He was fighting for breath. This was the seat of the disturbance.

She showed him flares of energy spewing from the vortex, passing as waves of coloured light across the sky, pushing great surges of heat into the atmosphere to cause wild storms. The vortex was comparatively quiet now, but if it should flare again . . .

He knew he had to get Con off the mountain, and quickly.

He asked, *where is it coming from?*

Akarata lanced him with red eyes. A series of powerful images slammed into his mind. Aelyr, fighting each other. The landscape around them rising and falling like an intensely blue-green sea. Scene after scene of battle, hopeless, pointless . . .

When she paused, he had no strength to send any pictures back to her. His brain felt bruised, drained. 'Gods.

The Aelyr are at war? Is that what Tanthe's gone into?'

More visions came, flowing across ever-greater canvases, spanning tracts of time. *The war will spread to this land – all the land will rise in chaos like the sea under the three moons.* Yet there was no emotion in Akarata as she showed him these things. She was not concerned; she was ancient and had seen everything.

Her wise eyes contained no sentiment, no evil either; instead, a keen alien intelligence that Rufryd identified with. *Not to blunder out in rage at every setback. Just to watch and accept.* And he realised, again, that what she was showing him was not the same as what she was actually telling him.

This wisdom, humans need too.

Then Rufryd understood what Rouna and the priestesses of Nuth had been trying to teach him, while he had been too busy hating everything and everyone to learn.

To stop judging. To open his mind.

The visions dwindled down to a simple picture of Rufryd and Con. *Since you have a purpose we will not take you as prey. What will you do, in your human way, to effect what you have learned?*

Rufryd looked out at the sweep of the stormy landscape far below Q'enartre's Throne. He saw weird lightning playing between the rolling clouds; the winged figure of Akarata looming over the swirling green chasm. He swallowed. He felt at once utterly despairing and lost, and yet calm. He showed her the same scene; himself crossing the Bhahdradomen plain. *What I intended to do from the start. I'm going into Vexor.*

Akarata dipped her long head. His answer seemed to please her. And then came an image that almost sent him slithering off the mountainside. The landscape was wheeling below him as if he were a bird. 'Gods!' He reached out to steady himself and found he'd grasped the edge of the dra'a'k's wing. It felt like fine velvety leather under his fingers.

You move so slowly, and have so little time. Days, searching for your companions. Days waiting for them to heal. Moons turning while you travel.

And we have to get down off the mountain first, he showed her.

I shall take you.

You?

I fly on the wind, cross the raging channels. Three nights, three days – you will be there.

Rufryd couldn't respond. He edged his way over the rock until he couldn't see into the terrible vortex any more, and he put his head in his hands. He was terrified and elated. *Why? To thank me?*

This is not a reward. It is necessary.

'Just one thing,' he said, trying uselessly to calm his leaping heart. *Take my friend Con off the mountain first. He's hurt. And there's something I need to collect. Then yes – take me.*

Con was angry, but Rufryd was pitiless.

'You can hardly stand up, let alone walk. You want me to treat you like an adult? Fine; that's why I'm leaving you here to get better. After that, you can do what the hell you like; it's called taking responsibility for yourself.'

Akarata had brought them one at a time in stomach-sinking swoops to the foot of Q'enartre's Throne, then Rufryd had carried Con to the door of the cottage. The old couple there took the boy in gladly; and if they saw the great queen-dra'a'k waiting outside in the storm-light, they said nothing. Perhaps they already knew her and respected her. Now Con was in bed in a tiny room, as comfortable as they could make him.

'You can have Halcyon,' Rufryd said more gently. 'I know you'll look after him.'

'Thanks,' said Con, and turned his face away. Rufryd hoped he wasn't crying, but suspected he was. Now everything seemed to have come full circle.

'If the shape-changers don't kill me, I'll come back. Okay?'

'Whatever,' said Con. He'd got that from Rufryd, as well.

Outside in the stable, Rufryd spent a few minutes rubbing Halcyon's ears. The stallion lipped at his pockets as Rufryd tried to tell him that Con would come to take care of him – as if he could understand. Then he took the blue-dove from her cage and slipped her into the breast pocket of his jacket, where she nestled quite happily and pecked a couple of berries from his palm.

Rufryd left without saying goodbye and stood on the slope of the meadow beside the cottage. Above him, Q'enartre's Throne brooded, keeping her secrets – and her mysterious communion with the menhir of Nilothphon – veiled in leaf-green light. Below, the flood still surged along the gully, brown with silt. Again Rufryd wondered about Dawn and Mirias; whether they were struggling to find him, or gone forever. He wished he were still at Tasqabad with Branq'elin in his arms, so he could tell her what he really felt about her. But he would be like Akarata, and not let any of it break him.

As he slipped behind a tree to relieve himself, he took a last, regretful look at the landscape. Then he was ready.

He let the dragon-hawk close her claws around his body and lift him into the air. He felt the wind rushing into his face and watched the dizzying tilt of the landscape spreading out below him, dwindling yet growing immense at the same time; and he left everything behind and fixed his gaze on the eastern horizon, watching for his first glimpse of Vexor.

Chapter Fifteen. The Basilisks of Calabethron

Helananthe stood on the highest battlements of the Amber Citadel – a tower above her private chambers – watching the weird green and blue flickering of the sky.

In summer Parione was hot, sometimes uncomfortably so, but winter usually brought crisp coldness and snow by Hollynight. Now that festival was past, yet the weather remained unnaturally warm, punctuated by violent storms and strange phenomena. Fervid winds streamed in from Thanmandrathor, clashing with cold winds from the north and throwing the atmosphere into turmoil. She clutched her cloak around herself, but the wind clawed at the edges.

Mawrdreth came from the doorway behind her, leaning on a crutch to support his healing leg. Reaching her, he wrapped his free arm around her waist.

'You're here again,' he said into her ear. 'Come back to bed.'

'I was on my way. You shouldn't have struggled up those stairs,' she said, mildly reproving.

'My leg's nearly healed. There's nothing I can't do now.'

'Well, that's true enough.' She smiled and turned in his embrace, raising both hands to caress his face.

Strangest thing. She had married Mawrdreth for political reasons, never thinking for a moment that he cared for anything other than Thanmandrathor. Helananthe saw herself as athletic, functional, even majestic when the occasion called for it; not attractive. With Eldareth it hadn't mattered, for he was hardly the most handsome of creatures himself, and they found something in each other much deeper than beauty . . . but she hadn't for a moment expected Mawrdreth to find her physically desirable.

So they'd shocked themselves and each other, within the first few nights of their marriage, by falling, if not in love, then at least into joyful, affectionate lust.

Helananthe was happy, and this frightened her. She couldn't afford to let her own contentment distract her from Aventuria. Sometimes she thought of Eldareth with a touch of regret, for he was braving perils on her behalf while she lavished all her attention on someone else; yet perhaps, in the end, it had been for the best.

Lord Derione and Lord Poel had worked efficiently together to organise a quiet and dignified wedding, followed by the coronation of the Queen's consort. King Mawrdreth.

King Mawrdreth. It had seemed strange at first, to be no longer alone, to have him there with her, not just a companion or lover but her actual King. Now, though, it felt right that he was beside her on the Sapphire Throne. She was still the reigning monarch and he could never overrule her; but she intended to share everything with him, so that, as far as humanly possible, they could take decisions together.

As for Lord Serpeth, he had accepted his failure with grace and had been a perfect gentleman about the whole thing. Self-preservation, perhaps, but Helananthe had sent him and his troops back to Eisilion with lavish rewards, so she was as certain as she could be of his future friendship.

'It's cold, and you have nothing on under this cloak,' said Mawrdreth. He slid his hand on to her bare waist to prove it.

'I'm not cold,' she said, turning again to look at the sky. 'I should be, since it's winter, but . . .'

'I'd tell you to stop worrying, but I can't. This is as much my concern as yours now. I wish I knew what was happening in Thanmandrathor. But Helan, standing out here and staring at the sky every night won't change anything.'

'Ah, now that's where you're wrong. Because if I watch for long enough I might begin to understand it, and then I should know what to do.'

They stood in silence for a while, watching the strange writhing of the clouds, feeling the pressure waves of distant thunder. Not true thunder, but the movement of vast energies she didn't understand.

'Some change is causing this,' she said after a while. 'I've consulted priest-seers in the Temples of Nuth and Nepheter but they all tell me the same thing. *Roth*-energies are being disturbed, but they can't tell me by what or by whom. What more can I do? I have sent representatives to the Aelyr realm and the Bhahdradomen land and all we can do is wait for answers. But waiting is driving me mad! I wonder if it's worth taking two days of my time to consult my friend Fox?'

Mawrdreth laughed. Helananthe had told him all about Fox the Seer. 'Do you really think it would help?'

'In truth, I doubt it. He's good but he's cruel, he puts all the responsibility on to you and gives you no help at all.'

'Cruel but fair.'

She laughed. 'True. I may receive some wonderfully enlightening vision or I may only get jumbled nonsense. I might go if things get worse, but there's too much to do here. The Bhahdradomen . . . I don't know what's to be done about them. So many . . .'

He kissed her head and spoke with the gentle seriousness she loved about him. 'You keep talking as if you're on your own, but you're not. You can and should unload at least half your duties on to me.'

'Thanks, love. This is what you've let yourself in for, marrying me,' she sighed. 'Bossy bloody woman who never stops worrying.'

'It's terrible,' he agreed, running his hand over her hip.

She leaned against him with a pang of happiness, caught his errant hand and pressed his palm over her heart. 'But I feel it here,' she said. 'The Xauroma. The land isn't happy, and it's up to me to put it right, but how can I when I can only guess at what's wrong? A few Bhahdradomen refugees can't do this. It's not *me* mistreating the land. The Aelyr, then? I don't know. Mawrdreth, don't you feel it?'

'Yes, I feel the storms, this tension in the air.'

'No, I'm asking you if you feel the Xauroma.'

'I don't know.'

'It's a pull inside, like a cord connecting you to the earth. It can be wonderful, or it can feel like it's killing you.'

He paused. 'Then no, I don't think so. Not yet.'

'Do you want to?'

He didn't answer at first. There was no obligation for the monarch's consort to be initiated into the Xauroma. Indeed, he couldn't receive full initiation, since that was reserved for the monarch alone; only Helananthe could make and uphold the covenant. But it was possible for him to be introduced to the Xauroma, as it were; to experience it, to swear fealty to it.

So far, Mawrdreth had not undergone this experience. They'd hardly spoken of it; the only time Helananthe had brought the subject up, he'd expressed unease and said he wasn't ready.

She pressed her hands to his shoulders, where his hair hung loose in brown waves, and looked into his long cat-green eyes. The more she knew him, the more beautiful he seemed to her. Difficult to believe she had ever considered him not to her taste. He wasn't the stern warrior he had seemed when he first arrived with his sister; or rather, that was not all he was. His proud face could express the warmest smiles, his tall muscular body was capable of amazing tenderness.

'Do you want to enter the Xauroma?' she said again, very soft.

'I don't know.' His eyes were apprehensive. 'I might not be worthy. I might not be courageous enough.'

'That's nonsense. You can't go only halfway with me! There are things I must learn. Secrets I only touched on at my initiation. I need that knowledge now, but as monarch there is no one I can confide in, not even Ariolne. I can share these secrets with no one except my husband. I need your help.'

Every time she looked at him, she knew she had made the right decision. Unlike Serpeth, Mawrdreth did nothing out of self-interest. All he cared about was the good of his land; not only Thanmandrathor now but all the Nine Realms. He and Helananthe might not have known each other long, but they understood each other completely.

'You have my help,' he answered. 'You have all of me, body and heart and spirit. I'll enter the Xauroma with you, Helan.'

'You're shaking a little,' she smiled, gripping his hand. 'It can be frightening, but exhilarating too.'

He bent his head to kiss her fingers. 'When?'

'Soon,' she said. 'I have much to do in the city tomorrow. And I think that you are not quite ready yet . . . but when you are, you'll know.'

Queen Helananthe walked through the streets of Parione, incognito in a plain cream cloak with the hood drawn over her hair. She looked ordinary, neither peasant nor noble; she could have been an artisan, perhaps, or a vine-grower from the southern slopes spending winter in the city. In this guise she moved unnoticed among the citizens of Parione. In parks and coffee shops, inns and galleries and markets, she spoke to people or eavesdropped shamelessly on their conversations.

Outwardly – despite the weather – everything seemed normal. The gracious life of the city went on. But sooner or later, every conversation would reveal the under-currents she had feared.

Her citizens were unhappy.

The influx of Bhahdradomen refugees was swelling beyond her wildest estimates. Each day, long processions of them came trailing over the hills from every direction to the camp in the Danen Valley. Her officers, who were monitoring their numbers, reported back to her with growing concern. The camp was spreading, flowing over the hills all around, reaching tentacles towards the city. Their demands for food were beginning to exhaust the nearby farms.

'This is not why we won the War of the Silver Plains,' she heard people saying. 'Who's paying for them to live on our land and eat our food? We're paying for it, that's who. It's a disgrace. Worse than a disgrace, it's beyond belief!'

'Send them to Vexor. What are they doing here, when they belong in Vexor?'

'Shoot them like dra'a'ks,' others said. 'I don't tolerate rats in my house; why should we tolerate these rats on our land?'

'They're not even really alive,' someone else whispered. 'Not as we are.'

'What's the Queen doing, allowing this? Even Garnelys – whatever you say about him and his blasted Tower – even he never invited the Eaters to live on our doorstep.'

Everywhere Helananthe went, she heard the fear threaded in their voices. Rumours were beginning that Bhahdradomen had been seen in the city itself.

'I've seen them,' she heard more than one citizen insisting. 'Little quiet figures whose cloaks turn the same colour as the street, so you can hardly notice them. But when you look at them your heart goes cold. It's like seeing a ghost. Seeing your death coming towards you.'

Some of them were parroting rumours, she could tell, but a few of them had that look in their eyes. The cold, creeping shock that only people who had truly seen and recognised the shape-changers could know.

Later, back at the Citadel, she sat on one side of her desk with Lord Poel on the other. His dark head was bowed as he took notes in his brisk, precise manner.

'Where on earth are they all coming from?' she groaned. 'I had no idea there were so many of them in these hidden pockets. How on earth are we going to keep feeding them?'

'We are working on the logistics of it night and day,' said Poel. 'It is awkward that they will only eat certain grains and fruits, of course. But we have good stores of food that can be moved to the west of the city, should the need arise.'

'Of course, people are saying I shouldn't be feeding them at all. But what choice do I have? I couldn't allow them to keep their flesh-animals. Neither can I allow them to starve. Great Goddess, surely people can see that? These Bhahdradomen are the equivalent of landless peasants; they offer no threat. If we can't be kind and charitable to our defeated enemies, what was the point of us winning on the Silver Plains in the first place?'

Lord Poel listened patiently to her outburst. 'I agree with you, ma'am.'

'It's just that there are so many of them. I never expected so many.'

'We could examine the possibilities of sending them to Vexor, but it will not be easy. It would take half the army to shepherd them across Thanmandrathor, which is an epic journey in itself. And then there is the problem of transporting them across the straits . . .'

'Never mind the fact that they don't want to go.' She leaned forward, folding her hands on the desk. 'Lord Poel, I hear rumours that they've infiltrated the city. Perhaps this is mere hysteria, but it needs to be investigated. I have even heard that they've been seen around a house in the old merchants' quarter. I know it's an unfashionable area, but that is taking lowering the tone of the neighbourhood to the limit.'

She had never been able to make Poel laugh, and this time was no exception. He was silent for a while, writing. 'I think it is unlikely. How could they possibly have purchased a house?'

'Well, I don't know. Perhaps they just colonised it, like

spiders. I know it's probably nonsense, but you could have it investigated, anyway?'

'I shall do so myself immediately, ma'am.'

Helananthe was softening towards Lord Poel. Far from showing any sign of humiliation or bad grace in his reduced position, he had proved helpful, loyal and hard-working. She was beginning to feel she had misjudged him. Slightly ashamed of her own pettiness in demoting him, she had praised his dignity and backed up her words by giving him greater responsibilities within the royal administration. She still didn't particularly like him, but her personal feelings didn't alter the fact that he was good at his job. She was sure, now, that he was not a bad man; that he had carried out Garnelys's orders in the loyal conviction that the old King's intentions were pure.

'Thank you,' she said. 'It's good to have so many conscientious people around me. But I need you here, not wandering the city or poking around among property deeds. Surely you can delegate this, can't you?'

But this was one matter Lord Poel could not delegate. 'What shall I do?' he said.

Zhoaah moved in the shadows of the empty house. It smelled of dust, old paint, crumbling plaster, decay. 'Panic?' he suggested. 'Ah, I see you've already started, my lord.'

'The house is not in my name,' Poel went on, dabbing a handkerchief to his forehead. 'I hid the ownership in a series of false names and guilds. I can go back and deny everything. But the Queen is suspicious. You have been seen!'

'Unfortunately, there are quite a number of us here now and we are not all as adept at camouflage as Gulzhur. People are bound to see us.'

'What shall we do?'

'Let the Queen come.'

'What?'

Zhoaah's pale face bore the whisper of a smile. 'Go to the Queen and tell her yes, there is a house full of Bhahdradomen in her precious city and she is welcome to come and look for herself. Let her try to evict us.'

'This is madness,' Poel gasped.

'Let us never have a competition, you and I, to see which of us is the more sane,' said Zhoaah. 'It will be far worse for you, my lord, if you try to hide everything and then get found out.'

'Worse for *me*?'

Facilitator opened his white, dry hands. 'We are only refugees from persecution. You are a palace official. Responsibility and blame go hand in glove, do they not, my lord?'

Disguised in plain cloaks, Helananthe, Poel and Derione made their way through the rambling streets of the old merchants' quarter. Half-seen through tangled screens of bushes and trees, long, pale mansions crumbled within neglected gardens. Helananthe made a mental note to revivify this area, or to return it to the countryside; as it stood it was a disgrace to the capital. Yet it had a mysterious atmosphere that intrigued her.

Both Derione and Mawrdreth had counselled her against moving about the city anonymously and alone, and they'd pleaded with her to send someone else to the house rather than going herself, but Helananthe refused to listen. 'I won't lock myself away in a gilded palace,' she had said. 'I will be a monarch in my own way, which means attending to my citizens and to the land. I'm not a deity. I'm human, and I am the land's servant, not its master.'

The house to which Poel took her was unremarkable. A big, shadowy, cold place that had not been lived in for some years. As they stepped over the portico and into the hall, she noticed an odour of age and damp, and a sweetness, like raw meat. It seemed deserted, but she imagined a whispering and bustling in rooms out of her sight. Either that, or her senses were overwrought.

'There seems to be no one here,' said Derione.

Poel cleared his throat and said, 'This is the house to which my investigations directed me . . .'

The hall was cavernous, with a wide flight of stairs and several large doorways whose doors had fallen off their hinges. The light was the colour of dust.

'Hello?' Helananthe called out, her voice echoing.

Something clawed her leg, making her start so violently that she almost kicked it away by reflex. She looked down in time to stop herself. Clinging to her hem was a small human-shaped thing, its white skin mottled with strange bluish shading, odd wattles growing between its neck and shoulders to give it a tortoise-like look. Then a Bhahdradomen appeared in the nearest doorway; a tiny asexual figure with a shroud-like garment wound round it. It came towards them, picked up the creature and carried it away without even looking at them. But the small one stared back over the adult's shoulder with unblinking, snake-like eyes.

'What was that?' Derione whispered.

'A baby,' said Helananthe.

'Hatchling.' Again Poel cleared his throat uneasily. 'They call them hatchlings, ma'am.'

'How do you know that?'

Poel didn't answer; another figure was coming soundlessly towards them, this one in a greenish robe. To Helananthe's astonishment he looked familiar . . . or were there dozens of Bhahdradomen who looked like that? 'Tzumezht?' she said.

'Yes, your . . . ah, Lady Vyne.' His tone hinted that he knew exactly who she was, but was going to play the game.

'What are you doing here? You were out on the hills.'

'I am trying to ensure that my countrymen are well looked after, my lady.'

Now she saw the others. They were crowding into every doorway and along the banister at the top of the stairs, all staring and silent. Gooseflesh shimmered over her shoulders.

'Our agreement was that you remained within the designated area in the Danen Valley.'

'My lady, we are grateful that you gave us the land. However, I recall no rule that said we must remain within it. Nothing was signed.'

That was true, she recalled in regret. 'Still, we had a verbal agreement and this was not part of it. You've entered the city without permission.'

Tzumezht's thin mouth clamped in a smile. 'My lady, if you will check your own laws, you will find that there is none stating that we need permission to enter the city.'

She was losing mastery of the situation. She looked hard at Poel.

'I'm afraid he's right, ma'am,' Poel said awkwardly. 'There is not and never has been any kind of statute forbidding the Bhahdradomen from entering Parione.'

Helananthe tapped her foot, furious at herself for taking laws for granted instead of looking them up. 'What are your people doing here, Tzumezht?'

'Existing.' His eyes seemed to fasten on to hers, drawing her in like long red worms of fire; then the feeling was gone and he looked merely pathetic, half-starved, harmless.

'I don't know that I can let you stay.'

'But we are doing no harm. We keep ourselves to ourselves.'

'All the same, you've been seen. The citizens of Parione are not happy about your presence. If you stay, you may find yourselves in danger.'

'We'll take that risk. We're settled here. There are hatchlings.'

'I noticed. Tzumezht, listen to me. Although the enmity between our people is far in the past, we cannot forget what happened to make the War of the Silver Plains necessary. You will never be accepted. If your numbers grow, you will want other houses, more land. I'm afraid the people of Aventuria will turn against you, and I shall not be able to protect you.'

'You can't stop us being killed? A handful of us in one isolated house, troubling no one, when all we ask is to be allowed to live here?'

Helananthe looked at Derione, who shook his head. Tzumezht had a wonderful talent for twisting her words. 'I'm sorry, but I see no way you can remain here.'

'We are legal tenants.'

'Of whom?'

'Ask Lord Poel.'

'Tzumezht, good sir, I'm inviting you one last time to leave here and return to your designated camp. Will you go?'

'I'm sorry, my lady, but no. We have every right to be here. If you want us to leave, you will have to evict us. Send your soldiers to slay us; we'll put up no resistance. Ah, but you would never do that. You could never slaughter a household of defenceless refugees, for where would that leave your pride in your humanity and kindness?'

His words slipped into her like a stiletto. Helananthe gave a grim laugh. 'What does your name mean, Tzumezht? Truth-speaker?'

'Prefigurer.' His answer was flat, literal and told her nothing.

'Well, you are right. Of course I wish you no harm. But if you insist on staying, I cannot protect you.'

She turned and strode out, Poel and Derione hurrying behind her. They walked in silence back to the road; but as soon as her feet touched the flagstones she swore vehemently. Derione, prim soul, looked shocked, but she took no notice.

'Right, the moment we arrive back at the Amber Citadel

362

we are going to check every line of the law and find some way to remove them – peacefully.'

'Yes, ma'am,' said Derione.

'And why did he say, "Ask Lord Poel"?'

Poel looked shamefaced; strange to see that expression on his marble countenance, yet because it was so unusual it looked utterly sincere. 'Ma'am, I have a confession to make. I tried to tell you before but I could not find the words.'

She stopped, hands on hips. 'Well?'

'The house belongs to a charitable guild of which I am patron.'

'Wait – are you telling me that house is yours?'

'No – no – not as such. It belongs to the guild. I only found out when I investigated the ownership. They do charitable work, ma'am, but they prefer to do so anonymously. It's true; the Bhahdradomen are there as legitimate tenants. And to be honest, ma'am, I support the guild in what they have done. They were only trying to help these wretched people who have nothing.'

Helananthe stared at him, completely dumbfounded. Finally she managed to speak. 'You've left me speechless, Poel. My goddess, I do believe those are tears in your eyes.'

Poel pressed his shoulders back, trying to regain his usual stiff demeanour. She added, 'I had no idea you were so soft-hearted. I'm stunned. I'm really . . . touched, almost.'

'All members of the guild prefer to keep their work secret,' he said stiffly.

'So I see. You certainly had me fooled.'

'Ma'am, I apologise if you think our charity has been misdirected. It was done with the best of intentions.'

'Yes, I'm sure.' She walked on again, pulling her cloak and hood tight against a sudden chill breeze. 'Enough, my lord, your secret is safe with me. You're telling me, then, that I have no grounds to evict them?'

'And indeed, ma'am, what harm are they doing?'

When she arrived back at the Citadel, Mawrdreth was not in their private chambers to meet her for supper as they'd arranged. Instead she found him in her office, sitting at her desk with a small, crinkled piece of paper held flat on the desk between his hands. Lamplight glistened on his hair, the amber walls, the gilded edges of the furniture. When he looked up, his face was grave, his thick brown eyebrows taut with shock.

'Love, what's happened?' she said.

'One of the blue-doves came back from Than-mandrathor,' he answered. 'The messenger brought the cylinder to me, so I opened it. I hope you don't mind.'

'Of course not.' She went to his side and slipped her arm round his shoulders. Her heart felt cold. 'Well?'

'My father's dead,' he said matter-of-factly. 'My sister has become Duchess. He was poisoned, it seems, by a . . . Bhahdradomen.'

'Oh, gods,' Helan whispered. 'Let me see.'

She read the message; two sides of tiny, rushed hand-writing that she recognised as Dawn's. A serving boy in the household who no one suspected . . . the Duke expiring of heart failure as the exposed shape-changer was killed in front of him. Strange storms emanating from Q'enartre's Throne. But the information was basic and every line Dawn had written – although she'd obviously done her best – only raised a dozen questions in Helananthe's mind.

'I'm so sorry,' she said. 'Tasq was a good friend of my grandfather's . . . some years ago, of course.'

'I knew that boy, Noli,' said Mawrdreth, pressing long fingers to his temples. 'He was just an ordinary boy like any other. A bit quiet.'

'That's what they said about Laphaeome,' Helan breathed. 'Love, I wanted you to help me on some points of law tonight. But I think it's better you just rest instead.'

'No!' He looked fiercely at her. 'I shall never be able to sleep. I'm going to help you. How much more evidence do we need that the Bhahdradomen are active?'

That was her first lesson that Mawrdreth must never be mollycoddled. He said no more about his loss, only worked intensely and calmly. Deep into the night they pored over huge tomes of law until the candles burned low and sheer tiredness forced them to stop. They were sitting on the floor on velvety rugs, surrounded by piles of books, the air filled with the musty odour of old paper and cracked bindings.

Helan groaned. 'I can't find anything, not one tiny by-law, that will enable me to turn those Bhahdradomen out of that house. There are no laws preventing them from owning or renting property. Why should there be? Our ancestors were concerned with them destroying and enslaving us, not buying houses! However, there *are* clauses allowing them to stay on the mainland.'

'But haven't they broken the conditions?' Mawrdreth asked sharply.

'They weren't allowed to cross the boundaries of their areas without just cause or permission of the monarch. But they claim just cause, and I gave them permission. We haven't a legal leg to stand on.'

'Pass a new law,' he said.

'That's a bit arbitrary, isn't it? I can't do that. The monarch can't just make up new laws to suit herself. Well, no, we could draft something and I'm sure the Sun Chamber would support me, but still, it would take months to pass it. And if they still refuse to leave, and I have to use force against them? They've put me in the most impossible situation. Half of me feels sorry for them, like Poel, and wishes them no harm. If they'd just vanish, I'd be so happy. But the other half of me, the responsible monarch – well, she has to think of her citizens. I have to put the good of Aventuria before any other consideration.'

'Even if it means being harsh with the refugees?' There was a hardness in his eyes, willing her to be resolute. His attitude to the Bhahdradomen had hardened.

'Yes. You have no idea how unpopular I am at the moment. "Even old Garnelys never let the Eaters live on our doorstep," they're saying. People are angry and restless. If I lose their trust, I'll never get it back.' She exhaled pensively. 'Should I have sent an army to Vexor, instead of a tiny deputation? Gods, if only I'd had some tuition from Garnelys or Galemanth on how to do the right thing. I had no idea this job would be so hard.'

She slumped over her crossed legs, rubbing her eyes. She felt Mawrdreth's hand on her shoulder. 'Your instincts and your judgement are sound,' he said. 'Sounder than theirs, I have no doubt. That can't be taught.'

'It's all very well learning by my mistakes, but in my position I can't afford to make any. Did you know, the Bhahdradomen never came as far as Parione before? Even the dreaded Ghaurthror of the Flies never conquered the Amber Citadel. The city was inviolate. Yet now, here they are, by stealth. They may well be harmless and innocent – but somehow, the Bhahdradomen are here. For the first time! How triumphant must they feel?'

'Helan, we've got to be tough. Maybe they are harmless, but they seem to be walking all over us.'

'That's it.' She shot to her feet. 'That's exactly it! The situation's slipping away from me. I must keep the upper hand or we're lost.'

'What are you doing?' he asked.

'We have to be prepared for the possibility that the Bhahdradomen's intentions are wholly sinister. They mustn't catch us out. We need weapons.'

'What kind of weapons?' He rose beside her, shaking creases out of his green and gold robe.

'I'll show you,' she answered. She laid her hand on his arm and looked into his face. 'We need to dress warmly and take a lamp. It's time, love.'

In the gloom of the underground chamber, the great

xauroth sphere rotated on its plinth, moaning softly. Mawrdreth was nervous, fascinated. He and Helan stood side by side in silence, wearing thick, dark, open robes over the flimsier palace garments beneath. His lamp splashed liquid light on the polished surface of the sphere.

'It's beautiful,' he whispered.

'I'm learning all its moods,' said Helananthe. She looked magnificent as always, her mane of honey-coloured hair rippling loose against the indigo material. She held her sceptre of office with the Orb of Clear Sight reflecting soft light on to her face. 'It's beautiful, yes, but so full of darkness and fire. I want to see it as the Zampherai described it; white crystal as clear as ice, with dragonfly lights dancing in its depths.'

He looked more closely then. The sphere had a greenish cast, as if the storms that clashed outside were echoed by flickers in its translucent core. Patches of blackness travelled through it and faded; they made him think of armies travelling across distant landscapes. Foreboding crept over him.

'Feel it,' she said, holding her palm a hair's breadth from the surface. He did the same. Ice-smooth coolness flowed from the globe; then to his amazement it seemed to slow down, warming under his hand like a loving cat. He gave a soft laugh of wonder.

'This is not the Xauroma,' said Helan. 'It is only a barometer that reflects its mood. The Xauroma itself cannot be seen or heard or touched . . . only felt.'

Suddenly the sphere uttered a terrible, mournful shriek. They both started violently and gripped each other. Green and red clouds roiled deep inside it, swiftly dissipating to leave the crystal dim again. Helananthe and Mawrdreth held on to each other in shocked silence. At last he said, 'What was that?'

'I don't know,' she said grimly. 'But Mawrdreth, you must know before you go any further . . . the Xauroma is under great strain. At my initiation, I felt the earth warning me that it may be more than I can do to hold it together. Perhaps I've failed already, and that is why the heavens are furious. There's a secret I must unlock before it's too late. Do you want to go on?'

He nodded emphatically. 'Wherever you go, I go.'

Helan moved around the sphere. She took out a strange, carved piece of obsidian, fitted it to a set of holes in a flagstone, and pressed it home. A lock gave. Seeing what she was doing, he helped her to lift the stone, revealing a well of blackness. She beckoned, and they began to descend the dark damp spiral of an ancient stair.

Mawrdreth was apprehensive, but not afraid. His lamp glistened on the gritty dampness of rock. Helananthe bore her sceptre like a second lamp, for the Orb of Clear Sight was glowing distinctly in the darkness.

As they reached the dome-shaped chamber at the bottom she called out, 'Andamanque!'

Mawrdreth shivered. The figure who appeared from a crack in the rock, in response to her call, was a tiny pewter crone with black hair straggling over her shoulders. Her cracked voice echoed. 'Who disturbs the Keeper?'

'Blessing of the earth upon you,' said Helananthe. She bowed and he followed suit. 'I bring my husband King Mawrdreth to greet the Xauroma and to unlock the tablets of knowledge.'

'He cannot go the way you went,' Andamanque said shortly.

'I know that, Keeper. But it is his right to swear fealty.'

'Indeed. Set your staff in the ground. Have him look upon it. If it please the Xauroma, its power will come to him . . .'

Mawrdreth was shivering with the chill of the air and the oppression of stone; the whole weight of the Amber Citadel above him. He looked at the Orb of Clear Sight and the vision came instantly, shockingly.

The Orb filled his vision like a moon and then he was tumbling into it, swimming dizzily through white light.

The whiteness darkened swiftly to a rich glowing red, like a heart . . . and on through purple and ink to darkest underwater green.

He was in the ocean.

What he'd sensed as the weight of rock now turned to the weight of water and he felt an immense pressure on his lungs. He gaped wordlessly. He wasn't breathing, yet this didn't matter; he was not in his body. Bubbles surged up past him like a million crystal orbs from cracks in the ocean bed and he saw red fires glowing deep in the fissures. Strange fish swam around him, mouths agape. He saw jewels – red, blue and turquoise – and realised they were not jewels but the triple eyes of huge sea-serpents.

Their great scaled bodies looped and thrashed around him. In a monumental ballet they were dancing out the pain of the deep places of the earth, revealing to him the unseen jewelfire burning where humans could never go, where even the vision of seers could not penetrate.

The water, they sang. *It will come through the water, the lakes and the streams and the wide slow rivers and the wild seas, the vast oceans. Do not forget us. Jthery . . .*

A single, gigantic serpent was surging towards him, jaws wide, the great cabochon between its eyes blazing ruby-red. Mawrdreth yelled.

At once he was jolted back into his body. He staggered, and found himself standing once more in the little underground chamber, with Helananthe holding his arm and the Keeper gazing keenly at him. The ruby-red eye remained; it was the Orb itself.

'What did you see?' Helan said anxiously.

He swallowed hard. 'Sea-serpents.'

'What?'

'I was in the ocean . . .' He tried to describe what he'd seen. 'They said a name . . . Jthery? Is that not the name of your cousin of Mithrain?'

She was looking at him in anxiety. 'Do you want to go back to our chambers and rest, while we talk about this?'

He shook his head vehemently. 'No. I was shaken, that's all. I didn't expect a vision so powerful. It was . . . intense. I wish I could tell you what it meant!'

The Keeper chuckled. 'One thing it meant is this; the Xauroma accepts you as the Queen's consort. It will let you in to help her. And she needs all the help she can get. Have you the other key?'

Helan reached into a pocket and brought out a piece of amethyst, shaped like a mushroom with several stalks.

'Good,' said the Keeper. 'Then I'll leave you.' She began to shuffle away, quickly lost in the shadows.

'Wait!' said Helan. 'Can't you help us to understand the slabs?'

The Keeper paused. 'The materials and the minerals of the earth are Zampherai matters. The words inscribed upon them are human business.'

She was gone. Helananthe let out a long breath that condensed in a cloud on the chilly air. 'Mawr, are you sure you're all right?'

'Yes,' he said firmly, annoyed at her asking.

'Good. Then help me. In here are the secrets I need to understand, if we are to protect our kingdom.'

She was bending down to a marble slab in the centre of the chamber. It shone creamily as if lit from inside. Pressing the amethyst key into the lock, she lifted the heavy lid and set her staff upright in a carved groove. At once the Orb of Clear Sight began to glow even more intensely crimson.

Mawrdreth looked on in complete wonder as she lifted a tablet of crystal out of the chest. It was beautiful; palest gold, translucent, inscribed with runes that channelled light in shining streams as she tilted it.

'Look,' she said, holding the oblong in front of the orb. 'Can you read it?'

He looked. He could make no sense of the flowing characters. 'No.'

'Damn. I hoped . . .'

'What language is it?'

'Ours. Paranian. I couldn't read it either, until my initiation. Now I can, but I still don't understand it.'

'Wait.' Mawrdreth stared at the fiery lines. Suddenly they resolved themselves into letters he knew, and he gasped in awe. '"Of the flying third came rains of fire, the tower whereof hath time, and time stitched back upon time, which by the power of Calabethron is rent . . ."'

'You can read it!' Helan cried.

'Yes, but I see your problem.'

'And so it goes on, making absolutely no sense whatsoever. Everything we need to know is in these tablets . . . if only we can interpret them correctly.'

Mawrdreth smiled. 'This will be interesting.'

'Don't look so pleased. It could take days, even weeks. I'm not even sure which of these slabs contains the most important information.'

'Which is . . . what?'

She knelt down, her shadow leaping on the rough, carved wall. 'The War of the Silver Plains was won only because humans had acquired or created some very special and powerful weapons to use against the Bhahdradomen. You will have heard of them. They were known as the Basilisks of Calabethron. Afterwards, they were hidden away so that no one foolish or ill-intentioned would misuse them. Only the monarch of Aventuria is allowed access to them – and as you see, even that has been made as difficult as possible.'

'You don't know where these weapons are kept?' he said, his voice low.

'Not yet, but what I do know is that that information is encoded in these tablets. Now all we have to do is tease the meaning out of them.'

Hours passed as they worked through the slabs line by line; Helananthe reading, Mawrdreth writing down possible interpretations (on paper they would later burn)

371

and trying to make sense of the cryptic phrasing. Gradually the tangled words became clear.

Mawrdreth was magical, Helan found; he could always spot the meaning in a sentence that had her tired brain in knots. Between them, they were achieving something that neither could have managed alone. The five most relevant tablets each had a simple diagram scratched at the bottom, like a fragment of a maze.

'A Basilisk to hurl fire among the enemy,' said Helan. 'Another to cast nets over the enemy. The lesser weapons that cast ice into their hearts . . . that sounds like the *mnelir* Tanthe had. The greatest of all . . . I'm not sure I've got this right, but it seems to say, the weapon that stops them folding time.'

'What does that mean?'

Helananthe pushed her hair behind her ear. 'I'm trying to remember what my history books taught me about the last battle on the Silver Plains. You know, I can't remember one clear description of the weapons they used. I got the impression that it was all done by sorcery, some kind of magic-lore that we've lost. Was that my bad memory?'

Mawrdreth shook his head. 'I read three history books while my leg was healing. You're right. The references to the weapons are few and highly cryptic, they don't describe any of them clearly nor say what their function was. Several great *roth*-mages entered the fray with mysteriously acquired powers, "Ashamta smote the enemy with fire." "Nilthorn stopped the *ghelim* in the air," and so forth.'

'Well, it's obvious. No one who *witnessed* the battle understood what they were seeing. Doubtless the mages themselves were sworn to secrecy. Only King Maharoth knew the truth.'

'To protect the secrets from our enemies.'

'It would seem so. Only the monarch is allowed this knowledge . . .' She looked at him and said drily. 'If we ever sort this out, remind me, won't you, to leave some clues to my poor children in the event of my premature demise?'

Mawrdreth stared back at her. She cleared her throat, suddenly awkward. 'Anyway,' she went on. 'The first thing is to locate these wondrous Basilisks. The next is for us to learn exactly how they're meant to be used. They must be dangerous, otherwise why would they be hidden? The last thing I want is to cause some dreadful disaster with them.'

He yawned, trying to stifle it. It must be nearly dawn and they were both feeling the lack of sleep. 'I've been wondering what these diagrams can be. They have numbers scratched on them.'

'Maps of some sort?' Helananthe said. 'But what do they refer to? Some part of the Citadel I don't know about?'

Mawrdreth laid one tablet on another and lifted the two up to the Orb-light. Suddenly the lines glinted with meaningful fire. He glanced at her, quickly placed the other three on top so that the designs were superimposed. With some effort, he lifted all five. This time, as the light shone through, it suggested a three-dimensional object, a strange comb . . . or a box with a domed top and prongs of different lengths . . .

'Gods, of course, it's a key like these other two!' Helananthe cried. 'It's a diagram of the key that will unlock the weapons! Mawrdreth, you're wonderful!'

'Then these numbers must represent its dimensions . . .'

'But where is it?' she said in dismay. 'It's not in this chest. The priestess didn't give it to me. I've never seen such a thing.'

'And where is the lock that it fits into?'

An hour later, stiff and frozen and beyond exhaustion, they had the answer.

'"After the War of the Silver Plains,"' Mawrdreth read out his translation, '"the Basilisks of Calabethron were hidden once more for safekeeping. The key was smashed, that the Basilisks shall be untouched. A new lock was formed, for which the key has not yet been made." Or rather, I think that should read, "Will not be made until the Basilisks are needed."'

'Great. So we have to get the key made ourselves.'

He looked through the layered slabs, turning them this way and that. 'It will take a stone-carver of great skill. A jeweller, perhaps. One we can trust to keep the task secret.'

'Oh yes,' she said mordantly. 'We can bring someone here, lock them up while they work, then never let them out again.'

'They don't need to know—' he began, but she started up with a gasp.

'Gods, of course! What am I saying! We have exactly that person on hand! She's a prisoner in the Citadel. Ysomir.'

He frowned. 'The woman who—'

'Yes, but she can shape stone like a Zampherai, so I've been told. Just when I least desired to hear about her skills and talents. But perhaps they'll prove useful after all.'

'And all we have to do is find the right stone for the key,' said Mawrdreth. '"The colour of the northern sea is this crystal, that of the fine seat standing double under leaves. Of this stone is that seat, and of this seat is that stone—"'

In a flash of revelation, Helan knew.

'The Sapphire Throne,' she whispered. 'It's main material isn't sapphire but lapis lazuli. It's telling us to make the key of the same stone and – Oh, goddess, Mawrdreth. I think it means that the weapons themselves are hidden under the Sapphire Throne.'

The sight of Ysomir never ceased to disturb Helananthe.

She appeared more peaceful every time the Queen saw her; always writing at the bare table, slim as a willow in her dull brown robe, her long wavy hair hanging forwards over one shoulder. The sun-kissed gold had gone out of it, since she had been locked away for so long, but it shone warmly like autumn leaves against the drabness.

As always, a reflex of anger and hatred kicked Helan's chest, that Ysomir could have stabbed Garnelys and yet be so unconcerned. It was a sort of irritation that bordered on jealousy.

The wardress announced the Queen. Ysomir flew to her feet, disconcerted. Good. A reaction.

'Your majesty?'

Helananthe, being considerably taller and bigger than Ysomir, could always intimidate her physically. She had to remind herself that this time, she'd come to ask for help.

'Sit down,' said Helan. 'Don't look so worried. I haven't come to interrogate you.'

Ysomir sat warily. The Queen took the chair opposite and waved the wardress away. Once they were alone, she placed a small bundle on the table between them.

'I understand you can carve stone. That you're very good at it.'

'I'm not bad, ma'am. My grandfather taught me. I haven't done any for a long time, since they won't allow me to have the tools in here.'

'Well, you'll be supervised, to make sure you don't do anything foolish.' Helananthe unwrapped the bundle to reveal a rough chunk of stone, intensely blue. Ysomir's eyes widened. 'This is the finest piece of lazurite I could find. I trust you'll be careful not to make a mistake with it. I have a drawing of a special carving I need made. The dimensions must be very precise. I don't think it's an easy piece. Can you do it?'

For the first time, life came to Ysomir's green-gold eyes. She looked at the stone and the carving tools with child-like excitement. She pored over the diagram that Mawrdreth had carefully drawn, adding the measure-ments in his neat hand. 'Quite difficult,' she said, 'but I can do it.'

'How long will it take?'

'It depends how hard the stone is.' She pressed her

375

fingertips to the lapis with a pleasure that bordered on the sensual.

'There isn't much time. I can wait a few days, but not weeks.'

'It will take as long as it takes,' Ysomir flashed back, looking up under her arched brows, not quite sharp enough to be insolent. 'Might I ask why you need it, ma'am?'

'No, you may not.' Helananthe was poised to stand up and leave, when Ysomir uttered a groan and swayed in her chair.

'*The key,*' she said. '*Ah, no, oh gods, they are coming again . . .*'

'I beg your pardon?' said Helananthe.

She saw a pale blue light flaring from Ysomir's fingertips where they touched the stone. A weird energy emanated from her, filling Helan with such unease that she wanted to flee. Ysomir sat back in her chair and her eyes rolled under the lids, showing only blank white crescents.

'Ysomir?' Helan said, jumping up. 'What's wrong?'

She was about to call the warder when the girl began to speak. Her voice sounded terrible, deep and slow and eerie.

'*I never had need of the key. Those days are gone, they are enemies no longer. They are our friends now. They always know when I am troubled. I can trust no one else. Aazhoth is a wise leader, I know that the Bhahdradomen are not my enemies, so I take them into my confidence and I feel the web of lies, the sticky lies that bind me to them . . .*' Her face became gaunt with pain. '*Lies. They promised . . . Garnelys the Kind may be forgotten but Garnelys who built the Great Tower and first forged true friendship with the Bhahdradomen . . . he is a King who will endure for ever.*'

Helananthe's whole being went rigid with shock. It sounded like her grandfather. Exactly like him. 'Ysomir!' she cried in panic.

The girl swayed and put her fingers to her forehead. 'Ma'am?' she said in her normal voice.

'What were you doing?' Helananthe sank back into the chair, her fingers white on the edge of the table. '*What were you doing?*'

'Oh no.' She looked stricken. 'No. What did I say?'

'Don't you know?' An emphatic shake of her head. The Queen took a deep breath, trying to think quickly, to be circumspect. 'I have heard that when Lynden and another friend of yours died, you claimed that they still spoke to you.'

Now her eyes were big and wary. 'Who told you that?'

'You wrote about it yourself. Is it true?'

'Yes,' Ysomir said hoarsely. 'They do.'

'And Garnelys? Does he speak to you?'

She paused. Shook her head. 'No.'

'Don't lie to me, dear. The others . . . are they still alive inside you?'

'Yes. And no.'

'I don't understand.' Helananthe was trembling.

Ysomir looked like a transfixed doe. 'They don't change or do anything. They stay as they were in life. They're like memories, but conscious memories. I don't know how to explain. Instead of flying off into nowhere, their *ethroth* came into me.'

'People you were close to.'

'Yes.'

'And you were very close to Garnelys, weren't you? Right beside him as he died, your hand holding the knife that was killing him. How can his *ethroth* not have gone into you?'

Ysomir was suddenly angry. 'Who told you about Garnelys?' she hissed. 'It must have been Saphaeyender. Tanthe would never have said anything. No one else knows. I made him promise not to tell you!'

Helananthe stared at her for several seconds. Eventually she said slowly, 'No one told me anything, dear. They didn't need to. I have just heard Garnelys's voice coming out of your mouth.'

The young woman's whole body seemed to loosen and slump with dismay. 'What did he say? No – no, I can remember. About the Bhahdradomen.'

'I find it amazing that Saphaeyender and Tanthe knew about this, while I did not. This is extremely serious. He should have told me. *You* should have told me!'

'I made him promise not to! I have nothing more to say!'

'Nothing to tell me – with Garnelys's memories inside you?'

'I knew this would happen. That you'd question me and question me. That's why I didn't want you to know, ma'am. Please . . . please, I can't talk about him any more.'

Ysomir's obvious anguish shocked her. Helan saw that unless she eased off, she wouldn't get her key. She placed her finger on the drawing. 'Has Garnelys informed you of what this is?'

'No. I've no idea.'

'Yet you said something that indicated he had told you . . .'

A wave of cold fierce passion went through Ysomir like a pulse of light. She said, 'Do you *really* want to know what Garnelys told me? Do you want to hear, and would you like it widely known, that Garnelys was not taken in by the Bhahdradomen but worked knowingly and willingly with them? He sold himself to them on a spurious promise of immortality! He knew what Laphaeome was. Not at first – but by the end, he *knew*.'

Helan was speechless. Eventually she managed to say, 'Make the carving for me, Ysomir, please. That's all I ask of you.' She got up to leave, feeling drained. She didn't trust Ysomir to make the key correctly, nor to tell her the truth, but she couldn't face any more arguing. 'If you require extra food while you are working or anything special, tell the warders and they'll see it is provided.' She took a few steps, half-turned. 'By the way, whatever you think you know, you must tell no one. Not the warders, not your visitors. Only me. Understand?'

She nodded stiffly. The Queen continued on her way but as she reached the cell door, Ysomir said quietly, 'Ma'am, you don't understand. When I first said, "The key," and "Oh gods, they are coming again," it wasn't Garnelys speaking.'

'Then who?'

'It was Maharoth.'

Darkness lay on the Sun Chamber. Rose and Leaf Moons cast their light through the great stained glass window, draping the floor in soft tesserae of blue and green, topaz and red. The Sapphire Throne gleamed darkly against the glow.

The King and Queen approached side by side and mounted the dais. The key gleamed blue in Helan's palm and her heart was leaden in her chest. If this didn't work, what next?

She had spent two nights examining the throne's jewelled surface, until she knew every inch of it, every single facet and cabouchon that adorned it. And at last she'd found what she was looking for.

All through the past few exhausting days, as she waited for Ysomir to carve the key, she'd been thinking of those dreadful words. If Garnelys had worked hand in glove with the Bhahdradomen . . . sold himself to them for a promise of immortality . . . that was bad enough, but if everyone *knew* . . . The disgrace to the Amber Citadel would never be overcome.

Ysomir, effectively, had blackmailed her into silence. She couldn't even tell Mawrdreth this. But she couldn't worry about Ysomir now.

She knelt down on the right-hand side of the throne and felt for the hidden place she'd discovered. A small segment that lay flush and seamless with the solid base of the chair, invisible unless you knew it was there. Now it sprang open to her touch. Beneath the flap was the keyhole; a flat square of marble with nine holes drilled into it.

Her mouth was arid as she held the key to the lock. The nine prongs married exactly. She pushed and the lapis block slid home with a satisfying crunch.

An unseen mechanism clicked. Suddenly the Throne itself felt unstable, and a thin black gap appeared beneath it.

'It worked,' she whispered.

She and Mawrdreth looked at each other. Then they began gently to push at the throne. It slid back, revealing a shaft. Blackness. Helananthe put her hand into the centre of the gap, feeling for a change of temperature, a draught. Instead she felt a strange energy rush through her – the Xauroma itself – and she knew that she'd been recognised. The shaft began to glow and she saw that it was not long, only inches more than the length of her arm, and that it terminated in a pocket about four feet across. This pocket glowed and shimmered, and she felt that she was looking at the fabric of another realm.

Mawrdreth gasped, pressing his head alongside hers to see inside.

'It's like a tiny portal, which only recognises us,' she said. 'So even if someone else had found this, they still could not have opened it.'

She couldn't see much through the glow. The compartment's strange fabric was actually some kind of crystal, full of shifting light. As her eyes adjusted to the brightness, she saw niches carved into it, as if each formed a perfect fit to a particular artifact . . . There were also lengths of silken rope that hung loose as if they'd been cut . . . she frowned. The niches were all empty. Where were the artifacts that should be lying snug in them? The Basilisks of Calabethron?

'There's nothing here,' said Mawrdreth.

Helananthe's hands flew to her face. Her elation drained away. Cold dismay and panic flashed through her and she cried out before she could stop herself. 'No!'

Mawrdreth reached past her into the shaft, lying flat on

the dais so he could get his hand right to the bottom. When he sat up again, there was a scrap of parchment in his fingers, and on it nine words in an unusual, flowing hand. *'Your pardon, seeker. Others have better use for them.'*

She sat on the lip of the portal, frozen. Mawrdreth stared and stared at the note. Inside her, heart-churning fear was growing by the second as she watched the consequences of their discovery arcing away from this moment into the unknown past and the terrifying future. Someone had known about the weapons and taken them – but who? Why? And *when*? And now her hopes of mastery had vanished and she had no means of controlling the Bhahdradomen, nothing to threaten or bargain with.

'Stolen.' Her mouth was so dry she could barely form the words. 'Nuth help us, some goddess-forsaken bastard has stolen them!'

Chapter Sixteen. Verdanholm

The battle of the Aelyr thundered across the plain, oblivious to Eldareth and his companions caught in the midst of it. Eldareth's head span with the shock of transition. The turmoil around him seemed overblown, dreamlike. Warriors in silvery webs of chain mail and garments the colour of dew or of dark sapphire were surging past on every side; swords clashing, spears flying. The plain on which they fought seemed to shake, and the air shuddered with unseen energies. The landscape flowed in and out of focus behind curtains of heat-haze, or sudden shimmering bursts of *roth* that splintered the light into rainbows.

Ghastly noises assaulted their ears; a cacophony of unearthly voices, stabbed through with metallic screams. Above, the sky trembled with waves of pale light.

An Aelyr woman fell dead right at the hooves of Eldareth's horse, a spear through her back, blood splashing the silver grass. Gany backed away nervously, and Eldareth gathered the reins, turning him, checking swiftly that his companions were still safely on horseback.

'Let's get out of this!' he cried.

Elrill had been on foot when they'd come through the portal, but he'd since vaulted on to Nefri's back. Jthery looked disorientated, but Tanthe had one hand on his reins, controlling his horse as well as her own.

The fighting Aelyr must have seen them. It was only a matter of moments before one side or the other attacked them. Eldareth saw a gap open up in the lines, and beyond it a rise in the ground that was clear of the battle.

'That way,' he said, but Elrill had seen it and was already urging his horse into a gallop.

In a tight-packed group they galloped, broke free of the battle, and surged up on to the rise. Here Eldareth reined in, making sure the others were all present and correct.

While the fighting ebbed and flowed below them on the plain, his main concern was their safety. His head swam, but he made a powerful effort to ignore it and clear his thoughts. He wanted to assess their situation, rather than simply turn tail and flee.

'Everyone all right?' said Eldareth. The eldritch noises of the battle were audible, but bearable at this distance.

'I think so,' answered Tanthe, out of breath. 'Nothing like as bad as it was last time. Just as well, or I'd be dead by now.'

'Jthery?'

Jthery looked white and dazed, but he managed to nod. 'A bit dizzy.'

'We'll wait here until we've got our bearings. No sense in rushing off.'

'And remember the landmarks, in the hope that we can find this place again,' said Elrill. A dark blue boulder, half-buried in long grass a few hundred yards below their vantage point, marked the portal's location. 'We shall wish to return to Earth, at some stage.'

'What's this battle about?' asked Tanthe, but no one answered her.

As Eldareth's head began to clear, the new realm stormed his senses. No question that this was not Earth. Colours, scents, the very feel of the air were different. The atmosphere thrummed with glittery energy, not all of it from the battle; the sun was high yet larger and less dazzling than the one he knew. It hung like a ripe apricot against a sky of indigo and a field of brilliant daystars.

In front of their knoll the plain curved away, a silvery bowl perhaps half a mile wide with woods clustering on both sides. Beyond the plain, directly in front of them, hills dwindled in smooth blue folds towards the horizon. On this shallow bowl, the opposing Aelyr sides were fighting.

They could hardly be described as armies, Eldareth thought; there seemed no organisation to the battle. On foot they swooped upon each other in scattered groups, long swords flashing. The fighting was swift, almost like a dance, leaving few casualties. He began to sense something deeper to it then, a delicate point-scoring strategy almost like a game of metrarch; but this was no game. The dance was directed by a deep, lethal fury on both sides.

Layers of strange sounds enhanced the unearthliness of the scene. A faint rushing noise that was like water, yet somehow electric; unhuman singing, screaming. Soundless displacements of light and air, a thrashing of energies caused by nothing he could see . . .

'Are they using weapons of some kind that work at a distance?' he said.

'It's possible,' said Elrill. 'But you must understand, Verdanholm and the Aelyr are part of each other. When we experience strong emotions, the realm itself reacts. It is quite painful to me.'

'We'd better move on, then,' Tanthe said anxiously.

Behind their knoll lay meadows and woods, with verdure of soft bluish greens sheened with silver. The main tide of the battle flowed up and down the plain, but several groups of Aelyr warriors ran past on either side of their knoll, very close – sometimes glancing up at them – yet ignoring them. No telling which was the best way to safety. A sinister music swelled in volume and Eldareth saw that on both wooded rims of the plain, long lines of Aelyr were standing under the trees, singing. Their voices were not beautiful but piercing and disturbing.

Eldareth turned to Elrill. From his expression it was obvious that the Shaelahyr was tormented by the discord, more so than the humans were. Eldareth remembered how Elrill's own people had brought down an avalanche by singing.

'Tanthe's right, we should be leaving,' said Elrill.

'That's not going to be easy,' said Eldareth. 'They're

down in the meadows and woods behind us, too. Whichever way we go, we're likely to blunder into a corner of it. Who are they?'

'Those in the grey are Fhelethyr,' said Elrill. 'The ones in dark blue and silver are Valahyr.'

'Why are they fighting?' asked Tanthe, anxious. She was touching Jthery's arm to steady him; he still looked pale.

'I don't know.' Elrill sounded grim. 'They've had their disputes in the past but to the best of my knowledge it has not come to war for centuries. This is the most terrible circumstance.'

'Rather a disaster, us stepping into the middle of it,' said Eldareth. 'Let's ride down a short way, so we're in a less obvious position. Is Jthery all right?'

'He will be,' said Tanthe. 'He's got the same problem I had, the first time I came through a portal. Trying to work out where he is.'

'I'm fine,' Jthery insisted.

They rode down the side of the knoll, which left them better concealed but less able to see what was around. On the plain the battle seemed to have passed its peak and was beginning to subside. The two sides were breaking apart and retreating to their respective edges of the plain; the Valahyr to the right, the Fhelethyr to the woods on the left. The piercing voices ceased and the singers vanished into the trees.

The plain fell quiet. Energies were still leaping about, but more softly now, gradually subsiding. Eldareth saw the figures of Fhelethyr warriors moving about on the battlefield to tend their fallen. Some Valahyr, too. But the two sides ignored each other, as if a truce had been called.

'Who won?' said Tanthe. There were tears on her face. Eldareth could think of no easy way to reassure her.

'I doubt that the war is finished yet,' said Elrill.

'Do you know where we are?' Eldareth asked.

'I think we are on the Plains of Hethryr,' Elrill answered. 'If that means anything.'

'I have seen maps and drawings of Verdanholm,' Eldareth answered. 'The geography corresponds very roughly to that of Aventuria. I know that much.'

Elrill sighed. 'My friend, I was not accusing you of ignorance. My remark, "If that means anything," was addressed to the fact that Verdanholm itself changes. No map can truly describe it.'

'What shall we do?' Tanthe said, her hand taut on Redbird's reins.

'Vanish, if possible,' Elrill answered. 'My position in Verdanholm is much the same as Eldareth's in Torith Mir.'

Tanthe looked shocked. 'Why, what have you done?'

'I am not accused of any crime, but the Shaelahyr, if you recall, are forbidden to enter Verdanholm.'

'Of course. I forgot,' Tanthe said stiffly. 'Maybe you'll even tell us why, one of these days. Would they arrest you?'

Elrill smiled mysteriously. 'They might try, but I should talk my way out of it. I'd rather it didn't come to that, however.'

'So you can talk your way out of it?' said Tanthe. 'Good. In that case, shouldn't we go down and help the wounded?'

Elrill looked from her to Jthery to Eldareth, a frown corrugating his white forehead. 'We'd be more sensible to save our skins than be charitable, but I'll abide with the majority.'

'I agree with Tanthe,' Jthery said simply.

'So do I,' added Eldareth. 'She's right, Rill. Dozens of Aelyr have already seen us. We might as well be of some use to them. It's our human duty.'

'As you wish,' Elrill said coolly, turning his horse.

They rode at a walk down on to the plain, then dismounted and went on foot, leading their horses. The Fhelethyr men and women began to notice them, looking up with subdued surprise rather than shock. Their grey and violet eyes were troubled, yet calm – almost serene, in

387

a grave way. Eldareth noticed Tanthe looking keenly at each of them and he suspected why. She was searching for a face – or even some element in their beautiful, oval faces – that was familiar, that resembled her own.

She was looking for her Aelyr parents.

He wanted to tell her not to, but there was no point; he'd only embarrass her. So he kept his counsel as they walked over the bruised, silvery grass. Even its scent was unlike that of grass at home; its poignant freshness was laced with a herbal bite. Rainbows sparked on the bent stems. The realm was as he remembered from his first, brief encounter, yet infinitely more vivid, and it caught at his heart.

No one stopped them. Presently they came to a wounded man who was alone. He was on his side, one arm covering his head. Tanthe knelt down on the grass beside him. Eldareth thought for a moment that he was dead, but as she spoke, he stirred.

'Hello, we're friends. We're going to help you.'

The Aelyr groaned and turned on to his back. His hair was brown with a lot of red in it, his eyes dark sapphires, his garments the soft dew-grey of the Fhelethyr. When he saw the figures above him he looked amazed and pushed himself up on one elbow.

'Humans? Who are you?'

'I'm Tanthe,' she said, smiling at him. 'We came through a *rothanamir* back there . . . never mind. Where's your injury?'

'My arm . . . I was bleeding, and the *faldatriu* . . .'

He had taken a sword cut across his upper arm, which was still oozing.

Eldareth and Elrill helped, but Tanthe did most of the work; made a tourniquet to stem the bleeding, gave him water and a tincture of chamomile sweetened with honey from her flasks. She asked, 'What was the other thing you mentioned?'

'*Faldatriu*?' Elrill said quietly. 'The voices. They're meant to disorientate. If the vibration resonates with your own *roth*, it will make you pass out. Even kill you.'

'Breyid's tits,' Tanthe said under her breath. 'I wish I hadn't asked.'

The Aelyr man seemed more shocked than badly hurt. It always amazed Eldareth that the Aelyr could at one moment be so human; at another, so alien.

As they tended the man, another Fhelethyr came towards them. It was a woman slightly taller than Tanthe, carrying a spear in her left hand. Her aquiline face was clasped with what Eldareth took for a moment to be a headdress; which he then saw was long, thick, feathery hair, like a mass of red scales each tipped with gold.

'Where are you from? Which side did you fight on?' she demanded.

'My lady, we have just come from Aventuria,' Eldareth said politely. He stood up and bowed his head to her. 'We blundered into your battle by accident and we fought on neither side.'

She studied them carefully in turn. 'Aventuria? Why?'

'It's a long story. We're hoping to find someone who might help us. Someone in charge.'

She laughed. 'No one is in charge of the Fhelethyr. Perhaps we would fight our cause better if we were that organised. You may as well speak to us as anyone.' She knelt down to the wounded man and said, 'Tial, how are you?'

'These people have helped me. It's good to see you, Nuanyr! How did we fare?'

The woman's mouth firmed into a smile. 'We won the day. Yes, the Fhelethyr are winning.'

Tial nodded, looking less than overjoyed.

Tanthe said, 'But what were you fighting about?'

Both the Aelyr fixed her with astonished, haughty looks, as if they couldn't believe she had asked such a question. Eldareth said, 'Tanthe, not now. My lady, we've done our best for your friend and we would be very grateful for your help. We're strangers to Verdanholm. I am Eldareth, my companions are Tanthe, Elrill and Jthery of Mithrain . . .'

'I'm Nuanyr.' She stood looking at them for several seconds, as if trying to decide what to do. Tial struggled to stand up; Eldareth helped him, holding his uninjured arm and easily supporting his slender frame.

'Well,' the woman said at last, 'if Tial can walk, you had better come with us. I don't know how to advise you. Come back to our camp, at least.'

'My lady, we are grateful,' said Elrill.

Nuanyr reserved an especially long, piercing glance for him. 'My lord, forgive this observation but you are plainly Aelyr yet I don't recognise your *eretru*.'

'I'm of the Shaelahyr.'

'Oh.' She looked astonished. 'That's why I couldn't tell. I've never seen a Shaelahyr before. But you were exiled . . .'

'And I had no wish to enter Verdanholm, believe me. But the time has come to breach such unwritten laws. I'm here in the service of a cause far more pressing than the petty quarrels of ancient history.'

She was motionless, taking in what he'd said. 'Well, if your presence here places you in peril, that's your concern, not mine. I have no quarrel with you.'

'Thank you, my lady. Nor I with you.'

'Come with us, then.' Turning, Nuanyr went on staring at him over her shoulder for a moment, then she began to walk towards the wooded rise at the plain's rim. 'You truly have been far from home, Lord Elrill.'

Deep in the woodland beyond the plain, there was a loose gathering of Fhelethyr resting between the trees. Tanthe looked them over, taking in everything with cautious wonder. The wood was a lush cave, filled with violet shadows; the trees were gnarled as oaks, covered with tiny silver-gold leaves. The ground undulated into hollows that were lined with thick grass and moss and navy-blue flowers with bright yellow centres.

And the Fhelethyr were exactly as her mother Aynie had once described them. Graceful as grey cats with watchful eyes. Their true colours were hidden, glinting beneath the cobweb surface. Tanthe had never felt more lumpenly ordinary; how was she to believe that she had their spirit in her?

They had no tents and built no fires. They sat in small groups on the grass, isolated from each other, though sometimes a man or woman would leave a group and go to another. There was an air of quiet alertness about them. Although they seemed unsociable by human standards, Tanthe knew she mustn't jump to conclusions. The Fhelethyr had different ways.

Now and then, others would come running through the trees, exchange a few words and pass onwards. Something was happening, but it wasn't clear what. Tanthe had given up asking.

They settled down once to eat, only for another group of Aelyr to come through the trees and tell them to move on. No explanation was given.

'What's happening?' asked Tanthe, dismayed. She was exhausted, the horses were too tired to be ridden, and Jthery looked dead on his feet.

'I'm not sure,' Eldareth said heavily.

'I thought the Fhelethyr won. Why are they fleeing?'

'You don't understand Aelyr warfare,' Elrill told her with a grimace. 'Both sides always claim victory. Neither side ever really wins. Attrition. This could go on for days.'

'Wonderful,' Tanthe said, gritting her teeth. 'Is it long since you were last here?'

'Many, many years,' Elrill sighed. He shot Eldareth a glance.

'What about you, Eld?' She suddenly realised he'd never really spoken of it, and she hadn't thought to ask him.

'You have been here before, haven't you? Some idea what to expect?'

Eldareth laughed. 'Yes and no. That's a strange story in itself.'

Nuanyr moved her group on a couple of times, before settling on a wide, deep hollow, guarded on one side by an outcrop of bluish rock. A tree clasped the rock with its roots and trailed its dome-shaped canopy over them. Here they rested and shared food. Tanthe longed for sleep; she fought to stay awake and not miss the conversation. As the evening wore on, others came in twos and threes to join Nuanyr and Tial, stayed a while then went on their way. Tanthe didn't learn their names.

As twilight fell, the rushing song of the stars grew louder, making the hairs stand up on her neck. She remembered the twilight in Falthorn's forest hall . . . This all felt so strange and yet terrifyingly familiar. It didn't grow fully dark; the light only changed to the sheen of starlight.

'So, what brings you to Verdanholm with your human friends?' Nuanyr asked eventually. Tanthe soon noticed that she spoke mainly to Elrill, and this annoyed her, although Eldareth and Jthery seemed not to mind.

'They needed my help to find a *rothanamir*, and a degree of guidance,' Elrill said, his tone neutral.

'To do what?'

'You're asking a lot of questions, considering you wouldn't answer mine,' Tanthe said spikily. Eldareth gave her a reproving look, made a subtle *calm down* gesture.

'It is not usual for humans to come here.' Nuanyr was unabashed. 'I don't sense that you wish us ill, but I must make sure.'

'Our friend Tanthe has been to Verdanholm before,' said Eldareth. 'Something was stolen from her by the Valahyr. We've come back to look for it.'

'The Valahyr!' exclaimed Tial. 'They have no conscience left. Stealing's the least of it.'

'So you've suffered at their hands, Tanthe?' Nuanyr asked thoughtfully. 'What happened?'

'It's a long story,' Tanthe murmured. 'I'd rather not go into it, if you don't mind.'

Now Nuanyr was looking at her instead of Elrill. Her expression changed, all her attention focussed on Tanthe like a cat suddenly captivated by the fluttering of a bird. 'What are you?'

'I beg your pardon?' Tanthe, who'd been leaning back on her elbows, sat up. 'What do you mean, what am I?'

'When I look at you I see a human, yet when I look into your eyes I see Aelyr.'

'Oh, don't you start!' She dropped her head on to her hands. 'I've had about enough of this! No one knows what I am, and I don't know what I am, either!'

Tial and Nuanyr both looked at her in shock. The woman touched Tanthe's shoulder. For all her imperious nature, she seemed kind. 'You helped Tial. We want to help you too. Don't be afraid of us.'

Tanthe found herself close to tears. 'I've been told that although I was born to human parents, my true mother was Fhelethyr and my father Valahyr. Don't you think I might have a valid reason for wanting to know what you are fighting about?'

There were other Fhelethyr around the edge of the group. Suddenly they were all listening intently. Nuanyr and Tial looked at each other. They seemed dumbfounded, which pleased her in a perverse way. 'What were your mother and father called?'

'Fiomir and Talthaliorn.'

All the Fhelethyr gasped audibly. Tanthe glared fiercely around at them.

'Oh, you've obviously heard of them, then. Any idea where they are? Because I'd do anything to find them, anything. I can imagine what my father looks like, because I've met his brother, Falthorn of the Valahyr.'

There were more soft exclamations. Nuanyr stroked the

side of her neck, a gesture of consternation.

'Yes, of course we have heard of them,' she said at last. Her voice was nearly a whisper. 'Everyone knows of them. They caused trouble and they vanished. And Falthorn is the one who is making war upon us – he and his mother and father.'

'Valthiell and Cielemne,' said Tanthe. 'Yes, I've met them too! Valthiell helped me get back to Aventuria last time, but only, I think, because he wanted to get rid of me. They're all frightened of Falthorn, especially . . .' She stopped herself saying Auriel's name. 'So, you do believe me?'

She felt the weight of everyone's attention upon her, but she didn't care. Anything to get at the truth.

'We believe you,' Nuanyr said at last. 'We never heard that they had a child, but it has been many years . . .'

'They had two,' said Tanthe. 'I have a brother, whom Falthorn is keeping prisoner . . . I don't think I should say any more. But have you any idea how I might find my parents?'

'If Elrill has no idea, then I have none.' Nuanyr's red and gold hair shimmered like a butterfly wing as she shook her head. 'They are only names to us, legends.'

'Why should Elrill know?' Tanthe eyed the Shaelahyr with suspicion. It wouldn't be the first time he'd kept her in the dark.

'I don't, Tanthe,' said Elrill.

'Were you told why they fled?' asked Nuanyr.

Tanthe shrugged. 'Their families disapproved of them falling in love with Aelyr of different *eretrue*. They had a huge quarrel with Falthorn and they must have thought he was going to kill them. However, I'm sure there's more to it than that . . . and I will find out the truth eventually.'

Nuanyr held Elrill's eyes for one of those strange, time-distorted moments that seemed to go on eternally. Then time shifted again, the gaze was broken.

'This is what the war is about,' Nuanyr said, the last trace of her haughtiness vanishing into sorrow. 'It's all part of the same tapestry. Your parents' reason for fleeing and the Shaelahyr's reason for being exiled – they're almost the same.'

Elrill said, 'We prefer to think that we chose to live in exile, rather than that we were forced. Our decision came first; the rest of Verdanholm tried to make it seem that they had pre-empted us.'

'Never mind who did what first!' Tanthe exclaimed. 'Why?'

'Simple,' said Elrill. 'We stood accused of loving the Earth too much.'

'They took sides, Tanthe,' Nuanyr added. 'When relations between humans and Aelyr began to break down, the Shaelahyr sided with the humans. Even fought with them against us. That's why they were told that if they preferred the inconstancy of humans to the love of their own kind, that's where they should stay.'

Elrill only smiled. 'We did so, gladly. The Fhelethyr tried to bring us back to the fold, the Valahyr to banish us forever. We didn't appreciate being bullied by either side. The accepting nature of humans was more to our taste.'

'Funny, I got the impression you didn't think much of humans either, when I first met you,' Tanthe said, folding her arms.

'That's unfair,' said Elrill.

Eldareth laughed. 'Is it?'

'Come now, Eld; how long have you and I been friends? It's true, the human race was less than thrilled that we had fought for them – which we did to keep them from being overwhelmed by the Aelyr. Our two peoples have never mingled well, and so we keep to ourselves in Silverholm. But we've always had human friends. Always tried to protect the Earth. I seem to remember that the Valahyr and Fhelethyr were reunited with us in that cause, two hundred and fifty-two years ago. Yet now, we are all at each other's throats again?'

'I don't wish to quarrel with you, my lord Elrill,' Nuanyr said solemnly. 'I'm trying to tell Tanthe what everyone else has failed to tell her. The Fhelethyr have done nothing wrong, nothing to deserve the hostility of the Valahyr. We have only continued as we have in the past; always moving across Verdanholm, creating new territory in front of us, never looking back. We want peace and quiet lives, as we always have. It's the Valahyr who have changed.'

She stopped, upset. Tial went on, 'This Falthorn has gained more and more influence among the Valahyr. Before that, like us, they had no leaders; they only had their circle of elders, which included Valthiell and Cielemne and was of no threat to us. But now, Falthorn has effectively become their leader.'

'That's what I thought,' Tanthe said softly. 'But my parents?'

'Patience. It's part of the story,' said Nuanyr. 'For thousands of years, Valahyr and Fhelethyr have agreed to differ on all kinds of matters. We fought rarely; usually we kept to ourselves and let the others live as they wished. But now, because we refuse to bend to Falthorn's will, the Valahyr are attacking us.' She drew several ragged breaths, finding the explanation difficult. 'They say that we are fleeing; they call us cowards. But we believe that they are the ones in the wrong. That they are actually siding with the enemy.'

'The enemy?' said Eldareth.

'Are you talking about the Bhahdradomen?' Elrill put in gently. 'The Eaters?'

'Eaters? Devourers!' Tial exclaimed.

Nuanyr's chin came up, defiant but desperate. 'Do you not know that the Eaters have never stopped attacking Verdanholm? They were quiet for a while after the War of the Silver Plains, but then they came back, ever more aggressive and insatiable.

'They can't be stopped. It's been tried, to our great loss. The Fhelethyr way is keep always on the move, weaving the new substance of Verdanholm in front of us as we go. By travelling, we keep ahead of the Eaters and never see them. Thus we keep ourselves and our children safe and at peace. It's the only true way, the only one that works. The Valahyr used to agree with us, but now they claim to have a better idea, a plan to stop the Eaters by negotiation – how can that end, except that they sell us all into death?

'And the third way was that of the humans, the Shaelahyr, and Tanthe's parents. To fight the Bhahdradomen.'

'What's wrong with that?' Tanthe frowned. 'The Aelyr fought with us in the War of the Silver Plains . . . didn't you?'

'Yes, but even then, we were divided about the wisdom of it. And afterwards, faced once more with the ingratitude of humans, we said "never again". Fighting wasn't the solution. It didn't work – not for Verdanholm, at least. How well did it work for Aventuria?'

'Quite well, until a couple of years ago.' Tanthe stammered out the answer, drowning in everything she'd learned.

'And now?'

Eldareth cleared his throat. 'Let's say there's been a certain amount of disturbance.'

'You see? The War did not work! If we throw ourselves against the Eaters in battle, we are merely stupidly sacrificing our lives while taking only a few of them with us! I cannot agree with Falthorn's policy of appeasement, but I can't agree with Talthaliorn and Fiomir either. It's said that they tried to raise support from both *eretrue* to fight the Eaters, with some mad idea of uniting all the Aelyr into a great army; that Talthaliorn quarrelled with Falthorn about it, and that's why he and Fiomir fled.'

A blond man on the edge of the group put in, 'I've heard that they stole something, and that's why they were being pursued by both sides. Part of the Jewelfire itself.' Tanthe fixed the young man with such a fierce stare that he recoiled, holding up his palms. 'That's all I know!'

'Rumours,' said Nuanyr. 'Meaningless. You can't steal something that's everywhere. Talthaliorn had as many mad notions as his brother, and he infected Fiomir with them. That's what the Fhelethyr say.'

'Well, they would,' Tanthe said softly. 'How well is your war against the Valahyr working, then?'

'We deplore it,' Nuanyr said fiercely. 'But if they attack us we must defend ourselves. Falthorn thinks we will just give in but we cannot. Unless the Valahyr leave us to live in our own way, we are facing the end of Verdanholm. The end of the world.'

They rested, but Tanthe's sleep was fitful and disturbed by weird feelings, unsettling dreams. She felt the hard edge of the *silvenroth* mirror under her fingers and dreamed she was asking Nuanyr, 'Could I use this to find my parents? Would they hear me?'

When she woke she remembered that she had given the mirror to Ysomir. Another mistake, probably, but she never knew the right thing to do until it was too late.

All the next day they stayed with Nuanyr and Tial, travelling slowly through the forest. Streams of Fhelethyr joined them, moving in soft processions like dragonflies along the forest paths. Tanthe thought about Aynie, wondering what her mother would think if she could see her daughter now. Not witnessing a Fhelethyr procession, but part of it.

'Where are we going?' she asked several times, but no one would answer her. Finally, though, she got quite fierce with Tial and he said, 'We're gathering for the creation.'

'What does that mean?'

'You'll see,' he said with a smile that nearly made her abandon her vow never to fall in lust with an Aelyr again.

The party stopped at last and took *sertance* – their evening meal – in a strange, ancient glade where three oaks, so old they seemed petrified like the trees of Elta

Arta, clung to the hem of a round, black pond. The surface was so still it was an obsidian mirror. Tanthe sat looking down into it, aware that the Fhelethyr were on their feet, beginning to dance and chant. They didn't ask her to join in so she remained where she was, looking at her face in the dark water. There was something odd about this place, a grey and papery quality, like a skin that needed to be shed.

'What was this strange tale you had about Verdanholm?' Tanthe said as Eldareth came to sit beside her. 'I know you don't like being asked questions about your past, but . . .'

He pulled a face. 'Ah, that. The fact that I believed I had been here before then discovered I had not.'

She blinked at him. 'I'm sorry?'

'I was young . . . I had made the acquaintance of Elrill and desired to travel into the Aelyr realm, but Elrill of course would not take me. I was in a remote part of Sepheret when I came upon two Aelyr in a forest – I thought they were Fhelethyr but now I realise they were of another *eretru*. They were small and bright, like fire, with a lot of gold and silver about them. They promised to show me Verdanholm and indeed they did . . . They brought me through a portal, only when I found myself on the other side, I was completely alone.'

'That must have been scary.'

'I was utterly terrified,' Eldareth confessed, smiling. 'The landscape was similar to this – unquestionably Verdanholm – but I was lost and could not find another living soul. That was my first taste of what tricksters the Aelyr can be. I thought I would be trapped there for ever.'

'What happened?' said Tanthe. Elrill and Jthery had joined them, listening. Elrill had obviously heard the story before.

'After many hours of fruitless exploration, I fell at last into an exhausted sleep. When I woke, I was back in the forest of Sepheret. Cold grey dawn, no sign of my little

golden friends.' Eldareth took a quick breath. 'I believe
now that I was never in Verdanholm at all. That they had
simply given me a vision. It seemed the most repre-
hensible trick at the time, but I wonder . . . at least they
gave me an accurate taste of this realm, just as I had
asked.'

Tanthe smiled. 'You're like Verdanholm, Eld.'

'In what way?'

'Full of surprises.'

They were all quiet for a while, tired. Jthery as always
was fascinated by the water, but after he'd sat for a while
with his fingers trailing in the surface he said, 'I can feel
nothing in there.'

'What are we going to do?' said Tanthe after a time. 'We
can't keep drifting along with these people. We either
have to find Falthorn or my parents.'

Elrill said, 'I've been talking with some of them. None of
them knows Fiomir personally. However, they may be
able to take us to join some Fhelethyr who know your
mother's family and can direct us there.'

Her heart leapt with hope. 'When?'

'Tomorrow, if the skirmish with the Valahyr is over.'

'Gods, that would be wonderful! I might feel we're
getting somewhere.'

Eldareth rested his hand on her shoulder. 'You're not
nervous of meeting Fiomir's family?'

'Yes, but they can't be as bad as Talthaliorn's. That
would be impossible. I feel that they'll help us.' She looked
up and noticed that the Fhelethyr were circling the glade
faster and faster, their voices rising, making the atmosphere ring with a charged resonance. 'Elrill, what are they
doing?' she said, suddenly uneasy.

Elrill looked up at the dancers, his face an ice-sculpture
against the lushness of the sky. 'This is the skill that the
Fhelethyr possess most strongly, and which the Valahyr
have always envied. To create Verdanholm from raw
Jewelfire . . .'

Tanthe felt the energy building, building. Jthery clung to her suddenly, soaking her sleeve with his wet hand and almost pulling her over. The air crackled. In front of them, where there were only trees clustering over a crease in the ground, new space appeared.

The crease, the trees, the air itself; all split softly open with a sound like the bursting of a fresh green pod. Tanthe couldn't even tell how it had happened. She only knew she was staring into a new pocket of woodland that, a second before, had not existed. The new-born glade had a pulsing shimmer, the rawness of a newly emerged butterfly. The air glittered. The Fhelethyr stopped dancing and ran into it, shouting and laughing like human children. They danced wildly and their colours were no longer greyish but fire-red, vivid blue-green, copper and dark gold.

Tanthe leapt to her feet, jumped clean over the pool and ran after them. She could hardly take in what she'd seen. A new part of Verdanholm being created.

Tanthe stepped into it and looked around in amazement. Unlike the older forest, the greens were intense and seemed to bask in spring sunshine. Yet she could see it changing before her eyes; swelling, hardening, becoming seamless with the surrounding forest.

She put her hands to her face and wept.

'Can you do this – just anywhere?' she said to the nearest Fhelethyr. 'Make Verdanholm infinitely bigger?'

No one answered. She went to Nuanyr and touched her sleeve. 'Now what have I said?'

Nuanyr pressed her lips together. She spoke in a whisper. 'It takes much energy, and the Jewelfire grows weaker every time. We don't like to speak of this.'

'Oh.' Tanthe let her hand fall, and asked no more questions. Nothing was ever what it seemed in this place. What she'd taken to be an act of joy, exuberant creation, was suddenly revealed to be a gesture of desperation and denial. She suddenly felt powerfully that the Fhelethyr were wrong to flee from the Valahyr and the Eaters.

Everyone was exhausted. The Fhelethyr from their working, Tanthe and her party from travelling. Verdanholm wove its spell over her and she didn't even remember falling asleep in a sweet green hollow, using Redbird's flank as a pillow . . .

Tanthe became entangled in a nightmare about her parents. All four of them were there. Small sunny Aynie, taciturn but kind-natured Eodwyth; and she'd loved them wholeheartedly, never knowing the secret they'd kept from her. And the other two were there, the ones she didn't know. Two shadows under grey veils. But in her dream they put back their veils and underneath they were wild, colourful, terrifying. Her father had flowing black hair like Falthorn and purple eyes; her mother's hair was red as autumn and flowed down to her hips, while her eyes were bright blue-green, like Tanthe's, and their faces were dazzling, like those of Nuth and Anuth.

In the dream, all four of them were making love. They writhed naked in a bower of arkh-wood trees, Talthaliorn with Aynie, Eodwyth thrusting himself into Fiomir . . . the two men kissing, the two women kissing, their tongues writhing like serpents. Tanthe squirmed in a stew of arousal and embarrassment, betrayal and confusion. She pushed at the image, trying to thrust it away, but it flowed around her and clung to her like honey.

She tried to scream.

She came awake in a sweat and saw dark figures standing all around the hollow, staring down at the sleepers. For a few seconds she thought it was an hallucination, part of the nightmare. Then her mind jumped to full alertness. It was real.

'Eldareth,' she croaked, shaking him.

He woke; Nuanyr and the others were stirring, sitting up. In the silver-blue glow of Verdanholm's night, Tanthe saw what the figures were. Garments of blue and black, more stiffly structured than those of the Fhelethyr, and edged in silver. Long straight hair, darkest brown or ebony. Violet cloaks. Cool eyes gazing down.

'Get up, please,' said one of the Valahyr. His voice sounded familiar. 'We have claimed this territory. Surrender yourselves.'

Nuanyr was on her feet, furious, but there was nothing she could do. A dozen swords were raised against them. The Valahyr began to relieve the Fhelethyr of their weapons; the four horses given to the care of Valahyr warriors. Eldareth, cursing under his breath, kept close to Tanthe and Jthery, protective as always; but she broke away from him.

She'd recognised the one who was in charge. Long dark hair, watchful eyes, a lynx-like ease to his movements.

It was her cousin.

'Ostarial!' she hissed. 'What the hell are you doing?'

He'd already seen her. He smiled. 'Hello, Tanthe. I didn't think you'd remember me. I always had a feeling you'd be back.'

'Bloody right I'm back. I bet you know why. I bet you had such a laugh at my expense!'

Ostarial raised his eyebrows. 'I'd forgotten how much you swore. Is that a human habit, or just you?'

'You bastard. You goddess-forsaken, motherless son of a shape-changer. What the hell are you doing to these people?'

This was the last way she'd wanted to meet the Valahyr again. She'd imagined striding back armed and powerful, with her friends at her side. Intimidating Falthorn into giving back her child. Instead here she was again; dis-armed, powerless, railing.

'Nothing. Just moving them. Prisoners of war. They won't come to any harm as long as they stay where they're placed. But you . . .'

'What?' she said.

Suddenly she could almost smell the forest hall again. It was on Ostarial's clothes. The scent of the air, the standing stones in the forest. The wet chill of an underground waterfall on her lips, the deceptive fragrance of the wine they'd used to drug her. She couldn't speak for terror.

He gripped her arm by the elbow and pulled her aside, so Eldareth and the others couldn't hear. 'Tanthe. No, what did Auriel call you? Fliyet.'

'Don't call me that! How dare you!'

'Tanthe, then. I don't know why you are so upset with me. I never did you any harm.'

'You work for Falthorn, isn't that enough?'

'Look, our beloved uncle has his ruthless streak and he didn't treat you well, I'll admit that. But he was doing it for the greater good. He's trying to save Verdanholm. All we're trying to do is make the Fhelethyr understand and cooperate.'

'What are you going to do with us?'

Ostarial looked in turn at Eldareth, Jthery and Elrill. 'I'm sure he'll be interested to know there are two humans and a Shaelahyr running about Verdanholm without his permission.'

'Since when do we need Falthorn's permission?' she said hotly. 'He actually rules Verdanholm now, does he?'

'We're at war, cousin dear. I'm sure your King is just as interested to know when there are Aelyr in Aventuria.'

'Queen,' said Tanthe.

'Whatever.'

'I want to see Falthorn. All four of us want to see him! That's why we're here.'

'Well, I'm sure he's going to be very delighted to see you. He never wanted you to leave, you know. Neither did I, Tanthe. We hardly got to know each other.'

'I think I know more than I need about you,' she retorted.

'I doubt it.' He smiled coldly.

'So, I suppose this means you're arresting us?'

'No,' said Ostarial, unexpectedly releasing her arm. 'I wouldn't dream of it.' He turned to the other Valahyr and called out, 'Take the Fhelethyr prisoner as usual. But not these four. Let them keep their weapons as a sign of our trust. They're coming with me of their own free will; guests of Lord Falthorn.'

Chapter Seventeen. The Heart of the Jewelfire

That was the last Tanthe saw of Nuanyr and Tial.

As she looked back, they were being herded away by the Valahyr troops, lost to sight among twenty or so other Fhelethyr. They went with quiet dignity, and never once glanced back at the humans. None of her companions said anything and she couldn't speak either; she felt torn apart by the sense of something unfinished.

Verdanholm seemed to Tanthe sometimes dreamlike, at others too real. Ostarial and seven of his Valahyr warriors accompanied her party on a long trek to Falthorn's hall. Back through the forest for a day or so, across the Hethryr Plain, through a narrower belt of woodland on the far side and then a swathe of rolling grassland. The landscape became high and stark, reminding her of the moors she'd crossed in Sepheret – arguing with Rufryd over the map, a thousand years ago, it seemed – but Verdanholm never ceased reminding its visitors that they were in another realm. The rocks were blue or green or a mottling of both, malachite and azurite mixed, and the sun slid above them like a golden lamp seen through a frosted screen. Occasionally, strange lights darted among the daystars, comet-like streaks that gave an audible hiss. Now and then she caught the long flanks of the hills shimmering as if they had changed briefly to water before settling back to rock again.

She expected them to arrive at the part of Verdanholm she'd known; the claustrophobic blue-green forest, with its mysterious standing stones and the forest hall rising out of the living trees. She dreaded it. Every time she thought of it, her heart raced.

Instead this landscape seemed greater and starker. The wind was fresh, pierced with changing scents of foliage and warm resins. At night, three small crescent moons curved across the heavens, an echo of the moons of Earth . . . were they the same moons, the same sun and stars, only seen from a different perspective?

On the fourth day of travelling, when they'd had an exhausting climb on to the long spur of a hill and there was still no sign of the forest she knew, Tanthe finally asked Ostarial, 'How much further is it?'

'Footsore, cousin?' he said. 'We are almost there.'

He stopped and waited for her; Eldareth, Elrill and Jthery walked behind, tired and silent. The Valahyr were leading their horses. They followed a path that ran along the top of a long ridge, with smooth grassy slopes falling away on either side. As they rounded an angle in the ridge, they came in sight of a great hill; and where the ridge joined the hill's flank, they saw a mansion poised on a high out-thrust of rock.

The mansion gleamed palest creamy gold above the auburn woodland that curved around its right-hand side and spilled down the hillside. As they drew closer, Tanthe saw that the edifice was built of living wood like the forest hall. But this place was more a palace than a mansion, rising in complex layers, balcony upon balcony, to a roof that seemed to be tiled with gold leaf. Pillars of gold and silver wood stood along its graceful porticos on every side.

It was a construction far more deliberate and complex than anything she'd expected of the Aelyr. A statement of power, perhaps, but also of exuberant beauty and free-flowing joy.

'Whose house is this?' she said.

'Ours,' said Ostarial.

'Falthorn's?'

'The Valahyr House of Valthiell and Cielemne.'

'But I thought . . .'

'That we lived in that draughty place you were in

before? No. Only for a short time, at least. That was made for Auriel, really.'

'The forest hall?'

Ostarial smiled. He loved shocking her as much as Falthorn had. 'No, the forest itself. That whole pocket of Verdanholm was isolated for Auriel, to contain him. One small portal led in and out of it, but Falthorn blocked Auriel's power to use it for himself. Took away the key to the door, if you will. That's why he couldn't leave.'

She thought of the Fhelethyr creating a glade, a pocket of space out of nothingness. She almost choked on her amazement. 'The whole forest was his prison?'

'He was perfectly comfortable there.'

'That's not the point, is it? He told me he'd tried to escape . . .'

'You'd go in circles,' Ostarial said, offhand. 'Run and run, and only find yourself back in the same place again.'

The silver-gold palace moved closer and closer. She felt her fear growing, branching into tendrils. 'Is Auriel still there?'

'Poor Auriel, still a prisoner. Is that what you're thinking? I believe you still feel sorry for him. Did you want to see him?'

Tanthe couldn't breathe for a moment. 'Not really, no. But I can't stand to think of him trapped and on his own. No wonder he was . . .'

'What?'

'I don't know. Weird. Frightened of Falthorn.'

'You didn't want to see him, anyway.'

'I shouldn't know what to say to him.'

'I expect he feels the same.'

She had the distinct feeling that Ostarial was laughing at them both. Anger rose with her fear. 'I hate your family. I can't be related to you, I want nothing to do with you!'

'And yet, here you are,' said Ostarial. 'You won't mind surrendering your weapons before we enter the house, for

409

reasons of courtesy. You may have them back when you leave, of course.'

Inside, the mansion smelled exquisite. New-cut wood, green and fragrant. A honeyed warmth, like beeswax. The rooms were large and full of light; the woven walls shimmered with silken bark. On the floor and the walls were tapestries, woven with designs of tiny leaves in green, gold and silver, or in violet, red and bronze. Colours of wondrous subtlety. Ostarial brought the visitors into a room that overlooked the valley. One long wall was open to a vertiginous balcony, while the opposite wall had a high gallery leading to other rooms on a higher storey.

'It's beautiful,' said Jthery. He went briefly on to the balcony, and came back again. 'There are gardens below, waterfalls and pools.'

His eyes were bright, his face radiant, his tiredness forgotten. Tanthe raised a smile, humouring him. She suspected that Verdanholm had woven its spell over him; he was obviously in love with the house already.

'A chance to remove these boots would be welcome,' Eldareth groaned. He sank down on to the tapestry seat of a bench.

'Always so prosaic, Lord Eldareth,' Jthery said. 'How can your feet ache here?'

'My back and my feet can ache anywhere, my lad,' he growled.

Silence fell. Tanthe suddenly found the tension unbearable. After all the weeks of anticipation and fury, the prospect of actually confronting her uncle left her weak with terror. 'D'you think Ostarial's gone to fetch Falthorn?'

'I hope so,' said Eldareth.

She was shaking from head to foot. She'd lost her nerve. 'You speak to him, Eld. I can't do it.'

He placed his hand on her back and looked gravely at her. 'Nonsense,' he said. 'You've had no trouble at all, so far, in spoiling for a fight with everyone we've met.

410

Falthorn is the one who really deserves your fury.'

'I know, but I've spent it all. I've got no strength left.'
Tanthe hugged herself. 'He's drained it out of me, before
I've even seen him.'

'It's still in you,' said Jthery, touching her arm. 'You're
not on your own.'

She filled her lungs with the bright air. 'This isn't the
way I planned it. He was going to see a strong Tanthe who
wouldn't stand any nonsense. Instead I'm just the same
cringing idiot I was last time!'

'You've never been an idiot,' Eldareth said brusquely.
'But it will help matters if you keep calm. *Pretend* to be the
strong Tanthe, even if you don't feel it. Don't let him see
he's hurt you.'

His matter-of-fact attitude was like a dash of cold water
on her face. 'Right. Thanks, Eld. I'll be okay.'

As they talked, Elrill was moving softly around the
room, thoughtfully taking in everything. Tanthe turned to
watch him.

'What are you doing?' she said. Her voice was harsh
with nerves. Elrill stopped and looked at her, his eyebrows
raised quizzically.

'You're pacing about like one of your cats. What are you
thinking?' she demanded.

'This is a Fhelethyr house,' he said simply.

She'd observed that the house had a light airiness that
she didn't associate with the Valahyr, but she'd been too
fraught with nerves to think about it. 'Do you mean that
the Valahyr have . . . taken it over?'

'I assume so.'

'I doubt the Fhelethyr gave it to them,' Eldareth added
drily.

'This is . . .' Elrill shook his head. 'Unprecedented. It's
not done. We don't claim territory or dwellings from each
other. There's no need. Verdanholm is big enough for all
the *eretrue*. Including the Shaelahyr, if ever we decided to
come back. Verdanholm is a vast realm.'

411

'Alas, no more,' said a voice from the gallery above them. 'Or it will not be, if we don't make efforts to preserve it.'

Falthorn was looking down at them. Tanthe's heart made such a wild bound of terror she thought she was going to pass out. He looked the same yet larger than life, as if her memory had somehow dwindled him. Same knowing smile and open grey eyes, the creaminess of his skin golden against the violet of his robe; long black waves of hair flowing to his waist, now lifting on the air as he came down the stairs towards them. She couldn't breathe. She could only think of how he'd used her and thrown her away afterwards. The power he'd had over her wreathed all around her like an odour of leaves and damp stone, sexual musk and blood.

'Ostarial told me you were here,' Falthorn said briskly, as if their arrival was routine. 'Tanthe, I'm glad to see you. How are you?'

His business-like manner stunned her. 'Fine,' she choked.

To her horrified amazement, he came to her and kissed her on the cheek. She was paralysed, couldn't stop him. Falthorn stood back and said, 'Will you make the introductions, my dear niece?'

'Er . . .' All the savage emotions that had brought her here had dissolved, leaving her adrift. She managed to reassemble her dignity. 'This is . . . my alleged uncle, Lord Falthorn of the Valahyr. We are here on behalf of Queen Helananthe of the Nine Realms.'

Falthorn's eyebrows rose in genuine surprise. 'A royal deputation! Tanthe, you've quite taken me aback.'

'My companions are Lord Elrill of Silverholm, Lord Jthery of Mithrain and Lord Eldareth of, er . . .'

'Parione,' said Eldareth.

'I think that they might prefer to speak for themselves,' said Tanthe.

'Very well.' Falthorn regarded Elrill with a smile as cold

412

as the white jewel on the shoulder of his cloak. 'Lord Elrill of Silverholm. Shaelahyr. Interesting. Without dwelling on the obvious fact that you are forbidden to enter Verdanholm, what are you doing here?'

'There are disturbances on Earth, which I suspect may emanate from Verdanholm. I came to find their cause, and to help my friends Eldareth and Tanthe. I come also in the hope of mending the rift between us – although, having witnessed your conflict with the Fhelethyr, my lord, perhaps I am being over-optimistic.'

'Lord Elrill.' Falthorn stepped forward and, to Tanthe's surprise, briefly clasped the Shaelahyr's hand. 'Everything is changing, indeed. We'll talk later. For now I'll give you the benefit of the doubt and take no action against you.'

Elrill bristled. He was used to being in charge of his own domain, Tanthe knew, and Falthorn had a wonderful talent for condescension. 'I'm grateful for your magnanimity, Lord Falthorn,' he said icily.

Falthorn shifted his attention. 'Lord Eldareth? Your name is familiar to me. Ah yes, Tanthe told us of your remarkable role in the war against Garnelys. To what do we owe this honour?'

Eldareth's eyes were narrow in his angular, weather-lined face. 'I'm here on the Queen's behalf to investigate the disappearance of her mother Princess Ghiseyma and her brother Prince Venirryen,' he said gruffly. 'They are reported to have been abducted by a party of Aelyr. Possibly Valahyr. No word has been heard of them since.'

Again Falthorn looked taken aback, but he quickly mastered himself. 'What has this to do with me?'

'Since you are a man of obvious wisdom and influence, we thought you might have some information on this matter.'

Falthorn stroked his chin. 'Interesting. This is all very interesting. A deputation from Earth, indeed. Why would I have abducted members of your Queen's family?'

'I wasn't suggesting you had, Lord Falthorn,' said

Eldareth. The two men glared hard at each other, two shards of flint, striking sparks.

'You shouldn't be surprised at us asking,' Tanthe said, gathering courage. 'The Queen knows everything you did to me. She's extremely concerned about it.'

'You haven't come to declare war, I hope?' Falthorn said mildly. 'We're rather preoccupied.'

'I want my child back.'

He looked at her, pretending blankness. She went on in a low, fierce voice, 'I know what you did to me! Forced me to have a baby, then stole it. I want it back.'

He looked straight at her, his eyes impervious and glacier-cold. 'We'll discuss this later. I owe you an explanation, of course, but this is not the place.'

Tanthe backed down, seething, but knowing the more she pushed him, the more he would humiliate her. So much for her righteous rage.

'Now, this young person . . .' Falthorn said, moving on. 'Forgive me, Jerith, was it?'

'Jthery of Mithrain.' He drew himself up, looking very young but calm, brave and as beautiful as a Fhelethyr with his red-gold hair dishevelled from the journey.

'What have I done to upset Mithrain?'

'Nothing, my lord,' Jthery responded. 'I'm of Queen Helananthe's family. I'm her cousin, great-grandson of the Duchess of Mithrain. I volunteered to come with my companions on the Queen's behalf.'

'Oh good. One of you who hasn't got a personal grudge against me. Welcome, Lord Jthery. Please—' Falthorn gave a rueful smile, opening his hands. 'You are welcome in my house. Make yourselves at home, take *sertance* with us. I'll talk to you all in turn. But for now, as you must appreciate, this conflict with the Fhelethyr is keeping me quite busy, so if you will excuse me . . .'

'This is so frustrating,' said Tanthe, throwing pebbles into a pool. 'I can't stand it.'

414

Falthorn had left them alone, apparently free to do as they wished, so they had gone outside to make sure the horses were being looked after. They found Redbird and the others grazing happily in a meadow behind the house. From there, they had made their way into the gardens that spilled in lush tiers down the hillside beside the house. Here, they hoped, they wouldn't be overheard.

She and Jthery were sitting on the mossy edge of the pool. Elrill and Eldareth stood nearby; Elrill leaning against some kind of birch with long bluish leaves, Eldareth resting one foot on a rock. Tanthe made to fling another stone, but Jthery stayed her hand. 'You'll disturb the elementals,' he said mildly.

The water was already turbulent, fed by a slender waterfall. She glared at him, on the verge of calling him crazy, but stopped herself. 'Sorry, Jey. But I can't sit and eat an evening meal with those bastards, making polite conversation as if they never did those vile things to me!'

'I don't see what the alternative is,' said Elrill. 'Falthorn said we are not prisoners. We're free to leave. But we'll achieve nothing if we do.'

'Not prisoners?' Tanthe growled. 'Don't you believe a word he says! He'll have some vile trick up his sleeve.'

'Then we have to be ready for him,' said Eldareth. 'If he is responsible for Ghiseyma's abduction, then we must bide our time until we can search the house and find some clue.'

'I'm sure that baby's not here,' Tanthe said miserably. 'I'd know if it was. I'd sense it. I still wonder if it was even real.'

Elrill took out the *anametris* sphere and turned it between his long fingers. It shone ice-white and perfect, but its gleaming inner layers were still. 'You must remember that Verdanholm is not all it seems on the surface.'

'And meanwhile we should be careful not to accuse Falthorn or his family of any wrongdoing,' said Eldareth.

'Play his game. Reassure him that Queen Helananthe regards him as an ally.'

Tanthe groaned. 'I sabotaged that plan as soon as I opened my mouth. But I couldn't help it. He used me and I can't pretend I don't hate him!'

'And if you tried, he'd know you were lying,' Eldareth said reasonably. 'But the fact is, Helananthe *does* want the Aelyr on board as allies, if at all possible. It's all right for you to be angry, Tanthe. He'll expect that. But we must present ourselves as wanting to sort it out in a friendly manner, rather than antagonising him.'

'Oh, cheers,' said Tanthe. 'So I look like a petulant kid who's dragged her big brothers round to threaten him, and instead you smooth it all over and end up patting each other on the back?'

'Something like that, yes,' said Eldareth. He grinned apologetically, making a rueful joke of it.

Elrill, however, fixed Tanthe with a hard, sombre stare. 'Eldareth's right,' he said. 'If the Bhahdradomen are rising, the last thing we want is to be making enemies of the Valahyr – especially one as powerful as Falthorn. There is more at stake here than your sense of personal injustice, Tanthe.'

'You know something, Elrill?' she retorted. 'For a man who doesn't want to make enemies, you've got a bloody funny way of going about it.'

The house had a great central hall on the highest level, with a gilded ceiling arching high above it and light falling through crystal panes set along the walls and in the roof itself. In the centre was a large, low, circular table of creamy wood, and here Falthorn's family were gathering for their evening meal. The atmosphere was informal, and they were sitting at the table on floor-cushions.

The first thing Tanthe remembered, as she nervously took her seat between Elrill and Eldareth, was how she'd felt the first time she had met these people. Elated and drunk on bliss, feeling she'd come home . . . that she'd found something unutterably wonderful. That memory made this encounter all the more bitter.

Her heart beat hard as they came in one by one, graceful in their deep blues and purples. Over thirty of them; some she'd seen before, some missing, some strangers. At last everyone was seated and there was no sign of Auriel. She was unutterably relieved, yet, paradoxically, stricken with disappointment.

Her grandparents, Valthiell and Cielemne, barely glanced at her from their position on the far side. Ostarial and her other cousins looked her over with a sort of amused contempt. They weren't overtly rude, but neither did they show her any warmth.

They were . . .

Oh, gods. As she realised it, she had to hide her smile behind the rim of her glass. 'What is it?' Eldareth whispered.

'They're embarrassed,' she whispered back. 'They never expected to see me again! I think I feel a bit better now.'

Tanthe felt her strength returning; she ate the delicious Valahyr food with relish, not caring whether it enchanted her or not. She sat calm and poised at the table, sipping her Aelyr wine – expecting it to disgust her, then pleased to find it didn't – and coolly making eye contact with each of them in turn.

The Valahyr were always the first to look away. Bastards, they all knew. They'd all been in on it.

'So, our good friends from Aventuria,' Falthorn said presently, 'what message is it that your monarch wishes to convey to us?'

'Her majesty the Queen sends greetings and blessings from the human realm to the Aelyr,' Eldareth said easily. 'She wishes you to know that there have been certain disturbances on Earth whose origin is unknown. Lord Elrill reported unprecedented movement of Bhahdradomen colonies across the Whiteveil Mountains towards

Paranios. And we have observed disturbances of the atmosphere which signal great disruption of *roth* energies. Then there is the unfortunate disappearance of her majesty's mother and brother, and the strange events of Tanthe's stay with you. She asked that all these matters be brought to your attention, in order to ensure full cooperation and to avoid misunderstandings between our peoples. The Queen wishes the alliance between the Aelyr and human races to remain firm and inviolable.'

Falthorn was quiet for a moment. His parents looked at him, silent and aloof, yet somehow leaning wordlessly upon him. 'And we wish for the same, naturally,' he said.

'Well, that is the situation on Earth. If you have any light to shed in return, her majesty would be grateful.'

'Yes, I have some light to shed, in case you are the slightest bit confused about our motives,' Falthorn replied. 'The Bhahdradomen are on the move, indeed. Verdanholm is under attack and until that threat is removed – much as I sympathise with your good Queen – I have no time to partake of Aventuria's problems.'

Eldareth raised his eyebrows. 'Yet you can find time to make war on the Fhelethyr?'

'All that I do is to protect Verdanholm.' Falthorn's tone was sharp. 'I wish your Queen well and every success in her endeavours, but I do not ask her help. Neither can I give her mine. Naturally, as her representatives, you are welcome to stay in my house for as long as you wish; but all my energies are bent towards protecting Verdanholm from her enemies.'

'We appreciate that.' Eldareth's tone was diplomatic.

'However,' Falthorn went on, smiling, 'Such members of my *eretru* as can be spared, I will place at your disposal to help investigate this abduction in any way they can.'

'And the matter of Tanthe's child?' said Eldareth. 'You can't deny that you are fully aware of that . . . strange circumstance. Indeed, you have not denied it.'

There was an audible intake of breath among the

Valahyr. Falthorn blinked, his crystalline eyes momentarily veiled. 'I hardly think that the *sertance* table is the right place to discuss such a personal matter.'

'But we may not have another chance, since you are so busy,' Eldareth replied, unmoved.

'Certainly I am willing to talk about it. But it's Tanthe's decision whether she wishes to discuss it here, or in private.'

Falthorn smiled encouragingly at her; she looked away, faintly sickened. 'In private,' she said gruffly.

Falthorn looked at Eldareth in triumph. 'It saddens me that some humans are determined to think the worst of the Aelyr, when we have common enemies who are more dangerous by far. To see us bickering over these minor matters would delight the Bhahdradomen, would it not?'

There was a murmuring of agreement among the Valahyr. As Falthorn went on, his presence and certainty seemed to light the whole room with fire. 'You surely must agree, Lord Eldareth, Lord Elrill, that our most important aim is to safeguard our existence. Everything I do – however bizarre it may seem to you, and I forgive you, for I know you lack the advantage of having my perspective on the matter – but my every action is laid down in the service of that one great goal. *To save our lives.*'

At the end of the meal, the travellers were shown to their rooms, four simple chambers that overlooked the gardens. By now Tanthe was exhausted. It was still light outside – the Verdanholm sun a huge flame-red lamp – but she was thinking longingly of sleep. As she set foot over the doorway, though, someone tapped her arm.

She turned. It was her grandmother, Cielemne. Her hair was drawn back from her smooth, ageless brow, a blue jewel gleamed on her forehead, her features were perfect yet somehow a little too pinched for beauty. She looked hard, aloof, unknowable. 'There is someone who wants to see you,' she said.

'Who?' said Tanthe.

'Come with me, dear.'

'It's not Auriel, is it?'

Cielemne wouldn't answer. She only looked at Tanthe with a hint of compassion and said, 'Don't be afraid. Don't be angry. It was all done for the best, as my son said.'

'I hate this,' Tanthe said. 'I hate being told I'm part of you, yet being excluded. You must really loathe my parents – or is it that I look and behave like a human?' The grandmother didn't answer. In a smaller voice she said, 'What was my father like? You must miss him . . . don't you?'

Still Cielemne did not reply. She took Tanthe to a lower level; a room similar to the one that she and the others had first entered, but with a different outlook over the valley and – to her surprise – books lining one wall. Cielemne left. And he was there, leaning against the crystal panes that gave on to the balcony, dressed in a long violet robe; his arms folded nervously across his stomach, his bare feet crossed as if he were somehow shielding himself from her.

'Oh hell, it is you,' breathed Tanthe.

Auriel came towards her, looking as alluring as he'd ever done with his long dark auburn hair streaming over his shoulders. 'They told me you'd come back,' he said softly.

'I thought – I thought you were still imprisoned in the other place.'

'No. Falthorn brought me with him.'

'Why weren't you at the meal, then?'

He gave a helpless shake of his head. 'I was afraid to see you.'

'Well, so you bloody should be!' she cried. She was beginning to tremble. Struggling to stay calm.

'And now you're here, I don't know what to say.' He looked down; not cold like the others but upset, at a loss. That made it easier for all her pain and rage to boil to the surface. 'You escaped, Fliyet. Why did you come back?'

420

'Oh, not for your sake,' she said viciously. 'After the thanks I got for trying to rescue you last time, I'm not falling for that one again. You can rot here.'

He frowned. 'But Tanthe, I tried to explain . . . I hoped you might not still be so angry with me . . .'

'Oh, did you?' she yelled. 'You bastard!'

The insult was lost on Auriel. To suggest he had made himself motherless, by turning his back on the Goddess, meant nothing to a race who had no deities. He looked at her with hurt incomprehension and his innocence made her want to hit him.

So she did. She flew at him, swinging her arm and landing a hard, open-handed blow across his head that sent him reeling into the wall. He caught himself and straightened up slowly, one hand pulling the tangled hair off his face. His eyes were glass-bright with tears. 'I'm sorry,' he said.

'Have you any idea what you did to me? Did you know?'

'I tried to tell you before you left . . .'

'No, I mean what you *did* to me!' She struck her breast-bone. 'You told me some rubbish before I left, yes, but I can't remember it all and who's to say it was even the truth? So try again! Did you *know*?'

He didn't answer. It was almost like shouting at a puppy, that pointless. But his sad eyes answered her question.

'What did Falthorn say, "Get your sister into bed so she can shell out this magical child, the quicker we can get rid of her the better"? That was your child too, Auriel! Gods, how could you? Haven't you got any feelings at all? Nuth curse you!'

He pressed the heel of his hand to his forehead. Strands of wild hair clung to his damp face; he was weeping, really weeping. 'Yes, Falthorn told me what would happen. He told me to seduce you . . .'

'Oh, and wasn't I a pushover! I hope you weren't too disgusted by the experience!'

'Fliyet, no.' He took a couple of steps towards her. 'You don't understand. It was easy, I loved you. None of that was a lie.'

'But you did lie! "We can't be fertile together," you said. You told me a blatant, deliberate lie and all the time you knew what was really going on, you were just Falthorn's dog!'

Auriel stared at her, tears running down his cheeks. Tanthe suddenly started crying as well. She couldn't stop herself. Auriel was grief-stricken and so was she, and she despised him and hated him and that made the feelings worse, because she still loved him . . .

They were moving towards each other – it only took a few steps – and her arms were sliding round him, and his round her, and they held each other so tight they could barely breathe.

'I hate you,' Tanthe said into his shoulder. She dug her fingers into his arms, pinching him. 'I'll never forgive you.'

'I'm sorry. I never meant to hurt you.'

'Why not just say no to Falthorn? Why do everything he says?'

'You don't know him,' said Auriel. 'I never could. He has all the power, and he terrifies me.'

She recalled the stark image she'd been trying to deny. Falthorn gripping his wrists as Auriel cowered on his knees before him . . . horrible, sickening image.

'Look.' Tanthe pulled him down on to a couch, one hand on his shoulder, the other holding his hand. 'He scares the shit out of me, too, but that doesn't mean I do everything he says. Why can't you stand up to him?'

As soon as she spoke, she saw how ridiculous the suggestion was. Auriel's beautiful eyes went blank with a fear that could only have come from long years of terror. 'I used to try. I told you I tried to escape, several times. He punished me.'

'How?'

'With *gauroth*. I can't describe it.'

'I don't understand. Was this physical? Did he beat you?'

Auriel shook his head. 'I wish he had; I could have borne that. He does something else, raises a dark whirl of energy that goes straight inside your head. It's the worst fear you've ever known. Like being trapped inside a nightmare that you can't wake up from, black mountains all around you, everything bleak and dead. Knowing that the Jewelfire itself is dead and your parents, everyone you love is so far sundered from you that you'll never find them again, never.' He was shaking feverishly in her arms. Tanthe's tears ran into his hair. 'It only lasts a few minutes, but while you're inside it seems to go on forever. The first time, I really thought I had been there for eternity. When I came out of it and saw Falthorn smiling down at me again, I almost lost my mind. After it's happened a few times, you don't have the will to fight any more. You'll do anything he says, just to avoid the punishment.'

Tanthe clasped him, kissing his cheeks and his mouth. He wasn't strong, but she couldn't go on despising him for that. Couldn't judge him, after he'd been terrorised and broken for years. 'I had no idea,' she said.

'It's a reflex, in the end,' he said bleakly. 'Falthorn doesn't even need to punish you any more. He only has to look at you. Like training a dog, as you said.'

'I didn't mean it. I didn't know.'

'So when he said to me, "You will seduce Tanthe, I need the child," I knew it had to happen. To think of saying, "No, I'm not doing it." It would have been easier to cut my own hands off. And I'm sorry. I'm so, so sorry, Fliyet, because I love you more than my life. You are all I've got, and that's how I serve you.'

'Bastard,' she said weakly, meaning Falthorn more than Auriel.

'I always hoped our parents would come and help me, but they never did.'

'They wouldn't walk into the trap,' she said. 'Or they couldn't.'

'So then I suppose Falthorn had the idea of creating this child instead.'

She couldn't speak for a long time. They clung together, crying. Eventually she blotted her nose on her sleeve and said, 'Did you ever see it?'

'The baby? No. They kept me away.'

'But it was real? It seemed like a dream.'

'I thought I heard it cry once . . .'

'And you don't know what Falthorn did with it? Him? Her?'

'Even if I knew, do you think I could tell you?'

'You'd better,' she said fiercely. 'I can be scarier than Falthorn, when I want to be.'

He shuddered faintly, not seeing anything amusing in her words. 'I think . . . I once heard them refer to it as . . . he.'

'A boy,' Tanthe whispered. 'All right, don't tell me any more. The more I know, the more real it seems and I can't bear it.'

'Neither can I.' He clung so tightly to her that she had to gently disentangle herself.

'Auriel, we have got to get you away from Falthorn. He can't be allowed to treat you like this! And we've got to find the child. Agreed?'

He nodded, but he looked utterly disconsolate. Tanthe tugged at his hair. 'Come on, haven't you got one spark of fire left in you, to fight this?'

'I don't think so.'

'Auriel!' she growled, angry again. 'What are you going to do, fucking curl up and die?'

'What do you know about me?' he retorted. 'Once Falthorn's had his way with you and you find out what it's like to live in fear every second of your life for years on end – then you can lecture me about fire!'

'That's better.' She laughed shakily. 'Add a few choice swear words and you'll sound just like Rufryd.'

*

Alone in his room, Jthery could not sleep. Moonlight slid through every chink of the woven walls and played brightly over the room. The sound of waterfalls in the gardens called to him. Eventually he got up and went out on to the balcony. Just beneath it was one of the supporting pillars of the house, a silken trunk with fresh leaves growing out of it. It was an easy matter to climb down, landing lightly in one of the upper levels of the garden; he did so as if sleepwalking.

Jthery made his way to the stream, which meandered all through the garden, flowing down from one level to the next in a series of rills, pools and waterfalls. He came upon a large pool lower down from the one where he'd sat with the others earlier. The water gleamed darkest sapphire, reflecting shoals of stars and two of the moons; Lily Moon full, Leaf Moon a crescent . . . he realised that he'd identified the moons automatically, before wondering if they were actually the same ones, or moons of Verdanholm mimicking those familiar to Earth? They were as beautiful. And under the water glided long blue and silver fish. Three worlds captured in one plane.

He dangled his fingers in the water. The fish felt his vibration, heard his soft call, and they came to him, swimming in circles round and round his hand.

Jthery laughed in soundless pleasure. This realm was so wondrous, he would have been happy to stay here for ever, to forget all that had brought him here. A thrill caught his heart and he felt, *knew*, that whatever mysterious lure he'd been following was about to reveal itself. His friends' concerns were not his. Something else had brought him here and it was close now, so close.

He was thinking it would be delicious to divest himself of his robe and lower himself into the water, when he suddenly heard the softest of breaths behind him.

He snatched his hand from the pool and looked round. Falthorn was standing there, an elemental carved from the Verdanholm night. Darkness with sparks of silver. Hair

425

flowing black around his strong face. Grey eyes full of stars; his sleeves pushed back from long, lean forearms, white and amethyst stones sparkling on his long fingers.

'Good evening, Lord Jthery,' said Falthorn. 'I hope I didn't startle you.'

'Er, no, Lord Falthorn. Well, a little. You were so quiet.'

'May I sit with you? It's such a beautiful night – all nights are beautiful here, of course – and I should like to speak with you.'

Jthery was instantly on his guard. Faced with Falthorn's overpowering presence, he was acutely aware of being young and lacking in the worldly wisdom of Eldareth, Elrill, or Tanthe, and that none of them were here to shield him.

'Has Tanthe been relating terrible stories about me?' Falthorn asked lightly.

'I – I don't know how to answer that.'

'With a "yes," I should imagine. It's all right. It's only to be expected. I don't really care what the others think of me, but I wanted you to know that I'm not an ogre. I should like *one* of you to know it, at least, and since you are the only one without prejudice, I'm afraid it's you, Jthery.'

He smiled. Jthery wondered why his approval was important to Falthorn. Perhaps it was unfair to assume the Valahyr always had a hidden motive. Falthorn seemed friendlier than he had before, relaxed and unguarded. 'I try to be open-minded, sir. To anything.'

'Anything?' Another humorous gleam. 'All I'm trying to do here is to look after Verdanholm. Nothing more sinister than that. Is it not a good cause?'

'Yes. Of course.'

'Then relax. Don't be frightened of me. Don't call me "my lord" or "sir"; we are equals. I love my realm, and I love my family, Jthery. And I am glad to receive human visitors, especially one as intriguing as you.'

Jthery felt his face turning hot. 'I'm hardly intriguing.

Just a very minor noble who's not above grooming the horses and making fires.'

'Yet you are the Queen's cousin. Heir to Mithrain.'

Jthery laughed. 'One day. My great-grandmother the Duchess is still alive and vigorous; she is to be followed by my grandmother, then my mother. I shall be an old man before I take the seat.'

'That must be frustrating.'

'Why?' Jthery was puzzled. 'I don't want to do it, anyway. I hope I'll feel differently when the time comes, but for now it doesn't interest me.'

'Power doesn't interest you?'

'It's not about power!' he said, shocked. 'Gods, I'd want that even less. People running round, obeying me? The idea is disgusting. No. It's the responsibility I don't want. It's frightening.'

'Then what do you want?'

Jthery considered. 'To keep Mithrain safe. So that we can always wander through the lakes in peace, and touch what really matters.'

'And what's that?'

'The water. To experience its energy, and all the elementals and spirit-forms that take shape from it. Water is life.'

'Water is life,' Falthorn repeated thoughtfully. He was quiet for a time. His reflection danced next to Jthery's in the surface. Jthery's own hair looked like a splash of rose moonlight. 'We want the same things, then.'

'Do we?'

'Yes. To keep our realms safe. It's strange, though, that you say power disgusts you. For I have seen the fish flock to do your bidding.'

'I expect they thought I was going to feed them.'

'No.' Falthorn gripped Jthery's right hand by the fingers, and lifted it. 'I saw *roth* flow from your hands. Your affinity with the water and the creatures that live in it is something wondrous. Don't deny it.'

427

Falthorn's eyes gleamed, so close to his that Jthery was unnerved. But there was something hypnotic in the Valahyr's face, a beauty and certainty of purpose that were very seductive. Idealism.

'It's nothing to be ashamed of,' Falthorn went on. 'Sometimes it is necessary to use a little power to achieve your aims. Command others. Even sacrifice a few, so that your own people may live. Haven't you ever done that?'

Jthery thought of the greenwolves that he'd summoned to save Eldareth. Some of the Torish guards and their horses must have died. Worse; he felt that Falthorn *knew*. 'Yes.'

'Well, then. Was it so terrible?'

'It *was* terrible, but . . .'

'It had to be done.' Falthorn nodded sympathetically. 'I know. You are a good-hearted man, I can see that. There is a great capacity for love in you. Are you married, handfasted, whatever it is you humans call it?'

'No.'

'I am,' said Falthorn.

Jthery found himself irrationally disappointed; and it seemed Falthorn saw this too, and found it amusing. He sensed that the Valahyr could see straight inside him and the feeling was intrusive, yet warm; not unpleasant.

'I am married to Verdanholm,' Falthorn went on. His lip curved in a smile both warm and self-mocking. 'I have had little time for lovers. I have never had a human lover. Have you loved one of the Aelyr?'

Jthery shook his head, his heart stumbling. 'No.'

'They say it's more exciting. Because we are the same in form yet alien to each other.'

'That's fascinating,' Jthery stammered. 'I suppose that would account for Auriel and Tanthe . . . although . . .'

Falthorn spoke over him, low and enticing. 'In this light I can't tell whether you are male or female. If I chanced upon you by this pool I might take you for a lovely Fhelethyr maiden, with hair as bright as the Rose Moon.

428

But then I see that you are a young man, and somehow your beauty is increased a thousandfold.'

Falthorn's shoulder was pressing into his. His face was the most compelling Jthery had ever seen, serene and god-like, yet somehow demanding. His black hair flared around his shoulders, haloed by a blue glow as if another figure were rising up behind him, formed of blue water . . . *Eshte.*

Your choices may save or doom us all.

Jthery caught his breath. The Goddess looked at him solemnly for a moment, and vanished. There was only Falthorn, wreathed in the warm ebony and sapphire of the night.

'I speak with an artist's eye,' Falthorn added, not quite breaking the spell; only shifting it. He was a master of that, Jthery soon found, drawing the conversation expertly along one path then abruptly diverting it over a cliff-edge. 'An artist, I think, is what I should have been, had I not devoted my life to preserving Verdanholm.'

He went on, talking at length about his love for the Aelyr realm; and as he spoke, Jthery felt himself being drawn deeper and deeper into the glamour, Falthorn's charisma weaving inescapable webs around him. All the time, Jthery was fully aware of his fall, yet he made no attempt to fight it. He knew it happened, that people contrarily fell in love with the one being who was least suitable, least obtainable, wrong in every way – but this was the first time it had ever happened to him. Over-whelming. Fighting it was unthinkable.

They talked for hours. The night seemed to go on forever; Jthery wished it would.

'You don't still think I am a monster, do you?' Falthorn said softly. 'I am acting for the good of my land and people. This I swear to you, on any god you wish to name. This I shall prove to you, over and over again, if you will only trust me.'

Jthery took a shaky breath. He was convinced, now, that

Falthorn was speaking the truth, that there was a purity and beauty in him that his companions simply hadn't seen. His heart swelled with revelation and he knew, in a quiet unfolding of wonder, that *this* was what he had been travelling to find. Eshte had shown him.

'Jthery?' said Falthorn, smiling. 'You look as if you've seen a ghost. Say something.'

Jthery shook his head. Couldn't explain. 'Of course I don't think you're a monster, Falthorn. It's obvious you aren't.'

'That's the sort of conviction I like to hear. So, we can be friends?'

Jthery nodded, finding it hard to speak. 'I'd like that.'

'Good.' Falthorn took his hand, and his fingers felt cool and strong and sensual. 'Because I have certain things to ask of you, Jthery. You will see me act in ways that appear strange, or wrong, or even rather cruel to your friends.' His eyes were intense and serious. 'I promise you now that, however wayward my actions seem at the time, there is good reason for them, that it's all for the greater good. In return, I need your assurance that you will do all I ask without question.'

Jthery had been ambushed. 'What sort of things?' he asked, uneasy.

'The odd bit of torture, bloodshed, unnatural magic—'

'*What?*'

Falthorn was laughing at him. 'Nothing like that. An errand or two, perhaps. The main one is that I need you to support me in front of the others; not to question me; to know that all I do is for the best of reasons. For I have a strange notion that we could be good companions. I would quite like you to stay here, for a while, at least. Does the idea appeal?'

'Gods, yes.' Jthery felt his pulse leaping against the pressure of Falthorn's hand.

'And do you trust me?'

'Completely,' Jthery said. He meant it. A fearful joy was

rising in him. This was wild, mad, dreadful, but he had to do it.

'Then will you do as I ask?'

'Yes. Yes, I promise.'

'I am so glad,' Falthorn said. His grip on Jthery's wrist eased, and his expression was warm, even emotional. 'I should like to see that pale *roth* playing around these fingertips again. Tell me about Mithrain, Jthery. Tell me about the water, and all its moods and energies, the elementals that live within it and how you communicate with them. I want to learn.'

Tanthe and Auriel slept together that night. It was only for closeness, they had no intention of making love . . . and she didn't know how it happened, neither of them instigated it, but somehow the embrace of friendship swelled and moistened and locked them together, and they were moving with each other, so delicately and slowly that they could almost pretend it wasn't happening.

'We weren't going to do this,' Tanthe groaned softly.

'I know,' said Auriel. 'But I don't think I can stop now.'

'Neither can I . . .'

Her words were lost in the sweet, slow, fiery deluge of satiation. It crept on her by stealth then flung her off the cliff-edge into convulsing, astonished ecstasy. But this time, thank the Goddess, no visions, no tiny white faces tumbling towards her through the cosmos. Purely sexual bliss and tenderness.

Afterwards, they held each other and talked until they fell asleep. Tanthe was glad it had happened. It had been somehow necessary, to exorcise her terrible memories of last time. Or rather, her terrifying *loss* of memory and time, where Auriel had haunted the gaps like some beautiful nightmare demon.

When she woke she felt surprisingly good. Rested, relaxed, optimistic. Propping herself up on Auriel's chest, she said, 'We've got to take you home with us this time.

Elrill will find some way to break Falthorn's hold over you. He must.'

He smiled sleepily. Then someone tapped on the screen that stood across the doorway, and moved it aside, and Falthorn stood gazing down at them.

Auriel froze. She felt him cringing, almost shrinking away, as if he wanted to vanish into the mattress. Her temper rose, and with it a wretched feeling of powerlessness.

'Well, this is a cosy scene,' Falthorn said with a smile. 'Quite the last thing I expected. No ill-feeling between brother and sister, then?'

'What do you want?' Tanthe snapped.

'I thought you wanted to talk to me.'

She was stunned. She'd thought Falthorn would do everything in his power to avoid talking to her. 'Yes, I do.'

'Well? Come, take a walk with me, Tanthe.'

'On my own?'

Falthorn put his fist on his hip. 'Stars above us, there's no need to be frightened of me. I've nothing to gain by harming you, have I? I'll give you a few minutes to get dressed. There is something I must show you. You'll understand everything then.'

Eldareth and Elrill were awake early, talking on the balcony that overlooked the gardens. Eldareth leaned on the satiny wooden rail, his hands clasped as he drank in the sweet air, the lulling music of running water and the eerie discordance of the cosmos. They'd decided to let Jthery and Tanthe sleep in for another couple of hours.

'Verdanholm can be very seductive,' Eldareth said. 'I can understand how Tanthe was tricked last time. This all feels so quiet and safe, you could forget what you came for.'

'That's true enough,' said Elrill. 'I feel it too, since I have been away for so long. It's an endless, quiet pain, to deliberately forsake one's home and ignore its call; but the call never ceases . . .' He sighed. 'However, we must not forget that we have a job to do. At least, being aware of the dangers, we won't fall prey to them.'

'What do you think Falthorn is actually up to?'

The Shaelahyr shook his head. His pale milky hair was rimmed by gold in the early light. 'I don't know yet. But one thing I'm sure of; he is sincere. He feels under threat and he is determined to safeguard the Valahyr and Verdanholm. I would feel the same in his position. I *have* done dreadful things, to protect Silverholm.'

Eldareth remembered how Elrill had sent his Shaelahyr to cause an avalanche, burying a troop of soldiers who were trying to enter Silverholm. A faint shiver went through him. 'Still, I wonder in what capacity he has assumed leadership? Like Helananthe, to serve and protect the land? Or is it power he wants?'

'We think of it as a human trait, wanting power. The Aelyr are, as a rule, above such base desires.'

'That's funny,' Eldareth said caustically. 'With us it's the other way round. Humans are sweet and innocent; it's the Aelyr who are arrogant and power-crazed.'

They laughed. Eldareth heard movement behind him and turned to find a lean golden-skinned Aelyr hurrying through the room towards them, long dark red hair flying, his brown eyes anxious. Eldareth had never seen him before, yet he looked familiar. The stranger came on to the balcony and placed one hand on his arm, the other on Elrill's.

'Lord Eldareth, Lord Elrill?' he said. 'I – I'm Tanthe's . . . brother.'

'Ye gods! Auriel?'

He nodded. Then Eldareth realised where he'd seen him before; months ago, in the Seer's hut, pulling Tanthe into the portal. Elrill fixed the young man with a withering stare, and Eldareth's first reaction was fury. But Auriel went on, 'I spoke to Tanthe last night. She's forgiven me for . . . I don't know how much she told you, but I did her harm and I'm sorry. I was forced into it and she knows that . . .'

'Well?' said Elrill. 'What do you want of us, more forgiveness?'

Auriel shook his head vigorously. He was as nervous as a bird, and their hard looks made him worse. 'She asked me to help you. Falthorn has taken her out, they may be gone for several hours.'

Eldareth swung round. 'Gods, is she in danger?'

'No, I don't think so,' Auriel said quickly. 'He wouldn't hurt her, he's far too subtle. He wants her to understand him, that's all. He's very concerned that people understand him and he only hurts them if they try to thwart him.'

'Really?' said Elrill. Auriel's eyes widened as if he expected the Shaelahyr to attack him; Eldareth was shocked, and Elrill's manner softened suddenly, as if he'd seen it too. 'Don't be afraid of us, Auriel. We're not like Falthorn.'

Auriel relaxed, by a fraction. 'I know. Tanthe told me a lot about you. She wanted me to tell you that she will keep Falthorn out of the house for as long as possible. But I – I didn't tell you this.'

'No, you didn't.' Eldareth gave a sombre smile, briefly clasped Auriel's shoulder. 'And neither did you tell us whether there is a specific part of the house in which we should concentrate our search.'

'The woodland side of the house, two levels below the *sertance* hall,' Auriel said, his voice falling to a whisper. 'There could be something there. But Falthorn hides things, you may not find anything.'

'Still, it's a start,' said Eldareth. 'Thank you, Auriel. Now go, before anyone sees you with us.'

He and Elrill moved softly through the warm, sunny rooms of the house, using the Fhelethyr rugs as stepping stones where they could, so that their booted feet did not echo on the wooden floors. They descended two flights of stairs; each level was broader than the one above, with more rooms and labyrinthine arrangements of galleries and walkways. Light penetrated everywhere; even to the inner corridors which shimmered green like a dappled underwater forest.

They passed one or two Valahyr on their way, but no one tried to stop them; only acknowledged them with polite greetings as they passed. The house was quiet. Elrill said, 'I hope this is not some trap they've set for us.'

Eldareth shared the hope, but didn't reply. They were in the very heart of the house now, underneath the central hall, and the rooms were dimly lit by lamps. One room led into another but all were deserted. They explored with an increasing sense of urgency.

Once or twice Eldareth called out, 'Ghiseyma?' but there was no response. 'This is hopeless. Unless we can get one of the Valahyr actually to betray Falthorn, we'll never find anything.'

He was edgy and close to giving up, when Elrill said, 'I feel something.'

'Where?'

'Close by. A trace of *anaroth* of some kind . . .'

They made a careful exploration of the seven rooms that led off this particular gallery, but all were empty. One screen he moved was a false feature; there was nothing behind it. 'I think we've looked everywhere. There's no one here. Damn!'

'There is a doorway you haven't tried,' said Elrill, pointing to the screen.

'Yes, I have. There's nothing behind it.'

'Try again.'

Eldareth shifted the light screen to reveal the blank wall, with its tracery of intertwined branches. Elrill took out the *anametris* sphere and brought it close to the wall. Suddenly the orb glowed ice-bright, its inner spheres sliding into motion, and the wall shone in response.

'But on the other side of this wall is just a corridor,' said Eldareth 'We've been in it. It was empty.'

Elrill only smiled. The fabric of the wall was melting to

shimmering white mist; the mist clearing to reveal a doorway. And inside was a chamber they had not seen before. It was too large for the space that should have contained it, brightly lit by a window that could not have been there, and furnished with tables and chairs and a bed all in silvery wood, tapestries of green, violet and silver.

On a stool sat a stern-looking but attractive woman with full grey hair swept up on to her head. She was weaving at a small tapestry loom. On the floor sat a boy of about ten or eleven in a green and gold robe, and he was reading out loud from a book, some kind of heroic myth about the Aelyr in Azura Maroc. His voice was loud and precise. '"And when the Fhelethyr wanderers came to Lapiszul . . ."'

Eldareth stood and stared. It was like seeing the curtain drawn back on an illuminated stage. Stunning in its colour and unreality.

'One of Falthorn's little hidden pockets,' Elrill said softly. 'He should have secured it better.'

At the sound of his voice, the woman and the boy looked up. Eldareth stepped over the threshold, felt the atmosphere change imperceptibly. The tiny realm-within-a-realm felt highly charged with the *roth* that maintained it. Elrill stayed in the doorway, holding the portal open.

'Princess Ghiseyma?' he said, bowing. 'Prince Veny?'

The woman stood up, her bobbin falling to the floor on a bright crimson strand. She looked well-fed and healthy, still the forceful and humorous woman he remembered. The boy rose too, glaring at Eldareth with a mixture of imperious wrath and excitement.

'Lord Eldareth?' she said, peering at him. 'Veny, are we dreaming? Strange things happen in this place, but this is the strangest yet.'

The child, a tall brown-haired boy, came striding up to Eldareth and pinched his arm so hard that Eldareth yelped. 'No, he's real, mother!'

Rubbing at the bruise, he grimaced and tried to ignore

the pain. 'Your Highness, I was sent by Helananthe to find you. Do you know where you are?'

Ghiseyma came towards him, brushing past her son. She moved with regal confidence, and her broad, comely face was unlined, alert and serious. 'I believe we are in the realm of the Aelyr.'

'Do you know who brought you here? How long you've been here?'

'Only that they were of the Valahyr, the party who took us from Eisilion. We've seen a man called Ostarial and a woman called Alviath, and others who bring us food and clothing. They speak of someone called Falthorn, as if they do his bidding. As to how long we've been here . . . Every day is the same. It could be a few weeks, but it feels like a year. Time passes in a confusing manner here.'

'Have they explained why they took you?'

Ghiseyma flattened her lips. 'That is the most frustrating thing of all! I imagine we are to be used as pawns in some game between the Aelyr and the throne of Aventuria, but of what nature, they will not say.'

'There's been no message, no ransom demand,' he said. 'I hope they've looked after you, at least.'

'Oh, they have treated us well – but gods, it is good to see you, Eldareth! How is Helan? I haven't seen her for so long. Do you know that she was once reported dead at sea? Then news came that she was alive. I don't think I can stand any more such shocks.'

'She's alive indeed, and well.'

'Never mind that,' said Veny. 'It's about time someone came to take us home, Eldareth! There's nothing to do here. Where have you been?'

Eldareth gave the boy a rigid grin. He'd been obnoxious as a five-year-old, and neither age nor captivity seemed to have improved his character.

'Veny!' Ghiseyma reproved him half-heartedly. 'I must admit, I'm relieved to see you, my lord. I'm a patient woman, but it's been hard on the boy.'

She came to Eldareth and clasped his hands. He didn't know the princess well, but they had always respected one another. There were tears in her eyes.

'Well, I've found you, ma'am, thanks to Lord Elrill. Alas, rescuing you may take a little longer. We're guests of Lord Falthorn but I don't think he'll take kindly to us spiriting you away. And we have two other friends to think of. We have to form a plan of escape. Until then—'

'Eldareth!' Elrill hissed. 'Someone's coming!'

'We know where you are now,' Eldareth said hurriedly. 'Be patient. We'll come back for you.'

As he stepped back through the portal, the young prince tried to follow him, shouting, 'This isn't fair! Take us home immediately! Mother, tell him!' – but Elrill gave a twist of the sphere, and closed the portal in the child's face.

Too late. There were armed Valahyr all around them, as if they'd melted from the walls. Their curved swords glinted dully, as dark as their black and indigo garments; violet jewels gleamed on their shoulders and on their broad, fair brows. Ostarial stepped forward, his cloak swinging. He looked pleased.

'Falthorn is going to be dismayed by this,' Ostarial stated. 'This is an abuse of his hospitality, and an act of aggression. I have no choice but to place you both in custody to await his judgement.'

Falthorn led Tanthe a long way on foot, a good two hours' walk, to a great hill she'd noticed from a distance. It was a long high ridge of steel-blue stone which reminded her of a picture she'd seen in Saphaeyender's books, the humped spine of a fantastical sea monster. All the way, Falthorn kept one arm across her shoulders in a mixed gesture of affection and control. She was afraid of him, couldn't help it. And the more she experienced Falthorn's power, the more completely she forgave Auriel.

On the highest point of the ridge, he stopped and said, 'Behold Verdanholm.'

She saw a flow of hills, sheened with green, blue and fire-gold. Deep valleys channelling amethyst rivers, sheltering the concealed wooden dwellings of the Aelyr. Forests, soft and rich as silk, with cliffs of white quartz towering from them. Circles and menhirs of rock that held deep, unknowable secrets. The sky was a vault of violet-blue glass, with its apricot sun and shoals of stars. Their music was clear, sharp and haunting. She saw disturbances, like those they'd seen over the battlefield; columns of tumultuous air that flashed with sudden rainbows, odd waves of light.

'More beautiful than Earth?' Falthorn asked softly.

Tanthe nearly answered yes, but stopped, for she loved Aventuria with a passion. 'I don't know. Different. Wonderful.'

He sighed. 'I might have known you couldn't give a straightforward answer. But yes, this realm is wonderful, and precious, and different to Earth. That's why I'm going to such lengths to protect it. Nothing else will save Verdanholm, believe me.'

From a leather sheath that hung on his belt he drew a telescope. 'Look more closely,' he said.

'At what?'

'The horizon. What do you see?'

Tanthe put the telescope to her eye. Its crystal lenses brought the landscape rushing close. Falthorn's hand was on her back and he turned her, directing her; she wished he wouldn't, but she didn't have the nerve to shake him off.

First he directed her to look at the horizon behind them, where the house lay. She saw the roof of the house, magnified; beyond it the pleated hills and the perfect crystal clarity of the skyline. But as he turned her slowly through a semi-circle, she began to see a strange greyness. A mere haze at first that she took for mist. Then as she scanned along the horizon, the land and sky appeared blurred with a slaty veil of smoke. A bruise . . . something wrong, something disturbing that filled her with unease.

'You see?' said Falthorn.

'What is it? A storm? A fire?'

'The Eaters.'

'What?' She went on studying the greyness and suddenly she saw what it was.

Nothingness. Verdanholm ended there, its substance ground to dust, or burned and streaming away into space as smoke and ash. Sickness kicked her stomach and she let the telescope fall from her eye.

Falthorn took it from her before she dropped it. 'The Bhahdradomen, the Devourers. Don't you know why they have that name?'

'For the way they destroyed Aventuria last time.'

'But Earth and Verdanholm are not the same. In Aventuria they consumed the grass, the trees, every living thing with such voracious appetite that they left nothing but dead earth behind them. *But the land itself remained.* That's the difference. Earth is stable, but Verdanholm is not.

'The Aelyr themselves created this realm. The creation goes on; we can make pockets of new space and land, islands of it like the one where I first met you. Our world is fluid and elastic. It is made of Jewelfire, *roth* that turns easily into matter and just as easily back to *roth* again. That's what the Devourers feed on.'

'Gods. You mean they are actually feeding on the land?'

'Turning it back to energy, and drinking it.'

'Are they the same as the . . . the Bhahdradomen we have on Earth?'

Falthorn lifted his shoulders. 'A different order of them, perhaps. Ones who feed on *roth* rather than on matter, more sophisticated and powerful, more dangerous. But all Eaters are capable of adapting from one function to another, as they deem appropriate. That's why they are called shape-changers, after all. So yes, in the end they are the same.'

She saw intense fire in his eyes and knew that he cared about this so passionately that he cared about nothing and no one else. 'How long have they been . . . ?'

'Always,' he said. 'Which is meaningless, since time here does not always move in a straight line. But the Eaters have always been destroying Verdanholm behind us, while we move ahead, expanding the realm as we go. This is hard for you to understand.'

'No,' she said. 'The Fhelethyr were telling me about it. We saw them do it.'

Falthorn sneered. 'The Fhelethyr!'

'Running away. That's what you think of them, isn't it?'

'Because it's true. They won't give up the old ways – always running from the Eaters. But this is exhausting us, and such a waste of the land that is lost. The Devourers are sucking out the Jewelfire faster than Verdanholm can regenerate it – which means that one day, there will be none left with which to create new land. It's already happening, only the Fhelethyr won't admit it. Yet the other way always fails, too. The Bhahdradomen don't understand the concept of war or defeat. They simply keep coming back.'

'They never really went away,' Tanthe said under her breath. Much as she hated to agree with Falthorn, she couldn't help it.

'And each time their activity increases on Earth, it increases here, too. What the Fhelethyr refuse to accept is that the Eaters are gaining on us. Their strength has multiplied. They're too voracious this time. The Aelyr cannot replace Verdanholm as fast as the Eaters are using it up. If we don't act, Verdanholm is going to be utterly destroyed.'

Tanthe stared at him. The zeal in his expression frightened her. 'What are you going to do?'

'I have worked towards this for many turns of the Earth. Since before you and Auriel were born. Everything I've done has been to this end. Your father and mother should have been helping me but, since they saw fit to dissent, I have managed perfectly well without them. I am going to make a bargain with the Bhahdradomen.'

'The Fhelethyr told me that, too. They think you're mad!'

'Wait until I've secured the safety of our realm – then let them tell me I'm mad,' Falthorn said flatly. 'They don't understand the Eaters. Negotiations have already begun.'

Tanthe's heart was beating hard. She pointed at the bruise. 'So why haven't the Bhahdradomen called a truce?'

'Because they are awkward, and don't believe I can deliver what I've promised. But I shall. It's why I captured Auriel, and used him to bring you to me, and created the child. Long, long forays into the heart of the Jewelfire – spirit realms you can't even imagine – brought the potential child to my notice. Without my intervention, it is doubtful that it would ever have been born . . . and in truth, perhaps it should *not* have been.' He smiled thinly. Her heart turned cold. 'A dangerous child, indeed. One that contains particular energies, a natural *roth*-mage who could become the greatest weapon against the Bhahdradomen in history. Now, what wouldn't they give to have such a weapon in their own possession? Quite a bargaining counter. I need levers against them, to ensure that they stick to the agreement. So I give them certain concessions, and in return they leave Verdanholm alone – for ever.'

Her hands flew to her face. She screamed, 'You're going to give my baby to the Bhahdradomen!'

Falthorn started laughing. 'Did I say that? Oh, it will take more than that, my dear. The Devourers bargain hard. I'm going to give them the Earth.'

Chapter Eighteen. Zhahgrament

Rufryd hung in Akarata's claws, the wind cold in his face. His gloved hands gripped the claw that encircled his chest, so he could hold himself in a comfortable position to watch the slow unfolding of the landscape. Above him, her great wings were a thundering canopy against the sky.

As they flew further from Q'enartre's Throne, the storms lessened and the weather grew colder. Rufryd's hair was whipped by sleet and wind; he was so cold he no longer felt it. For two days the dra'a'k-queen had flown. She would land to let Rufryd eat and rest, but never for long enough; he was so tired that he even slept in her claws as she flew on through the night.

Now the third dawn came and he saw a semi-circle of mountains, saturated green, their peaks patched with snow. Beyond them lay a vast plain. As he watched, the clouds broke and an immense curtain of white sunlight fell through, turning the steel-blue grass to a sea of shimmering diamond.

He caught his breath. He forgot himself in wonder – as he'd forgotten himself more and more often since he had met Akarata – and gasped, 'The Silver Plains!'

She showed him an image of battle. Human and Aelyr armies, battling ferociously against slow-moving, chameleon lines of Bhahdradomen who seemed strangely inert, yet immovable. The humans charged in tight-packed groups, some mounted and some on foot; he could almost smell their sweat, hear their raw shouts. The Aelyr moved like mist, uttering terrible, discordant howls; but they were loosely scattered so the Bhahdradomen easily moved among them, slaying them with weapons he couldn't identify but which spat green sparks. There were flashes of white fire, the stench of burned grass, *ghelim* screaming soundlessly above the battlefield . . .

A dreadful, disembodied voice began screaming in his ear. *'The Basilisks! The Basilisks!'* Not a human voice, but a Bhahdradomen in the throes of terror.

'Stop!' Rufryd cried, frantically trying to clear the image so she would understand he didn't want to see it. 'Stop. It's in the past.'

He closed his eyes. When he opened them again, the Silver Plains were deserted; peaceful, shining, desolate.

Beyond them, the land mass of Aventuria ended suddenly in a line of high cliffs. He heard the booming of the sea.

He strained to see Vexor, but Akarata dropped suddenly and landed, there on the silvery grass on the cliff-edge. *You still want to go on? Your last chance to stay.*

Stepping out of her grasp, Rufryd stretched his aching limbs. He hurt all over.

No. I'm going on.

Then rest first, and eat, and go safely.

Akarata's advice was wise; he didn't know what he would find on the other side. He didn't have much food left. Four days' worth, perhaps, if he rationed himself carefully. He ate a heavy potato cake and a strip of meat, feeding crumbs to Su. She seemed to eat almost as much as he did, looking out of his pocket with bright, perky eyes. He washed the meal down with water and a few mouthfuls of ale, slept for half an hour with the dra'a'k watching over him. But he was too edgy to sleep for any longer. He found a tiny stream where he had a perfunctory wash, shaved with the edge of his belt knife then splashed the earthy-tasting water on his face.

'I'm ready,' he said.

He stood within her claws, stroking the leathery skin. She took him up into the air again, with the vertiginous rush that he'd almost got used to – but not quite. The cliffs plunged away below him, so abruptly that he clung on in thrilling terror. And then there was nothing beneath him but foaming grey ocean.

Some time passed before he saw the cliffs on the other side. He hadn't realised the Vexat Straits were so wide, nor so perilous. There were no beaches, only the narrowest of rocky inlets where boats might be landed. He wondered how long it had taken for the exiled Bhahdradomen to be ferried across – or had dra'a'ks carried them, or even their own *ghelim*? Akarata showed him no image to satisfy his curiosity. There were only hostile waves crashing on the rock, and the dark pleats of the cliff drawing closer.

A brown plate of land tilted up to meet him. The dra'a'k-queen set him down and she was gone, wheeling away on the updraughts without looking back. Rufryd realised then that she'd already said her goodbyes on the other side.

In a daze he watched her gliding away, dwindling to nothing. The soil of Vexor felt spongy and friable beneath his feet.

He was alone.

He had his Aelyr sword, his bow and a few arrows left that were straight enough to shoot; his knife; a pack containing clothes that were no cleaner than the ones he had on, a map and the remains of his rations. His only companion, one small homing bird.

The cliff-top ran back into a high, flat stretch of land under a huge grey sky. A wind full of sleet blew steadily, though he hardly felt the chill any more. He was warm from the flight. The ground was black, tinged with the rust of primitive vegetation; lichens and mosses and wiry heathers, struggling to grow on exhausted soil.

The cliff was deserted, but he saw signs of the Bhahdradomen at once. Where his feet were planted, the soil began to seethe with the activity of unseen insects. He scuffed the dirt with his toe and there they were; great, pallid segmented things, writhing and digging. Eager to drag any dead or sleeping body under the earth as a nest for their eggs, food for their maggots. They were the parasites that lived on the Bhahdradomen flesh-animals.

Rufryd stared at them in a mixture of disgust and indifference. If the whole land was infested with them, it would be hard to find somewhere to sleep in safety.

He shouldered his pack and began to walk inland.

Within ten minutes, he saw a herd of the big fleshy creatures spread across the plain. He winced inwardly. Stopping briefly to string his bow, he went towards them. He wasn't used to cattle at the best of times – they'd mainly had sheep in Riverwynde – and these were not normal cattle. They were muscular and grotesque, with great square heads and tiny eyes, veins showing green under their hairless skin. Whether any were bulls, he couldn't tell; they all looked the same and all had horns, some rudimentary, others long and lethal.

They tore at the sparse vegetation with grindstone teeth, tearing it up by the roots, crunching soil and stones with each mouthful. If there had ever been trees on this plain, they were all gone now. And he saw that the animals were nothing like as bulky as the ones he'd seen in Ardharkria. In comparison they were thin, their flesh pulled tight over their bones.

As he began to weave his way between them, they stopped eating and stared at him with a weirdly knowing hostility.

Rufryd was holding his breath, walking on knives. If he just kept going it would be fine, he could get through them.

Then one broke away, came charging towards him. The ground shook under its hooves. It had four great horns lowered at his chest and he had seen a monster like this before, knew that arrows would only stick uselessly in its hide . . .

Rufryd set an arrow to the string, hauled it taut, and shot.

The arrow sank straight into the creature's eye,

skewering its brain. It went down, somersaulting with its momentum before its bulk hit the ground. Those around it scattered, trotting leadenly away.

Rufryd pushed sweat off his brow. He was shaking. One of these days his deadly aim was going to fail. The smell that emanated from the cattle was musty like rotting earth, and it was familiar, dragging up a dozen strange and horrible memories of Ardharkria. He ran to the fallen animal and retrieved his arrow, for he couldn't afford to lose it. He dragged it out, wiped it on the creature's hide and set it to the string again, watching for another attack with every sense primed.

'*Ashrach! Yr graukhim fethrouth!*'

The shout came from a group of Bhahdradomen; three figures wrapped in greyish rags who seemed to rise out of nowhere behind the herd. They must have been sitting on the ground and have seen everything.

They came towards him, looking alarmed and angry, shouting at him in a tongue he didn't understand. Their meaning seemed clear enough, though; he'd killed one of their animals, and they were furious.

Rufryd stood still as they came towards him, trying to judge the situation. Would they understand, if he tried to tell them he'd done it in self-defence? They seemed to be unarmed. He held his bow low, called out, 'I've come from Thanmandrathor. Do any of you speak Paranian?'

'*Asharrch, naraghahim nyr!*'

No, they didn't. They came on, their ashen skull-faces terrible, and he saw them pulling thin black objects from their belts. Spears, sticks?

Rufryd wasn't going to wait and find out. He drew his bow and let fly at the leader.

His arrow sank into the cattle-herder's shoulder, causing him to stagger. But it didn't stop him. As Rufryd made to draw a second arrow, another of the herders raised the thin black weapon and now Rufryd saw that it was a whip.

Before Rufryd could shoot again, the Bhahdradomen

447

lashed out. The whip's long tongue came snaking towards him, not striking him but hooking itself round him. Rufryd was taken completely by surprise. It seemed prehensile, tightening like a lasso around his waist, a greenish luminescence flashing through it. He felt a jolt of pain like an electric shock. All the strength went out of his body and he fell.

Looking up through a cloud of black stars, he saw the one he'd shot pulling the arrow out of his shoulder. Rufryd heard the crunch of cartilage as it came free. Then he passed out.

When he woke, he found himself in some kind of hut; a low dome of wattle and daub, with a supporting post in the centre. His head ached. A dozen odours wove through the air, earth and meat and mould and his own sweat and others he couldn't identify; unpleasant, but not unbearable. He tried to sit up and through the gloom he found a crowd of Bhahdradomen staring down at him. Merely staring, with bland green-brown eyes set in pale, greyish faces.

'I didn't mean you any harm,' he said. 'The bull attacked me.'

They only went on staring, clearly not understanding a word. When he pushed himself into a sitting position and slumped over his knees, they murmured and drew back. And he realised.

These people had never seen a human being before.

Rufryd started to laugh in sheer disbelief at his situation. He rubbed his face, then opened his flask and took a long drink of water – stopping suddenly to wonder if there was any clean water on Vexor.

His body was sore where the whip-like weapon had caught him, and there was a charred line on his jacket to mark its embrace. He felt in his pocket where the blue-dove nestled, found her warm and alive. Thank Breyid. They'd taken his bow away, but not his Aelyr sword;

didn't they realise what it was? They were inscrutable, unfathomable.

'I'm Rufryd,' he said, but none of them responded. 'From Aventuria. Parione? I was sent by Queen Helananthe. Gods, you've probably never heard of her. What kings would you know? Garnelys? Aralyth? Maharoth?'

At the last name they drew back, and a faint noise came from them; whispering or the hissing of breath; he couldn't tell. He shook his head in frustration. 'No, I'm not threatening you. Oh, fuck, surely there's someone here who can speak Paranian? I've come from Helananthe to see Aazhoth. Your leader, Aazhoth?'

He wasn't sure he'd pronounced it correctly, but the Bhahdradomen clearly recognised the name. They started turning their heads to look at one another, and as they did so they looked different, their skins turning paler, their eyes darker, and there was something at once reptilian and vulturine about them, and he began to feel really afraid. Shaking, he tried to get up and found he couldn't; instead he pressed back against the curved wall of the hut. He stood no chance of escaping. Were they going to kill him?

After a few minutes, a handful of them came forward; smaller, younger ones by the look of them. Whether they were male or female he couldn't tell; they seemed to be neither. Rufryd sat helpless as these creatures pulled and plucked at his clothing; taking courage from each other to poke at his arms and his face. He was reminded of boys tormenting a spider. They seemed at once horrified, wary and fascinated.

'Get the fuck off me!' Rufryd shouted. They flinched, but moved in again and he daren't incur the wrath of the adults by trying to hit or kick them. No, more than that; he didn't want to behave as the Than'drathians had to Noli. Enervation lay on him. Fighting it, he made another attempt to stand up and this time succeeded. His legs

449

shook under him. The youngsters went on pawing at him, smiling with their lipless mouths.

A gruff Bhahdradomen voice sounded at the back of the hut. At that, his tormentors scattered. The gathered watchers parted, and a new Bhahdradomen came marching through them and stared at Rufryd. Behind him was the cattle-herder whom Rufryd had shot in the shoulder.

The newcomer had some authority, from the look of him. He wore an ochre robe with a leathery cloak over it, and he carried a staff. The bald dome of his head was unhooded, skin matt and smooth like parchment of a dull orange colour, his small features close-set and serious.

'I'm Tsur, elder of this *tzcement*,' he said. Rufryd assumed that meant village, or something similar. His voice was thickly accented, but intelligible, to Rufryd's relief. 'I am told that you killed a *graukhim* and shot at one of our *domenim*.'

'In self-defence. I was attacked. I didn't mean to harm anyone.'

'Who are you?'

'I'm Rufryd Arthryn-son. I came as an envoy from my ruler to yours.' He made an effort to straighten up and speak with more authority. 'I barely set foot on Vexor and I've nearly been killed twice, then thrown into this hut and manhandled. Is this the best treatment a representative of the Queen can hope for? Oh, and this is what a human being looks like, in case you were wondering.'

'I have seen humans before,' Tsur said stiffly. He turned and gestured at the others, uttering sharp words in their own language. They turned and began to leave, shuffling out with considerable reluctance and throwing Rufryd many glances; some scowling, others impassive.

At last Rufryd was alone with the elder. 'Your Queen sends only one of you into Vexor?'

'There were four of us, to start with, including the – well, the Duchess of Thanmandrathor. We were separated. It's a long story. So I'm here alone, and I wish you no harm. All

450

I'm here for is to convey messages from the Queen to your leader, Aazhoth.'

Tsur glared at him, as if he'd committed a dreadful indiscretion.

'Your leader is called Aazhoth, isn't he?' said Rufryd.

'Aazhoth is long gone,' Tsur replied, with a strange grimace; whether this was anger or amusement, Rufryd could not tell. 'Our leader now is Vaurgroth, Lord of Light, Chosen of the Ancestor. It surprises me that your Queen does not know this.'

'I'm sorry, but it's news to me.'

'Still, as humans so rarely enter Vexor, perhaps it is no surprise.' Another odd smile flickered on Tsur's face.

'In that case, I need to find Vaurgroth.'

Tsur scratched his chin and murmured something in his own language. Then he said, 'He is not hard to find. He is always at Zhagrament; did they not tell you that? I shall have to decide what to do with you.'

Rufryd folded his arms and said sharply, 'With all due respect, it's not your decision. My presence here is between Helananthe and Vaurgroth. However, if I hadn't been attacked, I would have sought someone like you to help me. A Bhahdradomen in authority.'

Tsur seemed to respond well to a touch of flattery. He wasn't stupid, Rufryd could see that. He didn't think any of the Eaters were stupid, even the ones who'd stood gaping at him; just alien.

'I shall give you the benefit of the doubt, Rufryd Arthryn-son. It's in my power to keep you here and to kill you, for what you have done.'

'Yes,' said Rufryd, dry-mouthed.

'But if it transpires that your visit is of great importance between our two peoples, I don't want it said that I prevented your free passage across a land which, after all, still belongs to your monarch.'

Tsur dipped his shoulders in a half-bow, which rather took Rufryd by surprise.

451

'Thank you. You've made the right decision.'

'I shall guide you to Zhahgrament myself. A journey of a few days.'

'I'd be glad of that.' Rufryd was taken aback by the elder's display of courtesy, even if it was only to avoid the risk of upsetting a higher authority. 'But I really need to rest. That whip – whatever it was – felt like it nearly killed me.'

'As it is meant to,' said Tsur. 'Come with me. I shall take you to a more comfortable dwelling until your strength returns.'

Outside, Rufryd found a scene so desolate that it shook him. He was in a village of sorts; huts crowded around a flat, grey central space that was crowded with bleak-eyed Bhahdradomen. They stared at him as Tsur led him towards a larger hut on the far side. It struck him, suddenly, that they were so slow moving because they were weak and malnourished. There was no blade of vegetation to be seen. Their flesh-animals were living on roots and stones, and there was little flesh on them.

Rufryd recalled the shape-changers they'd encountered in the forest of Ardharkria, how their cattle had consumed everything, even the bark of the trees, leaving death in their wake. He saw that Vexor was dead, and that these people, too, were dying.

He didn't know whether to feel pity or contempt for them.

The hut to which Tsur brought him was hardly better than the one he'd left, but it was bigger and lighter, with hide-covered cushions and bolsters around the edges. Rufryd sat down, but felt uneasy. Did he dare to sleep with those hungry-eyed Eaters outside? Some of them angry with him, others merely . . . famished.

'You don't seem to have much to eat,' he said.

'You are correct. And what we do have . . .' Tsur stopped, as if he'd been about to give something away.

Then he said something in his own tongue. Rufryd nearly leapt out of his skin as an unmoving, pale shape in the shadows, that he'd taken for a bolster, suddenly leapt up and ran across the tent. It was a young Bhahdradomen, skinny and long-limbed, wrapped in a thin tunic of *graukhim*-hide. It busied itself at a table crowded with strange-looking vessels; Rufryd couldn't help staring at the odd way its legs were jointed, more like those of a bird or reptile. He looked away, recalling how they had stared at him. Presently the youngster brought Rufryd and Tsur tall thin cups of yellowish liquid. Its face was flat and rudimentary but its expression was eager to please; its skin was mottled with green and purple. Repellant, but harmless.

Rufryd took the vessel and looked suspiciously into it. 'What is this?'

'A liquor we make with water and herbs. I think it is not poisonous to humans.'

'As far as you know?' Rufryd swallowed. 'Oh well.' He raised the vessel, took a swig of the liquid. It tasted foul, like cold bitter tea, then pleasantly warming. If it poisoned him, he didn't really care. He had a feeling that Vexor was going to kill him, sooner or later.

The young one grinned up at Rufryd and said, 'Drink it? Good?'

'He speaks Paranian,' Rufryd said in surprise.

'I have been teaching him. He learns well. He is a good hatchling.'

There was a certain amount of affection in Tsur's voice. 'Is he your son?'

A veil came down over Tsur's face; complete incomprehension. 'Son?'

'Er – you know, your child.'

'Ah, I see. No, I don't think Vetru is of my hatching.'

'You mean you don't know?' Rufryd spoke before he could stop himself. Hardly diplomatic, to reveal his shock and ignorance.

Tsur didn't seem offended. 'I know a little of human customs, that you somehow label and keep offspring as your own. We cannot understand why it matters to you. Ancestor channels his creation through us, but it doesn't matter from which of us his hatchlings come. Although it is a pleasure, of course.'

Vetru smiled at his master, who stroked the youngster's naked head.

Rufryd didn't know what to say. He felt he'd stumbled into a world that got more complicated by the second. Vetru scampered away into the shadows. Rufryd said quietly, 'The first thing I shall tell the Queen is that you are in danger of a famine here. She doesn't know.'

'Perhaps she would have known, had she sent an envoy sooner,' Tsur said bitterly. His head came up and his eyes – so small their colour couldn't be made out – fastened on Rufryd's. 'Ah, but it was as much Aazhoth's fault as your monarch's.'

'How so?'

'Aazhoth was a coward. He bent to everything the humans demanded of us. He would not stand up to them in any matter. All he cared for was to avoid conflict.'

'Perhaps he was protecting you. Keeping the peace.'

'Protecting us? Then this is the result of his protection. The Bhahdradomen must move to live; if we are confined to one space, we die!'

Rufryd restrained himself from stating the obvious; that Bhahdradomen moving meant humans dying instead. 'What happened to Aazhoth?' he asked.

'He had to be brought down. If not, we should all have died. Vaurgroth deposed him.' Tsur's bald eyebrows arched in knowing insinuation. 'Vaurgroth is strong. Ancestor sent him to save us. Soon the famine will be over. A memory.'

'Is Vaurgroth well-disposed towards the Queen?' He suddenly wondered how Tsur knew of Helananthe, if she hadn't known about Vaurgroth.

'I'm sure he has no ill-feeling towards humans,' Tsur answered, with strange innocence. 'All Master of Light cares about is saving his *domenim*. His people. No one else will save us. Not your Queen, that is certain. Only Vaurgroth.'

They went on talking for a while. The liquor didn't poison Rufryd, but it did help to ease his soreness. He ate some food from his pack, offered some to Tsur, who declined. Later, as Rufryd was almost falling asleep where he sat, the Bhahdradomen said, 'You lie down and rest now. None will harm you. Vetru and I shall watch over you.'

Against his better judgement, Rufryd made himself comfortable on a pile of strongly-scented hide cushions. With a bowstring he made a tether for Su, so she could perch wherever she wanted but not fly away. Once she was settled, he went outside to relieve himself, then stretched out on the cushions and fell at once into a heavy sleep.

He woke sweating in sudden, heart-stopping terror. A sound had woken him. A dreadful, unhuman keening.

It was dark outside, but light flooded the hut from a dozen fatty candles. He sat up in a daze, not knowing where he was but recalling it was somewhere desolate, that someone was crying in pain . . . he sat up, and realised it was Tsur making the noise.

'Tsur?' he said. 'Are you ill?'

He saw the elder on the far side of the hut, sitting on the ground and resting back against a bolster that was covered in hairless white hide. He sat rigid, uttering a metallic groan that went on and on. There were other Bhahdradomen in the hut – two adults and Vetru – hovering about Tsur as if they were waiting rather than tending to him.

Still dazed with sleep, Rufryd dragged himself off the makeshift bed and stood up.

The others glanced at him, but said nothing. He saw in shock that Tsur was naked. His body was scrawny, a pale greyish-orange washed with candlelight, yet swollen around the abdomen. For half a second, his gaze connected with Rufryd's but he seemed unselfconscious about his situation. Rufryd felt awkward.

'What's wrong? Is he ill?'

No one answered him.

Suddenly Tsur lurched forward on to all fours, then drew himself up into a crouch. Rufryd didn't mean to look but he saw everything. Tsur threw his head back, thrust his seven-fingered hands between his legs. An egg began to appear. A leathery, mottled egg, squeezing like the bloody head of a baby from a stretched tube of skin.

Tsur strained. The egg paused, trapped at its widest part. Then in a rush it slid out, landing soft and heavy and wet in Tsur's own hands.

His groans stopped in a long, soft outrush of breath. He sat back in relief, eyes closed. At once, one of the other Bhahdradomen took the egg from him and began to wrap it in layer on layer of thin, ragged leather. Rufryd had the horrible impression that these were the skins of dead Bhahdradomen, stretched and tanned paper-thin.

The other adult covered Tsur with a blanket, but not before Rufryd had observed that the elder appeared to have no genitals. None he recognised, anyway. Only the ovipositor, which, having done its work, relaxed into a short, loose tube between the Bhahdradomen's thighs.

Rufryd stood there. He didn't know what to do. The wrapped egg was placed on a pad of material beside Tsur, and Vetru gave his master a drink.

'Er . . . is there anything I can do?' Rufryd said awkwardly.

Tsur waved a tired hand at him. 'Go back to sleep. This is nothing out of the ordinary. Another gift of the Ancestor . . . which will, I trust have a better life than we have had.'

'I should apologise,' Rufryd breathed.

'Why?'

'I – I thought you male. I shouldn't have made assumptions.'

Tsur frowned. 'What is that?'

'Er – male. Like me. But you're female?'

'You make no sense. I am too tired for this.'

'I'll leave you to rest.'

Shaken, Rufryd turned away and went towards his bed. He thought he wouldn't sleep; the only sound in the stillness was Tsur's thick, shallow breathing. But he lay awake only for a short time before sleep overcame him; and then he had the strangest dream that some creature was winding around him, holding him in a tight, bony embrace from which he couldn't escape.

He slept deeply and didn't wake until what felt like midday – although the Bhahdradomen seemed to have no obvious means of measuring time. Groaning, he sat up and scrubbed his face with his hands. Su hopped on to his shoulder, cooing. Tsur was up and about; he was seated in the centre of the hut with five *domenim* around him, talking quietly in their own tongue. There was no sign of the egg. No sign of anything that had happened last night. Rufryd wondered if it had been some ghastly hallucination brought on by the alien wine.

As he stirred, glances were thrown in his direction. He started; Vetru was at his elbow again, appearing as if from nowhere, offering him a drink. Rufryd took it and drank, so thirsty he didn't care what it was.

A lukewarm brew of herbs, this time without liquor. Tea. It didn't taste bad.

'Thanks,' he whispered. 'Your master, is he . . . well?'

Vetru didn't answer. He darted away, looking over his shoulder at Rufryd.

The others were rising and leaving the hut. When they'd gone, Tsur came to Rufryd. 'You must forgive me for our poor hospitality. We have little to offer, as you see.'

Rufryd laughed. 'No, it's all right. I'm just grateful you didn't kill me yesterday. That's good hospitality.'

Tsur's small features gathered into a smile. 'And now I must go back on my word. I said I would take you to Vaurgroth but I am indisposed. Last night was tiring for me and I must rest for a few days.'

'Oh. Yes, I see.' Rufryd floundered, wondering if he was meant to offer congratulations, or whether it was permitted to ask personal questions.

'It comes upon us very quickly, the laying, and sometimes there is no warning.'

'So you didn't know that you were going to . . .? I don't mean to be offensive, I'm sorry.'

'In what way are you being offensive? The egg was a blessing.'

'Where – where is it now?'

'In the hatching place, to be kept warm until the hatchling emerges. In ten days, usually, they emerge ready for imprinting. By then its role is decided.'

Rufryd thought of chicks at home, who would take the first object they saw to be their mother. 'You mean, you will have decided who is going to look after it?' Tsur gave him a look, which seemed to imply a communication gap. 'Teach it?'

'In a manner of speaking. Imprinting is learning, yes. How to be *ghelim*, perhaps, or *domenim*.'

'But you won't take care of it yourself? You said last night that the parents don't look after their own offspring.'

'It is not mine. It belongs to the *tzcement*.'

Rufryd didn't know why he felt so anxious about the unhatched creature's fate, but he couldn't help it. 'You'll want to see it, though, won't you? I would.'

Tsur shook his head patiently. 'I do not need to see it. It is not my possession. If I see it eventually, I may not recognise it as one that came from me. It doesn't *matter* that it came from me. This is very hard for you to understand.'

'Yeah. Just a bit. Because what about its . . . other parent? Don't they know or care about it?'

The elder looked at him with intense puzzlement. 'I am its sole progenitor.'

'That's not possible.'

Tsur's expression turned wary. 'You tell us what is and is not possible, when you know nothing of us? Humans are more unfathomable than I thought.'

'I'm trying to learn about you, that's all.'

'To what end?'

Tsur's flash of suspicion was like a spear-point, reminding Rufryd that he was among strangers, not safe. 'I was only curious. It's none of my business.'

The elder moved away to the high, round table and poured himself a drink from a tall thin carafe of yellow metal. It was something restorative, judging by the tiny amount he poured and the face he pulled as he swallowed it. 'You must leave today. My *domenim* are uncomfortable with your presence. I shall send three of them with you, and Vetru.'

'Vetru? But he's . . .'

'Little more than a hatchling, I know. But he is fond of you, and I trust him to escort you safely, and there is no other who speaks Paranian.'

Rufryd was uneasy about the idea. 'No,' he said quickly. 'I can't take him away from you. There's no need to send anyone with me, I'll find the way on my own.'

'You could. Zhahgrament lies at the centre of Vexor and it is not hard to find. But if ever Vaurgroth discovered I had let a human leave my *tzcement* to wander in Vexor without an escort . . .' Tsur raised his hands in a peculiar but clear shrug.

'I see. But how do I know they won't kill me?'

The look Tsur gave him was steady and honest. In spite of everything, Rufryd trusted him. 'They will protect you, not harm you. You have my word.'

*

Rufryd was glad to be on the move again, however grim the landscape that spread out before him. He had persuaded Tsur to give his bow and arrows back, though he feared he might lose them again before the journey was over.

Vetru loped at his side, seeming wildly excited to be on this journey. The other three villagers stayed in the background, like shadowy spies; keeping an eye on Rufryd, yet watching out for anyone who might attack him. Their presence made him nervous. After a time he stopped thinking about them, but he never forgot they were there, following, watching, haunting.

The sky was bleak, the air heavy with moisture. A cold, hard wind blew relentlessly across the high plug of land that was Vexor. They trekked across a bleak stretch of heath that was barren, cattle-sick. Even when the sun slipped through a crack in the clouds, it brought no colour to the scene. There was bare soil patched with rusty vegetation, oily rocks, the occasional cluster of wind-sculpted trees.

Here and there Rufryd saw herds of flesh-animals, being driven across the bleak land from one patch of scrub to the next. There was a little food left, but it would soon be gone. Rufryd wondered, then what will they do? Eat each other? Looking up, he saw what seemed to be dra'a'ks circling on the high currents. Then they turned all at once and arrowed away to the east. Not dra'a'ks. *Ghelim*.

'Not far to Zhahgrament. A few days. I take you,' Vetru repeated happily as they walked. He came only to Rufryd's shoulder, but would have been taller if he had held himself upright, rather than moving with an ape-like stoop. He seemed harmless enough, but Rufryd was already irritated with him. He would have done anything to have Con there instead.

When night came, they took shelter in a small thicket of trees and wrapped themselves in the hide cloaks that Tsur had given them. Their odour seemed to wrap itself constantly around Rufryd; the smell of the Bhahdradomen, musty and earthy and leathery, shot through with an unidentifiable sourness that for ever afterwards would make his skin creep.

He had hoped the trees had lost their leaves for the winter; but no, they were dead. There were a few leaves hanging from the tangle of shrubs around them, and even some broad-leaved weeds bravely struggling to grow on the bank of a tiny stream. The splash of green was lurid against the monochrome.

The three watchers kept their distance; Rufryd could not even see them in the twilight. Ignoring Vetru, he gathered a good pile of wood and lit it with his flint. It caught quickly. Despite the damp, the wood itself was brittle, as if it had been sucked dry. Rufryd huddled by the blaze, suddenly unable to stop shivering. Su perched on his rucksack, where he'd tethered her, and fell asleep with her head under her wing.

Vetru stared at the fire. Crouching on all fours, he seemed petrified.

'What?' said Rufryd. 'Don't you have fires at home?'

Vetru shook his head. 'I heard they have them in Zhahgrament. We have them sometimes, but only in—' he described a container shape with his hands. 'I only see this not often.'

Rufryd was too tired to compare domestic habits. 'It won't hurt you, unless you go too close.'

'Will you put your flesh in the fire?'

'Not if I can help it,' Rufryd said drily. 'We like to be warm, but you can overdo it.'

Then he realised that he'd misunderstood the question. Vetru was unwrapping a parcel of food; long pallid strips of raw meat. He peeled one off and began to eat it with a relish that turned Rufryd's stomach. But he had little food left of his own, only some hard cakes made of oats, honey and ginger that he was saving for emergencies, and to feed the blue-dove. He would have to start eating Bhahdradomen food eventually.

Vetru held the package out to him, his round eyes encouraging. Rufryd took a piece of the pale flesh, prodded its unyielding shiny surface, sniffed it. It had the faint sweet scent of offal.

'You're right, I'll try cooking it.'

The meat didn't taste bad when he dragged it out of the embers, half an hour later. It was tough and bland, but edible. Vetru sat watching him with bright eyes.

'I go to see Vaurgroth,' he announced excitedly, not for the first time.

'Know anything about this leader of yours, do you?'

'Ancestor send him to save us. We don't starve. We have all land, all . . .' Vetru waved a hand vaguely around his head. His spindly fingers with their big knuckles were like a cluster of gnarled twigs.

'All the sky?' said Rufryd.

'No, other place. Aelyr place.'

He coughed. 'Verdanholm?'

'All is ours. Vaurgroth promise. Follow Ancestor, he lead us to green land. *Graukhim* can eat, hatchlings grow.'

Rufryd wasn't sure what to say. If he said what was on his mind – that Vaurgroth had made a lot of empty promises in order to seize power – Vetru might take it badly. Probably wouldn't even understand.

'How old are you, Vetru?'

'Old? I came from the egg . . . three years ago.'

'Anthar's prick. You're only three?'

'I am not set in form,' Vetru said proudly.

'What's that mean?'

'I shall be, in one, two years. I shall be *domenim*, like Tsur. That is good. But I could have been *ghelim*. You know what is that?'

'*Ghelim*.' Rufryd grimaced. 'Yes. Bhahdradomen who have changed shape to look and act like something else. Dra'a'ks, or other animals – I don't know, they could be anything. The ones I saw were like dra'a'ks.'

Vetru nodded happily. 'That would be good.'

'Good? Why? They were like animals, they couldn't speak. They don't have normal intelligence, do they?'

The hatchling didn't seem to understand him fully. 'They are proud,' he insisted. 'Or *neshrim*.'

'What's that?'

'Shape is like humans.'

Rufryd thought of Noli. 'Oh, shit,' he whispered.

'*Neshrim* I would like.'

'No, no you wouldn't,' Rufryd said emphatically.

'I would! That is only for the higher ones, not for us. But I am glad I am not *graukhim*!' Vetru drew his knees up, giggling. He pointed at the charred piece of meat that Rufryd was working on. 'Be eaten!'

'Well, no one's going to make you be a cow, are they?' Rufryd thought he was sharing the joke, but Vetru became serious.

'Not now,' he said thoughtfully. 'Too late for me. But egg of Tsur might.'

'Might what?'

'When it hatches. Chosen to be *domenim* or *ghelim* or *graukhim*.' He spoke slowly, struggling for the words. 'Tsur tell me. Ones who sent for flesh-animals, they are happy to go. Serve Bhahdradomen.'

Rufryd's hand fell into his lap. He stared at the half-eaten lump of meat. 'You mean, hatchlings sent to look after the cattle . . . don't you?'

Vetru bounced impatiently. 'No, no. Become them.'

Rufryd leapt to his feet. He ran a good five yards before he threw up. When the spasms subsided, he stood leaning against the thin trunk of a tree, gasping, almost sobbing with an overwhelming desire to be at home . . . wherever that was. Anywhere. Even Parione was better than this.

Slowly, taking deep breaths all the way, he went back to the campfire and sat down with his head in his hands.

Vetru looked anxious. 'Rufryd?' he said, trilling the Rs. 'What is wrong?'

'We have a word, "cannibalism". It means eating your

own kind. I don't know where it came from because there's no human culture that does that. The word must have come from you.'

'Me?'

'Not you, Vetru, I mean from your people. You eat each other, for gods' sake!'

'No. Only the *graukhim*.'

'But they're imprinted when they hatch! They're Bhahdradomen!'

Vetru plainly had no idea what Rufryd was upset about. 'But that is what we have always done. We have nothing else to eat. We can't eat the grass and leaves. But the *graukhim* can because they are . . .'

'Adapted? Changed?'

'Yes, they are shaped to do it. They take . . . energy of grass and trees and make it that we can eat it.'

'You make your own people into farm animals.'

Vetru was beginning to look confused and sulky. Rufryd sensed the other three Bhahdradomen close by, listening, although they wouldn't understand. 'Why is this wrong?' said Vetru. 'Do your animals have choice?'

'No, but . . . but they are *animals*, not changed humans!'

'But the Bhahdradomen, we give ourselves for each other. Serve each other. It is a pleasure for us to be *ghelim*, to be *graukhim*, to be anything that serve our *domenim*! Humans are selfish. We are not.'

'Fine,' Rufryd said, holding up his hands to calm Vetru down. 'We do things differently. But I can't eat it. So what the fuck am I going to live on?'

'But the flesh is good. I cook in the fire for you.'

'No! Don't even think about it, I'm not hungry.' Rufryd folded his arms round his stomach. He was sweating. 'Gods, I feel terrible.'

Something had poisoned him, as he'd feared. Not the meat, for he'd been feverish before he'd eaten it . . . the water, then, or the Bhahdradomen themselves. Cramps knotted his stomach. Ten times or more, as the night dragged on, he had to rush into the undergrowth and void his bowels, cleaning himself as best he could with stream-water and the leaves that grew on the bank. By the time the pains eased, he was almost too weak to move. The fire had gone out but he lacked the will to relight it. He lay shivering with fever, feeling that he was going to die.

'What is wrong?' Vetru said, touching him warily on the shoulder. 'Why do you shake?'

'I'm frozen,' Rufryd said through chattering teeth. 'I'm ill.'

'I warm you.'

The young Bhahdradomen lay down behind him and twined his long limbs round Rufryd's, clinging like a vine. The feeling was confining, unpleasant. But Vetru pulled a cloak over them both and his thin body was warm, hotter than a human body. Rufryd slept.

When he woke he felt dizzy and thirsty, but better. He wasn't going to die after all.

Vetru lit a fire. He learned fast. Rufryd, unsure what had made him ill, got the youngster to boil the water over the fire in a metal bowl that Tsur had sent with them. Tsur had given them herbs, too, that made a reasonable infusion. He drank what seemed pints of this tea, made a meagre breakfast of an oat cake, then rose, ready to go on.

One of the other Bhahdradomen appeared, spoke softly to Vetru, then vanished again.

'They see you are weak. You can walk?' Vetru said anxiously.

'I'm going to try. I'm not staying here, however bad I feel.'

'You die?'

'Not yet,' Rufryd said grimly. 'Don't worry about me. I'm tough.'

They made slow progress that day, since Rufryd had to stop and rest frequently. His appetite was returning with a vengeance but he kept going more on willpower than anything, saving the last of the oat-cakes for Su. Sooner or later he would have to start eating Bhahdradomen food, or starve.

The bleak brown land began to rise, dotted with villages like Tsur's. If the fringes of Vexor were semi-deserted, now Rufryd began to discover the pattern of Vexor's population, which clustered ever more thickly about a central point. His Bhahdradomen escorts moved closely around him as they passed through each *tzcement*. Long curious looks followed him; some hostile, some inscrutable. But his escorts' explanation of his presence must have been accepted, for no one tried to stop him. On the contrary, he found only hospitality like Tsur's, an eerily passive tolerance of his presence.

That night, he ate the last of his own rations. The next night he accepted Bhahdradomen meat – made a fire and roasted it, much to the villagers' interest – and ate it, and managed to keep it down.

Each night, as they slept in small musty huts that were thick with the stench of *graukhim*-hide, Vetru twined himself around Rufryd and refused to let him alone. Annoying at first, it swiftly became infuriating. Yet he couldn't bring himself to shake the creature off. Vetru seemed to suck out Rufryd's will to resist. There was nothing sexual in his behaviour; so far Rufryd had observed no sexual interaction at all among the Eaters. Rather, he felt like a parasitic vine, desperate to absorb some essence of Rufryd's.

The villages all ran together into one great settlement, so crowded with Bhahdradomen that Rufryd began to feel hemmed in by them. Huts gave way to long, low communal dwellings, joined one to another in an unending maze, crowded with Bhahdradomen inside and out. One great *tzcement*, or a town? Rufryd could get no clear explanation out of Vetru, who had no frame of comparison.

The further they went, the denser the population

became. There was no escape. *Graukhim* wandered the spaces between dwellings – which were more courtyards than streets – and Rufryd saw other, stranger creatures which he realised were *ghelim*, Bhahdradomen twisted into other shapes. Some were poor copies, grotesques. Others were frighteningly convincing. Sometimes he would jump out of his skin at the sight of a wolf or a huge raptor – but their eyes always gave them away.

The Bhahdradomen here were of a different order. Less passive, better dressed. Their clothing was more elaborate, with layers of hide and a wool-like material dyed black or green or bleached white. Some of them glared at Rufryd in curiosity as they went about their arcane business, unable to decide whether he was human or an exceptionally convincing *neschrim*. They put him in mind of vultures, with their pallid skins tinged green or yellowish-grey. He would get the impression of wings rising over hunched shoulders, scaled skins, claws, then he'd blink and they were humanoid again. Pale with malnourishment. Living in crowds, in shoals. Their land was sick and they were on the verge of dying, and they knew it.

Rufryd felt sorry for them.

Further in, he began to see signs of industry. Furnaces smoked and he heard the ring of metal. The smoke smelled flat and bitter on the cold air. A sprinkling of snow fell and turned the community to a grey and white wasteland.

That night, they were taken in by a group of *domenim* who seemed to think Rufryd was royalty. He'd never known Bhahdradomen so excited to meet a human before; and they spoke a little Paranian, which gave Vetru the chance to show off. They gave him food other than the ghastly meat; there were cakes made of pressed meal and berries, and fish – real fish! It tasted of sawdust and mud, but he wolfed it anyway, washed it down with the usual watery, herbal concoction. He was beginning to have dreams of fruit and vegetables and roasted chicken, of fresh bread, milk and cheese, of honeycomb and Marocian wine.

The friendly ones talked to him for hours, but it was all about the greatness of Vaurgroth, the wonderful things he was going to achieve, the beauty of worshipping the Ancestor. Rufryd thought they were never going to leave. At last he and Vetru were given the corner of the communal hall and a pile of hide to rest on. Lamps flamed in the darkness; some of the Bhahdradomen never seemed to sleep. There were *domenim* moving around and talking constantly, the metallic murmur of their voices scraping the inside of his skull. With the three watchers from Tsur's village to guard him, however, they left him alone.

Rufryd let Su sit on his shoulder as he fed her with the oatcake he'd kept for her. Then he took out paper, quill and a bottle of ink, and began to write a message to Helananthe, keeping his writing tiny so as to tell her as much as possible.

'I'm alone in Vexor,' he began. 'I was separated from Dawn and Mirias in a flood, don't know if they survived. You may know by now that Duke Tasq is dead and Branq'elin remained at Tasqabad. Only one blue-dove left, so this will be my only message. Vexor is dying and the Bhahdradomen here have almost nothing, except a kind of dignity. Hard to understand them. They live in communities they call *tzcement* and their hatchlings are given to the community to serve it. No concept of parent–child relationship, not as we'd know it. Most amazing thing is that they've been friendly to me, in their own way. I've a guide, Vetru, who even looked after me when I was sick. They're alien, but I don't feel that they're evil. More cloying than hostile. But there are *ghelim* about, made to resemble Aventurian animals, so something is going on. There is some industry, metal work perhaps, but I don't know what they are making. The only weapon I have seen is a whip that has the power to stun. Bloody painful it was, too.

'They looked at me as if I was mad when I mentioned Aazhoth. He's been gone a long time. The new leader is called Vaurgroth and they are obsessed with him. He's going to save them, take over Aventuria and Verdanholm – though they don't look capable of taking over a cowshed between them. Their devotion to Vaurgroth is fanatical, though. Hope to learn more when I see him. Vetru is taking me to a place called Zhahgrament, which I assume is their capital.'

He stopped there, his eyes heavy with tiredness. Vetru was looking over his shoulder. 'What are you doing?'

'Writing to the Queen,' said Rufryd. He folded up the letter and put it in a pocket, to finish when he had more news. 'Can you read Paranian?'

'No. You tell her I am good?'

'Yes, I tell her you're very good. Go to sleep.'

Rufryd was so tired he dropped off immediately. When he woke in the morning, Vetru was wound so tightly to his back that he couldn't even sit up. He struggled to disentangle himself from the ropy limbs.

'Will you get the fuck off me!' he barked, close to lashing out at Vetru.

The hatchling unwound himself and leaned over Rufryd, his face bland with sleep. 'I keep you warm,' he said.

'I don't need you to. I'm not ill.'

'But we blend,' Vetru said softly.

Then Rufryd saw.

Vetru's complexion had turned paler. Pinkness was flushing into the grey-green skin. His features were more definite, his eyes darker, a sheen of hair on his skull the exact same chestnut brown as Rufryd's . . .

Rufryd gave a hoarse scream and scrambled away from

469

him. He thought of Noli, Con's friend, who had looked so utterly human until you really *looked* at him. Vetru went on smiling and Rufryd got the hideous impression that he was looking at a rudimentary, malformed reflection of himself.

'Don't!' Rufryd gasped, hardly able to breathe.

'What?' said Vetru.

'Don't imprint on me! You're not human, you can't be human. Don't even try it. Be what you are, for fuck's sake! Don't do this to me!'

Rufryd jumped up as he spoke, bundled his pack together, slipped Su into his pocket and rushed out of the hall. And then had to go back in again, for outside was an enclosed courtyard. He'd been calm for days but now a wild upsurge of panic possessed him and he strode frantically through the maze, looking for another way to the open air, hoping instinct would take him in the right direction. His escorts followed him like ghosts. Dozens of Bhahdradomen turned to stare at him with piercing, reptilian eyes.

He shoved his way through them. Blind panic filled him. Must escape their terrible eyes, the crawling alien aura of them, their writhing tentacles and white, poisonous spines . . .

He tried to run but it was too crowded. His terror subsided and his vision cleared, and he was still inside the maze, still surrounded by crowds of *domenim* who looked at him with varied expressions of surprise, curiosity and indifference . . .

A few seconds later, Vetru was trotting at his side again. No escape.

'Nearly there now,' he said brightly. 'I take you to Vaurgroth.'

'Oh shit,' Rufryd whispered. 'Nuth and Anuth help me. What the hell have I done to deserve this?'

Vexor was killing him, slowly and cruelly. Rufryd ate their

470

food but it passed straight through him, giving him no nutrition. He soon gave up eating their meat, for there wasn't much and Vetru needed it. Instead he tried to live on the soggy meal-cakes with berries pressed into them like drops of blood, the occasional bony fish. But it didn't matter what he ate, he was light-headed and hungry and growing weaker by the day. The cold gnawed into him. The Bhahdradomen themselves seemed to be sipping his vitality, with every smile or touch or stare. Especially Vetru.

They emerged from the tangle of communal buildings on to a stretch of heathland and Rufryd saw their destination; the black cone of a hill with long, low constructions splaying like tentacles around it.

'There is Zhahgrament!' said Vetru. 'There Vaurgroth is.' Suddenly the hatchling seemed nervous, his excitement turning to fear.

They began to walk over the cold, dark heath towards the heart of Vexor. This stretch of land was far from empty, however; there appeared to be an army encampment scattered across it.

Bhahdradomen moved between a tangle of pied tents. Rufryd looked around warily as he and Vetru passed by. These were the first clear signs he'd seen of military activity. These *domenim* wore uniforms of a sort; long soft tunics that turned the same colour as the heath around them, belts bearing lightning-whips and other weapons he didn't recognise; long black tubes, strange knives and lumps of oily grey mineral.

These warriors all had the same look about them, something dry and cold and fanatical. He noticed also that they appeared much better fed than the people he'd seen so far. Rufryd smiled bitterly to himself. Of course, Vaurgroth would be taking the best *graukhim* from the outlying *tzcements* and feeding them to his troops. Dra'a'k-like *ghelim* wheeled above the camp, which stretched as far as he could see on either side.

Rufryd shuddered.

Several times, Tsur's three *domenim* were stopped by Bhahdradomen officers, but after a brief exchange they would look Rufryd over and let him pass.

There was nothing passive or pitiful about the officers. They radiated power and anger like heat. He felt it flowing physically from them, sapping his strength even further.

Rufryd fastened his eyes on the black hill and went on.

Soon he saw that its sides were festooned with dwellings and foundries and unknown edifices that hung like wrecked webs from a great, cone-shaped tower. The tower crowned the peak and was the colour of smoke. It resembled a bad parody of the Amber Citadel. The clouds cracked and the whole scene was flooded with red winter sunlight.

In the sudden blood-wash of light, Rufryd saw crowds, legions of Bhahdradomen moving to and fro in the streets below the grey citadel. Swift and busy as ants they flocked about their business. The atmosphere was feverish. Rufryd watched with a sense of growing dread, feeling as helpless as a leaf in the face of a tornado.

By the time they came to the fringe of the settlement, Vetru was clinging to Rufryd's hand, more frightened than he was.

'I don't want to see Vaurgroth,' the hatchling whispered.

'You don't have to. What are you scared of, anyway?'

'He is made of lightning. You can't look at him.'

'He's planning to invade Aventuria, isn't he?'

'Of course,' said Vetru, as if this were the most natural and obvious fact of life.

Rufryd hadn't believed it could be real until now. Vexor had lulled him with its poverty and desperation. But here, at the core, he felt the shimmer of coiled power. 'Oh shit,' he said under his breath. 'Oh, hell.'

The Bhahdradomen who moved around them now were quick and busy and alert. They were dressed in fine, scaly skins that had come from dra'a'ks – or, more likely, from *ghelim* – and they wore adornments of feathers and crystals around their necks and waists. Their eyes were dark, their skin so translucent that the veins and bones showed through.

'The higher ones,' Vetru whispered in awe. 'Some are not fixed in form. They change as they will.'

He dragged hard on Rufryd's hand, forcing him to stop. Rufryd turned, shocked as always to see in Vetru a skinny, young, unfinished version of himself.

'You don't have to come any further with me,' said Rufryd. 'You've done your job. Take the other three and go home.'

'Cannot leave you,' Vetru said.

Rufryd stood still for a moment, feeling the eyes of the 'higher ones' moving over him, drinking him. He felt that they could see straight through him, and despised him and his doomed little mission.

Suddenly, walking among them, he saw a human being.

His heart rocketed in relief. Shaking Vetru off, he went striding toward the brown-haired man – only to stop dead in shock. The man glanced at him with whiteless eyes and moved on. Not human, but a facsimile. *Neshrim*, like Noli.

'I think I've gone far enough,' Rufryd said to himself, pushing one hand back over his hair, close to panic. 'I can see what's happening. I'll send Su and then I'm going home.'

A *domenim* walked in front of him and stopped. Rufryd tried to turn away but the Bhahdradomen reached out and touched his arm. 'We have been looking for you,' he said.

The creature that faced him was not much over five feet tall and had a bird-like face, pearly skin and the carriage of an old but wise man. His Paranian was perfect, even down to the precise accent of Parione, his voice thin and metallic. He smiled, but the aura of power and confidence that radiated from him almost knocked Rufryd off his feet. A necklace of grey stones gleamed round his throat and he leaned on a plain ivory staff. Behind him stood an entourage dressed in sharp black and white. Their eyes were crimson.

'You are the Queen's envoy? Rufryd Arthryn-son?' he prompted.

'Er . . . yes.'

'News of your arrival has reached us. We came to welcome you. I am Rhazagramen, which I think would translate as Counsellor. I am chief aide to Vaurgroth of the Fire, Master of Light, Chosen of the Ancestor.'

Gods, Rufryd thought in panic, why the hell didn't Helananthe send Eldareth or someone who could actually do this? With an effort, he put his shoulders back and tried to seem confident.

'Yes, I came on behalf of Queen Helananthe,' he said quietly.

'Then you are welcome. Come, I shall take you to Vaurgroth.'

Rufryd glanced round. Vetru and the other three – who seemed comfortingly familiar in comparison to the razor-sharp creatures that now surrounded him – had vanished. He had no choice but to go with Rhazagramen. The wall of Vaurgroth's lair – he could hardly think of it as a castle – reared above him, glistening with dull rainbows, a spectrum split by oil.

'You have had a long journey,' said Rhazagramen as they walked.

'Yes, long and tiring.'

'It is good of the Queen to send you to us.'

'She wishes to extend her greetings to your people,' said Rufryd, doing his best to sound like a royal ambassador. 'To see how things are in Vexor. If you have any matters you wish to raise with her majesty . . .'

'To pre-empt any misunderstanding between us.'

'Exactly.'

'Very good of her. Very good. A shame, then, that she sends her envoy fifty years too late, and with nothing to offer us. A poor specimen of an envoy who does not even know that Aazhoth is seven years dead and that Vaurgroth is our leader now.'

The atmosphere arched cold and echoing above them. They were in the huge gateway in the wall, and other Bhahdradomen were standing aside to let the Counsellor pass through. Energy pricked in the air and the sweaty light of lamps washed the walls.

Rufryd stared at Rhazagramen. Saw naked hatred in the Bhahdradomen's eyes. The shock of seeing the razor of loathing through the silken layer of politeness made him gag.

'I ask your pardon, then,' Rufryd choked. 'No one came from Vexor to tell us of the change.'

He'd made a mistake. Rhazagramen's eyes flared green as acid. 'No one from Vexor is allowed to set foot in Aventuria. How then is it our fault? Your monarch should have sent envoys to us, years and centuries ago. Now at last one comes! It is too little and too late. Tell her that, Arthryn-son, if she must have word from us. Your presence is less even than that. It is an insult!'

The Counsellor strode on through the long archway, his staff echoing on the stone floor. Rufryd was seething. He was bad at being conciliatory. Hopeless.

'An insult?' he said thinly. 'I've risked my life to come here, and what do I find? Something that looks remarkably like the Bhahdradomen preparing for war. Against humans?'

'You should not have come here.'

'Tough. I'm here. And you needn't bother scaring me with death threats. I'm not really expecting to escape with my life, anyway.'

The Counsellor stopped and faced him. 'We shall not stoop to killing you. It would be pointless. There is nothing you can do to stop Vaurgroth's machine, nothing you can tell your Queen that will save her. I am old, very old, but I thank the Ancestor that I lived to see this day; Aventuria struck down from her arrogant perch at last. My people allowed the simple privilege of eating, and moving freely, and ordering their own existence. The Silver Plains avenged. Humans destroyed.'

Rufryd caught his breath in the force of the Counsellor's hatred. 'I was starting to sympathise with the Bhahdradomen, until I met you. You're the first one I've met who actually hates humans.'

Rhazagramen laughed. 'Ah, we all hate you. I am too old to bother with good manners, that is all. Wretched bags of blood.'

'At least we don't fucking well eat each other. We don't give up our children to be turned into flesh-animals.'

The Counsellor hissed. His voice rang off the walls. 'I loathe your kind. Making righteous indignation from your lack of comprehension! You disgust me. You are split in half and you couple in grotesque attempts to merge yourselves. You make religion of your imperfection – your goddesses, your gods – trying to sanctify your repellent existence. You have no idea how we despise you – your maleness and femaleness, your revolting urges that drive all clear thought from your animal brains. The Bhahdradomen are perfect. We are made in the image of the Ancestor, whole and self-contained. We create life from within ourselves, by the Ancestor's grace, as and when the Ancestor wills it.'

'So you don't have to mate to reproduce? You don't have sex at all? And you're proud of that, are you?'

His thin lips curled in disgust. 'Ancestor be praised. We are complete in ourselves. You are like things cut in half, striving to be joined.'

'I think you're jealous,' said Rufryd. He gave a sour smile. 'Gods, that's it, you're jealous of us!'

The look of contempt that Rhazagramen gave him could have withered grapes on the vine. Slowly he turned and poked Rufryd's arm with a single thin fingertip, hard enough to bruise. 'Shall we see if you are this rude to Vaurgroth himself?'

The arched corridor ended. Beyond lay a vast enclosure, open to the sky, surrounded on three sides by the tall, curved sweep of the wall. Directly in front was the peak of the hill itself, sweeping up into a chimney shape that terminated in a crater. This crater was tilted slightly downwards, so that those below could see into its maw. It was full of whirling green and violet energy; not unlike the damaged portal he'd seen on Q'enartre's Throne. It filled Rufryd with foreboding.

The whole strange arena thrummed with power. It was invisible, yet it bounced off the walls and whipped round in a vortex. Vaurgroth's courtiers were Bhahdradomen of great power and skill, Rufryd saw that in the shine of their skin and the ice of their expressions. He felt like falling to his knees. They were proud and slow moving, with great veined heads, cold all-knowing eyes.

On a tall dais, some thirty feet below the crater, stood Vaurgroth himself.

The sight of him stole the last of Rufryd's strength, squeezed him white with fear.

Physically he was small. He wore a stiff robe of quilted red hide, with ornate touches, metallic jewels on the chest and the sleeves. The head was ice-white, with flushes of red and green moving like mysterious lights under the skin. On the skull was a pattern like a red spider's web, and a single slim white skein of hair sprouting from it, woven with bones and with knuckles of haematite.

He had a pet beside him, a thing like a tall dog that was covered in greenish-gold scales, but when Rufryd looked into its eyes, he saw that it too was Bhahdradomen, a *ghelim*, mutated to some whim of its master's.

But psychically . . .

Vaurgroth was a gigantic whirling cloud, a shadow made huge by powerful, flaring lamp. Rufryd had never used to be sensitive to such things but even he felt the *gauroth* that emanated from the leader. Now he was glad of his lack of sensitivity, for if he'd been like Lynden, it would have killed him. Losing all control, he collapsed and curled up in horror under the weight of that dreadful energy.

If it had a form it would be self-loathing. Power without conscience. A vampire that drained everything to feed its own insatiable appetite.

'. . . an envoy from Queen Helananthe of Aventuria,' Rhazagramen was saying.

'What has the Queen to say to me?'

Rufryd trembled. Vaurgroth had moved and was standing right over him. He couldn't speak.

The Master of Light laughed. 'I have this to say to her. *Enough.*'

'What?' Rufryd managed to drag himself into a kneeling position. All the Bhahdradomen seemed amused by his presence. Not the merest bit impressed or intimidated. They were laughing at him.

'I'm glad to see you are comfortable in that position. You will need to get used to it.' Vaurgroth's voice was as rich as the Counsellor's was thin. His tone was not hostile, but disconcertingly avuncular. 'Humans must learn that they have no divine right to Aventuria. Ancestor guided us to claim and rule and feed on that land. It is ours by right. Your forebears drove us out with tricks and sorcery, forcing us to exist on this barren square of rock. *My* forebears signed foolish agreements and gave in, like the *graukhim* they were. But that time is over, Aazhoth's order is swept away. Even Ghaurthror of the Flies, who struck such terror into human hearts in the days of glory, was a *domenim* of twigs, blind and foolish. We are strong now. And our suffering at your hands is over. I say again, *enough.*

'However, Rufryd my friend, there's no point in you returning to your Queen. You're dying; and even if you should survive the journey home, you will find us there long before you.'

To Rufryd's horror, Vaurgroth reached down and caressed his hair. He felt a crackle of static, a white buzz of nightmare suffusing his mind.

'You know, you're right,' Rufryd said desperately. 'Humans have been bloody stupid, not seeing what you were up to, not believing it!'

'I'm glad you agree with me,' said Vaurgroth, his tone warm. 'You seem a good young man. You sympathise with our grievances. Have no fear, we're not going to slaughter you all; humans like you shall be a great help to our cause.'

'I don't think so,' Rufryd whispered.

Vaurgroth didn't hear him. He was gliding away, his business with the Queen's envoy finished. Rufryd saw him as if from a very great distance and it seemed he was a hundred things at once; lightning and storm and wind and raging dark energy. Unstoppable.

Rhazagramen was grinning down at Rufryd. Others came and dragged him to his feet. They manhandled him out of Vaurgroth's presence, back along the stone archway, and threw him into the street outside.

He lay there for a time with dozens of Bhahdradomen walking around him. Not one of them paid him any attention. That was worse than anything; he expected to be feared, or reviled, or at least an object of curiosity. And he had been all those things. But to be ignored – never.

After a time he rallied his strength and crawled down the narrow street, until he managed to get to his feet and stumble to the edge of the grey citadel that was Zhahgrament. Where the narrow road gave on to the scrubby heath, he sank down beside a boulder. He felt that he didn't have much time. He drew out the unfinished letter and his pen and ink, and he finished writing the message.

His hand shook; his writing was scratchy, barely legible. But painstakingly he wrote everything he'd seen, and everything Vaurgroth had said.

He wondered, but how can the Bhahdradomen invade Aventuria? Do they have ships somewhere on Vexor's coast? I never heard that they were sailors . . .

Then he thought of the *ghelim*. Bursting out of the air in battle, vanishing again, as though some portal had spewed them out and sucked them back. Perhaps they didn't need ships or bridges or horses to travel into Aventuria. Perhaps Vaurgroth was planning something else entirely.

As Rufryd wrote, Vetru crawled up beside him and put his thin arm over his waist. 'What are you doing?'

Rufryd didn't answer. He finished the note, signed it; then rolled it up and slid it into the metal tube. Carefully – looking around to make sure no one saw him and stopped him – he slipped Su out of his pocket. She fluffed her feathers and blinked, voicing a mellifluous purr. He clasped the metal tube around her leg. She cooed obliviously; the last atom of sweetness in this terrible place, his last connection to life.

Rufryd kissed her beak, stroked her soft blue feathers. 'Breyid and Q'enartre and Nuth guide you, little one; all the goddesses and all the gods go with you.'

He flung her up into the air but she looped straight back to him. She was too tame. Gritting his teeth in bitter desperation he threw her again, higher and harder; and this time she fluttered and kept climbing into the grey void. Aching, he watched her winging away against the clouds. A small weak signal, a tiny messenger labouring too far, too late, to tell everyone what they already knew.

Chapter Nineteen. Loyalty and Mystery

All the way back to the house, Tanthe fought the urge to flee from Falthorn. She thought he might kill her if she tried – and why shouldn't he? What purpose did she serve now, unless it was to lure her Aelyr parents back to him? Her thoughts were in turmoil. She must tell Eldareth and Elrill what Falthorn planned but it didn't seem possible; he kept her beside him with her arm looped firmly through his and she had a feeling she wouldn't be allowed to see the others. She forced herself to appear calm.

On the long ridge of the hill, half a mile from the house, she saw something strange. A few Valahyr were gathered around a circle of turquoise stones, and between them stood a column of shimmering air. As she watched, sky-blue light rushed up through the column and she glimpsed a different scene, the ghost of a wall – there and gone so fast she couldn't identify it.

'What was that?' she said.

'Nothing,' said Falthorn. 'So tense, Tanthe. You had better have a drink when we arrive. We have various pleasant liquors that will relax you.'

'Relax me so much that I lose my memory for six months?' she said acidly.

'Be honest,' he said in a soft, confidential tone. 'Would you truly have preferred to experience every moment of your confinement? To feel the child growing, to form a relationship with it, to give birth, to see it taken away? You think you feel pain now? Actually you feel nothing. I clouded your memory to save you that pain, and it worked. In your heart, you don't truly feel that the child was real. Your indignation is a sham. I acted for your benefit, Tanthe.'

Her mouth opened as if he'd struck her in the stomach. No sound came out.

He tutted. 'You know, I still have hopes that when this is over you will understand what I've done and join the Valahyr of your own free will. You would be very welcome among us.'

'Like Auriel's welcome among you?'

'Auriel loves me.' Falthorn said it so easily that he had to believe it. 'So will you, dear. We'll sand the human edges off you, given time.'

'I'm perfectly happy with my human edges, thank you.' She swallowed. 'When are you going to do it?'

'What?'

'Give Aventuria to the Eaters.'

'Oh, that,' he said softly. 'Soon. Quite soon.'

They reached the house, climbed a flight of stairs to a balcony then entered the galleried room that overlooked the valley. There, to her surprise, he left her. 'Go up to the *sertance* hall if you are hungry,' he said matter-of-factly. 'You'll find refreshments there. I have things to attend to.'

Tanthe stood in fearful exhilaration as Falthorn left through one of the inner doorways. She was alone. At once she hurried up the stairs on to the gallery, up another flight and along the maze of corridors to their bed-chambers; no one there. She ran on through the house. Found the *sertance* hall deserted – food and drink still on the table for late-comers, but she had no appetite – and ran down again, searching room after room.

'Eldareth!' she called a couple of times. Why was it so quiet?

Coming into the room where she'd met Auriel the previous evening, she found Jthery sitting on the arm of a chair reading a book, his strawberry-blond hair hanging forward over his shoulder.

'Jthery!' she exclaimed. He looked up in surprise. 'Where are the others?'

'I'll take you to them,' he said.

482

'Well, hurry. I've got something really important to tell you all. I don't know what we're going to do.'

Jthery seemed unmoved by her urgency. He asked no questions; his face was oddly passive, his eyes bland. 'This way.'

He took her into corridors she'd never seen before, that snaked deep into the interior of the house. Here there were no windows, only a deep emerald light seeping in. 'Are you all right?' she said.

He smiled. A strange look, almost guilty. 'Yes, fine. Tanthe, something amazing happened . . . I'll tell you later.'

There were a handful of Falthorn's men and women idling in the corridors, but they seemed unconcerned by her presence. She took no notice of them. Jthery brought her to a large room lit with lamps whose crystal shades refracted the light into a white-gold dappling all over the silky wood of the walls and floor. It was a wide, open chamber with sections screened off and other doorways leading out of it. Here she found Elrill and Eldareth sitting cross-legged on cushions. They looked taut, restless, grim-faced.

'There you are, thank the Goddess!' Tanthe cried, rushing into the room.

They gave her no greeting. Eldareth actually groaned, and dropped his head in despair. Tanthe was confused, but too distraught to ask what he meant by it. 'We've got to leave,' she gasped. 'Go back to Earth and warn Helananthe. Falthorn means to give the Earth to the Bhahdradomen.'

Eldareth's head came up. He got to his feet, long limbs unfolding. 'What?'

Stammering, she told them what she'd seen.

He and Elrill stared at each other. Eldareth's face lengthened and pain clawed lines in his brow. Elrill hissed softly, 'Of course. Of course!'

'Come on, we have got to go back to Earth *now*!' Tanthe

483

said, pulling at Eldareth's arm. 'Get our weapons, get the horses. What on earth are you doing in here, anyway?'

'Oh, Tanthe,' Eldareth said heavily. He was shaking his head. It was only then that she finally realised something was wrong. Shadows moved in every doorway. Alarmed, she looked behind her and her heart sank in dismay.

Jthery had vanished. Instead the main doorway was filled with Valahyr warriors, holding dark, curved swords. Ostarial was there, smiling ruefully at her.

'Fuck, I don't believe this!' Tanthe snarled. Eldareth held her arm, reassuring or restraining her, perhaps both.

'Neither did we,' he said. 'Elrill and I found Princess Ghiseyma a few hours ago. Stupid. We should have known that Ostarial was following us. We've been under arrest ever since. You've just been led into the trap.'

'By Jthery?' she said. Suddenly she was so dizzy with frustration and despair she thought she would pass out. 'He can't have known what he was doing.'

'Oh, he knew,' said Ostarial, grinning.

'What's that supposed to mean?' Tanthe flared.

'You'd have to ask him. Our Uncle Falthorn is a man of strange tastes, it must be said. *Humans*!' He pulled a face. 'Calm down, cousin, because none of you are going anywhere until Falthorn gives the word.'

'You must tell me,' said Helananthe. 'Not only what Garnelys said to you when he was alive, but what he says to you now.'

'I can't,' Ysomir repeated. 'You promised you wouldn't do this.'

'I agreed to hold off until you'd made the key. That was all.'

'I take it the key did not unlock the thing you were expecting?' said Ysomir.

The cell was dark. The lamp threw shadows on to the wall, great black shades of the three women, Helananthe and Ysomir and the High Priestess Ariolne. Ysomir's eyes were bright with distress, her hands white on the edge of the table, but the more Helananthe questioned her the more stubborn she became.

Helananthe leaned forward, snarling her impatience. 'How many of them are there inside you?'

'I can't say.'

'You claimed Garnelys. Now you claim Maharoth! Where will it end? Will you have the spirit of every king or queen in history clamouring inside you?' She jumped to her feet and shouted, 'Do you expect me to believe this? Or are you simply intent on making a fool of me?'

Ysomir flinched. 'No! I didn't want you to know, because I knew you would do this! They're energies inside me, I can't make them do anything or tell me anything. I can't do it to order! If you are a fool, ma'am, it's only in that you won't listen to what I'm telling you!'

Helananthe was close to striking her. 'A *roth*-mage called Calabethron. Have you heard of him? Can you summon him into you?'

'No, I've never heard of him.'

'But you must have done, if King Maharoth speaks to you.'

'But he doesn't! I am not a machine to be used like this. I can't control it!'

Helananthe felt Ariolne's hand on her arm, warning and restraining her. She saw how close she'd come to losing all self-control. Sighing, she straightened up, folded her arms across her waist.

'You're being obstructive, Ysomir. Would you talk to Ariolne instead?'

'I don't want to talk to anyone,' Ysomir said hoarsely. 'Isn't it enough that I'm imprisoned? I want to be left alone.'

'Come,' said Ariolne. She rose, a slim cool figure in black. 'Let us leave. I don't think Ysomir can help us any more tonight, ma'am.'

The two women left the cell. The wardress shut the door

with a clank behind them as they made their way along the shadowy curve of the corridor.

'Ysomir is going to drive me insane,' said Helananthe.

'Perhaps you are expecting too much of her,' said Ariolne. 'Have you considered that she's telling the truth? That these dead spirits – if they are not a figment of her imagination – have no new information for you? She's afraid of you, ma'am, but she's stronger than you know. You'll never gain her cooperation by frightening her. You only make her dig her heels in.'

'Thanks for the lecture, good mother.' The Queen hissed her frustration between her teeth. 'Oh, I know what she's doing. It's the only power she has left, tantalising me with the promise of occult knowledge then withholding it. And I know that I'm the one who looks weak when I lose my temper. But it's only that there is so much at stake! Why can't she see that?'

'Leave her, ma'am,' Ariolne said softly. 'Concentrate on practical concerns.'

'A priestess tells me to be practical.' Helananthe grimaced.

'There is no one more practical than the priestesses of Nuth, who experience the Goddess as the very Earth herself.' They came to the steel gates that led out of the prison and back into the main body of the Amber Citadel. Ariolne held the lamp high as a warder let them through. 'In our rituals we travel deep into the darkest heart of Nuth, where most mortals would fear to go, and we look on her harshest face in our search for wisdom.'

'And?'

'She is angry. Sour energies are displacing the good. No one has heeded the warnings. A dark wind blows out of the past and it will tear the light away. So Nuth reveals.'

Chill waves of gooseflesh chased over Helananthe's body. 'Have you entreated Nuth to help us?'

'That is not how we work, ma'am, as well you know. We show her ourselves, and hope that she will reveal

486

herself in return. We don't ask her to intercede. We don't expect cheap miracles.'

'I know, I know. I meant that I thought she might have shown you what we ought to be doing.'

Ariolne was impassive, grave. 'Ma'am, she showed us that she, too, is in danger of destruction if the cold energies win.'

'How can a goddess be destroyed?'

'Easily, by being ignored and reviled. Yesterday a group of Bhahdradomen came to the Temple and said that they needed somewhere to worship the Ancestor.'

Helananthe stopped in her tracks. 'What? And what did you say to them?'

'We turned them away. We explained that they could not worship, on our premises, a god who would deny the existence of our gods. Nuth says this: "Yesterday you turned them away. Tomorrow you may not be able to."'

Helananthe shook her head, outraged. 'Never,' she said. 'I shall never let that happen! They become more impertinent by the day. Ariolne, you were right to turn them away and you must continue to do so. Would you send word to the Temple of Nepheter – indeed, to every temple in the city – that the Bhahdradomen must not be allowed to worship there?'

Ariolne gave her a haughty, sword-sharp look, as if Helananthe were trying to drive back the tide without noticing that it was already surging wildly around her knees. But she only said, 'Of course, ma'am.'

After she'd returned to the palace and parted with Ariolne, she went in search of Mawrdreth. She needed his bright optimism, not the High Priestess's pronouncements of doom. She needed his kind, clean spirit to cleanse Ysomir from her skin.

Ariolne's news had disturbed her more deeply than she would admit. Parione was under siege. The Bhahdra-domen refugees washed around its edges, venturing further along the city streets every day. Growing bolder, it seemed, though 'bold' was hardly the word she'd use to describe their demeanour. They attacked no one. They stole nothing. They were simply *there*, clustering on the roads that led into the city from the meadows, the vineyards and the lush hills that lay around it. Edging their way inwards.

Mawrdreth had been down with the army, which remained an uneasy amalgam of her own loyal but amateurish troops, and the official army that had fought for Garnelys. At her instruction, Mawrdreth had rallied them and set them to patrol the streets and keep the Bhahdradomen at bay. The refugees went readily when they were herded away, offering no resistance. Yet they kept coming back, as persistent as ants. They stood or sat in clusters along the roadsides, doing nothing, looking out of their blank mould-green eyes, as if waiting for something to happen.

The citizens of Parione were furious.

They were beginning to panic, Helan knew, and they blamed her for her failure to deal with the Eaters. Her meetings with the Council of the Sun Chamber were becoming increasingly rancorous, deteriorating as often as not into shouting matches between different factions however hard she tried to keep things calm. Helan had begun to dread these encounters. She was losing authority.

Her persecution of Ysomir, of which she was not proud, was born of sheer desperation. She wanted the shade of Garnelys, or Maharoth, or Hetys, or Calabethron – anyone – to manifest and tell her how to handle this.

Sometimes she cursed Garnelys. Thanks to his actions, people had lost their unquestioning trust in their monarch. They weren't afraid to challenge her . . . even to depose her? Perhaps that was healthy, in one way. She wanted them to trust her because she proved worthy of it, not because it was her due. But at present, all it did was to undermine her.

Each time she sat on the Sapphire Throne, it seemed to scorch her with its dark secret. Only she and Mawrdreth knew, but one day she would have to tell everyone the truth. The secret cache beneath the throne was empty, the Basilisk weapons lost, Aventuria defenceless.

Above the city, the great dome of the sky had cleared. The storms rolled away, leaving only a few flickers of greenish lightning gnawing at the eastern horizon. Under the icy calm of a blue, cirrus-streaked sky, Parione waited.

She found Mawrdreth in the Sun Chamber. He was at the Tree of Life window, looking out at the city through one of the clear panes. As she went to him and slipped her hand through his arm, he turned to her and smiled, but his face – like hers – was troubled.

'Any luck?' he asked.

'None,' she sighed. She told him about her fruitless encounter with Ysomir, Ariolne's ominous news. 'After we defeated my grandfather, I felt in charge,' she went on. 'I thought all conflict was over, peace restored for ever. I didn't see what was going on under the surface and now I'm paying. It's all slipping away from me and I didn't even see it happening!'

Mawrdreth held her but said nothing. He'd run out of things to say. He was brave and eager to please but so inexperienced . . . she would have done anything to have Eldareth there instead, then felt guilty for the thought. The prospect of another night spent in the caverns beneath the *xauroth* sphere, painstakingly deciphering the tablets – trying to discover the exact nature of the weapons that had been stolen, and instructions for recreating them – exhausted her. But there was no choice. She couldn't seem to sleep at all these days.

'Your majesty?' Her aide's voice echoed from the doorway.

She turned, trying to shake off her gloom. 'Yes, Lord Derione?'

He came striding towards her, businesslike but

animated. 'Ma'am, there is a messenger to see you.'

The Queen raised her eyebrows. 'I take it there is a good reason for you not dealing with it yourself?'

'I think you will wish to see her in person, ma'am. She has come from Verdanholm, bearing a message from the Aelyr.'

'Well, show her in immediately!'

The young woman who entered the Sun Chamber was small and slender, with long black hair and a creamy complexion with a touch of gold in it, a glow like diffuse sunlight. She wore black riding clothes and over them a soft open robe of indigo, held with a snowy jewel on each shoulder. Regarding her, Helananthe felt an eerie thrill. She was human-looking yet so obviously different. Shining, quick-moving, fey.

'Your majesty,' the woman began, bowing. 'I am Lady Alviath of the Valahyr. I come from the house of Valthiell and Cielemne, on behalf of Lord Falthorn. He returns the greetings extended to him by the royal party sent to him on your behalf, and he wishes you to know that he appreciates your concerns. Lord Falthorn requests that you grant an audience to him and his retinue at your earliest convenience.'

A bud of relief pushed up inside Helan. So Eldareth had reached Verdanholm safely. 'Of course I shall see him. Will Lord Eldareth come with him?'

'Ma'am, he will.'

The bud flowered into full-blown elation. Helan could have collapsed with joy. Eldareth was coming home. Now she could reopen a dialogue with the Aelyr, clear up all misunderstandings, regain the allies she so desperately needed.

She said cautiously, 'I suppose there is no news of my mother, Princess Ghiseyma?'

'I wasn't told. Your pardon, ma'am. I trust my arrival is not untimely or disappointing?'

'Far from it. My dear Lady Alviath, this news is more

490

welcome than you can know. I can only say, what kept you?'

Several days passed. Locked in their prison of living wood, Tanthe felt Verdanholm playing all its most deceptive tricks on her. There was no night or day, only the flicker of crystal lamps and the faint buzz of the stars outside. Time dragged, or made odd little leaps. Sometimes she was convinced that the room was floating in some strange blue-green limbo; she even felt it moving when she lay down to sleep.

She and Elrill and Eldareth talked endlessly, speculating on Falthorn's plans, dissecting every word he'd said to them. They discussed ways of escape, but none seemed possible. With the Valahyr constantly watching them, it was hard even to talk without being overheard.

Their captivity was civilised enough. They were brought good food and fresh clothes, and they were free to bathe in relative privacy behind a set of screens, where a chilly spring had been channelled to run first through a bath and then beneath a privy, both carved from green-veined marble in the shape of shells. But it was maddening being kept prisoner, especially when no one would answer their questions.

Their conversations began to go round in the same circles. They grew irritated with one another. Elrill frequently retreated into silence as glacial as his beloved Whiteveil Mountains, while Eldareth was restless and Tanthe venomous with frustration.

She woke from a deep, tortuous sleep. The meal the Valahyr brought them consisted of the foods they usually ate for breakfast – soft white grains wrapped in herby leaves, lemon-tasting fruits and thin biscuits that melted on the tongue – so she assumed it was morning. They sat in a tight group on the floor around the dishes, the better to talk without being overheard.

'How long have we been here?' said Tanthe.

491

'Nine days,' Elrill answered.

'How can you be so sure? Verdanholm plays tricks. The Valahyr might be playing games with us!'

'I am Aelyr,' he replied sharply. 'Verdanholm plays no such games with me.'

'Right. Nine days. I believe you.'

Eldareth breathed out heavily. 'I only hope Ghiseyma and the boy are well.'

'And what about Jthery and Auriel?' Tanthe said under her breath. 'I dread to think what he's done to them.'

'Alas, there are no Zampherai to break us from this prison,' said Eldareth. 'We're on our own.'

'I managed to escape last time,' said Tanthe. 'I wish I'd taken Ostarial's stupid head off while I had the chance. I knew this was going to happen, yet we all walked into Falthorn's trap anyway! I can't believe we were all so gullible – especially you two.'

Elrill did not respond to her insult. Carefully – so the guards would not see what he was doing – he drew the *anametris* sphere from a pocket of his robe and cradled it in his lap.

Eldareth gave her a sour look, but didn't take offence. 'Believe me, I'm more angry with my own powerlessness than ever you could be. I thought that a sword and a degree of cunning would always be enough to keep me out of trouble, but it isn't. All I could have learned from my mother . . .' he trailed off, frowning. Then he shook his head. 'Sometimes there is nothing to do but sit tight and wait. At least Falthorn hasn't killed us.'

'I don't think it's his style,' said Tanthe. 'He can't show off to us if we're dead.'

'I think he's more pragmatic than that. It seems we're more use to him alive. A few more for his hostage collection. So he must do something with us eventually, but when?' Eldareth breathed out through his teeth. 'I like action. The hardest lesson I've ever had to learn is patience.'

Elrill said, 'I hadn't realised just how powerful he has become.' He spoke thoughtfully, his attention fixed on the sphere. Tanthe saw it glowing through his fingers. 'And so quietly that no one knew. He must have been working for years. There is *gauroth* all around him, so strong that I could smell it. *Gauroth* is an energy that the Aelyr are sworn not to use. A terrible energy that is born of pain and cruelty.' He fell silent for a few moments. Then he said suddenly, 'There is a portal nearby!'

Tanthe started. She saw how bright and active the *anametris* was. Its inner shells were revolving, one inside the other, throwing off white glints. 'Where?' she said. 'Can we go through it?'

Elrill shook his head gravely. 'Alas, no. It is not in this room. It's outside somewhere, though not far away. It must be powerful, for the sphere to respond like this.'

He slipped the sphere away, before the guards noticed.

'Are you sure you can't create just a tiny portal with that?' Tanthe whispered.

'It's not possible.' Elrill gave her a stern look. He often seemed annoyed with her impatience, but she didn't care. 'The *anametris* helps us to find portals and to open them. However, a key is no use without a door.'

'I know. Sorry,' she hissed. She got to her feet and paced around the room, her boots echoing on the satiny planks of the floor. Turning, she saw a pale figure standing in the main doorway. It was Jthery.

'You made me jump!' she gasped. She rushed to him and seized his sleeve. There were Valahyr guards smiling behind him but she ignored them, pulling him into the room. 'Jthery, where have you been?'

He still had the same dreamy expression as before, when he'd led her into the trap. 'It's a long story,' he said.

'What happened? Are you a prisoner, or what?'

'I don't know,' he said.

Tanthe gave him a little shake. 'What's wrong with you?'

493

'Nothing.'

'Well, something's going on. You look as guilty as hell.'

His fair cheeks coloured. 'Falthorn sent me to speak to you . . .'

'Falthorn *sent* you? First you bring me down here to be locked up, now you're running errands for him. What's going on?' Tanthe was furious, gripping the front of Jthery's pale, embroidered robe. 'Why aren't you being kept prisoner with the rest of us? You're one of us, so why's Falthorn suddenly trust you?'

He looked away from her, a picture of awkwardness. 'Tanthe, not now.'

'Did he give you that milky wine that tastes of elder-berries, or are you sleeping with him?'

'Tanthe.' Eldareth came and gently pulled her away from Jthery. 'Give him a chance to speak.'

Flustered, Jthery said, 'He asked me to tell you that he's ready. We're going back to Earth.'

Tanthe, Elrill and Eldareth paused, looking at each other in shock. Then Eldareth shrugged and said, 'Well then, we'd better go with them. At last, something's happening!'

Briskly they followed Jthery out of their prison. The Valahyr led them along corridors and up stairs to the higher levels of the house. The daylight was blinding after their captivity, the colours shockingly vivid. They were relieved to be on the move, nervous of what was to follow. As they went, Tanthe walked beside Jthery, her hand through his taut, reluctant arm. Elrill and Eldareth were behind them.

'Well?' she whispered. 'Look, Jthery, I thought we were friends. Tell me what Falthorn's done to you. He's very plausible. Has he talked you over to his side, threatened you, bribed you?'

'No!' Jthery flashed back. 'He hasn't drugged or enchanted me, either. He didn't need to.'

Tanthe looked hard at him. 'You seem to have your wits about you. That's why I don't understand.'

Jthery shrugged, blushing at her scrutiny. 'I don't necessarily agree with what he's doing, but I can see why he's doing it. I've never met anyone like him, Tanthe, I'm sorry. I can't help it.'

'Oh, gods, don't tell me you've fallen for him! What is this, hero-worship or sex?'

'Keep your voice down!' he said. 'Do you have to be so outspoken? It's nothing like that. I admire him.'

'But he's a complete bastard!' Tanthe cried. The Valahyr guards gave her dark looks.

'No, he isn't. Even if he is, I don't care,' Jthery said stubbornly. 'It doesn't matter. Falthorn has this wonderful power about him, an aura. He's beautiful. He's strong; that's what people don't like about him.'

Tanthe was dismayed. 'He's really got to you, hasn't he? I didn't realise you liked men. I didn't realise he did, either.'

'Well, you don't know everything, do you?' Jthery said tartly. 'But I told you, we're not lovers! Not . . .'

'Ah, got you!' she exclaimed. '"Not yet", you were going to say. Being a tease, is he? I should have realised. Rufryd would say I'm too busy thinking about myself to notice such blatantly obvious things about other people and he's probably right. Of course, it explains a lot . . .'

'Like what?'

'Why Falthorn has no wife, despite being so wonderfully attractive. Why he got Auriel to seduce me instead of doing the job himself.'

'You're so cynical, Tanthe,' Jthery murmured. 'He's not this cold, hard person you seem to think. Not with me, anyway.'

'Oh, Jthery, open your eyes! He's using you!'

He glared sideways at her, angry and stubborn. 'No, he isn't. He's ruthless because he has to be, but he's so much more than that. Tanthe, he's what I came to find.'

She frowned. 'I was under the impression you came with us to look for Ghiseyma.'

'No. There was always something else. Now I know it's Falthorn, and the knowledge he's going to reveal to me. Something wonderful is going to happen.' Jthery was suddenly distant; focussed on his own dreams, blind to her nightmare. 'But if you're going to be like this, I wish I hadn't told you.'

'Fine, do what you want,' she said through her teeth. 'Just remember, when you see Lord Wonderful for what he really is – Tanthe says, "I told you so".'

They had come to a large chamber, flooded golden by the Verdanholm sun. Here Falthorn was waiting, with his family gathered around him and Auriel at his side. Seeing the prisoners, he smiled.

'I'm so sorry for the inconvenience you've suffered,' he said, for all the world as if he'd kept them waiting ten minutes, not ten days. 'You appreciate that I couldn't let you take my hostages away, nor could I risk you carrying warnings to your Queen. I trust you were comfortable?'

'We can't fault you on that,' Eldareth said. 'What now?'

'We're going to Aventuria. Just a few preparations first. Jthery?'

He went obediently to Falthorn's side. Falthorn put a possessive arm around his shoulders and smiled straight into Tanthe's eyes. His irises were like pleated ice around the intense black core of his pupils. Crystalline, ruthless, consuming.

'Jthery,' Falthorn said again in a gentle voice, turning to the younger man. 'Would you leave us now? Go to the garden until we've left; I shall be back within a few days.'

Jthery frowned. 'But I thought I was to come with you.'

'No, I want you to stay here,' said Falthorn. 'I don't need you in Aventuria, I need you in Verdanholm.' Jthery tried to argue but the Valahyr was insistent. 'Go. Be patient. I shall come back to you and you'll see that I kept all my promises.'

Reluctantly, Jthery did as he said. He gave Tanthe a last, painful look; then he was gone, his robe whispering on the floor as he hurried through the doorway. She glared after him. Turning her gaze to Auriel, she found him already looking at her; he appeared afraid and helpless, all the beautiful lines of his body limp with defeat. She saw that his wrists were bound together with manacles joined by a silver chain. Light sparked on the silver.

Behind Falthorn she glimpsed a strange object, a box some six feet high and four wide, covered in a shining cloth of gold. Tanthe couldn't tell what it was. There was something theatrical about it, the potential for a grand melodramatic gesture.

Several of the Valahyr seized Eldareth and Elrill, dragging their arms behind their backs and clasping their wrists with chained manacles like Auriel's. The two men struggled, but there was nothing they could do. The Valahyr would come to her next. It was her last chance.

Something snapped inside Tanthe.

She flung herself at Falthorn, aiming at his throat. She meant to strangle him. Her first blow was good; her fist took him straight in the larynx – the most painful place for human and Aelyr alike, judging by the way he doubled up, choking.

Auriel started away in shock. He didn't try to stop her. As Falthorn doubled over, she brought up her knee to connect with his chin. Her sight was crimson with fury. As he fell she leapt on to him, hands reaching for his windpipe. She was determined to kill him.

Half a dozen Valahyr hands closed on her, but they couldn't move her. Some wild power moved in Tanthe, born of fury.

'You'll give nothing to the Eaters!' she screamed. 'Not the Earth, and not my child!'

Falthorn's eyes glared up at her, red-rimmed. Her fingers began to squeeze his throat. He clawed at her arms but couldn't dislodge her.

The force that stopped her wasn't physical.

She saw it; a cylinder of dark mist that came flying out

497

of his forehead and straight into hers.

The *gauroth* hit her like a black wall. It flung her backwards, away from Falthorn. She threw up her hands but instead of hitting the floor she went on falling, her breath hissing out of her lungs in a soundless scream.

She found herself on a plain that was black yet seemed to glow. She was crawling on all fours, feeling that she had always been there and always would be there, weeping for something she'd lost. Something she couldn't even remember.

Pale figures moved on the plain. They met, spoke, moved on to the next figure and the next in a slow courtly dance. Terror filled her. The dance seemed meaningless but she knew it heralded a vast, unstoppable nightmare. The pale figures were exchanging information, making plans.

She turned away from them and began to crawl towards the mountains. Bleak slopes and bottomless valleys under an ebony sky, holding nothing but loneliness and despair.

'Help me. Help me,' Tanthe mouthed. She could make no sound. There was no one to hear her.

She felt years passing. Her mind was fragmenting. And she was still crawling towards the mountains. Still struggling to breathe.

Someone was calling a strange name, her own name distorted. 'Talanthyr, Talanthe.'

There were two faces looking down at her. A woman with an oval face, so like her own she might have been looking in a mirror. Warm, wise, anxious eyes, long dark red hair floating. A man who looked like Falthorn . . . his face longer and squarer, the eyes so pale they were nearly silver, his hair long and blue-black. He looked harsher than Falthorn and yet more honest.

Knowledge flashed like diamonds in her brain. These were her parents.

'Fiomir,' she said, reaching for them. 'Talthaliorn?'

They grasped her hands, lifted her up. The dreadful

landscape yawed all around them, changing like the sea but ultimately, eternally the same. Their hands on her were flesh, then liquid, then light passing through her; there and not there. Their voices were indistinct.

'Talanthyr, Talanthyriel,' said the woman.

'Mother?' said Tanthe. The word felt weird in her mouth.

'How did you come here?' Fiomir said. 'Did Falthorn take you too? We tried so hard to hide you. I'm sorry, so sorry.'

'Where is this place?'

'This is the *ezht*,' said the man. 'A place between the real worlds. Nowhere. Un-life.'

'What are we doing here?' Panic rose and seethed in her.

'Falthorn has trapped us here. He can't control us, so he trapped us.'

'No,' Tanthe sobbed. 'No.' But there was a weird joy buried inside her desolation. She'd found her parents. Her Aelyr parents. And there was so much to say but she couldn't say any of it because this was not real, this was a nightmare.

She saw a tiny white figure . . . how far away she couldn't tell. It seemed close enough to touch, then miles away. A slim Aelyr baby, but where its head should have been there was a ball of white light, like a sun.

'What's that?' she cried.

'That's the child,' said Fiomir.

'We must reach it,' Tanthe said. 'If we can only touch it, everything will be all right.'

She struck out towards the child like a swimmer, but her father caught her and spun her round. 'It's not real,' he said.

They held her. She looked into their lovely mysterious faces and she felt overwhelmed. To find them but to be trapped here for ever . . . oh, but to find them . . .

The universe jolted.

Her parents were whisked away from her on a tornado, fragmenting.

Tanthe found herself lying on the floor at Falthorn's feet. Reality rushed in, flattened her, crushed her chest so she couldn't breathe. She lay shuddering. The black plain and bleak mountains still shimmered in the back of her mind . . . she'd spent eternity there, how could she be here again? Her fingers groped at the silken floorboards. How could she have been so close to her Aelyr parents, only to lose them again?

There was a clink of chains. Auriel was bending down to her, trying to stroke her face without trailing the chains on her head.

'Fliyet?' he said softly. 'It's all right, you're back. You were only there a minute.'

She pulled herself up and clung to him. 'Our parents are there!' she said hoarsely. 'Trapped in the *ezht*!'

'No.' Auriel cradled her. 'You see things there that aren't real. That's what it's like. I never wanted you to find out.' The warmth of his arms helped bring her back to reality. Then the wretched Valahyr dragged him away from her and hauled Tanthe to her feet.

She stood dazed. Metal cuffs were clamped to her dangling wrists.

Elrill and Eldareth both had swords at their throats; clearly they'd tried to help her in spite of their manacles. Falthorn stared at her with narrow eyes.

'I can put you there and leave you there,' he said. 'It's worse than dying, believe me. But you know that now. So are you going to stop being tedious and come along quietly with us?'

Tanthe looked at the Valahyr lord and was, for the first time, completely terrified of him. Now she understood Auriel. She nodded, mute.

'Good. Let us go and reclaim Verdanholm.'

Chapter Twenty. Vaurgroth Rising

Eldareth was desperately concerned for Tanthe. He'd been horrified when she'd launched herself at Falthorn. He had tried to reach her – too late. Suddenly he knew what Elrill meant by the smell of *gauroth*. A burnt-metal stink, a crackle of darkness swooping from Falthorn's skull into hers.

Tanthe had only been unconscious a few seconds but when she came back, she was different. The light had fled from her eyes.

The grandparents, Valthiell and Cielemne, watched from the gallery above as Falthorn led his party out of the room. Eldareth glanced at them but they were inscrutable. Not daring to act for themselves, but happy to let their son do this dirty work for them? That was the impression he got. Or disapproving of their son's actions, but unable to stop him? Or, most likely, simply seeing him as their champion, their saviour.

Falthorn went in the lead, with Ostarial and ten or so of his Valahyr around him. The chained ones – Elrill, Eldareth, Tanthe and Auriel – moved in the centre, surrounded by more Valahyr soldiers. Behind them, another group of Falthorn's men and women were bringing the strange tall box covered in gold cloth. It tilted back to run on wheels, but they had a hard time manhandling it down the stairs and out into the gardens below the house.

Here, more Valahyr joined them. Others stood watching.

As they walked, Eldareth said, 'Are you all right, Tanthe?'

'I think so.'

'What did he do to you?'

'Sent me somewhere I never want to go again.'

'I hate to point out the obvious, but wasn't it just a little rash of you to attack a *gauroth*-mage in a roomful of his soldiers while all your friends are chained up?'

She groaned. 'I can't believe I did it. He's so powerful, Eld.'

'I know.' He thought, and now I can see all the wrong turns I have made in my life. Rejecting my mother's path because of what my father was . . . now I see that a sword was never going to be enough . . .

'A terrible place, Eld,' Tanthe said. 'I can't even begin to describe it. I never want to go there again; but I must.'

'What?'

Her head came up and her spirit rekindled, deep in her eyes. 'My parents are there. I don't know whether their bodies are there or only their spirits, but they are trapped. He couldn't make them come to him or bend them to his will, so somehow he's imprisoned them in the *ezht* instead.'

Auriel began to say something, but she turned on him.

'Don't, Auriel,' she said. 'I touched them, I spoke to them. I didn't imagine them. They were as real to me as you are!'

'A nice touch, the way Falthorn sent Jthery out of the way before the unpleasantness started,' Eldareth growled. 'I always suspected that lad was away with the faeries. But what possessed him to be such an idiot—'

'I feel sorry for him,' Tanthe said acidly. 'Even the *ezht* can't be a worse nightmare than being in love with Falthorn. That's Jthery's life, what's left of it, fucked up for good.'

A deep sound was shaking the air. As they climbed, Eldareth saw what looked like a heat-haze, rippling up into the sky with the ferocity of fire. Seen through it, the daystars shimmered. 'What's that?' he said.

'I believe that is the portal that set the *anametris* resonating,' said Elrill. 'A huge portal.'

As they came up on to the spine of the ridge they saw it clearly. It was poised on the highest point of the ridge, like whale-spouts Eldareth had seen in the northern ocean; a leaping fountain of aquamarine light. It was a good fifty yards across, dwarfing the standing stones that were its catalyst.

Elrill gasped. 'I've never seen a *rothanamir* of such size before. The *roth* needed to crack the fabric between worlds is vast. The portal on the other side must be of incredible power too, to balance this.'

'It is beautiful,' said Eldareth. 'There's no denying it.'

Valahyr swarmed over the hillside. There were a good number of Fhelethyr there too, Eldareth noted in surprise, mere spectators who were being kept well away from the main action. He noticed other Aelyr among them who appeared to be of *eretrue* he didn't recognise.

'I have a feeling that's what the war was about,' Eldareth said. 'To wrest control of this portal from the Fhelethyr.'

Elrill nodded. 'You could be right. It's probable that Falthorn discovered this to be the most powerful site for his needs. The house no doubt was a useful bonus.'

Falthorn led his party so close to the portal that its power made their hair stand on end. Heat came from it, and it boomed with deep, atonal notes. Here Falthorn paused for a minute or two. Then Ostarial said, 'They're coming, Uncle!'

A smaller column, smoke-grey, swirled inside the light; a second portal within the first. The tension among the Valahyr was palpable. It was the first time – apart from when Tanthe had hit him – that Eldareth had seen Falthorn look anything but relaxed. Out of the smoke appeared a group of ten figures, who quickly got their bearings and strode towards Falthorn.

'Q'enartre's teeth,' said Eldareth.

The newcomers were Bhahdradomen, but of no order he'd ever seen before. No downtrodden peasants, these.

Nine of them were dressed in fine, scaly skins of black and green, adorned with grey and black crystals. They carried themselves with the easy self-assurance of snakes; measured, watchful, regal and lethal.

But the one who led them . . .

He was dressed in scarlet, blazing like a red-hot sword. He was slim and straight, and although it was hard to tell the age of Bhahdradomen, he seemed young and dynamic in comparison to those around him. His face was ash-white, with fugitive colours moving beneath the skin. A long rope of white hair sprang from the dome of his head, but otherwise he was bald, his scalp tattooed with a red spider's web. He moved light and straight as a spear. No question of his status. Authority flowed from him, and soul-sapping radiance; a hunger that sucked in everything around it.

'Abomination,' breathed Elrill.

'That must be their leader,' said Eldareth.

'I thought Aazhoth was an ancient old fool,' said Tanthe. They were silent. Falthorn and the Bhahdradomen leader approached each other warily. They exchanged a measured series of salutes, to show each other respect without any loss of authority. Finally, and horribly, they clasped hands.

'Lord Vaurgroth, Master of Light, we welcome you,' said Falthorn. 'All is ready. The portal awaits you. Earth awaits you.'

'We've got to stop them,' Tanthe whispered.

'Lord Falthorn, you bargain hard,' said Vaurgroth. His voice was unexpectedly melodic yet disturbing. It crept pleasantly into the ears and lingered like the resonance of thunder. 'As of today we cease hostilities against the Aelyr and forgo all claim upon Verdanholm – providing you deliver what you have promised.'

'My dear Lord Vaurgroth, Aventuria is waiting for you.'

Vaurgroth's mouth split in a grin. The Valahyr lord and the Bhahdradomen smiled broadly at each other like serpents, joyful yet calculating.

'Then let us not delay.'

Falthorn turned and addressed the Aelyr on the hillside, directing his speech pointedly to the Fhelethyr and other *eretrue*. 'Today, all attacks upon Verdanholm by the Bhahdradomen have ceased. From this day on, Verdanholm shall be whole, peaceful and inviolate. You shall remember that it was I, Falthorn of the Valahyr, who ended the siege and set Verdanholm free!'

A wild song broke from the Valahyr; their equivalent, Eldareth thought, of cheering.

Side by side, Falthorn and Vaurgroth stepped into the portal. They were followed by their respective retinues. Then Ostarial and the Valahyr guards were urging their chained captives into the whirling light. Eldareth walked forward, noting the tense faces of his companions.

The sea-green light consumed them. There was a long step down, a whirling jolt, darkness and swimming dizziness. The air changed, becoming suddenly thick and cold. Eldareth checked that the others were alongside him, then he quickly looked around.

They were standing in what seemed to be a chimney built of marble. The walls were pale, the air grainy with damp and the stink of raw stone and soil. In a burst of inspiration, Eldareth realised where they were.

'This is the Tower,' he whispered. 'The Heliodor Tower!'

Helananthe couldn't bear to waste a minute. While she was waiting for the Aelyr party to arrive, she went to her private office and gulped down a cup of tea while she looked over the latest information on the Bhahdradomen problem.

The figures horrified her. She pushed the parchment pages at Mawrdreth and strode back and forth in front of her desk.

'These Bhahdradomen cannot all be from pockets on the mainland. There were never this many. I've studied the records. Even if they have been laying eggs like frogspawn there could not be this many! So how are they getting here?'

Mawrdreth looked up at her. He was exhausted, poor lamb. He worked ceaselessly and uncomplainingly, but she was sure he must regret marrying her. Even she couldn't have warned him that kingship meant not a life of luxury, but fear, sleepless nights, hours crouched in damp subterranean chambers, aching bones and headaches.

His face was grave. 'Helan,' he said. 'We know that in the old days they had the ability to move from one place to another in an instant. They could fold time in a small way, which enabled them apparently to step out of nowhere.'

'But that power was taken away from them. One of the Basilisk weapons destroyed it.'

'But they've got the power back.' Mawrdreth looked steadily at her. 'We know that they regained it at least two years ago, probably more.'

'I never wanted to think about this. Yes, the reports we heard of *ghelim* appearing and vanishing in mid air, helping Garnelys's troops to round up the conscripts . . . too horrible to contemplate. The Bhahdradomen are regaining their powers. Even if the weapons hadn't gone missing, they might not have held the shape-changers back for ever.'

'Do you think that your grandfather's counsellor took them? Laphaeome?'

'That's my worst fear,' she said grimly. 'If Laphaeome took them, if the Basilisks are in Bhahdradomen hands . . . That is the worst possible eventuality. Every effort I've made to find the truth has turned up nothing. Lord Poel doesn't know. Ysomir can't or won't tell me anything. Damn it!'

He said ruefully, 'Still, at least we *know* we're defenceless. If we hadn't taken the trouble to find out, we'd still be under the illusion that the weapons were close at hand.'

'True. Let's look on the bright side!' she said sardonically. 'Mawrdreth, we *must* reorganise the army.

The ill-feeling between the different factions has got to be combed out. And it's time our good citizens got off their arses and helped us to solve this problem, instead of bitching about my shortcomings . . .'

A strange sound made her pause. The air seemed to jerk tight with a snap, and a pale aquamarine light flickered in the window.

'What's that? Lightning?' They both hurried to look out of the window.

The disturbance centred on the unfinished Tower. In astonishment they watched light whirling up from its maw, felt the thunder of shock waves on the air. The walls of the Tower glowed and trembled.

'What the hell is that?' Helan breathed.

The light faded. The Tower was silent. She craned her neck, but from this vantage point she could only see the highest portion of the Tower.

'I've never seen one,' said Mawrdreth, 'but from all I have read and heard, I suspect that it may have been a portal opening.'

Helan was motionless, her fingers tight on the window sill. 'A portal within the Tower? Then it has been opened without my permission. It may well be the Valahyr party . . . in which case, it was wrong of them not to establish where they might be permitted to enter the Earth, and stupid of me not to have clarified the matter.'

'Well, we'd better go and see if it is the Valahyr,' said Mawrdreth.

'Yes. Come on.' She seized an embroidered over-robe and pulled it on, settling the heavy yoke on her shoulders and freeing her hair, which she quickly coiled up on to her head and secured with a sapphire clasp. At least she would appear more or less regal, when the Aelyr came. She hurried out into the corridor, yelling for guards to implement her command; a troop to be dispatched to the Heliodor Tower immediately.

They were a safeguard. If there were interlopers, the

guards would arrest them; otherwise they would provide an escort of honour for the Valahyr.

Of course, they must use a portal to come to Earth, but who could have created one in the unfinished Tower itself? Why would they even have thought to do that? It seemed sinister. Her nerve endings tingled with alarm. She should have asked Lady Alviath for more information instead of being so blithely trusting.

Ten minutes later she was in the Sun Chamber with Mawrdreth beside her. They sat on the Sapphire Throne, every inch the Queen and King of Aventuria. The sceptre bearing the Orb of Clear Sight was in her right hand, the royal circlet holding the blood-red almandine on her forehead. A number of courtiers were gathered about the dais, including Lord Poel. Palace guards stood to attention in the double doorway, resplendent in their blue and gold livery.

Derione entered. 'Ma'am, the Valahyr party are here. Lord Falthorn and retinue.'

'Any news from the Tower?'

'Not yet, ma'am, although it seems our visitors may have come from the Tower. I haven't ascertained it for certain. Your guard and officers were dispatched to investigate as you commanded, yet I can't understand why the two parties didn't rendezvous halfway . . .'

'Well, don't tax yourself about it now. Show Lord Falthorn in.'

There was a long pause before the party entered, though she could hear movement and voices in the antechamber. Then silence.

Lord Poel cleared his throat and exhaled, loud in the silence. She glanced at Mawrdreth, frowning; but at that point, Derione returned. He looked pale and puzzled.

'Lord Falthorn of the Valahyr of Verdanholm,' he announced.

The Aelyr man who came in was energetic and handsome, with black hair flowing on his shoulders as he strode

508

in and swept a graceful bow to her. Like his messenger before him, he had an otherworld sheen about him, but more than that; he possessed an aura of power and absolute confidence.

The ten men and women who came with him were armed, she saw, with swords in curved, jewelled sheaths. Lady Alviath was with them, but in the background now. All were dressed in ebony with touches of blue, violet and silver. She could only wish that her own army looked so lively and graceful.

Yet no sign of Eldareth and the others . . .

'Lord Falthorn, this is an honour,' Helananthe said. She wore a formal expression to conceal her anxiety.

'Your majesty, the honour is ours,' Falthorn answered in a beautifully resonant voice. 'We came as swiftly as our preparations would allow. Your envoys conveyed to us a number of concerns to which I can only respond in person.'

'And we are most grateful for your swift response. But my lord, have my envoys not returned with you?'

Falthorn smiled. 'Yes, they are all here.'

'Good. I should like to see them.'

'Of course, ma'am. They are in the antechamber. However, I wished to greet you personally before it became too, ah, crowded.'

She allowed herself a slight smile. 'It would be quite difficult to crowd the Sun Chamber, Lord Falthorn. However, I appreciate this chance to speak with you. My lord, we have a great deal to discuss. Would you prefer to rest first, and talk later in a less formal setting? Or shall we get to business immediately?'

'I beg to disagree ma'am.' Falthorn's smile changed imperceptibly from sun to ice. 'I think we have very little to discuss.'

She was instantly wary. 'Oh? The movement of Bhahdradomen, and *roth* storms, and the abduction of my mother and brother, not to mention my good subject

509

Tanthe's strange experiences in your household . . . this is *very little*?'

'I shall explain.'

'I wish you would.'

He raised a casual hand, at which one of his Valahyr ran lightly back into the antechamber. 'You wished to see your envoys. Here they are.'

Helananthe sat up in astonishment as her friends were brought in, surrounded by more Valahyr warriors. Eldareth, Elrill and Tanthe looked grim, but her worst shock came in seeing that their wrists were chained. She and Mawrdreth glanced at each other in confusion.

Helan stared at the chains in disbelief. There was a young man with them, obviously Aelyr, with long dark red hair. He too was manacled. But someone was missing. Jthery wasn't there.

'What on earth is going on?' Helananthe said, standing up. 'Am I seeing things?'

'I don't know, ma'am,' said Falthorn. 'What is it you see?'

'My friends appear to be manacled. What is this? Have they done something to offend you?'

'You'd better ask them that yourself. I shall allow you a few moments to talk with them.' Falthorn made a graceful gesture, but his impudence – in giving *her* permission to act – was deeply disconcerting.

Her chained friends were brought forward to stand alongside Falthorn. She descended the dais and went to them, hardly knowing what to say. Mawrdreth rose and followed, standing a couple of steps behind her.

Then she saw Eldareth's expression turn dark with disbelief. He was staring at Mawrdreth. Last seen being carried away with a broken leg . . . now here he was, blatantly presented to Eldareth as the new King, her husband. Her heart plummeted. Gods, she'd wanted to tell Eldareth in private, not to have him find out like this! But it was too late.

'Are any of you hurt? What's happening?' They looked

at her with glittering, fearful eyes, but none of them spoke. 'Eld?' she said warily.

His gaze met hers, dark and bitter. Helan felt dismay growing heavier in her by the second. 'What's going on? Did you find my mother?'

'Yes, we did, Hel.' Eldareth's voice cracked with pain.

'And? Is she . . .?'

'She's alive and well, as far as we know.'

Helananthe gave a quick sigh of relief. 'Then where is she?'

Eldareth hesitated. 'I'm not sure. She and the boy are prisoners of the Valahyr. We only saw them once, then we were arrested for our pains.'

'And Jthery? Is he a hostage too, or . . .?'

'He's alive,' said Eldareth. 'Apparently he has decided to take Falthorn's side in this, for reasons best known to himself. But the truth is, Jthery will probably find himself just another hostage, in the end.'

She turned on Falthorn. 'Why have you done this?'

'I didn't appreciate your choice of envoys,' Falthorn said off-handedly. 'Except for Jthery, whom I hope to find very pleasing indeed.'

Seething, she ignored the insinuation and spoke brusquely, 'I'm sorry if they've offended you, but you can unchain them now.'

'Ah, not just yet.'

'Where's my mother?'

'You'll see her, quite soon – and the brat.'

'So it was your people who took them? Why?'

'Ma'am, I want no conflict, no bloodshed between us,' Falthorn said in a tone of rueful sincerity. 'They are – how can I best put it? – insurance against war.'

Helan was trying very hard to stay calm, to understand what Falthorn wanted without antagonising him. She didn't want to seem panicky by calling for her guards at once. 'But Aelyr and humans are friends, my lord. Why should there be war between us?'

'Because there is something I must ask of you. I know you won't give it up readily.'

'Try me,' she said evenly.

'I want the Sapphire Throne.'

Helananthe's astonishment burst out of her as a laugh. 'What? Go to the furniture makers' guild, my lord. They could make you a fair reproduction, I'm sure.'

He held her gaze, cold and level. 'Don't mock me. That's not what I mean, and you know it.'

'Then what are you asking?'

'That you surrender the sovereignty of Aventuria to me.'

She gaped at him. Falthorn was dangerous, she saw that, but this was her territory and she felt on a more than equal footing with him. 'Your arrogance amazes me. You know that's impossible! What were you thinking of, my lord? That you could just snap up Aventuria for the glory of the Valahyr?'

'You have quite the wrong impression of me, ma'am,' said Falthorn. 'You think I am crazed with lust for power, a sudden whim to rule the Earth?'

'I don't know what to think,' she said narrowly.

'No. All that crazes me is the desire for my beloved realm of Verdanholm to be left in peace.'

'But we haven't touched Verdanholm. Never in our history have we launched an attack on your realm. What have we done to offend the Aelyr, that you come in here demanding to rule us?'

Falthorn's tone was sincere, urgent, and deadly serious. 'You misunderstand. I don't want the throne for myself. It's the price I must pay to ensure my people's future.'

Eldareth groaned. Falthorn turned to the prisoners and said, 'Go on, you tell her. I thought you'd be shouting it at the top of your lungs the moment we got here.'

Tears were running down Tanthe's cheeks. Eldareth's face was wrought with anguish. Then Helananthe knew that it was something so terrible that they *couldn't* tell her;

512

couldn't bring themselves to say it, not even to warn her.

Finally Elrill spoke with difficulty. 'Falthorn means to give Aventuria to the Bhahdradomen.'

'What?' She laughed incredulously, couldn't help herself.

'It must have been the way you said it, Lord Elrill,' Falthorn remarked. 'Try to put a bit more conviction into your tone.'

'Guards!' Helananthe called, her voice sharp and commanding. Falthorn and his followers would have to be arrested, that was clear. Two of her courtiers went racing out of the Sun Chamber – more out of fear than to make sure her order had been heard, she suspected. As she waited for the guards to attend her, she said, 'What do you mean by this?'

'Precisely what your Shaelahyr friend said,' answered Falthorn. 'While your land has basked in complacent peace, Verdanholm has been under constant attack by the Eaters. If I hadn't found a way to stop them, our realm would have been destroyed. It's a simple bargain. It took long years of planning and delicate negotiation, but at last they saw reason and agreed to it. They get Aventuria, they leave us alone.'

And even as she expressed her disbelief, she knew Falthorn was presenting her with a *fait accompli*. There were shoals of Eaters already in the city, passive, waiting . . .

The guards were not responding. Her own attendants stood in poses of helplessness. 'Lord Poel, summon the guards! Gods, have they gone deaf?'

Poel hurried to obey – accompanied by her three remaining courtiers, who were plainly terrified and desperate to escape – but as he passed her she saw a strange, narrow expression on his face, his eyes glistening like hot tar. Her heart was pounding. The threat of arrest didn't seem to concern the Valahyr in the slightest.

Now she was alone, except for Derione and Mawrdreth. Neither of them seemed to know what to say or do.

'Lord Falthorn,' she said reasonably, 'Aventuria is not yours to give.'

'Strange you should say that. What keeps the Nine Realms in human possession, after all?'

She hesitated. 'Our victory on the Silver Plains.'

'No. The Bhahdradomen's continuing fear of the Basilisks of Calabethron. That was their weakness. But they are weak no longer, and as for the weapons . . .' his voice fell to a whisper. 'I happen to know you've lost them.'

Helan caught her breath. She and Mawrdreth looked wildly at one another. 'How would you know that?'

Falthorn smiled. 'Because I have them.'

'You . . . ?' She caught her breath, shouted, 'Lord Poel! Where are the guards?'

But Poel was no longer in sight. She saw the guards standing motionless on either side of the double doors, their bodies relaxed and their eyes vacant. Dread thrummed through her. The Valahyr had placed some kind of glamour over them.

She turned to her last remaining aide and said, 'Lord Derione, fetch other guards and rally the army!'

Derione ran out, looking flustered and horror-stricken. Falthorn only said, 'It will do you no good. The troops you sent to the Tower will not heed you, any more than these palace guards will.'

'You can't have ensorcelled every soldier in the city.'

'No. Only those who tried to intercept us on our way from the portal. It won't be necessary to afflict them all.'

Mawrdreth had moved protectively to her side. She was glad he had the diplomatic sense not to intervene. He was inexperienced, but wise enough to know it wouldn't help her.

'If you have the Basilisks, you'll have to prove it,' she said. 'How did you take them?'

Falthorn only had to wave his hand at the Sapphire Throne and she knew that he wasn't bluffing. No one else could possibly have known where the weapons were secreted.

'It was not so hard to take them, while Garnelys was otherwise engaged. The mage Calabethron, who hid them after Maharoth's victory, thought he had placed sufficient safeguards around them – but he did not know me. I never even entered the Amber Citadel. A tiny worm of a portal was all that was needed, to connect my realm to the pocket beneath the Sapphire Throne.'

'And you had the nerve to leave a note,' Mawrdreth grated.

Falthorn grinned. 'Ah, you found it. I'll give you a sample of my handwriting, if it's further proof you need. So you have nothing with which to fight the Bhahdra-domen, even if you tried. They have painstakingly rebuilt their tower – teeth of Nilothphon, don't the Aelyr know it! – and you have no defence against them. If you still wish to be awkward, we could turn the Basilisks against you. Some only work against the Eaters, but others could be quite nasty. Not that I'd wish to do that.'

'Where are the weapons now?' Helananthe asked thinly.

'I'm hardly going to tell you that.'

Tanthe cried out suddenly, 'Oh gods, I've seen them!'

Everyone stared at her. Even Falthorn was plainly stunned. 'The first time I was in Verdanholm!' she went on. 'In Falthorn's chamber – there was a chest that seemed to be spilling over with white light. I touched it and it threw me halfway across the room! If only I'd known! Oh, if I'd known—'

Falthorn looked furious. 'Wherever the weapons were before, I can assure you they are not there now. Nor are they all in one place. It's a wonder my too-clever niece didn't kill herself.'

Helananthe was dizzy with horror. She would have done anything for a shot of Serpent Isles whisky. 'Are you going to give the Basilisks to the Bhahdradomen?'

'Of course not!' Falthorn huffed with exasperation. 'That would be idiotic, would it not? I need a lever against them, a lever to ensure that they remain on Earth and keep out of Verdanholm. Naturally, they are not happy at the weapons being in my hands – but it is a position they understand. I keep the weapons; the Bhahdradomen keep their bargain. A carrot-and-stick approach, as humans might have it.'

'And what if they try to steal the Basilisks from you?' Mawrdreth put in. 'They're bound to!'

'They won't. There has to be trust between us. I've promised them a token of good faith, which they shall receive in exchange for their guarantee never to renege on the agreement. An irresistible jewel. The child of Tanthe and Auriel, which carries the seed of the Jewelfire in its head. A child who is to become the only weapon that might actually destroy them. Not merely disable them; *destroy them*. Now, what would they not give to have that particular Basilisk in their own safekeeping?'

'It's a child, not a thing!' Tanthe cried.

'I created it. If not for me, it wouldn't exist.'

'And you're so bloody proud of yourself!'

Falthorn simply looked at Tanthe. Only looked, yet she went white, and her legs buckled. Eldareth and the red-haired Aelyr caught her and held her, trying to comfort her as she sobbed.

Helananthe felt sick. Mawrdreth's hand was on her shoulder – and Eldareth was looking daggers at Mawrdreth – but she shook him off. She'd never felt more alone. And she knew from Falthorn's manner, his matter-of-fact confidence, almost an irritation at having to wait for her to accept it, that he'd out-manoeuvred her. She was going through the motions.

'This is the position,' said Falthorn. 'You have no choice but to give up the throne.'

'No.'

Helananthe would never forgive the look he gave her

then; weary, contempt, as if she were nothing. And she saw then how fragile were her temporal powers, faced with those of an unprincipled *gauroth*-mage.

'It's time,' said Falthorn. He called, 'Lord Poel!'

The Valahyr ranks parted. Between them came Lord Poel, puffed up with nervous self-importance. And with him, a horrifying retinue.

Bhahdradomen. Thirteen of them.

They were nothing like the refugees she'd grown used to. They brought a precise cold smell with them, like metal. A greenish luminosity shimmered around them, as if they were so full of *roth* it overflowed and trailed after them. They moved like predators; now still, now quick as spiders, and they had the watchful, passionless eyes of dra'a'ks.

The humans watched them come in as if time were standing still.

Behind them came yet more of Falthorn's people, and they were pushing what seemed to be a tall chest or cage on wheels, covered in a golden cloth. The sight of it filled Helan with dread, almost more than the party of Bhahdradomen. Her immediate thought was that the Basilisks of Calabethron were in it.

The Bhahdradomen were vivid individuals. A soft-moving one, white as milk, human-looking. Another, hump-shouldered like a vulture, with skin so translucent his skull-face showed through horribly, his chameleon cloak blending into the background amber. One she recognised, with his hollow cheeks and horse teeth! It was Tzumezht again, who'd been the spokesperson for the refugees. Now revealed as one of the elite, a mage, a deceiver . . .

And the one in the centre, who wore burning scarlet . . . All the power centred on him. Physically he wasn't large but he gave a psychic impression of great size. An unseen tornado of force sheathed him, so that he seemed at once a pale, deadly snake in human shape, and a towering, raging storm.

Helan moaned involuntarily.

Their physical appearance she could bear. But their presence . . . their presence seemed to be sucking a vital essence out of her. Will-power, confidence, even her perception of reality.

Falthorn stood aside, letting the Bhahdradomen through. From alien eyes they regarded Helananthe with absolute authority, waiting politely for her to realise she was barring their path to the throne.

She breathed, 'Lord Poel, why did you not alert the guards to stop them?'

'No one could stop them, ma'am.' There was a look in Poel's eyes she'd never seen before, sweat standing out on the hard marble folds of his skin, his eyes narrow and glistening with anticipation.

Helananthe saw, with a rush of horror, that she should never have trusted Poel. Never let him worm his way back into her confidence. But she still didn't understand the game being played.

'May I present the new Bhahdradomen administration,' said Poel. 'Enabler Gulzhur. Facilitator Zhoaah. Prefigurer Tzumezht. Theosopher Rhazagramen.'

Helananthe studied them, particularly Zhoaah. He looked at her with such knowing eyes, and she thought of the description Ysomir and the others had given her . . . 'You're Laphaeome, aren't you? You're the one who corrupted Garnelys!'

'He needed no help,' Zhoaah said softly. 'He was already corrupt. I simply put wheels under him.' His eyes seemed to leak into her like ink.

She looked away, but immediately the scarlet-clad one filled her vision and held her pinned.

'And here is the new leader of the Bhahdradomen—'

The one called Rhazagramen put up his hand to silence Poel. It obviously wasn't fitting for a human to present him. 'Our leader, Master of Light, Chosen of the Ancestor, who has come to lead us out of exile. Vaurgroth of the

Fire. All of Aventuria shall bow down to him!'

The Bhahdradomen murmured in reverence. Helan felt she was about to go insane with disbelief. This couldn't be, couldn't be happening.

She took a step towards Vaurgroth. His aura physically buffeted her. Although he was shorter in stature, he seemed to be staring down on her from a great height, impervious and dismissive.

'Lord Vaurgroth, there is no need for this. I know your people have grievances. I sent envoys to reopen communication between us; did you not receive them?'

'One came,' said Vaurgroth. 'He was a poor, foul-mouthed specimen. My *domenim* speak better Paranian than he, and with greater eloquence. He said nothing I wished to hear.'

'What was his name? What happened to him?'

'Rufryd,' said Tanthe, with a sob in her voice.

Vaurgroth laughed. His manner was weirdly friendly, unless he was just being condescending. 'He is still in Zhahgrament, I imagine. He was not killed or mistreated while I was there. I have no interest in what happened to him.'

'We have tried to treat your people fairly,' Helan retorted.

'"Tried."' Vaurgroth's voice echoed in the great chamber. '"Treat." Madam, can you not hear the abhorrence of these words? It is not your position to *treat* us in any way, as if we were your possessions, animals towards which you pride yourselves on your kindness. That is why we are here. That is why I ask you to surrender the Sapphire Throne.'

'You will have to kill me for it!' she cried.

'We could,' said Zhoaah. 'We could also kill these.'

The tall cage was brought forward – not by the Valahyr now, but by the Bhahdradomen. As they manoeuvred it, liquid dripped out of the bottom and the stink of urine soured the air. Helananthe watched with growing alarm;

Eldareth and the others watched with grim despair, but without any hint of surprise.

Zhoaah flung back the gold cloth to reveal a tall white case with a pair of narrow doors. He opened the doors to reveal the gilded bars of the cage – and inside the cage stood her mother Ghiseyma and her brother Veny, clinging to each other.

'Very impressive,' Eldareth sneered. 'So you reveal yourselves as a pack of cheap conjurers.'

No one responded. Helan stared at them in horror and pity. Veny had wet himself. They looked dazed, as if they'd been drugged – but still alert enough to be terrified. 'Shall you see them tortured?' said Zhoaah. 'How much pain do you think they can bear before you give in?'

'Mummy . . .' Helan went to the cage and began to reach through the bars, only to find herself seized and dragged away by Gulzhur and Tzumezht. Mawrdreth leapt to her defence, Eldareth tried to break through the circle of Valahyr; there was a short struggle and then they all three stood helpless in the grip of the Eaters. She wanted to scream with outrage but her strength seemed to leak away into her captors' hands.

'Please!' Helananthe cried. 'Take the throne, only let them go.'

Ghiseyma stared at her daughter, as if to say, *how could you give up?* Her steely pride – even in this situation – made Helananthe want to weep. But her young brother's face curled up into an expression of purest contempt and he snarled, 'This is all your fault, Helan! *I* should never have given up the throne! I'll get it back and *I'll* be King!'

'Veny!' The hatred in his voice floored her. He'd always been a selfish child, but she'd had no idea how deep his jealousy ran. This was the worst, most horrible way to find out.

'Well done,' said Falthorn, as if she were a child who'd agreed to have a tooth out for her own good. 'Now you can go with your husband and your friends, and you will not be harmed. The Princess and the charming little Prince will stay in the custody of the Bhahdradomen, however.'

'No!'

'Your reward for your cooperation is that they will not be tortured,' Falthorn said matter-of-factly. 'Isn't that enough? Now, Lord Poel. Your moment of glory, I believe.'

Helananthe and Mawrdreth had been dragged away from the dais. Lord Poel began to mount the steps towards the bejewelled blue throne, visibly trembling with exhilaration.

'Poel?' Helan breathed. 'What the hell are you doing?'

'He's been very helpful to us,' said Zhoaah. 'I promised him a reward.'

'A puppet king upon the throne,' said Vaurgroth. 'An interesting idea of Facilitator's, that we let humans go on thinking for a time that they rule themselves . . . let the truth dawn upon them with delicious slowness. Zhoaah proposed your Lord Poel for this role, an idea he leapt at readily.'

Poel stopped on the top step and turned to savour the moment with a ghastly expression on his face.

Mawrdreth shouted, 'Deaf as well as vain! He called you a puppet!'

Lord Poel shifted a little, putting his shoulders back, staring over the captives with arrogant contempt. He'd heard the description and yet his greed for the Sapphire Throne overrode his pride.

'Indeed, he has served us well and capably and thoroughly deserves his elevation,' added Zhoaah.

'You bastard, Poel!' Helan roared, pulling against Gulzhur's hands. 'You goddess-reviled bastard! The house! All the time you swore Laphaeome had vanished, you knew where he was! Charitable work, my arse! You liar! I should have known!'

Poel's eyes met hers briefly, hard black diamonds. 'I had no choice. You are not a worthy successor to Garnelys.'

Zhoaah smiled. 'Tzumezht made a portal within the house to connect, via Verdanholm and by the grace of Lord Falthorn, with one our Master made in Vexor. Our *domenim* have been slipping silently through it ever since. A lesser portal in the house . . . a greater one within my Tower. For that is the Tower's purpose, to connect with other domains and channel energy, though Garnelys never knew it.'

'No doubt Lord Poel is ready to take up his new role,' said Vaurgroth.

The Bhahdradomen leader walked up the steps after Poel, sweeping one hand out as if inviting him to take the throne. Helananthe stood paralysed. She was watching her entire world fall apart, and blaming herself for all of it. More grief than she could bear.

'But then again,' said Vaurgroth, stopping Poel suddenly with his seven long fingers resting lightly on the usurper's broad chest. 'It was only an idea.'

Poel looked confused. 'Lord Vaurgroth?' He frowned

Vaurgroth's voice was gently modulated, but it pierced and crept into every crevice. 'The Bhahdradomen never came this far before. We never took the Amber Citadel before. This is the greatest day in our history. Why do I need a puppet king upon the Sapphire Throne,' Vaurgroth asked, 'when I can sit upon it and rule in my own right?'

'But my lord—'

'You've provided excellent sport. Now you've done enough, dog.'

Vaurgroth's fingers were held straight and hard and he punched them clean into Poel's breastbone. Through layers of material, flesh and bone. There was a wet crunch, a gush of blood pumping out with the rapid heartbeat.

Poel looked down in astonishment. His eyes were wide open and staring at the crimson slot in his chest. Then he fell back down the steps of the dais and his skull cracked on the marble tiles.

Helananthe could only watch, frozen as all her

companions were frozen. Her fellow humans, her subjects, her loved ones whom she'd failed so completely.

Vaurgroth of the Fire, Master of Light, Chosen of the Ancestor crossed the dais and seated himself upon the tall jewelled chair. He flexed his spidery fingers along the arms and looked out across the Sun Chamber. The Valahyr melted into the background, but the Bhahdradomen ululated in triumph.

Helananthe pressed her hands to her eyes and collapsed in unutterable grief.

'Ancestor is merciful,' Vaurgroth said warmly, 'even to humans. This is the first day of a new age of light. This day shall be remembered as the triumph of the Ancestor over darkness. And for the first time in history – we the Bhahdradomen taking our rightful place on the Sapphire Throne.'

Saphaeyender looked up. His pen leaked ink on to the page, staining the tortuous scrawl of crossed-out lines. His head ached from the strain of trying to write, his eyes stung, but a sound seized his attention and made him drop his pen. A change in the atmosphere. A hissing and chattering, like wind rattling the trees or like voices . . .

He looked out of the window and saw them.

A cluster of Bhahdradomen refugees right below his window. Changing. Growing taller, their skins filling with light, heads coming up and shoulders flexing back as if they were winged.

Saphaeyender watched, and understood. It was not their bodies that changed but their posture. Shedding their downtrodden passivity like a skin they rose up in response to some call humans couldn't hear, drinking from a source of energy he couldn't see.

He backed away from the window and stood in the centre of the room, hardly breathing. And all through the city the Bhahdradomen were looking up, opening their mouths to taste the light, sloughing their disguise, rising.

Ysomir felt it.

The voices inside her all cried out at once, and as she pressed her hands over her ears the static *roth* in the air felt like fur on her skin. Wild, she ran to the door and hammered frantically on it, shouting for the warder to come.

Someone came.

The face that met hers through the grille, however, was not the familiar female one she'd expected. It was not even human. Instead Ysomir found herself looking into the soft milky features and the wet black eyes she'd prayed never to see again.

The face of Zhoaah.

In Verdanholm, Jthery sat alone by the edge of a sapphire pool. He stared without focus through the blue-green leaves to the singing sky beyond. The carved gems of Eshte's gift were cold between his fingertips.

He was waiting for Falthorn to come back. The waiting seemed endless. Surely nothing bad was happening in Aventuria? Falthorn had sworn to salve their troubles, and he was too powerful to fail. Jthery clung to that.

In Falthorn's presence, it had been so easy to believe his promises. *All I do is for the best. Your friends will not be harmed. Trust me.* So many warm, reassuring words.

But alone . . .

Jthery shivered. Doubts crept in. Tanthe's dreadful revelation, her warnings, her harsh words, his friends' imprisonment; he'd chosen to dismiss all of it, to listen only to Falthorn. Couldn't bear to consider for a moment that Falthorn had lied.

But what if . . .

When he had seen Eshte rising up behind Falthorn, that first magical night, what if she had been giving not her blessing but her warning?

Different kinds of love wait for you; one is true, the other false and lethal. He sat up, rigid with dread and dismay. He'd forgotten those words until this moment. *The wisdom to know the difference . . .*

He didn't know. Falthorn had ambushed him with beauty and mystery and eloquence. What if this was the mistake, the lethal choice? No, Jthery told himself, I must trust Falthorn or I might as well drown myself.

In a turmoil of denial, Jthery plunged both hands into the pool, stirring the water, calling with all his will to the Goddess, *Eshte, come to me, guide me, show me I've done the right thing!*

But there was no undine in the pool. The waters of Verdanholm were chilly and silent. Eshte had abandoned him, turned icily away from him and left him to find his own way.

That was all the answer he needed.

Once again Rufryd tried to prise the Bhahdradomen's hands off his arms. The way Vetru clung to him, like an infant monkey to its parent, was driving him insane. What was wrong with him? Misplaced affection . . . or was he thirsty for human energy? Intrusively curious about Rufryd, absorbing his essence and become more like him, almost as if he were jealous of him being a human.

Rufryd was lying in a curve of the road in the shadow of Vaurgroth's tower, trying to sleep. After sending the blue-dove he'd collapsed there, so exhausted from hunger and his encounter with Vaurgroth that he couldn't move. He didn't care what became of him now. All he wanted was Vetru to leave him alone . . . yet nothing he did would shake the succubus off.

He twisted his head and looked into Vetru's face. Disbelief punched all the breath out of him. He looked even more human than he had before; his features more definite, his skin less translucent. Vetru looked . . . oh gods, he looked so nearly like him yet so disturbingly unlike. As if a poor sculptor had attempted to portray Rufryd's face.

All day they'd been aware that something was happening. The cone-shaped tower had glowed and rumbled. Streams of Bhahdradomen had gone in, and not come out again. Those that remained moved in an atmosphere of expectation. Passing each other they would stop, exchange a few words that sounded like the buzzing of drones to his tired ears, and pass on. Something was happening. Rufryd couldn't stop it. He didn't even care, yet misery overwhelmed him.

Now it was growing dark. If not for Vetru he would have been frozen.

Again he tried to disentangle himself, but Vetru only settled against his spine again, slipping his arms around him like ropes. Rufryd had no strength to resist. He so needed to sleep. Sleep . . .

From his position he could see the landscape; the low huts like ant-runs, the churned grey soil striped with shadow as if the red-hot claws of some beast had gouged and scorched the earth. Leaf Moon was full, bathing the scene in her dim greenish light. Against the glow, as if on some ruined stage, Rufryd saw the figures of Bhahdradomen moving.

He thought he was dreaming.

The silence was deep, yet he seemed to hear a song in his head. A deep hum, threaded through with a groaning chant and a sort of chattering, so faint he might have been imagining it, just audible enough to drive him to the edge of madness. And to this ghastly rhythm the Bhahdradomen were dancing; silhouettes against a greenish-grey glow.

They moved slowly, unfolding and stretching upwards with spidery limbs, and it seemed they danced under veils, like corpses rising inside their shrouds. These shrouds were translucent, tenting the writhing forms like dry stretched skin, papery membranes threaded with pulsing veins. Like insects they were changing, pupating, bursting out of their maggot form into something more powerful, poison-filled and exuberant in its strength.

Rufryd's mouth opened in an O of despair and grief. The scene filled all his senses with nightmare, and a distant part of him wept, knowing that this was a victory dance, that his mission had failed. Too little and too late.

There was nothing he could do but lie there and watch the Bhahdradomen dancing, writhing . . . rising.

END OF BOOK TWO

The story will be concluded in Book Three, The Obsidian Tower

EARTHLIGHT

A SELECTED LIST OF FANTASY TITLES
AVAILABLE FROM EARTHLIGHT

THE PRICES SHOWN BELOW WERE CORRECT AT THE TIME OF
GOING TO PRESS. HOWEVER EARTHLIGHT RESERVE THE
RIGHT TO SHOW NEW RETAIL PRICES ON COVERS WHICH MAY
DIFFER FROM THOSE PREVIOUSLY ADVERTISED IN THE TEXT
OR ELSEWHERE.

☐	0 6710 1605 9	Escardy Gap	Peter Crowther & James Lovegrove	£5.99
☐	0 6710 2261 X	The Sum Of All Men	David Farland	£6.99
☐	0 6848 6055 4	Brotherhood of the Wolf	David Farland	£9.99
☐	0 6710 1787 X	The Lament of Abalone	Jane Welch	£5.99
☐	0 6710 3391 3	The Bard of Castaguard	Jane Welch	£5.99
☐	0 6710 1785 3	The Royal Changeling	John Whitbourn	£5.99
☐	0 6710 3300 X	Downs-Lord Dawn	John Whitbourn	£5.99
☐	0 6710 2193 1	Sailing to Sarantium	Guy Gavriel Kay	£6.99
☐	0 6710 2191 5	Beyond the Pale	Mark Anthony	£6.99
☐	0 6848 6041 4	The Keep of Fire	Mark Anthony	£9.99
☐	0 6710 2192 3	The Last Dragonlord	Joanne Bertin	£6.99
☐	0 6848 6051 1	Dragon and Phoenix	Joanne Bertin	£9.99
☐	0 6710 2208 3	The High House	James Stoddard	£5.99
☐	0 6710 3749 8	The False House	James Stoddard	£5.99
☐	0 6848 5828 2	Green Rider	Kristen Britain	£9.99
☐	0 6710 2190 7	The Amber Citadel	Freda Warrington	£5.99
☐	0 6848 5825 8	Into The Darkness	Harry Turtledove	£9.99
☐	0 6710 2189 3	The Siege of Arrandin	Marcus Herniman	£5.99

All Earthlight titles are available by post from:

Book Service By Post, P.O. Box 29, Douglas, Isle of Man IM99 1BQ

Credit cards accepted. Please telephone 01624 675137,
fax 01624 670923, Internet http://www.bookpost.co.uk or
e-mail: bookshop@enterprise.net for details.

Free postage and packing in the UK. Overseas customers allow
£1 per book (paperbacks) and £3 per book (hardbacks).